I0590073

SPIRIT OF THE BAYONET

2

ODYSSEUS

TED RUSS

Published by Chinook Publishing LLC.

First Edition: 2025

ISBN: 979-8-9986894-2-0

Cover design & interior formatting: Mark Thomas / Coverness.com

For Tony.

ODYSSEUS

Somewhere between Earth and the Asteroid Belt

2072

Chapter One

The command station on the bridge of the *Odysseus* was a testament to the engineering efforts that had kept the old ship running to and from the asteroid belt for nearly thirty years. Decades-old equipment, still doing its job, sat beside state-of-the-art systems in a wide horseshoe-shaped console that wrapped around the command chair. The setting appealed to Paul. It was good to know that he was not the only subject of multiple retrofits.

"Sir, all cycle inspections for the week completed," Paul said as he floated up onto the bridge. "No discrepancies noted."

Captain Nathan Drake hovered before the large forward window, his back to the command station, the infinite void stretching out before him. He wore his navy-blue dress uniform, merchant spacefarer captain rank on his shoulders. More than a year into the voyage, and it was still the only thing Paul had ever seen him wear. But the gold buttons and piping, like many things about the captain, had grown on him.

Drake stretched one magnetized boot down to the floor to gain purchase and turned his thin body from the window. Decades in space had wrecked him. He was as skinny as a skeleton and paler than a cadaver.

"Anything interesting this week?" he asked, taking the inspection sheet from Paul.

"Actually, yes. One closet on the bottom level of the Utility Module contained a couple dozen pairs of leather combat boots."

"Leather combat boots?"

"Yes, sir. And ten boxes of black shoe polish."

"Only the military," Drake said with disgust, his dark, well-trimmed beard unable to conceal his scowl. The black hair contrasted starkly with his pale-white skin.

Paul nodded in agreement.

"Seriously, Prisoner Owens. Who the hell brings useless leather combat boots on board a space freighter? They would do no good on Mars or anywhere else. They are purely ceremonial."

Drake shook his head.

"And I can just picture those dumb bastards shining their useless boots for months. Please tell me you didn't do that shit."

"I only did as I was told, sir," Paul said with a shrug.

"See that the boots are destroyed."

"I will, sir."

"I suppose you've earned your ration, Prisoner," Drake said, pushing off from the floor toward a locked utility closet on the far side of the bridge.

The bridge was part of the command-and-control module, or C&C, that sat on top of the bridge tower, a narrow superstructure that rose fifty meters from the top center of the *Odysseus'* hull. The shoebox-shaped module enclosed two levels, offering two thousand square feet of weightless, pressurized crew area. The bridge took up the top level of the C&C, and it was from there that Drake commanded his ship. The bottom level of the C&C held a small medical bay with one of the ship's two MedPods, the captain's private quarters, a galley kitchen, and a storage area.

Captain Drake smiled as he returned to Paul with a large silver flask.

Paul smiled back to conceal his unease. The captain had started sharing his personal store of bourbon with Paul almost fifty cycles ago. At first, it was novel and fun. And Paul liked bourbon. The shots mellowed Drake out, and he would talk about his decades underway. Once the old man got going, he could talk about spacefaring for hours. Paul would float there next to the captain, sipping on bourbon and only half listening as he gazed out of the forward window at the void.

Now Paul thought the old man drank too much.

Does it really matter? Paul thought. *Doesn't the executive officer run everything at this point?*

Paul still loved that forward window, though. The wide, curving floor-to-ceiling glass presented a 180-degree field of view in the direction of flight. The top of the *Odysseus'* forward hull stretched out below for more than a kilometer. In the distance, the Habitat and Utility Modules spun around like they were attached to opposite tips of a large propeller fixed to the nose of the ship.

The stars were legion, but there was no visual reference close enough to indicate that they were hurtling toward the asteroid belt at over thirty thousand kilometers per hour. Looking out the window, it seemed to Paul that the *Odysseus* was caught in the doldrums of space. Derelict, lonely, and beautiful.

"You know they laid this old girl's keel in 2043?" the captain said, gesturing out of the large window at the ship. "Almost thirty years ago."

Paul did know. He had heard it dozens of times.

"She was built in high lunar orbit, but has spent most of her time out here, running to the asteroid belt and back," Drake said. "She was the second M Class freighter to be commissioned, and now that the *Perseus* has officially been declared lost, she is the only big factory ship left and the longest serving of her line. They brought her executive officer on line in 2044, and she was underway to the belt for the first time the next year."

The captain gestured at the great window.

"You know, if she had been built just a few years later, we'd be floating here looking at a bullshit multi-mode display system instead of out into all of that."

Drake held his flask in front of his face and opened it. He jerked it forward and back quickly, ejecting a small blob of golden-hued bourbon. It quivered and flexed for a few seconds before stabilizing into a perfect sphere, spinning inches in front of Captain Drake's head.

Captain Drake leaned forward and sucked the floating orb of bourbon between his teeth into his mouth and then exhaled with a satisfied, "Aaahhhhhhh…"

The captain looked at Paul. "Give me a window any day. I hate to think of looking at some damn machine's interpretation of all that, rather than the real thing."

The captain handed the flask to Paul with a wink.

"Thank you, sir."

Paul ejected a large shot of bourbon out of the flask. He looked at his distorted reflection in the liquid and then swallowed it, enjoying the sugary burn as it went down. He handed the flask back to the captain.

They floated in front of the window, alternating shots of bourbon.

"Do you know the last time I walked on solid ground?" Drake asked.

"No, sir."

"Guess."

"Ten years?"

"Twenty."

Paul looked at the captain with raised eyebrows.

The captain nodded proudly. "Not Earth or Mars or even an asteroid in over twenty years."

"Where was it?"

"What?"

"Your last solid footstep."

"Earth. Back in 2052."

"Do you miss it?"

"Miss what?"

"Earth."

"Not really. There are some people I miss. But I don't miss that nasty planet."

"That's a long time," was all Paul could think to say.

"There was a time when NASA thought spending that length of time in space wasn't possible. They thought that men and women would go crazy." Drake handed Paul the flask and looked out of the window. "But me and my generation of spacefarers proved them wrong. Sure, we got skinny, worried constantly about cancer, and turned as pale as ghosts. But we didn't care. We lived among the stars in a stark, apolitical, and beautiful universe that was trying to kill us. And we loved it."

The captain sounded more morose than usual to Paul.

"I know you think I'm a fool. That I'm weird. Well, you're fucking right. I'm a goddamn spacefarer. I've had comets fly within one kilometer of my ship. I've hauled asteroids that were so dense it took all engines at max burn a week to get us moving at a detectable velocity. I spent three days drifting in space, tethered to my ship, when an EVA went pear-shaped. Fires. Reactor leaks. Decompression incidents. And, in the last few years, goddamn pirate attacks. Shit that would make an Earthsider piss their pants. But I loved it all. And I don't care that I look like an emaciated walking corpse now. Small sacrifice."

The captain looked from the window.

"Don't act like you don't know what I'm talking about, son! Look at you, for Chrissake! Look what you let them do so you could serve. I mean, they reversed some of it, of course. But…"

The captain got quiet, sensing that he had gone too far.

But Paul was long past caring about his augmentation scars. The incision where they'd peeled back his scalp and put the brain interface cap in place was now a thin, hairless scar that encircled his head above his ears like a crown. The gap left by the removal of the rectangular data-communication module at the base of his skull had healed, but hair would never grow back there either. Paul did not try to conceal the scars. He kept his hair closely cropped, so the marks were always visible. The battle-suit chassis attachment points at his major joints had done more damage. But his clothes usually covered those scars.

It was the absence of feeling that still bothered Paul. The expansive, multispectral, high-velocity feeling of belonging was gone forever now. And it was an absence that he knew the captain would not understand. So, he would smile and shake his head in an it's-OK gesture at the captain.

Paul knew it was coming then. The captain asked him to tell his stories.

"Come on, son. I know it was a world of shit for you. Just tell me a little. It's only out of respect that I ask."

Paul declined, as he did every time, but not without a twinge of guilt. He felt indebted to Captain Drake. The Fly It Off program was only open to prisoners convicted of nonviolent crimes. Paul had been an exception. Drake could have denied his assignment. Ultimately, crew composition was up to a ship's captain. But the old man had let Paul aboard.

Even so, Paul shook his head and said, "I'm sorry, sir."

Paul's melancholy face, staring at the stars through the large window, pained the captain, and he gave up quickly. "At least we each served, son," Drake said, holding a hand over his heart. "Me in space, you in the mud… But we each served."

Paul usually left about then, and the captain would drink alone on the bridge afterward. Paul, back in his room, would meditate before going to bed to stave off the nightmares. So far, despite the captain's bullheaded insistence on bringing the old shit up, Paul had not had a single nightmare since he'd boarded the *Odysseus* more than a year ago.

"I love it out here," the captain said before Paul could turn to leave. "But it's different now. It's perverted. By those damn things."

Drake gestured angrily at one of the patrolling inspection-and-repair bots passing slowly from right to left about twenty-five meters in front of the window. It was one of the midsize units, twenty meters in length. It had the egg-like appearance of most of the IR bots: sensory equipment on the forward, thicker end of the asymmetric oval, and main propulsion on the more tapered aft section. Two utility arms were folded against its belly, like the talons of a bird in flight. The unit used its maneuvering thrusters to keep itself pointed directly at the bridge's window as it slid slowly by. It was scanning the structure for integrity and wear and tear using ultraviolet and infrared spectrums. It was the kind of thing that always made Paul smile, reminding him of his unit and the amazing things they had done together. As the bot passed the middle apex of the large window, the captain raised both hands, middle fingers extended. "Fuck you!"

Paul chuckled. He looked down and past the offending IR bot, at the long forward length of the *Odysseus*. A handful of other IR bots were going about their patrols, looking for trouble. Their small size and quick movements further emphasized the *Odysseus'* seeming lethargy.

"You know, the son of a bitch never asks my permission for any of this activity," the captain said angrily. "Every cycle, I watch swarms of those sneaky weasels prowling up and down my ship. I don't get so much as a 'how do you fucking do' from the executive officer. I hate it."

Paul knew Captain Drake was getting worked up when he referred to the XO by his full title. Drake said "executive officer" in a voice that dripped with sarcasm and anger. On any other ship, a captain's executive officer was his right-hand man, trusted above all others. Not on the *Odysseus*.

"The truth is, I don't even know how many of those damn things are aboard my ship. I think the rat bastard has been making more in the factory since we got underway. He's making a damn army!"

"You get the inspection logs, though, right?" asked Paul.

"Of course. But what else do you think they are doing?" the captain asked ominously. "They're damn sure not telling me the whole story."

Paul shook his head and rolled his eyes as he handed the flask of bourbon to the captain.

The captain's face was dark as he took the flask. "Fuck you, son. Used to be that spacefaring was a brotherhood of adventurers. We were crafty survivors facing long odds in an empty universe. I didn't care that no one on Earth, the Moon or Mars gave a shit. I knew they just wanted the commerce to flow, their cargo to show up on time. Didn't bother me. I knew where I fit in. Knew my part. Knew my role. Had authority. Now, though…" Drake took another large shot and swallowed hard. He rubbed his eyes and then looked at Paul.

Paul could see that the captain was getting worked up.

"I felt something off about this ship the moment I came aboard, you know," the captain told Paul.

"I know, sir."

"It was only about a month before you prisoners showed up. The Company brass called me in and asked me to take command of the *Odysseus*, to take her to the belt and back. I was serving orbital dry-dock duty on Lagrange Four, waiting to command the next Romeo Class freighter, the *Satulah Queen*, on her maiden voyage. She had been promised to me."

Drake shook his head and then took another big swig of bourbon. He handed Paul the flask.

"But the *Odysseus*' captain had fallen ill," Drake continued. "Hit with the cancer. It was a sudden thing, and the Company didn't want to miss the departure window. They didn't have anyone else. They tried to pump my ass full of sunshine and compliments, going on and on about how important the mission was to the Company. About her being the last of the big factory ships.

"I wasn't going for it. I told them no. 'You take the *Satulah Queen* away from me, and I'm done, goddamn it!' I yelled. I was so loud, I bet they heard me down on Earth."

Drake chuckled at the memory.

"After the meeting, though," he continued, his smile fading, "A friend of mine working in flight scheduling told me that there were no other belt-and-back command billets slotted to open up for at least two years. I was in a precarious position. If they decided to truly fuck me, I would have been stuck on that stinking orbital facility or, worse, Earth." Drake looked at Paul to make sure he was getting the severity of the situation.

Paul nodded.

"So, I swallowed my pride," Drake said, looking back to the window. "I ate my words, apologized, and took command of the *Odysseus*. I loved spacefaring too much to give it up, despite my chapped ass."

Paul resigned himself to staying a little longer, even though he had heard this part of Drake's story many times. He ejected another swallow of bourbon from the flask. It hung in front of the window like a small golden planet. The captain had always been good to Paul, and Paul had heard horror stories about the treatment of prisoners on other ships. Letting the captain vent background chatter for Paul's contemplations of the void through the glorious forward window was a small price to pay.

"And you know what?" the captain said, staring at the stars and not expecting an answer. "When Captain Drake takes command of a ship, it's a sacred goddamn thing. She's my ship now. I love her, and I'll get her and my crew to the asteroid belt and back safely, on time, and at a profit."

"I'm counting on it, sir," Paul said.

"The *Odysseus* is a strange old girl, though," the captain said with a rueful laugh. "In so many ways. The damn XO, for starters."

Paul stared out of the window, trying to ignore the captain.

"Look, Prisoner," the captain said, undaunted. "No one is going to make it to the belt and back without a powerful artificial intelligence continuously monitoring and controlling a ship's systems. And I have worked with some good ones in my time, AIs that I considered shipmates.

"But I knew this one was a little off the first time I talked with him. I knew his software had just been updated, so I tried not to dwell on it. Sometimes it takes a few cycles for those changes to get digested and smoothed out. But after our preflight planning meetings, I was convinced he was different, a little strange. So, I called a buddy.

"He's one of the best maintenance engineers in the fleet. He tore the C&C apart." Drake looked around in satisfaction. "Took out every communication and monitoring device from here down to the tube airlock." Drake pointed down through the floor at the main body of the *Odysseus*, a sly smile widening on his face. "Before anyone knew it, he had ripped out the XO's eyes and ears up here and installed a few good, old-fashioned, un-hackable mechanical switches." The captain pointed at his command chair, where he had shown Paul, maybe a dozen times, the switch that enabled the speakerphone and videoconferencing camera.

"Most everywhere else on the *Odysseus*, except some parts of power and propulsion, the XO can listen in and often see everything. Not so on my bridge. The XO can't hear or see shit in here unless I key the mic." Drake looked at Paul and nodded with satisfaction. "He has his chamber. I have the bridge."

The satisfaction faded, and Drake's face clouded with doubt.

"But sometimes I wonder," he whispered, his eyes darting nervously around the bridge.

Paul had had enough.

"Well, sir," Paul said, reaching a foot to the floor. "I'm going to hit the rack. Been a long cycle. I appreciate the bourbon, sir."

The captain nodded, but grabbed Paul's shoulder to stop him. He gestured with his eyes and head toward the IR bot that was still in view. It was passing right to left now and almost to the edge of the window.

When it finally slid out of view, the captain reached into his tunic and pulled out a folded piece of paper. He thrust it into Paul's hand. Drake held a finger over his closed mouth to make sure Paul knew not to talk.

Paul nodded and pushed off the floor to leave.

Back in his quarters, Paul shook his head, remembering the captain's nervous look. He read the captain's note.

They are out to get me. They are out to get all of us. We are trapped on this space freighter with a diabolical threat. I do not intend to go easily. I am very close to having what I need. But I sense that we are in more danger than ever. If I am killed before I can prove what he is plotting, you must know that it was the executive officer and his minions. You must avenge me and protect the crew!

Paul walked over to his bureau and pulled open the top drawer. He lifted a stack of folded T-shirts and grimaced. Dozens of paranoid notes that Captain Drake had given him over the past cycles lay in a pile.

This is why they should limit a person's time in space, Paul thought.

He threw the latest note onto the pile and put the T-shirts back on top.

Paul closed the drawer.

Crazy old man.

Chapter Two

aul woke the next cycle two hours before the all-hands meeting, as he always did. He rose, showered, and sat for his morning meditation before making himself a pot of coffee. He stood for a few moments holding a cup of the warm beverage, staring at the leather-bound book on his desk like a man sizing up a wrestling opponent.

The book lay in the center of an old wooden military field desk. Faded olive green with metal fittings, the sturdy rectangular table stood on four folding legs under the one small window in Paul's quarters. A simple metal chair was pushed under the center of the table, in front of the leather-bound book. The chair was also olive green, or was decades ago. Now, dull aluminum showed through numerous dents and scrapes.

Paul pulled out the chair and sat down.

The stars pinwheeled slowly on the other side of the window as the Habitat Module corkscrewed through space. This was his favorite place to be on the *Odysseus* - In his chair, at his desk, in his quarters. Alone.

The Habitat and Utility Modules were added to the *Odysseus* after she returned from her maiden belt-and-back voyage in 2048. The first Battle of Santiago had taken place the previous year, and tensions with China were high. The contest of superpowers, both military and commercial, was extending out into the solar system.

The Pentagon wanted the ability to put troops on Mars and gave Space Command the mission of getting them there. The soldiers had to be able to fight upon arrival. They couldn't be soft and gooey from nine months or more of zero gravity, so Space Command ordered the retrofit of all merchant space freighters with troop-carrying habitats. The large M class ships, like the *Odysseus*, got the biggest modifications.

The Habitat and Utility Modules were pressurized to one atmosphere and spun around a center hub gear, providing one G. The long truss structure that spun them around contained an enclosed and pressurized passageway with a ladder called the "Traverse."

By 2050, during the height of the misguided preparations for war on Mars, each M Class freighter had up to ten of these rotating habitat assemblies stacked on its nose. That war never happened. The bloody stalemates on the African and South American continents were costly enough in lives and treasure that both China and the US lost their appetites for direct conflict in space.

Rather than a battlefield, Mars turned instead into a nearly lawless commercial boom planet for the countries, corporations, and privateers able to get there and to the asteroid belt beyond it. As a result, most commercial ships were transitioned back to just one spinner assembly, like the *Odysseus*. The spinner offered much more space than needed for a freighter crew, but pressurized compartments with induced gravity were so valuable that the Company had left it in place. Besides, it would have been expensive to remove, and the Company was sometimes able to charge for passage to or from the belt.

Both the Hab and the Utility Module had three levels. The bottom level of the Hab housed a medical bay with the ship's second MedPod, as well as crew quarters and a small mess facility. Paul lived on the bottom level with the rest of the prisoner crew members. They each had private quarters that were palatial compared to a military prison.

Crew quarters filled the second level of the Hab, which also had its own small mess facility. The regular crew members lived on the second level.

The Utility Module, over a hundred and fifty meters away on the opposite end of the traverse, was designed to store weapons and military gear. Now it was used for food, spare parts, medical supplies, and other gear the crew wanted to have nearby. It was a much more convenient location than a kilometer or more away down the tube in a beat-up container clamped to the ship's hull. At least half of the UM was still full of abandoned and unknown junk, accumulated over decades. That was where Paul had found his desk and chair, in a storage section full of map stands, filing cabinets, old field tables, and metal chairs.

Paul looked down from the window and took another sip of coffee, trying to get his mind ready.

Besides the leather-bound copy of *Adauchi* in front of him, there were two other books, one on each side of the desk. To the left, a large Japanese-to-English translation volume and a thick leather-bound journal on the right. His scribbled translation efforts filled the first couple dozen pages of the journal.

Paul was working his way through *Adauchi* the old-fashioned way—word by word, on his own, with nothing but pen and ink and the books on his beat-up desk. No AI. He had thought the more than three-years there and back would be plenty of time.

More than a year in, he was not so sure.

Paul set down his coffee and got to work.

After an hour of translating, Paul changed into his duty uniform and hustled to the all-hands meeting.

Chapter Three

My name is Manji Saito, student of School Hiroaki, friend of Hiroaki Ashikaga himself, and the only survivor of the Battle of the Covered Bridge.

I apologize to the reader. I am a warrior. I am not a writer.

I wandered as a rōnin, a masterless samurai, for many years, fighting in many battles for different sides. I was wounded badly in the Siege of the Seven Swans. I would have been killed had it not been for the bravery and skill of an older rōnin named Kusunoki. He saved me and was wounded in the process. We both lay bleeding as the siege concluded. Both in pain. Both happy to be alive.

Our side was victorious. Kusunoki and I were taken to a small village to heal. It took me many months to recover. During this time, Kusunoki's stories were my only diversion. He was a master storyteller. He told them well, and for many hours at a time. I lay on my bed and looked at the ceiling, listening to them.

Kusonoki spun tales about School Hiroaki. In those days, it was heard of only in whispered rumors. A school of the famous general and sword-fighting master, Hiroaki Ashikaga. Kusunoki claimed to be a member of the school. He claimed to know Hiroaki himself. Kusunoki claimed that he was not really a rōnin. Instead, Hiroaki and the practice were his master.

Sadly, Kusunoki's wounds were grave. He descended into fever. His stories became more fantastical. Then he stopped speaking. Eventually succumbed. In his last lucid moment before dying, Kusunoki asked me to carry his body back to Hiroaki's school so that he could be buried with his brothers. I still did not believe his stories. But Kusunoki saved my life in battle. I was honor bound to try.

I spent a week trying to remember every detail that Kusunoki had told me. I wrote my notes in a small journal so that I would not forget. I also drew a map that resembled, as closely as I could manage, the route into the hills that Kusunoki had described.

I wrapped Kusunoki's body and rigged it on two long poles. One end rested on my shoulders, the other dragged on the ground. I put Kusunoki's katana and a note he asked me to give Hiroaki into my sack and set out on my journey.

Chapter Four

The captain convened an all-hands meeting on the top level of the Hab at the beginning of each duty cycle.

The top level was divided into two sections. The forward section was the largest. In it, two swiveling command chairs faced a large floor-to-ceiling multifunctional display. It was possible to command the entire ship from this forward command section if control was given over from the captain's bridge. It was an impressive facility. Paul hated it. He preferred the bridge, with its rambling landscape of old and new equipment and large window.

The aft section of the top floor was a large meeting space. A conference table surrounded by a dozen chairs sat in the middle of a windowless room. There were a couple of multifunctional displays on three of the walls. The fourth wall was adorned with a map of the solar system. It was a simple map but provided Paul with something to consider when the all-hands meetings got boring, which was most of the time.

Paul entered the meeting room and took a seat that afforded him a view of the map of the universe.

Drummond was already seated, sifting through files on his tablet computer. Drummond did not acknowledge Paul's entry and continued to ignore him after he sat at the table.

That was fine with Paul.

Mathew Drummond was the ship's CFO and second-highest-ranking officer on board. He was charged with making the voyage as profitable as possible for the Company. Drummond looked much older than his early thirties. His brow was always furrowed with concern, and his face pinched with anxiety. Balding and skinny with a small paunch, he looked slight next to the military convicts.

Paul did not understand why Drummond was so stressed out. He never had to participate in any of the maintenance or inspections, and he certainly never had to do any of the more dangerous tasks, like extravehicular jobs. Still, the man walked around like he was being stalked by something. Any time Paul saw Drummond, he was glued to his tablet display, monitoring the Bloomberg Belt Market feed and running cargo, factory, and negotiation scenarios.

"Top of the morning, bean counter!" Regas said as he stepped into the room. McNeeley and Hahn, laughing, were right behind him.

"I've told you not to call me that, Prisoner," Drummond said, not looking up from his tablet.

"I know. I'm sorry," Regas said. "I'm just kidding. I'm just kidding."

Belen Regas was a former Combat Corps corporal serving twenty years for desertion, theft, and drunk and disorderly conduct. A veteran of two deployments with an exoskeleton battalion, he had been awarded the Purple Heart and a Silver Star for valor. His parents had immigrated to America from Athens, and he was the first generation of his family born in America. Tall, muscular, and handsome, he was the epitome of masculine Greek beauty and a tragic disappointment to his parents.

He was also petty, hypercompetitive, easily offended, and drove Paul crazy.

Regas looked at McNeeley and Hahn. They tried to swallow their snickering.

McNeeley was a short, fat slug of a man. He was so out of shape that even on the *Odysseus*, where the blistering chill of the void kept the old girl cold at all times, he was always sweating. His brow, armpits, and the fold between the bottom of his man breasts and the top of his belly were always wet. He was the kind of specimen that Paul could never believe had made it into the military, much less thrived for a few years. McNeeley was not a Combat Corps veteran, of course. He had been part of the big administrative beast, working as an armorer, taking care of weapons and equipment.

The problem for McNeeley was he didn't take great care of the weapons and equipment. He was serving fifteen years for selling army equipment on the black market. With the Fly It Off program, he would be a free man when they got back to Earth.

Hahn was a wiry kid from Kentucky who wore an outdoorsman's full beard. He was tall, though not as tall as Regas. Hahn exuded the quick and assured demeanor of a country boy. Paul could picture him shooting squirrels, jumping from rock to rock, and driving too fast in an old pickup truck. Paul had the sense that Hahn would have made an excellent infantryman had events played out differently in his life. As it was, though, he was serving seventeen years for dealing drugs in the barracks.

They had all been strangers when the *Odysseus* had left high lunar orbit. Now, though, Paul could see that McNeeley and Hahn belonged to Regas. They followed him around like puppies.

Regas looked at Paul. "Good morning, Captain Jigsaw," he said with false regard and cheerfulness as he sat down.

In a former life, Paul would have sprung across the table at the word "jigsaw." But that part of him seemed a million years away. Regas had called him that since their first day on board, trying to offend. Paul never objected. He didn't care about those things anymore.

"Hello, Regas," Paul said.

Althea walked in.

All eyes, other than Drummond's, locked on and followed her.

Dressed in her customary baggy utility uniform with multiple pockets, she succeeded in obscuring most features of her five-foot-five frame, but enough swells and curves made it through the camouflage to excite. And she was unable to hide her beautiful face. Ink-black hair cut in a swooping asymmetrical bob framed large, expressive eyes and full lips. She never wore lipstick, but it was easy to imagine.

An advanced melding of organic, mechanical, and electronic systems, Althea was the ship's administration and counseling officer. Her role was twofold. First, she assisted the executive officer in the administration of shipboard operations and served as the XO's embodied representative when the *Odysseus* was in port or docked with another ship. Her second but most important role was to serve as counselor to the small crew.

Althea's programming was optimized around behavioral observation and therapeutic communication. Years of deep space travel was hard on humans, and the shipping companies had learned the value of conversation and counseling over the course of so long and isolated a journey as a belt-and-back, even when the muse was a machine. And particularly when the crew included military inmates. The counseling initiative was, therefore, accelerated when the military's Fly It Off program started.

Paul looked across the table at Regas, who made no effort to hide his lust. He worked his lips and craned his neck to get as much of Althea as he could.

Paul wondered for the hundredth time about the wisdom of putting so attractive a synthetic on board a long space voyage. Althea was indistinguishable from a human woman. He had been around high-fidelity synthetics often in the military, so he appreciated their utility. *But why make all her organic stuff so damn good looking?* he thought. *Only an engineer who had never deployed into the real world, or real space, would do such a thing.*

Cooley walked in and scanned the table.

As boatswain, Floyd Cooley was in charge of all nonrated crew member activity, discipline, and training. It was his job to turn the four inexperienced prisoner crew members on their first space voyage into capable stevedores before they docked at the belt. It took a little over a year and a half to get to the belt. Plenty of time, he hoped.

This was Cooley's second belt-and-back voyage and his first serving as boatswain. He looked the part. Cooley kept his sandy-blond hair cut short and his goatee neatly trimmed. Six years of spacefaring had thinned him out some, but he was religious about his exercise regimen and stayed in the gravity of the Hab as much as possible. He was not muscular like Paul and the other prisoners, who were little more than a year off of Earth. But Cooley looked like an Olympic athlete next to the captain.

Cooley nodded to Althea before passing his eyes over Drummond, who did not look up. He then looked from Regas to McNeeley and then Hahn, daring them to crack wise. Satisfied, Cooley looked at Paul and put his notebook down. He checked his watch: 0759 hours.

Rather than sit, he stood as he waited for the captain.

He didn't have to wait long.

"Attention!" Cooley commanded as Captain Drake entered the room at 0800 hours.

Everyone at the table sprang to their feet. Cooley stood at attention as well.

Drake took his time. When he got to his chair at the head of the table, he looked at each crew member in turn.

"Prisoner Regas," Drake said, staring at the tall military convict.

"Yes, sir," Regas said, head snapping toward the captain.

"What have I told you about uniform discipline?"

"Sir, the discipline one attends to their uniform is the same discipline one attends to their ship."

There was no edge, irony, or rebellion in Regas's voice. Regas knew that the captain was not a man he could fuck with, that he and his petty minions, Hahn and McNeeley, were nothing in Drake's world. Less than nothing. The captain could, here, now, at this table, order Regas jettisoned into the void. It would be done, and no one would question it.

That enraged Regas.

But he didn't show it.

Regas had been stupid in the past. That was why he was standing on the *Odysseus*, millions of kilometers from Earth. He was flying off a conviction for being stupid. He had promised himself he would never be stupid again.

"Check your uniform, prisoner," the captain said as he sat down.

The room stood at attention while Regas checked his uniform. The left breast zipper of his utility suit was unzipped.

Drake shot Cooley a disappointed glance.

"Sir, may I make the correction?" Regas asked Drake.

Drake waited a heartbeat before saying, "Do so."

Regas zipped up the pocket and returned to the position of attention.

"Sorry, sir," Regas said.

McNeeley and Hahn shifted on their feet slightly, nervous for their alpha.

The captain shook his head and shifted his eyes from Regas back to Cooley.

Cooley nodded slightly to say, *I'll deal with it, sir.*

Drake looked unconvinced.

"Take your seats," the captain said.

Everyone sat down.

The leadership sat in the same seats every time. The captain at the head of the long oval table. Drummond to the captain's left. Cooley to the right. Althea sat next to Cooley.

The prisoner crew members filled in the other seats.

"XO, we'll begin," Captain Drake said.

"Very good, sir," the XO's voice came over the speakers. "The all-hands meeting is now in session for this, the three hundred and eighty-fifth mission cycle, and is being recorded in the ship's log."

"OK, Mr. Drummond," the captain said. "Go ahead."

"Thank you, sir," Drummond said, still not looking up from his tablet. "All economic work streams are green for this cycle. Voyage forecasts remain yellow. Belt negotiation simulations and factory-planning scenarios place belt departure forecasts all between ninety-seven-point-eight and ninety-eight-point-six percent of revenue plan, and between ninety-six-point-eight and ninety-seven-point-nine percent of profit plan."

Out of the corner of his eye, Paul could see the captain's face darken.

"Unfortunately, factory output dropped to eighty-six-point-three percent for three hours during the previous cycle," Drummond continued.

"What happened?" the captain asked. "A five percent swing in factory output is a big hit."

"We would have hit ninety-plus percent had the appropriate materials made it to the mouth in time," Drummond said, looking down at his hands.

Paul thought Cooley was going to reach across the table and punch the

CFO. The boatswain's face reddened, but the XO chimed in before he could speak.

"With respect, Mr. Drummond," the XO said. "Mr. Cooley and I were quite clear that a major payload transfer operation takes a minimum of five hours' notice to be conducted safely."

"How much notice did you give them, Mr. Drummond?" the captain asked.

"Two hours," Cooley answered, daring the CFO to contradict him.

Drummond looked up. "Mr. Cooley is correct, sir."

Drake waited for him to continue.

"I was trying to take advantage of a surprising level of heavy metals and rare elements detected in an asteroid as it was processed by the factory. My forecasting algorithms suggest that there will be a higher-than-average demand for precision drilling equipment at the belt when we arrive."

"We've been through this before, Mr. Drummond," Captain Drake said, weariness in his voice. "There are many moving pieces to this ship and her operations. She and the crew cannot turn on a dime just because your spreadsheet asks them to. The *Odysseus* is not a damn day-trading platform!"

"Yes, sir."

The captain leaned forward in his chair and turned his head toward the CFO.

"I remained concerned, Mr. Drummond. That financial performance is still forecasted below one hundred percent, and I see no evidence to suggest you have a plan to get us back in the green."

The captain glared at Drummond, who nodded nervously.

The lack of response angered Drake.

"You do realize, don't you, Mr. Drummond, that you have a very narrow reason for existence on my ship?"

Drake did not wait for Drummond to respond.

"Your only reason for being is to maximize the Company's financial return on this voyage," the captain continued. "To achieve that purpose, you have only four basic inputs you need worry about."

Drake held out his hand and counted each point with a bony finger as he walked through them, the edge in his voice increasing with each point.

"What to transport from Earth to the belt, what to produce in the ship's factory on the way to the belt, what cargo to select and bring back to Earth from the belt, and what to make in the factory on the long voyage back to Earth from the belt."

The captain let his four fingers hang in the air in front of Drummond for a moment before continuing.

"You get two bites at the goddamn apple," Drake said, volume rising. "When the *Odysseus* docks at the belt, and when the ship arrives back in high lunar orbit. The only thing left to be done at those two points in time is unload the old girl, sell what she's got, and tally the final number!"

The captain was yelling now. Everyone looked down at the table, scared to make eye contact with the enraged officer.

"Any voyage that does not score at least a hundred percent to financial plan is a failure! It is a failure for the Company, and a failure for the crew! Small to no financial share after four years in space is a hard goddamn blow, I can assure you! But it is nothing compared to the indelible tarnish that stains each crew member's career and reputation!"

The captain pointed at Drummond, who was shaking in his chair.

"We crew the Company's only remaining factory ship! Get your act together, Drummond!" the captain yelled. "I want a green forecast within seven cycles, or I will arrange for your replacement at the belt! Do you understand me?"

"Aye, sir."

The captain stared at the CFO as he leaned back in his chair.

"Very well," Drake said, his voice returning to normal. "Thank you, Mr. Drummond."

The captain looked around the table as if remembering there were people other than him and Drummond in the room.

"Mr. Cooley?" the captain said.

"No maintenance or inspection anomalies to report. In terms of training, we've just completed the extravehicular activity module, which puts us slightly ahead of syllabus. Anticipate no issues having Owens, Regas, and Hahn fully trained by the time we get to the belt. They are green across the board. McNeeley failed his second attempt at the EVA practical exercise."

McNeeley swallowed hard and looked at his hands, which were folded on the table. More sweat than usual beaded on his brow beneath his bald head.

Drake sighed. "Prisoner McNeeley," he said with disgust. "By my count, this is the third module you have required multiple attempts to satisfactorily test out of and advance."

McNeeley wiped the sweat from his forehead, but did not raise his eyes to meet Drake's gaze. Hahn and Regas looked straight ahead.

Paul shared a furtive, *what-a-piece-of-shit* glance with Cooley.

"Prisoner McNeeley," the captain said in a low voice.

McNeeley's eyes jerked up.

"Yes, sir?" he said.

"My patience with you is exhausted. If you don't pass the EVA practical within the next three cycles, you're done. I will not approve your Fly It Off credit, and you will forfeit your one-tenth share. Do you know what that means, Prisoner?"

"Yes, sir."

Everyone knew what it meant.

McNeeley would get no credit or pay for his four-year tour of service on the *Odysseus*. He would return Earthside and go back to serving his time, which would not have decreased a single day since his departure.

"I'll take this time to remind all of our prisoner crew members," Drake said, swiveling his head back and forth as he spoke, looking each of the prisoners in the eye. "The captain of a space freighter is the final approval authority for all Fly It Off program participants. My approval is not and never will be a rubber stamp. Is that clear?"

"Aye, sir," the four prisoner crew members said in unison.

"Good," Drake said, before turning to Cooley. "See that it happens, Mr. Cooley. If Prisoner McNeeley does not pass the EVA practical, it will be reflected on your voyage efficiency report."

"Aye, sir," Cooley said, staring at McNeeley. "Consider it done, sir."

Paul felt sorry for Cooley. A boatswain's voyage efficiency report was all-important. A good one meant a larger share and career advancement that made the long years in space worth it. A poor or even average rating meant career stagnation and a reduced share.

For Cooley to be put at financial and professional risk because the Fly It Off program had saddled him with McNeeley was some real shit luck. McNeeley was undisciplined, weak, of low intelligence and even lower morals and motivation.

And extravehicular activity was for real.

Paul had been through the most demanding training and combat situations the military had to throw at a person. Still, being outside of the *Odysseus* with just a pressure suit between him and the insatiable void was unnerving. There were so many ways to die. Quick ways. Slow ways. Painful ways. And some ways a person would never even see coming. Add a few complex maintenance or other tasks, and EVAs were the thing that everyone on board dreaded the most.

So, Paul couldn't blame McNeeley for being scared, but he still didn't like the fat asshole.

"XO?" the captain said, moving on. "Anything to report?"

"No, Captain Drake. All monitored systems nominal."

Drake nodded and glanced at Paul.

Paul looked down at his hands.

"Miss Althea," the captain said, not bothering to conceal the loathing in his voice. He looked down at his notes as she spoke.

"Crew health remains strong, Captain," she said. "No concerns at this time."

"Thank you," Drake said.

The captain looked around the table.

"I'll open the meeting up to anyone at this point. Any concerns or issues we need to discuss as a crew?" The captain waited for a moment before saying, "Very well. XO, this all-hands meeting is concluded."

"Noted, sir. Transcription ended."

"Attention!" Cooley said. Everyone sprang to their feet as the captain stood up.

Drake pushed his chair back into place and said, "I appreciate everything everyone is doing to keep us safe and underway. Let's make this a safe and productive cycle. Carry on!"

The crew stood at ease as the captain left. As soon as the door closed behind Drake, Regas spoke. "Hey, Mr. Drummond. If we catch up to the revenue plan, can we discuss increasing prisoner shares?"

Drummond ignored Regas. He gathered his tablet and papers.

"Hey," Regas said, a slight edge creeping into his voice. "Did you hear me, Drummond?"

"That's enough, Regas!" Cooley said sharply.

"Whoa! Hey," Regas raised his hands in a friendly surrender gesture. "I'm just kidding. He knows I'm just kidding. Right, Mr. Drummond?"

Drummond exited the room without acknowledging Regas.

"At ease, Regas!" Cooley said.

Regas saw the anger in Cooley's glaring face. He nodded at the boatswain and shut his mouth.

"McNeeley," Cooley said between his gritted teeth. "Come over here, you fat, useless slob."

Paul walked out of the room, fleeing the irritating antics and attitudes of his fellow prisoners. He was ready to immerse himself back in the *Odysseus'* solitude.

Captain Drake was waiting for him.

"Prisoner Owens!" Drake yelled as Paul walked toward the aft ladder.

"Yes, sir?" Paul answered, coming to a halt.

Hahn and Regas, stepping out of the meeting room, sped by and down the aft ladder to begin their cycles. They wanted distance between themselves and the captain's ire.

"I noted a discrepancy on your last inspection report," the captain said in a gruff voice as he stepped in front of Paul. "What have I told you about inspection reports?"

Paul was puzzled, but popped off with the first thing that came to him. "Sir, an inspection is not complete until the report is rendered."

"Exactly!" the captain said, raising his voice as he poked Paul in the chest with his bony index finger. "So why the hell am I still dealing with incomplete paperwork from you?"

Confused, Paul stayed silent.

"Damn it, Prisoner!" Drake said, frustration welling up. "The *Odysseus* has been ridden hard for a long time. She's ferried troops, done a few belt-and-backs, and hauled cargo to Mars. And I think every crew that she took on board left some of their shit behind. She is a mess!"

Drake poked Paul in the chest again as he spoke. Paul stood at attention, wondering how many times he had heard this speech before, and why the captain was so worked up.

"Well, the old girl is ours now. We're going to take care of her, and part of that is inventorying her burden."

On the next poke, Drake unzipped Paul's left breast pocket.

"Do you understand me?" Drake demanded.

Paul looked down, puzzled.

"Answer me, Prisoner!"

Paul looked up. "Sir, I don't know what you are talking about."

"That's your damn problem, Owens," Drake said, poking Paul again in the chest. "You don't know what I am talking about."

On the last poke, the captain shoved a note into the pocket and made a show to Paul of looking at the zipper.

This is ridiculous, Paul thought, realizing what was going on.

"Do you understand me, Prisoner?" Drake said, taking a step back.

"Yes, sir. It won't happen again."

"It better not."

Paul nodded.

"You are dismissed, Prisoner," Drake said.

Chapter Five

Paul, something is very wrong. I suspect that there has been a deviation in our course and that the XO is responsible. How? For what purpose? I do not know. I should have my calculations completed in a day or so, and then you and I should meet to discuss. Please trust me this time when I say that something is very wrong. Meet me in power and propulsion, section ten, transfer room 105, in two cycles. 2030 hours.

Paul tried not to scream as he stood in his quarters. He held the captain's note in one hand and his forehead in the other.

Maybe it's time for me to tell someone about all this, Paul thought as he walked over to his bureau. He opened the top drawer and placed the note in the growing stack under his T-shirts.

But who?

Paul walked over to his utility closet and pulled out his pressure suit. He was going to knock out his inspection first thing this cycle. He mulled the situation over as he donned his suit.

I guess I tell Drummond? He is second in command, after all.

Paul stood up straight in disgust at the thought.

No way. That guy is an idiot.

He grabbed his helmet and headed for the aft ladder.

Paul's inspection assignment for this cycle was a shipping container on the aft end of the ship almost two kilometers away, near power and propulsion. It would be a long float through the tube.

Perfect. I could use a little time to think.

Seen without cargo, the *Odysseus'* two-kilometer-long hull looked like a bony, disembodied spine, and her cargo rigging system, which ran along the bottom of her hull, looked like a series of stunted ribs. These ribs were as effective as they were strange-looking, though, and could secure any type of modular container as well as entire asteroids.

A maintenance and cargo access passageway, called "the tube," ran the length of the ship on top of her skinny hull, giving the crew access to the numerous compartments as well as the cargo and rigging systems. The tube was twenty meters in diameter. A ladder ran along the top of it, and a utility tram, used for hauling loads, ran its length along the starboard side. At regular intervals along the bottom of the tube, hatches gave access to cargo rigged to the ship.

The tube was not pressurized and required a full suit. Even so, Paul liked to go there and drift aft, snooping around the cargo. Open one bulkhead, and he'd see a stained and ugly container that had traveled to and from the belt with the *Odysseus* for decades. Open another, and he'd gaze on a gleaming thousand-ton asteroid full of exotic metals. From the outside, when fully laden with a cargo of odd-sized containers and massive asteroids, the *Odysseus* looked more like a collection of drifting space junk than a spacecraft.

Paul made his way up the aft ladder to the first level of the Hab and then walked to the middle bulkhead to access the traverse. He twisted his helmet on before starting his climb. The traverse was pressurized, but it was easier to climb the 66-meter ladder to the hub wearing his helmet rather than holding it.

Paul's weight reduced as he climbed until he kicked off of the ladder and floated up into the center chamber called "the hub." He paused there.

He liked to float in the zero gravity of the hub and listen to the low-frequency thrum of the massive gears driving the two arms of the spinner.

Most of the *Odysseus* was silent, doused in vacuum. But in the hub, Paul could hear the old girl working. He liked it.

Paul activated the air lock and worked his way into the tube.

He had learned that with a firm kick and one or two strong arm pulls on the ladder along the way, he could float from one end of the tube to the other in about twenty minutes. It was a relaxing and contemplative way to move through the tube.

If I tell anyone, it will be Cooley, Paul thought as he floated aft.

Cooley reminded Paul of the good noncommissioned officers he had known in the Combat Corps, each a unique but familiar cocktail of coach, disciplinarian, dictator, and older sibling. They were the glue of every good unit. Cooley was the *Odysseus'* glue.

Why does it even matter, though? So what if the captain is a paranoid drunk? The XO runs everything anyway. He's not going to let anything bad happen to the ship or us.

Paul reached the center of the ship and passed beneath the bridge tower airlock as he debated the situation.

Crazy old man.

By the time Paul reached his destination, he knew what he was going to do.

Nothing, he thought with a nod. *I'm not going to do a damn thing. I didn't come here to join a crew or be part of any drama. It's not my problem.*

Paul opened the bulkhead to access the container. Empty.

He shook his head at the sight and chuckled to himself. Early in the voyage, this would have sent Paul into an impotent rage: suiting up and shagging his ass two kilometers through the tube to confirm a shipping container was empty. Now it seemed like a good way to start the cycle.

Paul closed the bulkhead and started back to his quarters to complete the paperwork.

Chapter Six

ater that cycle, at the end of Paul's duty period, he walked toward Althea's quarters on the middle floor of the Hab. It was time for his mandatory counseling session.

Paul gritted his teeth as he walked. The sessions always came at the most inconvenient time of cycle: either at the beginning, when he did his best translating, or at the end, when he was tired and just wanted to hit the rack. This cycle, it was the latter.

Paul had met Althea for the first time on the top level of the Hab the day he and the rest of the prisoner crew members had reported to the *Odysseus*. She'd briefed them on her role and capabilities in a matter-of-fact stream of high-tech psychobabble. Paul was confident that, given his background and all that had happened, someone at the Company or Space Command had routed Althea, the latest-model counseling synthetic in the fleet, to the *Odysseus*. The last thing anyone needed was another high-visibility incident involving Paul Owens. He didn't care. He had earned the reputation and precautions. And he was grateful to the Geek and Captain Drake for getting him into the program and on board the *Odysseus*.

So, as Althea ran down a list of her own abilities like someone describing the features of a car, the only thing Paul was thinking was that she was beautiful.

She was short, coming up to about Paul's chin. Though he knew her flesh had been grown in a lab before encasing her mechanical parts, her skin exuded warmth and looked inviting to the touch. The oversized and pocketed utility suit she wore allowed only hints of her true shape. But for a group of convicts who had been locked up for years, a hint was all that was required. Hahn and McNeeley grinned like schoolboys as Althea spoke. Regas leered at her. At one point, he'd even licked his lips, causing Paul to roll his eyes.

This must be a mistake, Paul thought at that first meeting. *Somewhere in the fleet, a brothel ship is puzzling over a homely, professorial, middle-aged male companion, and we've got this lap dancer trying to navigate four crazy, horny, convicted fiends. Another bang-up job by personnel command.*

A couple of his army buddies had been fans of synthetics as temporary companions. Paul wasn't, though he did see the practical advantage for soldiers who spent most of their lives in war zones. And the stories he heard left no doubt that the synthetics performed at a high level of sexual expertise. It wasn't that he didn't like sex; synthetics just didn't do it for him.

Nothing did it for him anymore.

He wanted nothing to do with Althea. He wanted nothing to do with anyone on the *Odysseus* beyond what his duties mandated.

So, he was disappointed to learn that all crew members had to sit for a counseling session with Althea at least once every ten cycles. That was the minimum. Crew members could do more.

Paul made it clear to Althea from the beginning and on every subsequent interaction: he would attend the sessions, but he had no intention of ever participating.

Paul sighed with resignation as he reached her door. He adjusted the small satchel on his shoulder and stood up straight, squaring his shoulders as if preparing to take a punch. Then he knocked.

Althea greeted him with a smile.

"Hello, Paul," she said, stepping aside to let him in.

The door to Althea's quarters opened into a small sitting room. It was furnished with a large, comfortable sofa that sat against the wall and faced the only window. Two chairs sat opposite the sofa on the other side of a small coffee table beneath the window.

Paul walked in without greeting her. He sat down on the sofa and pulled the leather-bound book and his translation journal out of the satchel.

Althea sat in a chair.

Paul checked his watch and then opened the leather-bound book.

"Remind me what your book is about, Paul," Althea said in her most inviting voice.

Paul answered, but did not look up. He had learned that Althea's price for leaving him alone was a few minutes of friendly chatting.

Well, chatting, at least.

"It's an old text. Written by a rōnin, a masterless samurai, sometime in the early 1500s, during the Sengoku period, when the fighting was really bad. It was only recently discovered, during the excavation of a newly discovered Sengoku-period military compound in Japan."

"What is it about?"

"The leader of a fighting school and his students."

"What happens to them?"

Paul looked up from the book. His face was tight with irritation. He glared at Althea to make it obvious that this was the end of the friendly chat.

"I don't know. I haven't finished it yet."

Althea nodded.

Paul returned to the book.

He studied the pages and tuned her out, pausing now and again to write himself a note in the margin.

Every session for the past year was like this. Paul entered the room without greeting Althea. He sat on the sofa and tolerated several minutes of talk before descending into silence and working on his translation.

Althea, accustomed to the pattern and taking no offense, folded her hands in her lap and sat quietly, watching him work.

Forty minutes later, he stood up and left without saying goodbye.

Chapter Seven

I dragged the body of Kusunoki for many weeks. I walked through the hills and small villages, following the map I had drawn from Kusunoki's fantastic stories. Along the way, I asked those I came across if they knew of the school.

Those I asked denied any knowledge of such a school. They laughed at me. It was a common delusion, they said. They offered to let me bury Kusunoki in their village graveyard. It had been almost a full year since the Siege of the Seven Swans, and the battle was now well known across the land. It had brought a measure of peace. They would be honored to have his body rest with them.

I refused. I continued to walk.

After forty days, fatigue made a coward of me. I wanted to stop. I felt foolish. I was dragging the body of Kusunoki down a narrow road in the woods many miles from the nearest village. It would have been easy to bury Kusunoki in those woods. To give him a peaceful grave many would have been grateful for.

I stood still for many minutes, staring into the woods and trying to convince myself it would be OK. There was not, after all, a School Hiroaki. So, in fact, I could not fulfill my vow. Therefore, it was no dishonor to break it.

"So it is true!" a voice called from behind me.

A man approached on the road. He walked with a horse. He was an older man, I thought. In his fifties, perhaps. He wore simple clothes and a single katana on his waist.

"I heard about a crazy rōnin dragging a body from village to village and through the hills," he said. "But I did not believe it."

He walked up and stood next to me, taking my measure. He chuckled at what he saw.

"I seek School Hiroaki," I said. "Do you know it?"

"There is no such thing," the man said. "It is a myth."

I nodded in exhaustion.

"Why do you drag that body behind you?"

"It is the body of my friend Kusunoki. A hero of the Siege of the Seven Swans. I owe my life to him. His last wish was to be buried at School Hiroaki, where he studied. I promised to fulfill this wish."

"Then he has bound you to folly," the man said with a chuckle.

This angered me. But I had no strength left.

"Nonetheless," the man said. "I would not see a traveler burdened in this way and not help. I appear to be going in your direction. We could put your friend's body on my horse until the next village. Then we must part ways."

I nodded my assent. "I am grateful."

We walked in silence for a few miles before the man asked me, "What will you do if you cannot find the school?"

"I do not know."

"What will you do if you find it?"

"I will bury my friend," I said. "And I will give Hiroaki my friend's katana and a note meant for him."

"And then?"

"I do not know."

"You are rōnin, are you not?"

"I am."

"Would you tell me about the Siege of the Seven Swans?" the man asked me. "Tell me how your friend saved you."

Happy to be free of the weight of Kusunoki's body, I did not mind telling the man the story. For the next few miles, I described the siege to him. I described all of our preparations and all of the violence. I described the moment when Kusunoki saved me. I described our wounds and convalescence in the village. I told him of Kusunoki's crazy stories and of my vow and, finally, of his death.

The man listened closely. When I finished, he nodded.

"Thank you for telling me," he said.

We walked in silence for a long time after that. The man was lost in thought, and I was no longer in the mood to talk. Remembering Kusunoki had saddened me. I did not know what I would do when I reached the next village.

"Stop," the man said.

We came to a halt at a remote spot on the narrow road.

I looked at the man to ask what the problem was, but he gestured at me not to speak. He whistled the call of the kingfisher and waited.

From the woods came the call of the snipe.

The man smiled at me and whistled the call of the kingfisher again.

Four armed horsemen stepped out of the woods, guiding a riderless horse behind them.

I reached for my katana, but the man put his hand on my shoulder.

"Relax, friend," he said. "These are my students."

"Who are you?" I asked, hand still on my sword.

"My name is Hiroaki."

Chapter Eight

After the session with Althea, Paul climbed down the aft ladder to the third level. It had been a long cycle and he was ready to hit the rack. He walked through the crew galley on the way to his quarters. Regas was holding court.

"Now listen to how I wrap it up, guys," Regas said with excitement.

Hahn and McNeeley listened to Regas as he worked through a document. He was standing at the end of the table, reading in a proud and sure voice.

"We, the prisoner crew members, do, therefore, request our pay be increased to a full share in recognition of our outstanding and worthy service."

"So good," McNeeley said.

"I know, right?" Regas said.

Paul filled his water bottle. All of their heads turned toward him.

"You should get in on this, Owens," McNeeley said, his belly straining his sweaty T-shirt.

Paul ignored him.

"Seriously, Owens," Hahn said, stroking his beard. "You should get in on this. At least sign it so the captain knows it is unanimous."

"Come on, Jigsaw," Regas said. "How about a little crew unity out of you for once?"

Paul turned around like a tired parent.

"What are you idiots up to now?" he asked.

"We're demanding a full share," McNeeley said.

"That's right." Hahn emphasized his words with a cocky nod of the head.

Regas smiled and crossed his arms. "Who is the idiot now?"

Paul belly laughed.

Hahn and McNeeley sagged. Regas glared.

"Fuck you, then, Jigsaw. You'll be sorry." Regas turned back to face the table. "He'll be sorry, guys."

"Do you guys really think you are getting screwed?" Paul asked in a patient voice.

"Hell yes!" Regas spun around to face Paul. "We are being exploited. You are just too stupid to see it."

"That right? Who held a gun to your head and made you sign up for the Fly It Off program?"

"That's not the point!" Regas said, raising his voice. "You know as well as I do, there is a freighter crew shortage. Command can't fill the billets without us. And if they can't crew the ships and man the belt operations, the Chinese will have dibs."

"Exactly!" Hahn said, snapping his fingers. "Chinese don't play. They just press poor bastards into service over there. They got no problem crewing their damn fleet!"

"And if Command does not crew its fleet, the Chinese will dominate the asteroid belt and get all the energy resources, precious metals, and exotic materials."

"You've been studying hard, I see," Paul said with an insincere smile. "I'm impressed."

"It's the truth! No one in their right mind would sign up for this if they didn't have to. Four years on this piece of shit? It sucks!"

"And it's dangerous," McNeeley said. "There are a thousand ways to get killed on this death trap."

"Yeah!" Hahn nodded emphatically. "Killed, lost, or taken by pirates. Look at the *Perseus*! Gone forever. We could be next."

"And for what?" Regas asked.

"For your freedom, you idiots," Paul reminded them. "Three years of credit for every one year of duty. It's a good deal."

They looked at him, unable to argue the point.

"You're doing fifteen, right, McNeeley?" Paul asked.

McNeeley nodded.

"How many you got left?"

"Ten."

Paul shook his head.

"You'll be a free man when we get back. Don't let him screw this up for you," Paul said with a nod toward Regas. "I don't see this bullshit playing well with Captain Drake. The cranky old man might get pissed and kick you out of the program, give you zero credit. Then what?"

McNeeley looked from Paul to Regas and then back to Paul.

Regas saw the doubt welling in McNeeley's eyes.

"You wanna be a rich free man?" Regas asked McNeeley. "Or a poor free man?"

"Rich," McNeeley said.

"That's right," Hahn said.

Paul shrugged. "Good luck with that."

"Don't listen to this stuck-up jigsaw," Regas said, turning back to the table. "He don't know shit. And he's doing life, anyway. He's going right back to a cell when we get back. What does he care?"

Paul turned to leave.

"You sure you don't want to sign?" McNeeley asked Paul, leaning to his side so he could see around Regas.

"I learned a long time ago," Paul said as he walked toward the door. "To never trust a barracks lawyer."

"What if he can get us a better deal, though?" McNeeley asked, gesturing at Regas.

"Then he wouldn't be on this ship with us."

Chapter Nine

Belen Regas laughed as he skinned the frog alive. He was twelve years old at summer camp. He had led a small group away from the campsite during lunch and caught the little dark-green frog by the pond.

"Oh, my God! So gross!" a girl screamed as he pulled on the dark, rubbery skin. Pink and white flesh resisted the separation.

He held the frog's skinless rear legs in one hand as he tried to pull its skin off over its head like a sweater with the other. He grunted with effort.

The two girls ran away from the scene.

Three boys his age stood around him. They squinted, horrified but unable to look away, knowing it was wrong but not knowing what to do.

"Belen," one of the boys said, almost in a whisper. "Stop it."

"Shut up, Carlos!" Regas yelled, furious at the challenge.

He let go of the frog's skin with one hand, maintaining his grip on the tortured amphibian's legs with his other, and lunged at Carlos.

"If you love frogs so much, why don't you kiss it?" he said as he slapped Carlos in the face with the dying frog.

Carlos yelped as the other two boys turned to run. Carlos ran after them, crying as he wiped frog bits from his mouth.

Mr. Watson, a camp counselor, heard the commotion. He saw Regas standing by the pond and shook his head. *Crazy, that kid,* he thought to himself as he walked toward the cruel boy.

Regas saw him coming. "You're lucky, you little bitch," he whispered to the frog as he tossed it into the pond.

"Belen!" Mr. Watson said. "What was that?"

"Nuthin."

Mr. Watson looked at the disturbed water where the frog had landed in the pond and sunk out of sight. He shook his head at the young boy. "Belen…" he started. Then he stopped. The kid looked back at him, hands in pockets, unafraid. Almost taunting.

Mr. Watson turned and walked away. He was tired of dealing with Belen Regas. *No wonder his parents signed him up for eight weeks of summer camp,* he thought. *I wouldn't want that little shit around, either.*

* * *

Corporal Belen Regas woke up in the aid station. He was thirty-two years old on his second combat deployment. He couldn't see anything.

"I'm blind!" he yelled. "I'm blind! I'm fucking blind!"

"No, Corporal!" a voice said as he felt hands restrain him. "Corporal Regas, listen to me! Your eyes are fine. We bandaged them for your comfort. They were full of sand when they brought you in," she said.

"Sand?" Regas asked, lying back down.

His mind was fuzzy. Blurry thoughts passed by, just out of reach. Gradually, he remembered where he was. He was a squad leader. There had been a firefight. Had they won?

"Your helmet was destroyed by the blast. It's a miracle you survived."

"Fuck!" Regas shivered as blinding pain cleaved his forehead. He gripped the rails of the bed.

"Easy," the voice said. "Your brain has sustained a terrible concussion. You need to rest."

"How long was I out?" Regas whispered through the pain.

"Two weeks. The last week of it was induced, though. We had to keep you sedated because of all the brain swelling. You're a strong man, Belen. You took…"

Her voice faded away. Thankfully, so did the pain.

* * *

A month later, Corporal Regas walked into his company commander's office and saluted.

"There he is!" the captain said, returning the salute. "Regas the killing machine." The captain grinned and gestured at the pair of chairs. They both sat. "How do you feel?"

"Good. Thank you, sir."

"No more headaches?"

"Not nearly as many, sir," Regas said, nodding.

"Good," the captain said, smiling. "You're a lucky soldier. When that vehicle went up, I thought we'd be scraping you off the roof. I still don't know how you survived."

"Me either, sir."

"And, my God, son," the captain said, shaking his head. "The way you attacked them. I've never seen anything like it."

Regas just nodded. The truth was, he had enjoyed it. But he knew that he wasn't supposed to admit that.

"How is the lieutenant?" Regas asked to change the subject.

"He is going to make it. But it's going to be a long road back for him." The captain's face darkened. "You saved his life, you know. I'm putting you in for a Silver Star."

"Thank you, sir." Regas met the captain's gaze.

The captain nodded and looked at Regas for a long moment.

"Look, Corporal," the captain said, knowing there was no good time to tell him. "I'm sure you're wondering. We got the results back."

Regas said nothing. He could tell where this was going.

"You didn't get picked up for the Centaur Corps. I'm sorry. I know you really wanted it."

Regas resisted the urge to yell at the captain, to tell him he didn't know shit, to tell him that it was a fucking crime the Centaur Corps was not taking him. What a bunch of fucking idiots.

But, truthfully, Regas had expected it. It was just like the Academy. He never really had a chance. They tolerated his application and then denied it with pleasure. They couldn't deny his enlistment, though. And they couldn't deny he was the best killer in his unit. He loved it. He was good at it. He should have been welcomed into the Centaur Corps with wide-open arms. But they were just like the rest. Idiots.

"Any feedback why, sir?" was all Regas said.

"No, son, they rarely give out that kind of information. It's a simple yes or no."

"I understand, sir," Regas said.

The captain looked at the crestfallen soldier. "Look, Corporal Regas," he said. "You know you're in the running for squad leader when we rotate back. I know the lieutenant feels strongly about it. That would be another stripe. You'd be a sergeant, with a bright career in front of you."

Regas nodded. That was something. But it did not take away the sting.

"Am I dismissed, sir?"

"Sure, son," the captain said.

Regas stood up and saluted. The captain stood and returned the salute. He watched as the corporal left his office.

To join the Centaur Corps, an enlisted soldier had to serve a successful combat tour and then pass the rigorous assessment process. A tortuous one-month endurance test that ended in an extensive psych eval for those who made it that far.

Centaurs were augmented human soldiers. Not only was each centaur a $100 million investment by the military, it was a considerable physical upgrade to the human. Not the kind of upgrade you wanted to make to a person of unstable or otherwise undesirable mental makeup. The conditions and situations that Centaurs were exposed to were excruciating for even the strongest of constitution. And the damage they could do if they went haywire was extensive.

The captain walked back to his desk, sat down, and leaned back in his chair.

On his desk sat a file with Regas's name on it. The captain closed his eyes, remembering what it said.

CLASSIFIED—Though physically and tactically well qualified, psychological evaluations of Corporal Belen Regas reveal a lack of stability, a quickness of temper, and a tendency toward antisocial behavior. This combination of factors calls into question his ability to be loyal to his comrades, unit, or chain of command. This deficiency is exacerbated by his underdeveloped conscience and strong ego. Corporal Belen Regas is not fit for duty in the Centaur Corps.—CLASSIFIED

The captain remembered Regas fighting his way through the ambush to get to the lieutenant, who had been riding in the lead vehicle. When Regas charged forward, there was a moment of hesitation by the rest of the unit. It was chaos. Multiple vehicles had been hit, and there were so many enemy.

But Regas cut through everything in his way.

At the time, it had thrilled the captain. The courage. The will to win.

In retrospect, he wondered if he had seen some of what Regas' psych eval had described. He remembered looking for Regas when it was over. The medevac drones were cycling the wounded back to base, and the captain was not sure if Regas had been hurt or not. He found the corporal near the prisoners.

Half a dozen enemy had survived the skirmish and been captured. Stripped of their exoskeletons and armor, they sat on the ground, arms bound behind their backs inside a hastily assembled concertina-wire perimeter. Two soldiers stood guard over them.

The captain found Regas circling the POWs like a shark. He walked slowly around the captives, just outside the wire that encircled them. He held his bayonet in his right hand.

"Corporal Regas," the captain said, approaching. "Any injuries you need to have checked out?"

No response.

The captain stepped in front of Regas, who stared at the POWs as he walked.

"Corporal!"

Regas stopped and slowly swiveled his head to the captain.

"Sir?"

"You OK, son?"

"Yes, sir." Regas turned his head back toward the prisoners. "I'm fine."

"What are you doing?"

"Was just thinking, sir."

"About what?"

"Old pictures I've seen from the Vietnam War. You know they used to cut the ears off the enemy and make necklaces out of 'em?"

"Uh-huh…" The captain looked from Regas to the POWs and then back. "Well, we're not going to do that today, Corporal. If you are not hurt, I need you back on convoy security. We've got to get to the outpost before dark."

At the time, the captain had not thought much about Regas's comments. People said all kinds of weird shit in combat.

Now, he wasn't so sure.

* * *

Regas seethed as he left the captain's office.

The Combat Corps was the elite fighting arm of the US military. Formed after the disaster in Santiago, it was the unified fighting force that took the place of the fragmented special-operations community. Taking only the best, the Combat Corps was the most important and most honored branch of the modern military. The Combat Corps was made up of Centaurs and soldiers, and they were not created equal. The Centaurs were the elite. They were meldings of man and machine that could rain down death and destruction on an astounding scale. The Centaurs were the ones that counted. Wherever they went, they were in command. They were the real show.

Rather than full augmentation, the infantry component of the Combat Corps received epidermal electronic implants that were not much more than tattoos that sensed vitals and conveyed information to the exoskeletons they wore and fought in. In addition to working for the Centaurs, they did the shit details. The infantry missions, MP duty, convoy security, etc. These were important jobs. But still shit details.

Regas hated taking off his exoskeleton and armor at the end of a mission. He was back to being human. He knew that his destiny was to be a Centaur. He had waited as long as he could before applying.

Less than 5 percent of applicants made it through the assessment. Less than 5 percent of those ultimately made it through the training and augmentation process to become true Centaurs. Nonetheless, Belen Regas had been certain he was going to make it. He deserved it. His family had not had the money to send him to college, and he had not been able to get into the Academy. That was the first time the military had failed to recognize his greatness, and he never forgave that first offense. But the prospect of joining the Centaurs had helped him to move forward.

He realized now he had been a fool. It was rigged. Always would be.

He did not know what to do. That made him angrier.

Two weeks later, Regas was on a security patrol with his squad. It was their final mission. The next day, they would start the process of rotating back to the States. As they walked through the dusty streets, Regas spotted an open door. Usually, when they patrolled through a place, it was locked up tight. No one wanted any trouble with the American infantry.

Regas peered inside the open door. He thought he heard a noise inside, the shuffling of feet, perhaps. He turned sideways and crept with bent knees in order to get the bulk of his armored exoskeleton through the doorway. When he straightened up and turned into the room, a frightened male teenager looked back at him.

Regas leaned his rifle against the wall and pulled out his bayonet.

* * *

Four months later, Corporal Regas was drunk at the NCO club back at Camp Lejeune. He sat on his stool, ordering beer after beer. The waitress felt increasingly uncomfortable serving him. But she could tell he was one of those guys. A little crazy from what he had seen and what had happened to him, and not one who walked away politely after being cut off. It was easier to just keep serving him and call the MPs when he wasn't looking. They would be here soon.

Regas guzzled beers but was unable to swallow what had happened earlier that day. He sat hunched over at the bar, sagging under the weight of his indignation. He got madder and madder as he replayed the day's events over and over in his head. He punctuated each insulting memory with a large swallow of beer.

He remembered waiting in the battalion orderly room. He was so excited, it was hard to sit still, so he stood in the corner.

"Corporal Regas!" the major had called from his office.

The captain was a major now. He'd been promoted a month after they got back. Everyone was getting promoted. Today was supposed to be Regas's turn.

He snapped to attention and entered the major's office. Regas walked up to the major's desk and saluted.

"Sir, Corporal Belen Regas reports as ordered."

The major was sitting at his desk. The sergeant major and new lieutenant were seated in chairs just to the left of the major's desk. Regas had heard his old lieutenant was still in the hospital. He should be released soon, but would never be back on combat duty.

"At ease, Corporal," the major said, returning Regas's salute.

Regas felt fantastic. He knew his uniform looked perfect, and he had nailed the interviews earlier in the week. Now, finally, was his moment.

"Corporal," the major began. "We want to thank you for stepping up and applying for the squad leader position for third squad. It's the charge-the-hill attitude we've come to expect and rely on from you."

The major smiled nervously and glanced at the sergeant major.

That's when Regas knew. Fucked again.

"But the truth is, son, we are going to go in a different direction with third squad. You have demonstrated…"

Regas's mind went blank with rage. His head sagged and his arms went limp by his sides, leaving the position of at ease. He couldn't hear a word the major was saying.

"Fuck!" Regas heard himself shout.

"At ease, Corporal!" the sergeant major said, flying out of his chair. He was a salty old enlisted man, someone whom Regas actually respected. "You will maintain your military bearing, soldier!" the sergeant major yelled at Regas, closing the distance between them in an instant. Regas could smell the sergeant major's breath.

The new lieutenant sat stunned, eyes wide, in his chair.

The sergeant major's anger bumped Regas back from the edge. Just barely. He stammered as he tried to say his piece.

"I just don't get it, sir. I am the best soldier in this company. Period. You know that. I fucking saved my lieutenant's life when no one else would leave cover. What else do I need to do?"

Regas's voice was pleading. He heard it himself. He was ashamed.

The major gestured at the sergeant major to back off a little. The old NCO took half a step back, but maintained a glaring overwatch of Regas.

"Son," the major said. "I'm going to be as honest with you as I know how to be. You deserve that."

The major stood up and walked around his desk. He leaned back against it in front of Regas and crossed his arms.

"You are a good soldier, Regas," the major began. "But you are damaged, son. And not just from the combat. That leaves a mark on all of us. And we're all filthy from it. But you…"

The major paused, deciding if he should measure his words or not.

"Look, we've heard about the ears, the questionable battlefield killings, the way you bully other soldiers. We've never investigated, son, because we need you out there, outside of the wire with us. Every unit needs a crazy-ass killer like you. And I'm damn glad you're ours. And you did save the lieutenant. I don't forget shit like that. None of us do."

The major looked around the room. The lieutenant nodded. The sergeant major just stared at Regas.

The major uncrossed his arms and sighed. "But there is a difference between a good killer and a good leader. And stripes are for leaders, son. Not murderers. There is no way I'm giving you sergeant's stripes. Ever."

It was the finality in the major's voice that enraged Regas now as he sat drunk on a stool at the bar in the NCO club. The major's voice, more than his words, told Regas that his dreams were dead, that he didn't have a purpose anymore, that he wasn't good enough.

"Can I get another goddamn beer, please?" Regas yelled. The waitress looked at him from the other side of the bar.

Regas felt a hand on his shoulder.

"Evening, Corporal," said the MP. "Why don't we call it a night?"

Regas turned around on his stool to face the two military policemen. They each smiled at Regas with hey-we've-all-been-there grins meant to lower the tension. They were relaxed, not expecting a confrontation.

Big mistake.

Regas' beer mug shattered on the face of the nearest MP, shredding the flesh of the young man's cheek and knocking him unconscious.

In the next heartbeat, Regas kicked the other in the groin. Hard.

As the shocked MP bent over in pain, Belen broke his nose with a punch to the face. He fell backward, blood spraying on the floor.

"What the hell are you doing?" the waitress yelled at Regas.

He glanced at her and then scanned the NCO club. The small crowd was stunned by the sudden violence. No one was making a move for him yet.

Regas bolted for the door.

"Someone stop him!" he heard the waitress yell.

No one followed him.

* * *

Regas ran. He knew he was done.

He snuck off post that night, avoiding the gate guards, and then bought a bus ticket. He didn't go home. That was the first place the MPs would be looking for an AWOL soldier.

It was an overnight bus to Baton Rouge. Regas did not sleep at all, kept awake as his mind lurched from anger to shame to sadness and back to anger. The shame faded first. Then the sadness. All he had left when he got off the bus in Louisiana was anger.

Two months later, he was still on the run. Regas was living in a South Texas town, trying to figure out how to cross the border without getting picked up, when the MPs caught up with him. A few days earlier, he'd gotten in a fight in front of a convenience store where he had been hanging out, being rude and confrontational while he mulled over his plan. A hapless, smart-ass teenager had drawn his ire with loud music and a sneer. Regas beat him, would have killed him had two truckers not intervened.

It got him noticed.

Getting noticed got him caught.

"You dumb fucking son of a bitch," the major said to Regas when the MPs returned the disgraced corporal in handcuffs.

Regas just stared back at him from behind the bars of his prison cell. He imagined himself on the other side of the bars, pounding the smug officer into a bloody pulp. Then he would step on the unconscious man's head and grind it into the concrete floor. Then—

"Are you even listening to me?" the major asked.

Belen's eyes came back into focus and swiveled to meet the major's.

"You were AWOL for longer than thirty days. We're still at war, so that is called desertion. It's punishable by death."

No reaction from Regas. He would not give the major that satisfaction.

The major, who had been called into the brig to sign paperwork after Regas's return, was flabbergasted. Sadness came over his face. He shook his head, turned, and left without saying goodbye. It was useless.

The court-martial took half a day. Regas got twenty years for desertion, theft, and drunk and disorderly conduct. He sat in his cell afterward, not fully understanding what had just happened. He knew he had been charged with multiple counts of aggravated assault. But he had declined court-appointed counsel, so he hadn't really followed why those charges seemed to have gone away. He knew enough to know that he had gotten lucky, though. Those crimes carried decades more time in jail. As it stood, he'd still be a little over fifty when he got out.

The night before they shipped him to Leavenworth, he found out the source of his good luck.

"You're a lucky prisoner," a guard told him, delivering his dinner.

"Doesn't feel like it to me, sir," Regas said, taking the tray of slop and returning to the corner of his small cell.

"Shit," the guard said, shaking his head. "If that lieutenant of yours had not appealed to the judge, you'd have gotten about a hundred years for all those violent-assault charges."

Regas looked up from his slop.

"I guess you guys served together?" the guard asked.

"Yes, sir."

"I read the account of that day," the guard said, shaking his head slowly and raising his eyebrows. "Sounds like it was some serious shit."

Regas nodded, recalling. It seemed like a million years ago. Was that his best day ever? Would he ever feel like that again?

"Your old LT appealed to the judge. Made a case on your behalf. You know, all the damage you got up here." The guard pointed at his head. "Gave a long speech about how he lost his legs, but you lost your way. Told the judge how we treated our combat vets was shit. How it wouldn't be right to put you away forever."

Regas looked at the guard, wishing he would shut up, and then went back to eating his slop.

The guard chuckled. "Shit worked, I guess."

Two days later, Private Belen Regas was processed into the United States Disciplinary Barracks at Fort Leavenworth. Less than a year later, he applied to the Fly It Off program and was accepted due to the nonviolent nature of his convictions.

Chapter Ten

aul sat down at his desk at the beginning of the cycle. He felt good. It had been a good meditation, and he was ready to translate.

He opened *Adauchi,* his place marked by a letter he kept folded in its pages. The handwritten note was short and Paul started each translation session by reading it before setting it to the side. Then he took a deep breath and gazed at the dense Japanese text. Such a long way to go.

A rapid succession of jolts ran through the floor, accompanied by strange banging sounds. Both stopped as quickly as they began.

The loud shriek of the ship's decompression alarm startled Paul.

Paul jumped from his seat toward his utility closet.

"Attention on board, there has been a decompression event on the command-and-control module," said the XO in his ever-unperturbed voice.

Paul yanked his pressure suit out of the closet.

"The Hab and Utility Modules do not share life-support systems with that section of the ship and have not been compromised, so I have terminated the alarm," the XO announced.

"What is the status of the captain?" Paul yelled as he continued to don his pressure suit.

"I am trying to determine the captain's status. But at this time, the bridge has lost all atmospheric pressure. I have dispatched IR bots. They will be on station in two minutes."

"Damn it," Paul muttered.

He pulled on his helmet and activated the seal. Paul then turned and headed for the middle ladder.

Drummond and Althea stood gawking as Paul climbed through the second level.

"What are you doing, Paul?" Althea asked.

He ignored her and kept climbing.

Cooley, almost two kilometers aft in the tube, transmitted on the ship's intercom as Paul worked his way to the hub.

"Captain Drake, can you give us your status?" Cooley transmitted.

"Prisoner Owens. What are your intentions?" the XO's voice asked over the intercom in Paul's suit.

"I'm going to the bridge."

"I don't think that is advisable," chimed the XO. "My IR bots will be there in ninety seconds. Shouldn't you wait for Mr. Cooley's instructions?"

"Fuck you. I am headed that way." Paul pulled hand over hand on the traverse's ladder. His weight decreased, and he sailed upward as he neared the center of the hub.

Paul flew into the center hub and activated the airlock. Once in the tube, he grabbed the ladder and yanked repeatedly, increasing his speed. He barreled through the tube toward the C&C.

"Captain Drake, this is Prisoner Owens. Can you give us your status, please?"

No response.

"Owens, where are you?" Cooley called on the radio.

"In the tube. Headed for the bridge."

"Me too. I'm coming from PPM. Meet you at the airlock. All other crew members stay put. I repeat. All other crew members stay put. XO, any clarity on the captain's status?"

"Negative, Mr. Cooley. As you know, I am unable to monitor the C&C. Furthermore, he was not wearing a bio-monitor when the incident occurred, so I am getting no information from him."

"I want a report as soon as your IR bots are on-site," Cooley demanded.

"Of course."

Paul and Cooley were in sight of each other now and closing in fast. Paul reached up to the ladder rungs on the roof of the tube to slow himself. Cooley did the same.

They met under the bridge tower airlock. Cooley opened it and went up first. Paul followed. They sailed up the superstructure's ladder.

They were almost to the C&C air lock when the XO spoke up again.

"Extensive damage to the bridge, Mr. Cooley. Total loss of atmosphere. Captain Drake is dead."

Chapter Eleven

Captain Drake floated in the middle of the bridge. Most of his head was missing, as well as his left arm, which was severed cleanly just above the elbow. Bits of blood and fleshy debris orbited the captain in a cloud of frozen gore.

"Oh God," Cooley said.

Paul closed his eyes and shook his head. "Damn it," he mumbled from behind Cooley.

"Oh, Captain…" Cooley's voice choked with emotion.

"Any idea what happened, XO?" Paul asked. He touched the toe of his right mag boot to the floor for traction and eased next to Cooley, who floated motionless, staring at the captain's disfigured body.

As Paul passed the boatswain, he put a hand on Cooley's shoulder and got his attention. He and Paul locked eyes.

Tears welled in Cooley's eyes. But he gave Paul a thumbs-up.

"I'm good," Cooley said.

Paul nodded and turned back toward the captain. He dropped a mag boot to the floor and pushed off.

"It appears that we were struck by a group of meteoroids," the XO said. "In addition to the bridge, we have sustained damage to multiple hull sections and cargo containers. The factory was damaged as well. No indications of fire at this time."

"That's good," Paul said.

Fire on a spacecraft was a death sentence.

"Inspections are still underway," the XO continued. "But we have counted over two dozen hull penetrations so far. Aside from the bridge, however, no other pressurized sections have been compromised."

Paul approached the captain's body. It floated upside down relative to him and Cooley, rotating slowly. More than half of the captain's head was gone. Only his right cheek and ear remained.

Paul reached out and grabbed the captain by the shoulders. He pulled Drake toward the port-side and turned the body right side up as he pushed it against the wall. Paul let go of the captain for a moment and grabbed a cargo strap from a nearby utility closet. He secured the body to the wall so that it would not continue to float around the bridge while they made a plan.

The action snapped Cooley back into mode, and he helped Paul. Then they both inspected the damage.

Paul tried to ignore his quickening pulse and clammy hands.

The port side of the bridge looked like it had been shot open by a machine gun. There was a gaping, ragged hole large enough for a person to pass through, surrounded by numerous smaller holes. The penetrations radiated out from the large hole, pockmarking the entire port side with small glimpses of the void. Paul gave up counting. There must have been over a hundred holes.

He and Cooley turned to look at the starboard wall of the bridge. The holes were mirrored on that side. The mighty *Odysseus'* body had not slowed the galactic projectiles at all. They had passed through her, and the captain, in an instant and had kept going. Forever.

Paul and Cooley locked eyes again and shared rueful shakes of the head.

"Damn," Cooley said, looking back at the captain.

At least he died instantly, Paul thought. *Brain vaporized before it could register pain or fear.*

A flash of light outside the pierced hull caught Paul's eye. The inspection-and-repair bots were getting started.

"Mr. Cooley, I estimate that repairs to the bridge will take several cycles," the XO said.

"Got it. Proceed, and we will take care of the captain."

"That's really not necessary. I can have the body transferred to storage and—"

"XO, you know that is not what the captain would have wanted," Paul said. Cooley nodded.

The XO hesitated for a moment and then said, "As you wish."

"We will need some towels and a body bag," Paul said. "It's going to get messy when he starts to thaw out."

"I will have Althea bring you the necessary supplies," the XO said. "May I ask your intentions for the captain?"

"What does his file say?" Cooley asked, though he knew the answer.

Every spacefarer was required to fill out a last will and testament before leaving Earth. This file included disposition of remains, if there were any.

"Burial in space," the XO answered.

"Then those are our intentions. Please notify Drummond."

"Aye, Mr. Cooley."

Paul and Cooley floated in the depressurized command-and-control module with the captain, waiting for Althea to show up with cleaning materials and a body bag. They stared in silence at the captain. It seemed to Paul like a long time since he had been that close to a dead body, to a fallen comrade. He felt the familiar discomfort and sadness begin to creep into the edge of his mind. The anxiety was there, too. He did not want to remember.

The air lock opened down on the C&C's first level, startling Paul and Cooley. Althea glided up through the passageway onto the bridge, two large utility bags in her hands.

"You guys OK?"

"Fine," Cooley said.

"Can I help you with this?" she asked as she handed Cooley one of the large utility bags and pushed the other toward Paul.

"No."

"I'd really like to help." She looked at Paul, the concern on her face obvious, even from within a pressure-suit helmet.

Paul ignored her.

Althea floated nearby, observing as Cooley opened the utility bags. The IR bots worked silently just outside of the module, sparks erupting from their efforts on the *Odysseus'* hull.

Paul was motionless as he looked at the captain's bloody fragment of a head. Memories exploded in his mind. The blood. The torn flesh. The pain and fear. The cries for help.

"Paul?"

Althea's hand on Paul's shoulder startled him. He realized he had been staring at the captain. He was shaking. Paul turned and looked at Althea floating next to him in her pressure suit.

"What do you want?" He was irritated now.

"I want to help you. Let me help you guys with this."

"We'd rather take care of it ourselves," Cooley said.

"Are you sure? I think—"

"Althea, please!"

Paul realized he was shouting at her. Embarrassment flushed his face.

Cooley gave him a look as if to say, *I just got my shit back together. Don't lose yours.*

"I'm sorry," Paul said, shaking his head.

"Althea, I really appreciate you bringing the stuff," Cooley said. "But I need you to leave. Now."

Althea looked at Cooley. Then back to Paul, who was now unzipping one of the utility bags.

"Yes, sir."

But she did not leave right away. She floated motionless, still looking at Paul.

He tried to ignore her. Then he glared at her through his helmet visor and pointed at the passageway.

"Call if you need anything," she said as she turned and left.

Paul and Cooley got to work. Cooley went first to the storage unit down on the first level and retrieved a pressure-suit repair gun. Back at the captain's body, he sprayed the remains of the captain's head while Paul held the body steady.

The aerosol-propelled fiber-and-adhesive compound bound itself to Drake's flesh, sealing the gaping bloody cavity. It was not a technique one would ever use on a live person's wound, given its toxicity. But since it was designed to instantly restore integrity to a damaged pressure suit, Cooley figured it would contain the captain's lifeless blood for the next few hours, until they set the old man on his final journey.

"Go to his quarters and get a new uniform," Cooley told Paul.

"Aye, sir."

Paul touched a mag boot to the floor and pushed off toward the passageway down to the first level.

He went to the captain's closet and retrieved a new dress uniform. He also grabbed the captain's saber and formal hat.

Cooley had cut off the captain's tattered clothes by the time Paul returned to the bridge.

They put Drake in the new uniform, being careful not to allow any of the suspended frozen blood drops to cling to the new outfit. They pinned the left sleeve back on itself beneath the severed arm's stump. Then they gently pulled the black body bag over the captain and zipped it up.

"Mr. Cooley," Drummond called on the intercom. "Can you… um… give me a, um, status, please?"

Cooley made eye contact with Paul. But to Cooley's credit, he didn't break. He didn't say, "Now I've got to report to that asshole." He didn't make a face or even roll his eyes slightly. In that glance, Paul could see Cooley make the reluctant transition to a new captain. One who was unsuited for the task.

"Aye, sir," Cooley said, looking away from Paul. "Prisoner Owens and I have secured Captain Drake's body and prepared it for burial. We were going to make our way back to the Hab with it."

"You are bringing it here?"

"Yes. I assumed we'd do the ceremony from the air lock there. Did you have something else in mind, sir?"

The lowest level of the Hab, the floor where Paul and the other prisoner crew members' quarters were, was equipped with an air lock in its forwardmost section. It was useful as an on- and off-loading access point when the *Odysseus* was docked. But underway, with the spinner rotating, it wasn't very useful for anything other than emergency egress. It would be perfect for the captain's burial.

Cooley waited for the CFO's response. Nothing.

"I figured, that way, we wouldn't have to suit up and you could easily say a few words to the crew, sir," Cooley said after a moment, hoping to unstick Drummond.

Silence.

"In a brief ceremony, sir," Cooley added.

"Yes," Drummond responded. "Um… I concur. Proceed."

"We're on the way now, sir. Probably need about half an hour to get through the tube and get Captain Drake's body into position." When it became clear that Drummond was not going to acknowledge his last transmission, Cooley said, "XO, let me know when the bridge repairs are complete."

"Of course, Mr. Cooley," the XO responded.

Paul and Cooley floated through the tube, pushing Captain Drake's body in front of them.

* * *

"Ding-dong the son of a bitch is dead, eh, fellas?" Regas said with a chuckle.

"Stow that shit, Regas," Cooley said with a glare in Regas's direction. He and Paul had just finished setting the captain's casket down in the Hab air lock.

"Hey," Regas said with a friendly shrug. "I'm just kidding. I'm just kidding. He was a nice guy." Regas winked at Hahn and McNeeley, who chuckled.

It was hard to tell if they were amused or embarrassed by Regas's behavior. Either way, Cooley was pissed. Paul would not have been surprised if Cooley spaced Regas along with the captain. He would not have been opposed.

Paul and Cooley stepped out of the airlock and took their positions with the rest of the crew. Paul activated the bulkhead, sealing the living area off from the airlock.

Drummond shuffled his feet and adjusted his glasses. He was in agony. Paul had seen this before. Someone thrust by death into a role they were not up to. They knew it. Their unit knew it.

Regas, Hahn, and McNeeley stood on one side of the narrow passageway facing Paul, Cooley, and Althea on the other. Drummond stood at the end of their small formation, in the middle of the passageway, facing the air lock. Through the glass, they could all see the captain's casket sitting on the floor of the air lock.

Everyone waited for Drummond.

The pause was awkward.

Regas smiled. He stared at Drummond the way a schoolyard bully stares at his next victim. Hahn and McNeeley alternated their eyes between Regas and the CFO. They were nervous.

Cooley's hand rested on the handle of the large utility knife on his hip, the one he had used to cut the captain's bloody uniform off. Cooley glared at Regas, daring him to say or do something stupid.

Regas moved his eyes to Althea. They roved over her, head to toe and back and then down again.

Paul felt the slightest shift in Althea's posture. She stiffened in resistance to Regas's assaulting gaze while putting on a show of ignoring him.

Cooley couldn't take it anymore. He looked at Drummond and said, "You can begin now, sir."

Drummond coughed. "Y-yes. Um… of course."

He pulled a piece of paper out of his flight-suit breast pocket and unfolded it slowly.

"We are gathered here on this cycle to bid farewell to Captain Nathan Drake. Born on Earth in 2022. Killed in the line of duty on this cycle, in the year 2072. We, um, thank him for his service."

Drummond folded the paper and placed it back into his pocket.

He looked at Paul and said, "OK, Prisoner Owens."

Paul looked at Drummond and then at Cooley to be sure.

Cooley looked at Drummond and then back to Paul. His face was a mask of sadness and disgust as he nodded at Paul.

Paul pulled the lever, activating the air lock. The lights on the other side of the bulkhead flashed red for ten seconds in a countdown before the outer doors opened. When they did, the violent rush of escaping air launched the captain's coffin. It leapt out of the airlock and sailed into the void.

Paul watched it for as long as he could. It was gone in seconds, impossible to discern among the stars.

Chapter Twelve

aul woke up screaming. He tried to jump out of bed, believing it to be a pile of bodies. He had thrashed in his sleep, tangling his legs in the sheets. He fell heavily to the floor, which helped clear his head. It was the metal floor of the Hab module spinning on the front of the *Odysseus*, not that dusty village square. He lay on the cool floor for a few minutes, drenched in sweat and panting.

"I'm on the *Odysseus*," he said quietly to himself.

"Is everything OK, Paul?" said the XO over the intercom.

"Yeah. I'm fine." Paul rubbed his eyes.

"You sounded very alarmed. I hope you understand I don't eavesdrop, but if certain parameters are exceeded, I do check in just to ensure that—"

"I'm fine, XO. Just please let me wake up in peace." Paul stood up and walked to his bathroom.

"As you wish, Paul. My apologies."

"I'm definitely on the *Odysseus*," Paul grumbled to himself as he stepped into the shower.

Paul let the warm water run over him as he stood motionless. *Haven't had that dream in a while,* he thought. He looked at his hands. They were trembling. He began to get angry. His mind raced.

I can't fucking believe this. I left Earth to isolate myself from the triggers. To get the fuck away from anything that would remind me. I've worked so hard to get my shit together. I get out here, and a man gets his head taken off and I'm picking brains out of my clothing. Are you fucking kidding me!

"Paul. Are you OK?" It was the XO. Paul realized he had been screaming in the shower.

"Um… yeah… Thanks. I'm good."

"Very well. Please let me know if you need anything."

"I need you to leave me the fuck alone."

Paul sat down in the shower. He closed his eyes and did his breathing exercises as the warm water ran over his body.

By the time he'd left the shower, toweled off, and gotten dressed, Paul had de-escalated himself from enraged down through panicky to just anxious. He dove into his daily ritual, sitting for a longer-than-usual meditation before making himself a pot of coffee. He sat at his desk with a cup.

His watch alarm clock chimed.

"Fuck!" Paul muttered. *I just sat down to translate.*

But when Paul looked at his cup of coffee, no steam rose. Hadn't he just poured it? He grabbed the cup. It wasn't warm. He dipped his finger into the coffee. It was cold. He looked at his watch.

It had been forty-five minutes. He had ten minutes until the meeting Drummond had scheduled.

"Shit," he muttered.

* * *

"Attention!" Cooley said as he entered the room ahead of Drummond.

The room sprang to attention.

Cooley walked to his seat. Drummond walked to his and sat down.

Cooley cleared his throat. Drummond looked at him.

"Oh," Drummond said. "Yes. Please be seated."

Regas glanced at McNeeley and Hahn, who just managed to hide their snickering. Cooley glared.

"Mr. Cooley," Drummond said, glancing quickly around the room. "You may conduct this meeting, if you will."

"Aye, Captain," Cooley said.

"Congratulations," Regas said before Cooley could continue. Regas wore his most friendly smile to disguise his act of disrespect.

"Excuse me, Prisoner?" Cooley said.

"I'm sorry, Mr. Cooley," Regas said, still wearing the bullshit smile. "Just seems like we should acknowledge Mr. Drummond's—I mean, Captain Drummond's—promotion, shouldn't we?"

Paul looked at Cooley, wondering if he would explode. Then he looked at Regas. Paul noticed that Regas's left breast pocket was unzipped, just like last time. Paul knew it was not a coincidence.

"Prisoner Regas—" Cooley began.

"It's OK, Mr. Cooley," Drummond interrupted him. "Let's just get on with it. We've got less than six months to the belt. When we get there, we'll let the Company know what has happened, and they will have resources, including people, that I am sure will be very helpful."

It was clear to everyone that Drummond was hoping that a new captain would come aboard at that time. Space Command always had experienced senior officers posted at Belt Station for contingencies like this one.

But his comment did raise another question.

"Has the Company not already been informed of the incident, sir?" Paul asked Drummond.

Drummond glanced at Cooley and then looked down as he said, "No, Prisoner Owens. They have not."

The crew exchanged looks.

"XO, please review the damage report for the crew," Cooley said.

"Yes, sir," the XO responded. A three-dimensional schematic of the *Odysseus* sprang to life above the table's holo-display. Red highlights blinked in dozens of areas, including the bridge.

"The *Odysseus* was struck by a total of one hundred and seventy-one meteoroids across her entire length. There were two main clusters, however, that caused most of the damage. One was concentrated aft of the hangar, below the tube."

Red circles appeared around two areas on the *Odysseus'* floating image as the XO outlined them.

"And the other was concentrated on the bridge. This is the meteoroid cluster that killed Captain Drake."

"At what angle did the meteoroids strike us?" Paul asked.

"The meteoroids struck the *Odysseus* at eighty-seven degrees off of flight path." As the XO spoke, red lines traced the meteoroids' paths passing through the *Odysseus* on the table displays.

"Damn near a perfect broadside," said Paul.

"We'd have been fucked if anything had hit the spinner," Regas said.

"Indeed, Prisoner Regas," the XO said. "A large enough strike to any part of the spinner would have created a severe out-of-balance situation that I would not have been able to control. It would have torn itself apart. We'd have lost both the Habitat and the Utility Modules and likely suffered severe damage to other parts of the *Odysseus*."

"Please continue with the report, XO," Cooley said with some irritation in his voice.

"Full atmosphere and environmentals have been restored to the bridge, but most of its command-and-control capabilities remain offline. Twenty-seven percent of hull perforations have already been repaired, and I estimate we will be at one hundred percent in less than five cycles."

As the XO talked, the 3D *Odysseus* schematic image rolled and expanded to show the precise impact areas.

"Cargo damage assessment is not yet complete but so far looks limited primarily to raw materials. The factory was only slightly damaged and is fully operational again. Communications systems, however, were heavily damaged, given their location aft and below the tube."

"That's not good," Paul said.

"You're right," responded the XO as the image zoomed in. "This is the main communications antennae array site. Five small meteoroids impacted this area, damaging our ship-to-ship communications antennae and destroying our long-range antennae array. The ship-to-ship antennae can likely be repaired, and we should be able to achieve seventy-five percent capacity."

"That's great, XO," Regas said in a sarcastic voice. "Especially since we are at least fifty million kilometers from the nearest ship, and the range of that antennae is, what? A couple million kilometers?"

"You are correct, Prisoner Regas."

"What about the long-range antennae?" Paul asked.

"The long-range antennae array was damaged beyond repair," Cooley said.

The crew sat silent for a moment, staring at the image of the *Odysseus* floating over the large table.

The long-range antennae array served two purposes. First, it allowed the *Odysseus* to communicate with the Company back on Earth and in the belt whenever there was a need. This included the Bloomberg Belt Market feed. Drummond nearly cried when Cooley had explained this to him.

Second, it transmitted the *Odysseus'* location and other data on a regular schedule. This data provided the Company with situational awareness that enabled it to warn of hazards and known pirate activity, de-conflict flight paths, and effect rescue if needed. Without this communication link, the *Odysseus* was on its own in the void until it made it to the asteroid belt.

The *Odysseus* suddenly felt much more remote.

"Any other good news, XO?" Regas asked.

"No. That is it. As tragic and irritating as this situation is, it could have been much worse."

"I thought these shipping lanes were constantly reviewed for foreign object violations like this," Paul said, turning his head toward Cooley.

"They are," the XO said. "Command takes care to plot courses that are out of the way of all known meteoroids and other hazards."

"Fuck load of good it did us," Regas said.

"The void is infinite," Cooley said with a shrug. "It is too big. There's too much stuff out there. And, unfortunately, the usual method of discovery is a collision like this."

"I have recorded the meteoroid cluster," the XO said, "as well as calculated its new trajectory as a result of the collision with the *Odysseus*, and will upload it to command as soon as I am able."

"You mean when we dock at the belt?" Paul said.

"Unfortunately, yes."

"OK," Cooley said. "So, as we discussed, Mr. Drummond is serving as captain. I will be adjusting our training and maintenance schedule in coordination with the XO as he completes the damage assessment. The old girl is going to need a lot of repairs, and we are going to have to pitch in. The new cycle watch and duty schedule will be posted in a few hours."

Cooley looked around the room and then at Drummond, who was looking at his tablet computer.

"Sir?"

"Yes, Mr. Cooley?"

"Will that be all, sir?"

"Oh," Drummond said. "Yes. I think so."

"Then are we dismissed, sir?" Cooley asked when it was obvious Drummond still didn't get it.

"Yes." Drummond looked back down at his tablet. "You are dismissed."

The crew stood up and began to leave. Drummond stayed in his seat.

"So, no other promotions, then?" Regas said to no one in particular. "Damn."

McNeeley and Hahn snickered.

Althea and Paul were the last to filter out of the room. As they neared the door, Paul gestured to Althea to go ahead of him.

She hesitated. "Paul. How are you feeling?"

"Fine."

"Are you sure? The XO told me you have had a rough time sleeping."

"I'm fine, Althea," Paul said with some irritation. "I promise. Just leave me alone."

He pushed ahead of her and walked out.

Chapter Thirteen

ater that cycle, after his duties were complete, Paul went to the fitness room. Located across the hub on the top floor of the Utility Module, it was a decades-old facility that was part of the original retrofit of the spinner. "The military doesn't go anywhere without a weight room, beer, and porn," Captain Drake had said about the facility. Used often by previous crew members, it was one of the grungiest rooms on the *Odysseus*, and certainly the worst smelling. Despite years of cleaning by sanitation bots, the smell of sweaty soldiers persisted.

Paul visited the fitness facility every other cycle. Occasionally, he would get on one of the old-style treadmills, but usually he lifted weights.

He did both that cycle, hoping a good workout would help him sleep.

Paul woke up screaming anyway.

He thrashed himself awake but managed to not fall out of the bed. But he was stuck. He lay in sweaty sheets, unable to move. He could not speak. Could not break his gaze at the ceiling. Brains floating in the bridge, entrails dragging through the dirt, aircraft falling in flames from the sky, a pile of dead foot soldiers, a bayonet slicing, rockets flying, bullets impacting. Kill after kill. His brain cycled from image to image to image as he relived it all... He started to tremble. He was being swallowed by it.

"Paul." A voice called from the void.

He couldn't find it.

"Paul," Althea repeated.

He felt a hand on his shoulder.

"Paul," Althea said tenderly, but with some force to get through to him. His head swiveled quickly, and she met his gaze.

She was sitting on the edge of his bed.

His eyes were wide and darting back and forth. His breathing was rapid. Althea noted his pulse rising.

"Paul, you are in your quarters on the *Odysseus*, and I am here with you." She maintained eye contact, beckoning him back.

"You're safe, Paul."

His wide eyes narrowed slightly. His breathing slowed. He recognized her.

She gave him a few minutes to breathe before whispering, "It's OK."

"I can't believe it. I thought I had gotten far enough away from it." Tears ran down his face. His voice quivered with pain. "How fucking far do I have to go to get away? They are all around me again."

Althea grabbed his other shoulder and gently turned him to face her squarely.

"No! I know it feels that way. But it's just you and me here. In your room. On the *Odysseus*. Together."

Paul looked around nervously. "I know. I know. I just…" he stammered. Then he locked eyes with Althea.

Althea nodded. "I won't let you get lost again, Paul. I promise. I've got you. But you've got to meet me halfway."

Paul nodded. Then he sobbed.

Althea sat next to him, hand on his shoulder, for the next hour. When Paul was spent and had fallen asleep, she stood up carefully and left.

She closed Paul's door. When she turned to go back to her quarters, Regas startled her.

She stopped herself just before running into him.

"Can I get some room service also?" Regas said, taking a step closer, one foot almost between her legs. He towered over her, head angled down, eyes running over her body.

"Have a good evening, Prisoner," Althea said sharply, moving to step around him.

Regas matched her step to the side, blocking her path.

"Come on. It ain't fair. Why does the jigsaw get special favors?" Regas stared at Althea's breasts and rubbed his chin.

"If there are issues you need my assistance with, you may schedule a time through Mr. Cooley," Althea said without emotion. "That is the policy."

Regas dropped his hand from his chin and adjusted his crotch.

"I ever tell you how much you remind me of someone I knew? It was my first deployment, I think."

Althea stayed silent, not taking the bait.

"Some*thing*, actually. A synthetic. My squad and I found her when we were patrolling behind a jigsaw unit that had carried out a major raid the night before. Who knows? Maybe it was Captain Jigsaw's unit?"

Regas gestured past Althea at Paul's door.

"Those guys were always in and out without coordinating with anyone, so how would I know?" Regas said with a shrug. "All I know is they killed a lot of people. The little town was all shot up. It was a mess. One of the other guys heard her. She was inside a bombed-out building, kneeling over a wounded civilian, administering aid. The four of us snuck up on her."

Regas chuckled at the memory.

"She looked kind of like you. Black hair. Skin work wasn't as good as yours by a long shot. But nice titties. She was missing a hand and about half that forearm. A couple of wires dangled out of her stump. But, other than that, she was good to go. You guys don't really bleed as much as we do, you know."

An ugly smile spread across Regas's face.

"I went first. Then I went again when the others were done. We tied it up and hid it in a closet in that shot-up house. I mean, we couldn't tell anyone else in the unit about it. They would have worn it out in a day. We kept it a secret. Just our squad."

Regas paused, as if recalling one of his fondest memories.

"The fellas got mad at me, because within a few days, I had broken her up pretty bad. I didn't care, though. In fact, I liked it better that way. I didn't care that she didn't have a head anymore. Or that the one leg bent the wrong way."

Regas's eyes roved all over Althea as he spoke.

"It got to be ridiculous. I mean, it was really broken. I didn't care. But that's when the rest of the unit found out about it. You know what my commander did when he heard?"

Althea kept her face placid, knowing that he would feed off any reaction.

"He laughed! Thought it was hilarious."

Althea looked down.

"I bet your jigsaw captain would have laughed too," Regas said in a mocking whisper. "So, you see," he said, hand reaching out to her. "I've got stuff I need to talk about, too."

"Prisoner!" Althea slapped his hand and stepped back. "Let me pass or I will report this incident."

"Incident?" Regas said, raising his voice. "What incident? I haven't gotten shit. It's the jigsaw who you've been fucking." Regas pointed at Paul's room with growing anger. "You're the one who should be reported!"

Althea squared her stance, preparing for violence.

"That will be enough, Prisoner Regas," the XO said over the hallway speakers, startling Regas. "I asked Althea to visit Prisoner Owens's quarters for medical reasons."

Regas looked at the speaker in the ceiling and then back to Althea.

"Return to your quarters this instant, or I will report this incident to Mr. Cooley and Captain Drummond," the XO said.

Regas stared at Althea, who met his gaze with defiance.

"No problem, XO," Regas said, letting his eyes rove over Althea one more time before he slowly backed down the hallway. "Nice talking to you, Althea."

EARTH

Chapter Fourteen

"I am not happy about this, Cyrus."

Fiona Malloy stood behind her desk, looking out the floor to ceiling windows of her top floor midtown Manhattan office. The expansive windows lined two entire walls of the corner office, coming together in a dramatic apex behind her large, dark modern desk. She looked down at Central Park. The green space stretched away to the north, surrounded on all sides by encroaching grey buildings. Thousands of feet above the park, reflections of the rising sun sparkled off of the multitude of delivery and taxi drones coursing above the city. Behind Fiona, wide flat screen TVs lined the other two walls and a large conference table with seating for twenty sat in the middle of the room.

She shook her head slowly in frustration.

Cyrus Thane stood behind Fiona on the far side of her office next to her large conference table. His bald head and longish, well-groomed and greying beard gave his face a distinguished but oversized appearance. Everything about Thane gave a slightly exaggerated impression. He was dressed in one of his many tailored, double-breasted suits that accentuated his athletic build and six-foot-four height. This one was steel blue. Without a tie, his crisp white open-collared shirt and ivory pocket square hinted at the end of a well-handled day at work, even though it was only seven AM.

He stood motionless behind Fiona, studying her silhouette as he often did when she was not looking. Dressed in a form-fitting pantsuit, charcoal grey with a faint blue pinstripe, her lean frame cut an angular, determined figure against the view of Manhattan. Her long brown hair was pulled back in a tight bun as usual, accentuating her shoulders.

Cyrus was a good eight inches taller and over a hundred pounds heavier than Fiona. But she still intimidated him.

And aroused him.

Thane had never known anyone like her. She was smart. Sexy. Rich. Powerful. Ruthless. At only 37 years old, she was one of the dominant forces in the international defense industry, an industry that typically destroyed newcomers.

It irritated Thane that, in the almost seven years he had worked as Fiona's contracted head of security, he had developed feelings for her. Many carnal, of course. But some unlike any he had felt for a woman before, like *devoted* and *protective*. A lifelong bachelor - *If the military wanted me to have a wife, they would have issued me one, amirite?* - These were the things he had never really felt before and was uncomfortable with now. Things he certainly never talked about. To anybody.

Because Thane knew damn well, he could never act on them, and would never be satisfied. Fiona was of the highest caste, a member of the small and privileged America he would never be a part of.

Thane took off his uniform after spending twenty years of his life "defending freedom." It didn't take long as a lower middle-class civilian with a government pension for him to realize it was all bullshit. He had been duped. America was a stratified caste system, less fair and more soul crushing than the communist society he and his comrades had fought against for decades. All that really mattered was money. Period. How much you had. How much you could spend. How much you could borrow. The virtues he had structured his life around - duty, honor, country - were false idols conjured by the monied commercial interests to manipulate simple, earnest kids like he had been, to serve and defend the system that kept a tiny upper caste swimming in privilege and wealth. Thane fell for it. But at least he had survived. Barely. Many of his comrades had not.

Thane was 38 years old when he retired from the military with twenty years of service. Not over the hill, exactly. But late in life to realize you'd been a sucker. So, realizing he had an extremely narrow set of marketable skills - killing people and breaking things, Thane applied to the highest paying private military contractor he knew of. DredSkill.

Fine, he thought. *I'll be a mercenary. But I won't be poor.*

Now, less than six months from his fiftieth birthday, he rated joining DredSkill as the best decision he had made in his life.

DredSkill recognized Thane's experience and potential immediately. What they had not understood was Thane's deep desire to be rich. They quickly realized, however, that this guy would take any job, anywhere, to make money. He had no qualms or personal redlines. Within his first year at the outfit, he was the highest paid operator, known for only taking the highest paying gigs, no matter how dirty or wet the job.

So, when Fiona Malloy reached out needing help of the most dangerous and discrete kind, DredSkill put Cyrus Thane on the job.

He did some bad things for her. Really bad. Things that only a few living people knew about, including Fiona. Especially Fiona.

Thane liked to think that the secrets, the things he did for her, were a kind of connection to Fiona. At least he felt it. He also knew those things could never be mentioned. Ever.

So, really, he didn't know how she felt about it all. That frustrated him. Sure, he knew she was glad he did those things for her, that it all worked in the end. He knew she was glad they were still secret. And he damn sure knew she wanted them to stay secret.

But how did she *feel* about it?

Did she realize he would do more if she asked?

So, because of all of that, it was a relief to him to be re-assigned. Sort of.

It was clearly not a relief to Fiona.

Thane stood next to the conference table in a stance he would have called parade rest in his previous life as a soldier - feet shoulder-width apart, hands clasped together in the center of his back. He found the posture worked well in his civilian professional life to help defuse angry clients.

It wasn't working this morning, though.

He could almost see the anger radiating from Fiona's tense shoulders.

"I would have thought the eye-watering sum of money I pay you guys assured me some measure of continuity," Fiona said to him without turning her head from the window.

Fiona had appeared on the defense industry scene like a thunderbolt in the summer of 2066 when one of her young start-up companies, Spitting Metal, secured the largest defense contract in history. Fiona and Spitting Metal were immediately designated high value intelligence and disruption targets for the Chinese, Russians and other adversaries. They were also juicy corporate espionage targets for Lockheed Martin Boeing, Raytheon and the other old school defense industry perennials. The big, slow goliaths had been surprised by Fiona's success. Their surprise had quickly turned to insult, and Fiona found herself besieged on all sides.

Unsettled by her newfound notoriety and high profile, Fiona moved to upgrade her security posture. Determined End States, the holding company that owned Spitting Metal and the rest of her military AI portfolio, had a small corporate security team. But Fiona wanted more robust capabilities.

The distasteful crisis with Musashi's Ōkami on the southern cone taught her the virtue of having discrete options and reach in a crisis, and had led her to Dredskill, a low profile but accomplished international private military contractor. From her first outreach, DredSkill's leadership recognized the opportunity in a relationship with Fiona Malloy. They assigned Cyrus Thane, one of their most experienced security executives, to her with a clear charter - "Whatever she needs." And though Fiona almost lost her nerve several times, Thane handled the situation better than she could have ever hoped.

Pleased with the outcome of that initial, very sensitive engagement, Fiona expanded her relationship with Dredskill when things accelerated for Spitting Metal. They now provided comprehensive corporate security services for

Fiona's entire business empire, all at Thane's direction.

Almost seven years later, all parties were pleased.

Today, though, DredSkill was promoting Thane and moving him off of Fiona's account.

Or trying to.

Fiona turned from the window and looked at Thane, a hand on one hip.

"So, let me make sure I have this straight," she said, raising the other hand to count with her fingers as she spoke. "My most sensitive and risky private security requirements have been well handled. My businesses have not suffered a single security incident or other penetration. DredSkill is making trainloads of money. You must be, let's be honest, viewed as the Firm's most successful security professional since the boss lady herself. And you are enjoying the role of wealthy playboy in New York City."

Thane held parade rest and dared not smile, but he loved the fact that she was taking this so badly. Would she miss him?

"You guys seriously want to put all that at risk?" Fiona added, acid in her voice. "Because all it takes is one fuck up."

Thane did not take the rhetorical bait.

"How about you, Cyrus?" she asked in a more personal tone. "You think this is a good idea? You're on board with this change?"

"Don't worry, ma'am. I handpicked my successor. I have known him for fifteen years. We served together, and I personally recruited him to DredSkill. He's been with the Firm for five years and has handled some of our most demanding and complex jobs."

"But is he discrete?" Fiona asked, turning from the window and leveling her eyes at Thane.

"Yes. He wouldn't work for the Firm if he was not."

Fiona stood motionless, eyes boring into Thane.

Thane let a few heartbeats go by, holding her gaze.

"Give him a chance," he finally said. "You will like him."

Fiona's jaw clenched.

"If you don't like him, you just say the word, and we will fix it. Also, I will stay involved as an advisor to both him and you. This will actually end up being an upgrade, I promise."

"Uh huh," Fiona said, finally turning away from Thane and looking back out the window.

Thane fidgeted and looked down at his Berluti buckled monk shoes. He had learned that when Fiona was mad, it was best not to push. He took a few even breaths and then looked back up at her.

"Would you please at least meet him, Miss Malloy?"

In seven years, he had never called her by her first name.

Just when he thought she was ignoring him, she said, "Fine."

Thane tried to stifle a sigh of relief.

"Thank you."

Fiona turned from the window and walked toward her desk.

Thane took the cue and left her office.

* * *

Fiona sat at her desk and stewed after Thane left. *This new guy better be good,* she thought. Shaking her head to clear it of irritation, she checked her watch. It wasn't even eight AM yet. So, not yet 2pm in Italy.

She picked her cell phone off her desk and swiveled in her chair to face out the window as she called Eugene. She pictured his Italian villa, Mio Posto, as the phone rang. She loved stepping out of the main house, a converted barn, into the garden behind it. A low stone wall encircled Eugene's favorite herbs and flowers, which radiated out in semicircular planters, from an old bird bath, always burbling with fresh water spilling from the small fountain that fed it.

A path wound out of the garden, passing through an old iron gate that clung to the stone wall. Fiona loved to follow the long, meandering trail, appreciating its hidden sitting areas and views of the rolling Tuscan hills. There was one spot in particular, her favorite, that she found herself gravitating to each day when she visited her brother.

A large stone bench sat beneath an old gnarled olive tree. Eugene told her he thought the tree was a few hundred years old, because he could not get his arms around its knobby, twisting trunk. The ground declined gently to the south and the patchwork of olive groves, vineyards and fields stretched far into the distance. Fiona liked to sit there with coffee in the mornings, watching the long shadows shrink, revealing farm houses and barns in the distance. In the evenings she would sit in the same spot with a glass of wine, watching the shadows lengthen, gradually dousing the view in darkness. Sitting in that spot, eyes resting on the horizon, she felt more at peace than anywhere else in the world.

Eugene noticed Fiona's affinity for the quiet spot. When she returned for a visit a few months later, she found that he had had her name carved into the bench. A gesture that brought a tear to the global defense industry titan's eyes.

That was during what she now thought of as the good times for her and Eugene, just after she had narrowly averted disaster with Spitting Metal and his villa. The business was doing well and the ugliness, the things she had to do, seemed as if they would stay behind her in the past.

That was before she learned what Pruden was up to. That the sphere was missing. That Musashi was missing also.

And it was before her falling out with Eugene.

Now, she sat in her chair listening to his phone ring and thought about the last time she sat on that bench, almost five years ago, just before their big fight.

They had not spoken since. And she knew they would not speak today. Eugene would not pick up.

She let the phone ring until his voice mail answered and then hung up. She stopped leaving messages a few years ago. Doing so always left her feeling even sadder than when she called, and she doubted he listened to them. But she knew he would see that she had called. He would know she was thinking about him. Maybe one day he would call her back.

Chapter Fifteen

"Miss Malloy, your two p.m. is here," the receptionist said, her voice tentative as she leaned her head into Fiona's office.

Fiona looked at her watch and frowned. She had forgotten about this meeting. Ordinarily, she would have been looking forward to it. Sort of.

But now, with the Quarterly Business Review at the end of the week, she had too much to do and—

"MALLOY!" The distinctive boom of General (Ret) James "Bear" Harriman filled Fiona's office. Her assistant looked at her apologetically as the stocky retired general in the tailored dark grey suit and Persol 649 photochromic sunglasses strode past her toward Fiona's desk.

Fiona forced a smile, wondering for the hundredth time why she'd started this charity… though she knew exactly why.

"Still all work and no play, I see." The general looked around Fiona's office and then back at her receptionist. "We gotten her laid yet?"

The receptionist fled the scene.

Bear looked at Fiona and shrugged.

Fiona could not resist chuckling as she stood and shook the general's hand. His trademark coarse enthusiasm, cloaked in Wall Street polish, always made her smile. The fifty-six-year-old divorcé, with his well-coifed, salt and pepper, just-a-little-longer-than-regulation head of hair and ever present stylish glasses gave off a worldly, appetitive vibe that reminded her of Thane.

"Good to see you, Bear. Thanks for coming."

"Don't fucking thank me. You're the boss, remember?"

Fiona chuckled again and gestured at her seating area.

Following the general, she marveled, as she always did, at the fluidity and grace of his movement. He set his leather briefcase down and settled into one of the oversized leather chairs, shooting her an easy smile that gave no hint of the hardship he had endured - losing both legs in Schofield's doomed offensive in South America in 2067. When he accepted the role of director, she made sure he got the most advanced prosthetics available - full artificial flesh housings with enhanced synaptic proprioception and virtual gyroscopes.

The old warrior wore them well.

"Aw shit," Bear said. He gave Fiona a just-a-minute look as tapped the side of his glasses and stood back up.

Fiona shook her head in respect at the old general's back as he stepped away and answered the call. No one else on the planet did that to Fiona Malloy. Ever.

She took no offense, though. She had known what she was getting when she picked the Bear to lead the Warrior Renewal Initiative.

"WERNER! How the hell are you? Look I'm meeting with my boss. Can you make it fast?"

The general turned and looked back at Fiona, offering her a what-the-hell look and shaking his head as if the caller was the most insolent person he had ever had to deal with.

"Yeah?" He turned back around. "Really? Well, it's about goddamn time!"

The general put his hands on his hips and nodded vigorously as he listened to the other end.

"Uh, huh. Yeah… OK… Yeah.

"Look, Werner, I think she'll be real pleased. Real pleased. But you know I can't promise you that.

"Uh, huh… I understand. I'll try. I really will. I feel good about it.

"Thanks again, buddy. I gotta go. She is busting my balls.

"You too, you old bastard."

The general turned and headed back to the seating area.

"That was Werner Müller, chairman of Rheinmetall over in Germany." The Bear smiled as he sat down. "He says they are good for five million bucks to be a premier sponsor of our golf tournament."

Fiona's eyebrows raised. "You serious, Bear?"

"Yes, ma'am." The general's eyes crinkled as he smiled. "He wants all the golf balls to be branded Rheinmetall. I figure no brainer, and told him OK."

"What was that last bit?" Fiona asked. "What did you tell him you'd try?"

"Oh, he wants a one-on-one breakfast with you at the tourney."

"For five million dollars? Yeah. Tell him he gets some cheesy eggs and bacon with me."

Bear shook his head.

"No, ma'am."

"No?"

"Trust me on this one, ma'am. He's good for a million more. No doubt about it. Gimme another few weeks to string him out."

Fiona leaned back in her seat, nodding her head in respect at the Bear.

"But, look, that's not why I'm here, ma'am." The general grabbed his briefcase, opened it, and pulled out a small tablet computer. "Which of these damn monitors is available?" He asked, waving at the numerous video screens streaming market updates.

"Use that one," Fiona said, gesturing at the largest of her wide-screen monitors. It went blank at her command.

"I think you are really going to love this," he said with confidence, gesturing from his tablet to the big screen.

Fiona settled into her chair and steadied her breathing. She hated these things.

The screen went black for a moment.

Then a date appeared.

"August 11th, 2070."

A somber male voice started speaking.

"We knew it was going to be a fight."

The image of a mountain side battle faded into view. The green tint of the night vision imagery was grainy. The image faded in an out, washed out by intermittent explosions. Tracers and directed energy beams lanced back and forth across a dark shape that Fiona recognized as a shattered and burning hexacopter.

"But we also knew it had to be us. No one else was close enough."

Soldierbots and troops in exoskeletons slugged their way up the steep rocky incline of a mountainside, striving to reach the downed aircraft.

The assaulting troops began taking hits. Several were engulfed in flames while others broke apart under withering, well-aimed fire. Earth and body parts were thrown in the air. Despite the cleansing effect of the monochromatic night vision, it was awful to watch.

"We paid a price, but we got there in time," the voice continued. "We pushed the enemy back and extracted the survivors and… And those that didn't survive.

"I remember looking around that smoking hillside while we waited for extraction and thinking how lucky I had been."

A series of large explosions washed out the screen.

The voice chuckled sadly. "Feels pretty stupid to say that now."

The camera jerked back and forth abruptly and went black again.

"I woke up two weeks later at Walter Reed."

The image of an intensive care hospital room faded into frame. Tubes and IVs snaked into a bandaged body lying in the bed, nurses in attendance. The camera lingered just long enough for Fiona to grasp what happened.

The wounded soldier had no arms.

The image faded and changed. A young man with a bruised and scraped face sat in a chair flanked by two nurses working on stumps where his arms should have been.

"Recovery was hard."

The nurses worked on the shoulder stumps with metal instruments. His face contorted in agony.

"But the worst was my little girl."

The image changed back to the hospital room. Colorful balloons and flowers circled the bed. A woman, stood over the bandaged, armless man as a young girl, maybe four years old, stood next to the bed raising her arms.

"Not being able to pick her up and hold her…" The voice cracked with emotion. "That made me want to die."

Now the image was of the disfigured soldier in a physical rehabilitation setting. He was wearing awkward metal arms with clumsy mechanical mitts for hands. His face was a knot of frustration as he tried to pick up a towel.

"The prosthetics the VA gave me were worse than nothing. They were insulting. They…" the voice cracked again. "They scared my daughter."

The screen faded to black.

"I was actively planning how to kill myself."

The screen stayed black for an extra beat before the sound hopeful music broke out and the screen blossomed in happy pastel colors that morphed into the scene of the young man, miraculously, walking down a wooded path holding his daughter in one arm, and his wife's hand in the other. Shafts of morning sun struck his arms, illuminating the flesh with a warm glow.

"The Warrior Renewal Initiative saved my life."

The daughter bolted from her father and ran, laughing with joy, toward the camera.

The scene cut to another physical therapy room, one that was clearly superior to what had been seen so far. Happy nurses were attaching a state-of-the-art, artificial flesh covered arm to the smiling soldier.

The camera zoomed into the soldier's right shoulder. The prosthetic's flesh reached out to his scared stump, forming a tight seal as high-tech specifications and buzzwords flashed across the screen.

"Self-adhesive organic bonding."

"Full spectrum tactile sensing."

"Adaptive learning and constant optimization."

"My wife got me into their program somehow. It has been the most amazing, God-given experience. The arms they gave me truly gave me my life back."

The scene shifted quickly from one happy circumstance to another. The soldier was tying a ribbon in his daughter's hair. He was caressing his wife's cheek. He threw a football.

"But as amazing as the prosthetic technology is, the people at WRI are even more amazing."

Images of the battle leapt back on the screen.

"This has been a hard journey. Harder than I could ever have imagined."

Images of the hospital. Of his daughter crying.

"But I made it."

He was walking, holding his daughter's hand.

"And I would have never, ever made it without Warrior Renewal Initiative."

A close up of the soldier's healthy face. An American flag, superimposed behind him, billowed in the wind.

The soldier snapped a salute, his hand indistinguishable from a real one. The camera zoomed closer and closer to his extended fingers. His gold wedding band sparkled. They looked so real.

A young hand, his daughters, reached into frame and took his.

"Please consider giving to their worthy cause."

The image of the father and daughter's hand faded away, but the flag remained. Over the image of the flag, the words, "The Warrior Renewal Initiative Golf Tournament" appeared as rousing music played in the background.

The general gestured and stopped the video.

He turned and looked at Fiona.

"Well?"

Fiona's eyes were locked on the screen. She blinked a few times and turned to look at him.

"Damn, Bear. That was something."

"I thought you would like it. I know it is some powerful stuff. But it needs to be told. That soldier in the video, Jamie, is amazing. And what a family! I am flying them out to the tournament. He's an impressive speaker. He'll be the keynote the second night."

Fiona nodded.

"I wish you would reconsider being in one of the videos, ma'am. Or just getting out there more. It's such great work we are doing. And it is all because of you."

Fiona shook her head and stood up.

"No. That's not what this is about, Bear. I've told you that from the beginning."

The general shook his head as he stood.

"I know. I know, ma'am. But you'd be good at it. And you deserve the recognition."

Fiona waved her hand in frustration.

"I said, no."

General Harriman's back straightened.

"I'm sorry," she said. "I just… I see something like that and I just can't think about the topic of credit or 'getting out there.' It's just not…"

Bear held up a hand. "I won't mention it again, ma'am."

"Thanks."

"I just want you to know, though," he leaned in toward her and smiled a mischievous smile. "That I know you are doing a lot of good here."

Fiona felt the kindle of something warm inside her at the comment. Then remembered all that she had done.

"Shit." He shot Fiona another apologetic look as he stepped away and tapped his glasses. "This is Bear."

Fiona turned and looked into the blackness of the wide screen monitor. Her grandfather had ridiculed the charity at first. Which only strengthened her commitment to it. Then decided it was a "smart move." Which made her want to quit it immediately.

She knew it was hopeless. There was no balancing the ledger. She was too black from it all. But doing some good felt good, which was something. Now, though, it hurt to be around it. It made her think too much. All the damaged and ruined bodies. There was no amount of gifted limbs that would staunch the flow of blood and pain. She would stop if she could, but was in it now. And, surely, the only thing worse than starting a charity to try to balance the ledger was to then shut it down when it was doing good, just because it made you uncomfortable.

"Sure, Jim," the general's voice snapped her back.

She turned to look at him.

"I understand and have some ideas. Let me call you when I get to my car.

"OK, then. Yep. Bye."

Bear turned back to Fiona.

"Sorry. That was Morgan Whitfield."

Fiona, her thoughts clinging to her, just nodded

"Longbow Dynamics?" the general said with a hint of impatience, raising his eyebrows.

"Uh huh," Fiona tried to muster interest. She knew the general was on Longbow's board.

The general stepped closer and said in a quiet, conspiratorial voice, "He's trying to get the finance committee to approve a big acquisition."

"Uh huh."

General Harriman sighed. He studied Fiona for a moment. He put a hand on her shoulder. "What the hell is going, kid? You OK? Usually that kind of thing is catnip to you."

"Nothing. I'm good. Why?"

Bear, leaving his hand on her shoulder, leaned in closer. "Bullshit. I've been leading people for almost forty years. I've led them to into battle, into the boardroom, and into a few really good titty bars. It's my job to know when they are dragging and I am good at my job. What's going on?"

Fiona smiled wearily.

The general took his hand from her shoulder and crossed his arms.

She fought it. But it came out anyway. "Where was that soldier injured? Where was that battle?"

"The Southern Cone."

Fiona's chest tightened. Of course, it was the Southern Cone. It was always the Southern Cone. For her, it all started and ended there. Always.

"Why?" General Harriman asked.

"Sorry? What?"

"Why do you ask?"

"No reason, really. Just wondering."

Bear's eyes narrowed.

Fiona shifted on her feet.

"Tell me, general. Does it ever strike you as distasteful, or at least ironic?"

"Does what?"

"Being well paid by huge corporations that make money selling deadly weapon systems that kill and wound people, while directing my charity that serves wounded veterans."

"Not in the fucking least," he said with certainty. "I'm good at both. Why deny either of my services?"

Fiona shook her head, like the answer didn't work for her. She looked at the floor.

General Harriman reached out, put a finger under her chin, and gently lifted it.

The fatherly gesture almost made Fiona cry. She blinked rapidly to make it go away.

"Listen to me, kid," he said, dropping his hand from her chin to his side. "You didn't make the world this way. And you didn't choose your gifts. You're a ballsy broad that gets shit done and I, for one, am glad you are doing what you do, giving smart, kick ass machines to our warfighters."

What if I did have a hand in making the world this way?

Fiona nodded and stepped back abruptly.

"It's always good to see you, Bear."

The general hesitated for an instant, but let her off the hook.

"You too, ma'am. I do appreciate the opportunity. I hope you know that."

"I do. And I am glad you are on it. Can I show you out?"

"Hell no."

The general shook his head and started out of her office.

"I fought my way through First and Second Santiago. I can sure as hell find my way out of a goddamn civilian office."

General Bear Harriman stopped at the door and looked back at Fiona.

"You really should think about getting laid, ma'am."

He left in a peal of laughter.

Fiona stood still in the general's wake for a moment, unsure if she respected him or was repulsed.

She knew she repulsed herself.

Chapter Sixteen

Maximillon Seager stepped out of the elevator at 8AM into the top floor lobby of Determined End States. A large modern reception desk sat directly opposite the elevator bank. One of the two receptionists looked up.

"Mr. Seager," she said, smiling. "Please follow me."

The receptionist led him across the large lobby and into a hallway. Max took in the modern, luxurious space as he followed. Plush leather couches and loungers established cozy seating areas along the way. Abstract art hung on the walls and ample natural light flowed in through tall windows. The place felt more like a successful hedge fund than defense industry behemoth.

Max, though, looked exactly like what he was - a combat veteran of twenty years of service. He kept his dark hair closely cropped, which lessened the impact of his greying temples and his eyes were black with no discernible pupils. His sturdy body stood about five-foot-ten and moved with the economy of motion of a soldier that had learned the value of always conserving one's energy.

Max wore a black suit over a dark grey shirt as usual. No tie. The two-buttoned jacket had side vents, providing quick access to concealed weapons. His most distinctive feature, though, was his right hand.

The metal prosthetic was sleek and perfectly proportioned. The color of well-worn gun metal, the artificial hand caught the eye as it swung back and forth against black fabric in Max's easy stride.

The receptionist gestured at Max as they reached the end of the hallway.

"Please wait here for a moment, Mr. Seager," she said, before continuing into the large office that lay beyond the open door.

The receptionist returned a moment later, smiling as if hugely relieved.

"Miss Malloy will see you now, Mr. Seager," she said, gesturing toward the office.

Max nodded and walked into Fiona's office.

She met him in the middle of the room, near the conference table.

"Fiona Malloy," she said without enthusiasm, extending her hand.

"Max Seager." He shook her hand.

"I notice you are equipped with a prosthetic," Fiona said as she took her seat at the head of the conference table. She gestured for Max to sit.

Max sat with a seat between she and him. His fully articulated, metal-sheathed right hand extended from the cuff of his dark grey dress shirt.

"Yes, ma'am."

"What happened?"

"The Chinese blew my right arm off in South America."

"I see. I'm sorry."

Maximillian shrugged. "You should see the other guy."

Fiona's face was an expressionless mask. Inside, she stifled a chuckle.

"Santiago?" she asked.

"In that vicinity."

"So it's an entire arm assembly, then?"

"Yes. The blast tore it right of the socket. So this new one goes from here," Max's human hand pointed at his robotic hand. He ran his pointer finger all the way up his arm to his deltoid. "To here."

Fiona nodded in approval. "That's a very advanced prosthetic."

Fiona had become an expert in robotic and cybernetic technology and knew good gear when she saw it.

"Yes, it is."

Max thought about his first prosthetic as he met Fiona's expressionless gaze. It was not as nice as this current one. It was a joke. An insult, really. A worn-out old piece of over-used equipment that lacked any nerve junction or even haptic feedback. But Max knew he had been lucky to receive it. It was all the VA hospital had. Plenty of similarly wounded veterans left Walter Reed with just a stump. A travesty in these days of augmented soldiering. America would spend the money on their Centaurs to send them out, but not on its wounded veterans coming home.

Thane raged when he saw it.

"Don't you fucking worry about it," Thane told him. "As soon as we get your DredSkill on-boarding paperwork done, I am personally walking you into the Firm's shop."

A month later, Max had this beautiful new arm, courtesy of his new employer who wanted its operators to be well equipped.

That was five years ago.

"Must have been expensive," Fiona said.

"It was," Max said with a nod.

"Fine. But why leave it like that?" She asked, gesturing at his metal appendage. His hands were folded together on the table in front of him. His interlaced fingers alternated between flesh and metal alloy.

"Like what?"

"Most people have their prosthetics encased in artificial flesh these days. They have come a long way with the technology. It's nearly impossible to tell it's a prosthetic and offers several sensing upgrades that are similar to true sense of touch."

Maximillian nodded.

"They offered me that stuff," he said.

"And you were not interested?"

"No. Like I said. It is what it is. I lost my arm in combat. I'm proud of my service. I'm not trying to pretend it didn't happen. Besides, not everything the flesh feels is all that pleasant."

"And you know Thane from the service?"

"Yes, ma'am. We served in the Army together. He was—"

"Well, I am sure he told you I am not happy about this change."

"He did. I can assure you—"

"No, you can't," she cut him off again as she stood up from the table.

Max stood up as well.

"We'll proceed on a trial basis," Fiona said over her shoulder as she walked back to her desk. "Thane will brief you up on the job."

Fiona pulled her chair out and sat down.

"Please show yourself out. I have a meeting with our chairman tomorrow and have a lot left to do to prepare."

* * *

Later that evening, Fiona sat at her desk reflecting on Max Seager.

She liked the fact that Max did not wither easily or try to please. She had found that, for the most part, she only met two kinds of men in the business world. The first saw her as a business goal, the stupendously successful member of the Malloy family they would do anything to do business with. The other kind saw her as the beautiful woman in her early thirties they wanted to bed.

Maximillian seemed to fall into neither camp. He was inscrutable to her.

Inscrutability was not a quality she liked to have around her.

But Thane had asked her to give Max a try.

Cyrus Thane.

She swiveled her chair around to look out the window and thought about Thane.

He was unlike anyone else in her life. Ever. A military combat veteran, he was different from the smooth-talking generals she worked with. He had been an enlisted man, and took on the world in the no bullshit manner of a someone that had commanded troops from the front, not from a safe, comfortable command center. He was straightforward and full of appetites. He had scars and tattoos and could tell you stories about each one. His Viking-like beard was borderline ridiculous but worked for her, she had to admit. Thane's forearms, like the rest of him she was sure, were wrapped in taught, weathered skin that barely contained the coursing veins just below the surface. His eyes were grey with deep crow's feet that spoke of hard times and little sleep. He was, to her, gorgeous. And, though she never let it show and never acted on her attraction, she liked having him around. Fiona loved to listen to his ribald stories of New York City bachelorhood, which he told with zero hint of shame. She liked to imagine what could have happened if they had met somewhere, some night, in the city in different circumstances. She liked to imagine it in detail.

Then there was what they had done together. What she had paid him to do. It had saved her. Saved Eugene. But she was ashamed of it. In those few moments when she let it creep into her mind, it immobilized her. The waves of remorse and regret crushed her. She had not let herself go there in a long time. When she did, she reminded herself that it was her grandfather's fault. He had pushed her to the edge, dared her not to act, underestimated her. But in the end, she had found those decisions easier to make than she would have ever thought possible. She would do anything to protect her brother. Always had. Always would.

What she remembered most, though, about that time, was how decisive Thane had been. Ruthless. Unhesitating.

She remembered how she felt when he looked at her and said, "Don't worry, ma'am. I understand. I know what to do."

At that moment, Thane was a stranger to her, just assigned to her that day. But something about him and the way he spoke lifted her burden and replaced it with the sudden understanding that she was no longer alone. Since her father died, Fiona had been navigating the world and fighting against her grandfather alone. Even with Pruden by her side, she had been on her own. And Eugene, before he rejected her, had been more liability than comfort, someone she had to worry about and protect.

It was as if, trapped alone in the heart of the labyrinth, Fiona had rounded a corner to find Cyrus Thane, a fierce protector, emerging from the shadows. Finally, she had an ally. A decisive, ruthless, unhesitating ally.

Fiona almost came undone as the sensation washed over her. But she held it together until Thane had walked out of her office. Then she broke down sobbing.

Thane flew to South America that night. He got it done.

Now she missed him.

And that pissed her off.

Chapter Seventeen

he Determined End States main conference room faced east. Through the large windows one could catch glimpses of the Queensboro Bridge, the East River and large aircraft stacking up miles in the distance, waiting their turn to land at LaGuardia. The coursing, ever present cloud of delivery and taxi drone traffic flew above and into the distance.

Fiona was not looking out the windows at the moment, though. She sat next to her grandfather at the head of the large conference room table. Dozens of people, including a ridiculous number of her grandfather's executives and assistants, as well as a handful of the top vice presidents from her own organization, sat at the table and in chairs pushed against the wall. At the other end of the room, her Chief Financial Officer stood in front of a large wide-screen display presenting Spitting Metal's quarterly performance numbers.

Every quarter, her grandfather, Robert Malloy II, came to Fiona's headquarters for a quarterly review of the Spitting Metal business. Fiona always marveled at the number of executives and assistants that followed the old man. A few years ago, she referred to them as "the Sun King's sycophants" as she vented to her top leadership about the vagaries and politics that surrounded her grandfather. "It's like the fucking halls of Versailles over there," she railed. The nickname stuck.

The derisive nickname was the only thing fun about the quarterly meeting. Her grandfather combed through every aspect of the Spitting Metal business in painful, intrusive detail. In the week leading up to each QBR, Fiona's staff would work themselves into a stressed-out panic as they prepared. Fiona would hide her irritation as she talked them down each time. It was hard for her to relate to people that feared her grandfather, when the only thing she felt for the old man was a burning hatred. Fortunately, the business was doing extremely well and exceeding every forecast. Fiona could not imagine how bad the meetings would be if it were not.

The worst part of the quarterly business reviews for Fiona was that they served as a humiliating reminder to her of the indentured servitude she lived under.

Fiona barely listened to her CFO. She knew the numbers by heart. Her mind drifted as she looked down at the top of the large conference room table. She had it custom made when they first moved into the building years ago. Made from the salvaged metal of World War II aircraft, it was the kind of piece that revealed itself slowly. At first glance, it seemed sleek. The top, an enormous expanse of hammered metal aircraft skins, flattened and encased in a thick layer of clear epoxy resin, looked almost like the silver scales of a massive fish. Closer attention, though, dissolved the sleek appearance and revealed tantalizing hints as to what the aircraft sections had been through. Bullet holes, scrapes, and dents testified to combat, violence and mishap. Some sections bore fragments of painted nose art, insignia and warnings providing splashes of color.

This morning Fiona stared at a particular rivet in one of the weathered metal sections in front of her. She thought about the rivet being shot into place over a hundred years ago and there it was today, still holding, still imprisoned. Like her, fixed. Unable to move. Unable to get away from her grandfather.

She stole a glance at him. The man was ninety-seven years old, but it didn't show. Sure, he looked old in that general, he-is-an-older-guy way, but he did not look like someone with close to a hundred years on the planet. Access to the best longevity therapies in the world helped, as did the hard Malloy bloodline. Even back in the nineteenth and twentieth centuries, the Malloy men were known to live to a hundred.

Now? Fiona feared that, with longevity therapies and the well-protected lifestyle of a multi-billionaire, the vile old man might go another twenty years or more. The thought flamed a sense of panic within her. She did not know if she could make it that long.

The success of Spitting Metal, and early demise of Musashi's efforts, had won Eugene back his beloved Mio Posto, averting a disaster. But it had been a pyrrhic victory for Fiona. She often wondered, other than the resolution of Mio Posto, if she would have been better off having failed and lost all of her money than be in the position she was in now - a minority owner in the successful defense contractor at the mercy of her grandfather's whims. Her B Class shares were illiquid and only an outright sale and change of control would convert them to cash. And her grandfather would never sell or allow a change of control. Not because he cared about the company or its success in any way. He was already a billionaire many times over. But because it allowed him to continue to control and punish Fiona. She knew he would never willingly give that up.

On paper, Fiona's ownership in Spitting Metal made her a very wealthy woman. But she had no way to access the estimated half a billion dollars. Her grandfather loaned her money against the value of her equity. Charging a very low interest rate, he never turned down a request from her. It was galling and painful for Fiona, to have to sit with the old man and take from him, like a prisoner in a cage, a minuscule portion of the vast wealth that her boldness had created, and that he now lorded over like a vampire.

He had made vague statements in the past about some kind of exit for her when Spitting Metal had achieved some goal or size that he was never specific about. She regarded those statements as mirages, conjured by the old man to manipulate her and keep her working her hardest. The only dim hope she held onto was that when he did eventually die, the estate would divest, triggering the change of control that would vest her ownership and set her free.

Ten, twenty or more years from now.

An eternity.

But she had promised herself that she would not quit. She was determined to do her best, to bide her time, to outlast him, and see what opportunity fate afforded her. She knew one thing - she had earned her bad karma.

"Roberta," her grandfather said, jolting her back to the meeting. "Do you agree with his forecast?"

"Yes, of course," Fiona said, not missing a beat. "We are all confident that the sea trials will go well and should finish on time."

She looked down at her lap for a moment, swallowing her distaste for her first name. She hated that he insisted on using it. But she would not give him the pleasure of her protest.

Her grandfather smiled.

"Good," he said.

She raised her eyes to meet his.

Robert Malloy II stood up from his chair. He buttoned his suit jacket and straightened his tie while the room waited. One of his assistants stood up quickly and pulled the chair away. The old man scanned the room for a moment. "Good work. All of you."

Fiona cursed the swell of pride she felt at her grandfather's praise. She glanced around the room noting, with deep annoyance, the words had the same effect on everyone in the room.

"I do want to challenge this team, however," Malloy said, stepping back from the table and walking slowly around towards the large display. "To be bold and exploit your enviable position. You have it much easier than we ever did with Malloy Markets."

Stopping in front of the display at the opposite end of the table from Fiona, Robert Malloy II put one hand in his pocket and gestured with the other.

"You see, Malloy Markets is a consumer business. We sell products every day to individual consumers," he explained unnecessarily. Everyone knew Malloy Markets, the largest retailer in the world whose supercenters were in every decent sized town in America and encompassed grocery, department, pharmacy and outdoor goods.

"We have to win our customer back over and over and over again," he said. "We have to prove we understand them, their lives, what they need and value. Every damn day. And if we don't do it, our competition will. As sure as the sun will rise, tomorrow the American consumer will need milk, eggs, underwear, blue jeans and all manner of other bullshit. But they do not have to buy it from us. If we stop working at it, stop trying to win their business, we will vanish.

"You lucky bastards, though," he said, sweeping his pointing finger around the room. "You sell to the government."

A smile broke across the old man's face.

"Your buyer is a public servant," he said, as if he were uttering a terrible slur. "Someone that works for the government because it was the best job they could get. Or, even better, because they felt it was their patriotic duty."

Malloy chuckled.

"They wake up, shower, get dressed, go to work, and you know what? They get to work with you, Spitting Metal, the most advanced defense contractor in the world. And they are rewarded based on how well they work with you, how successful your projects are. None of them are incentivized to make you compete for or re-win the business. Your customer is not shopping you, not comparing you to the business across the street."

"So, I want you to know that I am not satisfied. At all. There is so much more to be taken."

He looked around the room slowly.

"I expect you to seize it," he said, reaching out as if snatching something in front of him, then pulling back his fist and shaking it.

Robert Malloy II smiled.

"Thank you, all," he said. "I look forward to next quarter's review. Now, if you would excuse me, I would like a word with my CEO in private."

Everyone sprang to their feet. Malloy walked back to the head of the table as the group made their way out of the conference room. Soon he and Fiona were alone. She took a deep breath and then swiveled in her chair to face him.

"Another good quarter, Roberta," he said, taking his seat.

"Thank you."

"I meant what I said, though," he said, leaning back in his chair.

"Don't you always?"

The old man chuckled, enjoying her barbs.

"Yes, I do."

Fiona closed her notebook of meeting materials. "How can I be of service to my chairman?"

"Nothing required for me. I just wanted to provide you with a private moment in case you needed to borrow money."

Chapter Eighteen

Cape Canaveral Space Force Station,
Florida

"What the hell, Hartwell?" Lieutenant General Nasir, the Geek's boss and a three-star general at the Pentagon, yelled over the phone. "You are not General Eisenhower, for chrissakes! You're just a damn one star. I don't want you burning any more time and budget flying dipshit lieutenants down to Canaveral and spending hours interviewing them. I don't give a damn who walks into your office next. Whoever they are, guess what? That's your new aide. Are we clear?"

"Yes, sir," the Geek said, looking despondently at the speakerphone on his large desk.

"Good. Now, if you will excuse me, Hartwell. I've got to tend to matters that are actually relevant to our national defense. Goodbye."

"Goodbye, sir," the Geek said. But the line was already dead.

Mrs. Johnson, Hartwell's administrative assistant, sat across from him on the other side of his desk and looked back at him with a sad mix of disapproval and concern.

Abigail Johnson was a Department of the Military civilian that had just celebrated her thirtieth year of federal service. A tall, trim black woman who moved with the grace and purposefulness of a ballroom dancer, Mrs. Johnson had served as the Technical Space Programs Commander's administrative assistant for seventeen of those thirty years. She came from a family of service.

Her late husband had been a colonel and her son and daughter both currently served in uniform.

Technical Space Programs Commander was typically the first assignment for a promising, newly promoted one star. If successful, the general would serve two to three years in the role, get selected for promotion, and move on to their next assignment and second star. Mrs. Johnson prided herself on the fact that every one of "her brigadiers" had gone on to get their second star.

She had been excited when it was announced that Brigadier General Wallace Hartwell, hero of the *Bluestone*, was going to be the next TSP Commander and her new boss.

He was not what she expected. His scarred stump of a right hand was consistent with the character she had conjured in her mind. But the rest of him was not. Short, a little overweight, and wearing glasses, he did not radiate the instant and imposing air of authority that most general officers did. He was unassuming and observant. She learned quickly that when he spoke, it was the product of thought, not ego, which she liked and did not always observe in senior officers. The man was highly intelligent.

She learned just as quickly he also had a stubborn contrarian streak. Used to being underrated, he was the sort of person that, once they had decided something was right, would not abandon their point of view in the face of rank or pain or reason.

General Hartwell was her tenth brigadier and would be, she had assumed, a good one to end her career on. Now that he had been in role for a little over a month, Mrs. Johnson worried he was going to break her winning streak.

For his part, Hartwell knew that she did not understand him yet. And he knew that she thought he was a geek.

She wasn't the first to think that.

The Geek had been looking for a new aide since his first day on the job. His current aide, Lieutenant Rowe, was being promoted to captain and shipping out for service on Lagrange Station Four in three days. Rowe was a decent enough aide, but Hartwell wanted something more in this next one.

General's aides typically served two years in role, so he would be stuck with whoever he picked for a while. Despite the benign, intentionally bureaucratic title, Technical Space Programs Commander, was a highly sensitive role with direct national security impacts. He wanted to get this right.

A general's aide was a critical piece that could make or break a flag officer's time in role. An aide provides direct support of all kinds to their general and performs a nearly infinite variety of tasks that are vital to the success not only of the general themselves but also to the unit they command. A general's aide serves as a direct link between their general and other high-ranking officers and personnel, requiring the aide to be an excellent communicator as well as professionally discrete. Aides often find themselves coordinating at a high level with other agencies and military units, demanding a high level of organization and laser-like attention to detail. General's aide was a high-pressure job.

Most important to the Geek, though, was that his aide be philosophically in sync with him. In addition to demanding, the general's aide role was also high-visibility, and nearly always resulted in promotion and selection for desirable follow-on assignments. Lieutenant Rowe was very good at it, but there was a glint of careerism in his eye that the Geek did not like.

He had interviewed a dozen candidates and had not found one he felt good about. The Geek was running out of time.

"When are our next interviews?" he asked Mrs. Johnson, lifting his eyes from the speakerphone.

"Tomorrow, sir."

"How many do we have coming in?"

"Just one, sir."

The Geek grimaced.

"She actually looks very promising, sir," Mrs. Johnson said in a coaxing voice. "I am sure she will make an excellent aide."

"Can I see the list of candidates we have not spoken with yet?"

"No, sir," Mrs. Johnson said gently.

The Geek looked at Mrs. Johnson. She met his gaze, imperturbable.

The Geek turned his head to look at his right shoulder epaulet with its embroidered star.

"I'm still a general, right?"

"At the moment, sir. Yes."

"Great," the Geek said, swiveling his head to look back at Mrs. Johnson. "Then send me that list, please."

"Very well, sir," Mrs. Johnson said, standing up. "Will there be anything else?"

"Not at the moment, Mrs. Johnson. Thank you."

The Geek swiveled in his chair to look out the large window behind his desk. It offered an expansive view of the Kennedy Space Center. Two miles away, the newest launch facility towered over the vast expanse of Floridian flatness, beyond which lay the endless, flat Atlantic Ocean. A dozen more facilities stretched out behind it. Most had vehicles standing tall on their pads in various states of preparation. There were two launches tonight, like most nights. Hartwell loved watching the launches. They never got old.

Mrs. Johnson hesitated a moment, looking at her new brigadier with his back to her, his knotted and scarred hand on the armrest, his attention on the launchpads.

She turned and left in silence, closing the door behind her.

What am I going to do with this one? She thought.

Chapter Nineteen

eneral Hartwell regarded the young lieutenant from behind his desk as she walked into his office and saluted.

"Sir, First Lieutenant Michelle Ryuk reporting for interview," she said.

The Geek waited, as he liked to do. Most superior officers return salutes quickly. When one didn't—it could rankle people.

Those were folks, too easily rattled, that Hartwell did not want. He learned that the hard way on the *Bluestone*.

Ryuk stood like a statue, dark, thoughtful eyes forward.

Good, Hartwell thought. He returned the salute.

Ryuk dropped her hand to her side and stood at attention.

Here again was an opportunity to cast out the obvious chaff. Most senior officers would tell a junior, "at ease," quickly so that they could relax. It was off-putting to be held at the position of attention longer than necessary.

Hartwell stood and assessed the young Korean American lieutenant as he walked around his desk. Compact and lean, she exuded a wiry strength. Her face was intense, symmetrical, framed by a sharp bob of jet-black hair cut just above the collar.

Standing in front of her, Hartwell looked over her uniform.

"Quartermaster Corps," he said.

"Yes, sir."

"Why?"

"Amateurs study tactics, sir. Professionals study logistics."

"Uh huh," Hartwell said, laying the skepticism on thick. He had, of course, thoroughly reviewed her resume. But he continued to stare intently at her uniform, as if trying to decipher it for the first time.

"Airborne school, I see," he said.

"Yes, sir."

"Why? That is not a skill the average quartermaster needs."

"I wanted to qualify at something dangerous, sir. Something stressful that required me to apply my training or get hurt. I think it is important, as military professionals, that we work and remain proficient at mastering the discipline and skill versus stress and danger equation. Even those of us that work in combat support roles."

"Uh huh."

The Geek continued to scan her uniform slowly.

"Combat exoskeleton expert's badge?"

"Yes, sir."

"Why?"

"Because I qualified expert in combat exoskeleton, sir."

"No shit, Lieutenant," Hartwell said, walking away from her and sitting back down at his desk. "I mean, why did we spend money to train you to that skill level?"

"You didn't, sir," Ryuk answered. "I was sent to the exoskeleton school as part of my convoy tactics training. I worked hard on my off time to achieve the expert skill badge."

"Why?"

"I don't do anything half ass, sir."

"Uh huh."

The general made a show of opening her file. He flipped through the first few pages before leaning back in his chair.

"Very well, First Lieutenant Ryuk," he said, allowing his weariness to seep into his voice. "Please go see my admin, Mrs. Johnson. She will give you your next set of tasks. You and I will reconvene here in exactly two hours."

Ryuk remained at attention.

"Post," the general said.

Ryuk saluted.

The general returned it quickly, and the lieutenant left the room.

Half an hour later, Hartwell stepped out of his office. Mrs. Johnson looked up from her desk.

"Mrs. Johnson," Hartwell said, walking up to her desk.

"General," she said, standing up with her pen and pad.

"What do you think?"

"Well, sir. I think if you don't take this one, General Nasir will not be happy."

"I know that. But what do you think of her?"

"I'm serious, sir. A one-star general's aide is usually selected after a resume review and a thirty-minute interview. You have to be reasonable."

"Just your initial impressions."

Mrs. Johnson sighed. She put her pen and pad down on her desk and leaned into the general. "There's a fire in that one," she said in a low voice. "She may be what you are after. Let's see how she does on your exercises."

"I had the same feeling," the general said with excitement. He rubbed his hands and walked back toward his office.

Mrs. Johnson shook her head and sat back down.

Later that afternoon, Lieutenant Ryuk concluded her final presentation to the Geek and Mrs. Johnson. She had been given three problem sets; one terrestrial resupply scenario, one orbital crises scenario, and one data analysis problem. She aced all three.

Mrs. Johnson beamed, happy that her new brigadier's ridiculous process was over and she could get on to the task of training him right.

The Geek wore an inscrutable face.

"Could you give us a few minutes, Mrs. Johnson?"

Mrs. Johnson's smile dissolved. Her face became stern.

"Don't you need me to take notes, sir?" she asked in a leading voice.

"I'll keep my own notes on this part. Thank you."

"Very well, sir." Mrs. Johnson smiled at Ryuk and said, "Well done.

Congratulations," before walking out of the general's office.

"Thank you, ma'am," Ryuk said as the door closed.

"A general's aide typically serves in role for two years," Hartwell said. "If selected, do you know what you would want to do afterwards?"

"Yes, sir. I want to serve in space. My application has been in for a year now."

"I see," Hartwell said, an approving tone sneaking into his voice. "Why?"

"I've always wanted to be an astronaut, sir. Always. I feel lucky to be alive now, when so much is going on in space. I just want to experience it and do my part."

The general nodded and an awkward silence settled in the room as he thought about what he wanted to know.

Ryuk looked down at her hands.

Finally, the general looked at Lieutenant Ryuk. "How was Officer Assessment and Training for you?"

"Oh," Ryuk said, surprised by the question. It had been two years since she passed the gauntlet. "It was tough, sir. Really tough. But, in a lot of ways, the best experience of my life."

"In what ways?"

"Well, sir. It was hard, of course. Hardest thing I have ever been through. There were plenty of days that I did not think I was going to make it. So, having that to draw on, knowing how much I can take, is something that will stay with me forever, I think."

Hartwell nodded.

"Who was running the program when you went through?"

"Colonel Shapiro, sir," she answered. The shiver in her voice confirmed for Hartwell what he had heard. Shapiro was tough.

"I had Filson," Hartwell said.

"Holy shit, sir! *The* Colonel Filson?"

Hartwell smiled at her reaction. "Yes, that one."

"Wow, sir. I don't even know what to say. He is a legend. I have heard the horror stories."

Hartwell nodded and then held up a finger to make his point. "Well, I have heard horror stories about Shapiro as well. I would not want to do some of the shit I have heard he puts classes through."

Ryuk smiled. Every junior officer wants to know that the old guard respects what they had to do to earn their commissions.

"How many started your class on day one?" he asked her.

"One thousand two hundred and five."

"How many graduated?"

"Three hundred and one, sir," she answered, pride showing in her eyes.

Hartwell nodded with approval.

"Tell me about your classmates," he said.

"They were the best. It's weird, there are O.A.T classmates of mine that I really did not like at the time. But if they called me right now and needed something. I would be there. No question."

"How many from your class made Combat Corps?" Hartwell asked.

"One."

"Tell me about them."

"His name was Mathew. He was a military brat. His father had seen combat as an exoskeleton company commander."

"From a tough bloodline, then," Hartwell observed.

"He was special. By the end of O.A.T., we all knew it was him. I…"

Ryuk's voice trailed off. Her mind flooded with memories.

"What is it, Lieutenant?" Hartwell prodded.

"Sir, I'll tell you the truth. I went into O.A.T. knowing it would be the hardest thing I'd ever faced. But I was skeptical of all the stuff you hear about how it changes your perspective. By the time I graduated, though, after getting to know Mathew, and going through everything we went through together, I got it. I know I only have the slightest inkling of what he is going through in the Combat Corps. What they all go through every day."

Ryuk paused. The Geek thought he saw a wave of memories wash over her.

She took a deep breath and said, "If he needed something, and therefore if any of them need something, there is nothing that can stop me from getting it to them."

"I'll tell you the funny thing, Lieutenant. That feeling never goes away. If anything, it gets stronger the longer you serve. Filson's evil genius changed the whole damn military."

Ryuk smiled with respect at the mention of Colonel Filson again.

"And it's a good thing it did," he added.

"What about your class, sir?" Ryuk asked. "Who was the Combat Corps selectee from your class?"

"We had two."

"What? I've never heard of that happening," Ryuk said with surprise. "Two? I thought it was always only one."

"I have never heard of it happening again, either." Now it was his turn to be washed over by memories.

"Paul Owens and Kata Vukovic," he added, mostly to himself as an aching sadness welled within him.

Ryuk's eyes got wide at the name.

"I was peer witness for their induction ceremony," the Geek added quickly with a forced smile to shake the sadness.

Ryuk nodded with respect at the general's statement.

Hartwell watched as a troubled look came over the lieutenant's face. He knew that Paul Owens was the topic of several military ethics classes required of newly commissioned officers.

"Yep," he said with sadness. "That Paul Owens."

Ryuk looked at her hands.

General Hartwell stood up suddenly.

Ryuk jumped out of her chair.

"Thank you for your time, Lieutenant. We will be in touch."

Chapter Twenty

Michelle Ryuk got the call from General Hartwell about a week after the interview.

"Lieutenant Ryuk," the Geek said. "You impressed me. I'd like for you to be my aide."

"I would be honored, sir," Michelle said, smiling and pumping her fist in the air.

She spent the next two weeks preparing to relocate to Canaveral and filling out endless background checks and security clearance paperwork. Mrs. Johnson pestered her multiple times a day, chasing down this form or that, trying to accelerate the process. Ryuk started to wonder if she would be working for General Hartwell or for Mrs. Johnson.

She also wondered why such an extensive background and security clearance process was required. The Technical Space Programs Command seemed to be mostly about research and administration of space navigation aids. Not national security level stuff.

When she reported for duty at Canaveral, she learned the truth.

"Tell me, Lieutenant. What is the biggest challenge we have in the Space Transportation and Logistics Command?" he asked her, both of them sitting at his large conference table on her first day.

Ryuk thought for a moment before answering.

"I would have to say, just keeping track of everything out there, sir," she said, gesturing at the map of the solar system on his wall.

"You're right," he said with a smile. "It's just too damn big out there. There is no way to keep track of it all because most of it is just an infinite stretch of empty. And it's not just our problem. It's everyone's. The Chinese, the Russians, the Europeans, the Indians—all of us are trying to track our assets and maybe a known pirate or two. Each country has invested hundreds of billions of dollars in the effort. And that's not even counting any of the private commercial and civilian monitoring.

"Thousands of antennas and sensors," the Geek continued, gesturing around in the air as he spoke. "Tracking technologies of all kinds based down here on earth, up in orbit, along the major trade routes, on and above Mars, circling the sun, and out in the asteroid belt. All being managed by countless AI systems.

"But it's all piecemeal." The Geek shrugged. "And focused primarily on the unmanned shipping convoys and other high dollar activities. No one has a complete view. We might as well try to illuminate a stadium with a flashlight. It's hopeless."

The general shook his head.

"So the US Military started the Vishnu Stare program about ten years ago. A covert espionage and technology program that targets other, non-US space monitoring networks to expand our situational awareness."

"Targets, sir?" Ryuk asked.

"We hack into the other systems. Foreign, domestic, civilian, corporate, anything we find that might be useful. We suck their information into our database, and then bang all kinds of algorithms against it."

"I see."

"In terms of the sheer volume of information we are stealing, it is the most successful American intelligence operation in history. And it gives us the most complete picture possible of what is going on out there," the Geek pointed over his shoulder at the map of the solar system.

"It's still woefully incomplete, mind you. But it's better than anyone else has. And it is an advantage we must maintain. That is why the program is classified above top secret."

Ryuk met the general's gaze and nodded.

"Much of what I do around here is eyewash to cover up what we are really focused on, which is the administration and careful exploitation of the data Vishnu Stare provides based on the intelligence priorities of the National Command Authority."

"Wow," Ryuk said softly.

"Yep," General Hartwell said. "As my aide, you will be exposed to some of the most sensitive intelligence the United States possesses, intelligence that is given directly to the president. You will become familiar with Vishnu Stare sources and methods. And you may become the target of foreign, corporate or pirate intelligence efforts."

"Do other countries, or corporate interests know about the program?"

"There are… rumors out there," the Geek said, speaking carefully. "There have been close calls and good guesses that were never confirmed. But, no. We do not believe the program has been compromised."

General Hartwell looked at Lieutenant Ryuk.

"Welcome to the program, Lieutenant."

Chapter Twenty-One

"Good morning, sir," Mrs. Johnson said as the Geek walked through the front doors of the Technical Space Programs headquarters, Lieutenant Michelle Ryuk a step behind him. Located in the heart of the Canaveral launch facility, the simple and unassuming five story building that served as TSP headquarters belied the nature of the unit's work. There was no dramatic signage outside. No hulking spacecraft propped up on display. No bragging slogans emblazoned on banners. There was not even a building address number posted. In fact, the only bit of color on the outside of the building was the American flag, which flew from reveille to taps.

Inside, the walls on the first floor, decorated with old maps and photos of Cape Canaveral over the centuries, created an intentionally mundane atmosphere. Like a sleepy post office or land survey consultancy.

The extensive security, though, hinted at something more.

"Good morning, Mrs. Johnson," the Geek responded with a smile.

Johnson was old school. If her general was in town, she got to the office before him and met him at the door.

Michelle was new to her role, and learning how demanding the life of a general's aide can be. Only a few weeks into the job, she had started riding to work with the general when they were not traveling. The twenty minutes in the car together gave them a chance to get a grip on the general's day before getting to HQ.

Mrs. Johnson fell in behind Hartwell next to Lieutenant Ryuk as the general took his time through security, submitting to the same layered processes as everyone else, as he greeted and chatted with the security personnel.

Johnson and Ryuk always used this time to discretely confer on the general's day.

"He is addressing the Congressional Committee on Space Trade Security today at oh nine hundred hours," Mrs. Johnson said, leaning in toward the lieutenant as the general handed his briefcase to the guard who opened it to check for unauthorized data devices. The briefcase then made its way on the conveyor beneath an Xray and chemical detection scan.

"Yep," Michelle said. "I re-read his remarks last night. He is ready."

She smiled at the guard as she handed him her satchel.

"Then he has his session at eleven hundred hours, of course."

Michelle nodded.

"The QSIR is due to General Nasir by end of day."

"Yep," Ryuk said, one eye on the general as he swiped his ID card and stepped up to the retinal scanner. "The general has already written his summary. But I am chasing down one last report from the field for him."

"Who are you waiting on?"

"Colonel McDade. Civilian shipping liaison."

Mrs. Johnson nodded. She was expecting that name. "I will call his admin, Sabrina, as soon as we get to the office."

"Thank you," Michelle said, swiping her card and then placing her right eye in front of the scanner.

"Do you think he is going to go to the Brevard County Chamber dinner this evening?" Mrs. Johnson asked, nearly in a whisper.

"Not a chance. His daughter has a volleyball game tonight."

The general stepped into the final, full body biometric scanner.

"I wish he would go at least once," Mrs. Johnson said. "He misses out on too many networking opportunities."

Michelle nodded in agreement.

"You know how he is about his family time."

"I do," Mrs. Johnson said.

Michelle followed the general through the biometric scanner as Mrs. Johnson stepped around it. She had been through half an hour earlier.

The lieutenant grabbed the general's briefcase and her own and walked to the elevator, where Mrs. Johnson was already holding the door open.

The Geek finished chatting with one of the enlisted guards and joined them. Mrs. Johnson stepped in last and pressed the button for the fifth floor.

After a bumpy first month, the trio had found their rhythm. Lieutenant Ryuk proved herself to be a highly effective aide. Furthermore, she was adept at navigating Vishnu Stare program and its outputs. She had impressed the Geek with her ability to pull her own insights from the vast amount of raw intelligence the program threw off and he started including her in his daily session.

Mrs. Johnson's ability to work the bureaucracy, to anticipate its needs and knife through its obstacles, was without equal. As Hartwell and Ryuk came to understand this, they increasingly deferred to her recommendations and coaching.

As for the general, his heart, fight, and competence wrapped in a disarming, easy-to-underestimate exterior endeared him to his supporting duo.

The elevator opened onto the fifth floor. More guards were positioned at the opening doors. Rather than salute their commanding general, they left their hands on their weapons, per Vishnu Stare standing operating procedures for the fifth floor. They recognized the general, his aide and his administrative assistant, but challenged them anyway.

"Good morning, sir," the NCOIC said, hand on his pistol. "Looks like another day of wind and rain."

"Not according to the Cherokee calendar, Master Sergeant Qureshi," the Geek responded.

Qureshi's hand dropped from his pistol, and he smiled. "Good morning, General Hartwell," he said in a more genuine tone of voice.

"Morning, Stephen."

The challenge and password for fifth floor access changed every eight hours, at 6AM, 2PM and 10PM. At the moment, the challenge was "Rain," and the password was "Cherokee." Had the general not answered the challenge correctly, he, Ryuk and Mrs. Johnson would have been detained. And not gently.

The trio walked down the hallway that split the building along its short axis, dividing it in half. General Hartwell's office was at the end of the hallway, Lieutenant Ryuk and Mrs. Johnson's desks sitting outside the door. The wide hallway was lined with pictures of spacecraft of all types. Probes, freighters, gunboats, science vessels, long haulers.

The hallway divided the building into two sides. The north side contained offices and work spaces for the team of scientists, engineers and intelligence analysts who teamed with the Vishnu Stare AIs to turn the gargantuan stream of stolen data into useful intelligence. The team worked in three rotating ten-hour shifts. The shifts overlapped by an hour at the beginning and end to allow for collaboration and effective work stream hand offs. The north side of the building buzzed 24 hours a day with the thrum of conversations, presentations, arguments and normal office banter.

The other half of the floor was controlled by yet another guard post in the hallway midway between the elevators on one end and General Hartwell's office on the other. Access to the south side was tightly restricted. Only those that passed another retinal scan on the spot and were authorized by General Hartwell in person at that moment could pass through the doorway. And then, only after another scan for unauthorized devices and with General Hartwell's in person escort.

Those that gained access stepped into the United States Intelligence's holy of holies.

Called the SolarScope by the handful of people that knew of it, the room was deceptively simple. A large, dark circular chamber, fifty feet in diameter, with a domed ceiling. The room's floor declined slightly toward the center, where a dozen leather reclining chairs sat around a large, circular conference table.

The heart of the room was its sophisticated holographic projection system, which immersed occupants in realistic 3D images of planets, moons, asteroids, spacecraft and other objects detected and tracked by Vishnu Stare. The display was dynamic and could be used to search the database and model scenarios. This was done through voice interface with Vishnu Stare's powerful AI.

Nicknamed, "Vish," the search and analysis AI layered the most advanced theoretical and observational models of the solar system and universe on top of the intelligence data to make the system as insightful as possible. Without Vish, the system's deeply penetrating and far-flung hacking tentacles would simply be spewing data into an inchoate pile that increased in size every second. The SolarScope brought Vishnu Stare to life, and Vish made the data sing with insight.

General Hartwell winked at the SolarScope guard desk as he walked by, Ryuk and Johnson in tow.

"Good morning, team," the Geek said to them.

"Morning, sir," the NCOIC said.

Lieutenant Ryuk and Mrs. Johnson followed the Geek into his office. Mrs. Johnson paused just inside the door as Michelle followed the general to his desk. She handed him his briefcase and then walked back to stand next to Mrs. Johnson.

"Sir, your first meeting this morning is the National Security Council stand up meeting at oh eight hundred. Then the Congressional Committee on Space Trade Security at oh nine hundred," Mrs. Johnson said.

"Got it. Thank you," the Geek said, standing behind his desk. "And you will chase down Colonel McDade, LT?"

"Yes, sir," Michelle said. "You will have his civilian shipping report shortly."

"Thank you, LT. Also, I'd like you to join me for my session today."

"Roger that, sir."

The general's "Session," was a standing briefing from Vish in the StarScope chamber officially called the "Daily Inner Solar System Intelligence Update and Assessment." The very few people that knew about it referred to it as "the session." Taking place at the same time every day when the general was not traveling, 1100 hours, it was the reason for the role of Technical Space Programs Commander. General Hartwell was tasked with mastering Vishnu

Stare's output and infusing it into American space operations in a way that was useful, but not detectable. Hartwell was the sole arbiter of what made it out of the system.

When Lieutenant Ryuk started as his aide, Hartwell had her background check upgraded and worked to get her the highest-level clearance possible so that she could attend the sessions with him. He didn't take her in for every session, but he took her enough so that she maintained a general awareness of what was going on in the solar system. That way, if anything happened to him, or if he needed her to represent him in a national security situation, she had enough context to be effective.

For the first half hour of the sessions, Vish briefed the general on several categories of intelligence, starting always with the disposition of Chinese assets in the solar system, then allied assets, then confirmation of American assets. Next, Vish covered all known pirate locations before diving into a commercial activity such as mining, shipping and manufacturing. Finally, Vish gave an assessment of any ongoing emergencies or potential hazards. The sessions usually concluded with a question and discussion period in which the Geek pursued items of concern or interest.

Ryuk knew the gravity of the sessions and felt honored and humbled the general included her.

"I'm going to spend some time reviewing my remarks for the committee now," Hartwell said, pulling a folder from his briefcase. "Please hold my calls."

"Will do, sir," Mrs. Johnson said.

"Oh, last thing," the general said, holding up his good hand, index finger extended. "I really need your help today, guys. I've got to get to my daughter's volleyball game on time."

Mrs. Johnson nodded.

"You can count on it, sir."

"Thank you." General Hartwell smiled and sat down, already focused on the draft of his remarks.

Mrs. Johnson and the lieutenant closed the door behind them as they left his office.

Chapter Twenty-Two

eneral Hartwell and Lieutenant Ryuk sat at the conference table in the middle of the SolarScope chamber looking up at the 3D holographic display above them as Vish ran through the session.

A grey band of what looked like glowing dust particles encircled the room. Representing the asteroid belt, the band of diffuse light seemed to scrape against the dark chamber walls. Inward from the belt, Mars, Earth, Venus and Mercury occupied their relative locations to each other and to the sun, which hung at the center of the room above the conference table. Earth Moon Lagrange Station Four and other key American facilities throughout the inner solar system were marked with green 3D icons, allied in blue, Chinese and Russian in red.

A sparkle of multi colored icons spread throughout the planets. The location of every ship, drone, probe, wreck and hazard known by Vishnu Stare. Thousands of them.

Sitting at the conference table looking up at holographic rendering, one could see the throbbing pulse and patterns of inner solar commerce. Convoys of ships flowed out to Mars and the belt and back, bearing billions of dollars of material, from finished to freshly mined, back and forth. Clusters of ship icons in the belt indicated the exploitation of particularly rich mines. The larger asteroids, like Ceres, Vesta, and Hygiea, hosted small outposts and a handful of ships were always nearby. The two Lagrange bases, one Chinese, one American, were obscured by swarms of docking and departing ships. The Moon bore its own cloud of arrivals, departures and orbiters. Earth, though, was the most busy, nearly invisible behind a glowing swarm of symbols.

"Getting and spending…" the general would often mutter in a sad tone when he and Michelle sat down and Vish first fired up the projection. "Getting and spending."

Lieutenant Ryuk loved the sessions. Her imagination flared as she listened to Vish work through his briefing topics. The names of ships, asteroids, and facilities, the vast distances, the exotic cargos all called to her. She hoped her assignment with General Hartwell would help her get a duty station in space. Something on Lagrange Station Four would be amazing, or maybe the Moon. She didn't care. Hell, she would scrub the floors on a nasty freighter if they let her. She just wanted to get out there. The daily sessions fueled that desire. She often walked out of the chamber feeling like she was vibrating with excitement. Sometimes it was hard to bring her focus back to her earth-bound job.

When Vish gave his piratic activity update, though, a sense of disquiet ran through Ryuk. She wondered what happened. Did pirates simply love space more than Earth? Emptiness more than people? Were they betrayed? Or were they traitors? She could not understand those that refused to come home, that lived in space serving themselves rather than their country, preying on their fellow spacefarers rather than helping them.

"Finally, sir, I am tracking one emergency situation at the moment," Vish said.

Ryuk shifted in her seat.

"Oh?" The general sat up.

"Yes, sir. There has been a mining accident on Ananke."

The holographic display shifted, yanking a section of the asteroid belt closer to the conference table and then zooming into an irregularly shaped asteroid until it was the size of a large beach ball.

"Ananke was discovered in 1872 by Edwardo Palisa. It is a large rocky asteroid with a diameter of 167 kilometers. A Chinese state sponsored corporation established mining operations there in 2061. Twenty-seven hours ago, a Chinese military ship initiated a course change followed by a max burn acceleration toward Ananke."

As Vish talked, a red course line blinked and elongated from its origin toward the asteroid.

"The ship acted with the customary Chinese military signals discipline. No SIGINT was gained from it, though European Space Agency telescopes did capture imagery of its acceleration burn for a sufficient amount of time for us to plot its course."

"Two hours later, a Chinese civilian science ship began transmitting un-encrypted voice calls to Ananke and to the Chinese military ship," Vish continued. As he spoke, a second glowing red icon appeared.

"Radio intercepts from this Chinese civilian ship were very informative."

"How were the signals intercepted?" Hartwell asked.

"The Chinese science ship was very undisciplined," Vish answered. "They made several transmissions trying to confirm the situation. They finally went radio silent after initiating their acceleration burn. But their signals had been picked up by an Indian cargo hauler that happened to be close enough and in a favorable relative antenna orientation,"

"The radio intercepts, combined with the rare instance of two Chinese ships initiating course changes and maximum acceleration burns in a short time window and toward the same objective, gave me pause. I therefore conducted a focused search of recent intelligence hits at the same time and location and found a civilian Japanese radio telescope source that confirmed elevated radiation levels emanating from the mine on Ananke."

"Those damn Chinese nuclear drill bits," the Geek mumbled.

"Indeed, sir."

"Estimated casualties?"

"Unknown, sir. But historical intelligence on the Chinese mining operation on Ananke estimates the onsite staffing to number between twenty-five and fifty souls."

The Geek shook his head. "Poor bastards."

"I further estimate the evacuation capacity of the two ships enroute to Ananke to be ten to fifteen."

"Ten to fifteen each?" the Geek asked.

"No, sir. Ten to fifteen total."

Michelle looked at the general. His narrowed eyes were focused on the holographic image of Ananke.

"The entire mining site is being jammed now," Vish said. "No radio signal intelligence is making it out."

"At this point they are probably using tight beam laser communications to avoid signal leaks," Hartwell said, studying the enlarged image of Ananke.

"Agreed, sir."

The Geek chuckled ruefully. "They must be mining something pretty damn valuable."

"What do you mean, sir?" Michelle asked.

"They are trying to hide the fact this is going on," the general said, taking his eyes off of the imagery and looking at Michelle.

"Would the Chinese ever ask us for help?" she asked.

"Oh, sure. There have been plenty of times the Chinese have asked for help. And there have been plenty of times they have helped us. I'd say we've each rescued hundreds of the other's spacefarers."

"Do they really have to request help to get it?" Michelle asked.

"No. The traditions and expectations for rendering aid out there in space, to anyone that needs it, are strong. They are derived from those that have existed for centuries down here at sea. If you are able to help another seafarer, you help."

"So, they are going to let dozens of people die just to keep what is in their mine a secret?" she asked, disbelieving that the calculus could be so cold.

The general's face darkened and he did not answer. He turned his head from Michelle and looked back at the holograph of Ananke.

"There is one more relevant source involved, sir," Vish said. "And it is HUMINT."

"Go on, Vish."

"A deep Human Intelligence penetration within the Chinese Space Science Agency confirmed the radiation leak on Ananke and the involvement of the Chinese Science ship. This source estimated there to be forty-seven souls on site at the time of the accident."

The general nodded to himself. His elbows were on the conference table. His good hand gripped his burned hand, rubbing it rhythmically.

"Do we have any ships nearby, Vish?" Lieutenant Ryuk asked. "Close enough to help?"

"We do. There are two American flagged ships nearby that are close enough to assist with the evacuation of Ananke in a timely fashion. If—"

"That is enough, Vish," the general said. "Anything else we need to cover today?"

Michelle looked at general Hartwell, surprised he had interrupted Vish. Hartwell rubbed his forehead with his burned hand.

"No, sir."

"Thank you." The general dropped his hand to the table and looked at Michelle.

Michelle waited. The enlarged 3D image of Ananke, several feet across, hung above the general's head. Icons for the two ships and the doomed mining facility glowed red.

"We can't help them," Hartwell said.

"Why not, sir? Vish said we have two ships within range."

"What happens when those ships show up to help, LT?"

"They would save lives," Michelle said, leaning across the table.

"They would." Hartwell nodded. "And that would be a good thing."

The general leaned back in his chair and sighed.

"And what do you think would happen when the Ministry of State Security asks themselves, 'How did those miners get so lucky? How did the Americans show up just in the nick of time?'"

Michelle straightened in her chair, her lips tightening and brow knitted.

The general let the question hang.

"Um…" Michelle started. "I think…"

"Vish, was there any possible way for us to know about the crisis on Ananke on our own? Without Vishnu Stare intelligence?"

"No, sir. There was no relevant American asset located close enough that could possibly have any indication of the crisis on Ananke."

Michelle leaned back in her chair.

"Think about it, LT," the general said in a resigned voice. "When State Security goes and talks to their version of Vish, and they ask it for a theory on how we knew to divert our ships just in time to help, what do you think it will say?"

Michelle sat motionless.

Hartwell let her off the hook.

"Vish, if you were asked that question, what would you say?"

"Sir, if asked that question, I would have to answer that the most plausible explanation involves intelligence and potentially espionage."

The general nodded.

"Vish told us what his sources were," Hartwell said, holding up a finger from his good hand as he ticked them off. "First, Indian intercepts of a Chinese science ship's transmissions that we then siphoned away from the Indians without them knowing. Second, imagery from an ESA telescope asset that we stole from our allies. Third, Japanese radio telescope data that we obtained without their approval or knowledge. And, finally, a flesh and blood human spy embedded in the Chinese Space Agency working for us that is sending us timely information under threat of discovery and execution."

General Hartwell held the four fingers up for a moment for emphasis before setting his hand on the table. He leaned forward in his chair. "That's about over a dozen countries that would be royally pissed off if they heard the conversation we were having right now."

"The bottom line is that we cannot let anyone know what we know," the Geek said. "Unless there is a plausible cover story for how we know it."

Michelle looked back at the general in silence.

"Vishnu Stare is too valuable to jeopardize. In situations like this, it's not fun. And for me, personally, it hurts. Remember, I have been the guy out there, fighting to keep my crew alive. I know how cruel the void can be. But I am not here to make myself feel good. I am here to do a job. And so are you, Lieutenant."

Lieutenant Ryuk took a deep breath and nodded.

"I get it, sir," she said. "Same calculus, different variables."

"What do you mean?"

"For them it's a super valuable asteroid mine, for us it's a super valuable intelligence program. And for both of us, the lives of dozens of people can't compete."

ODYSSEUS

Chapter Twenty-Three

Paul sighed heavily as he stepped in front of the door to Althea's quarters. It was late in the cycle, and he was showing up for a counseling session. He wasn't scheduled to see her for another six cycles, but Althea had told him, and he agreed, that he needed it. The captain's death had unearthed a lot of things he had worked hard to bury.

Despite Paul's certainty, he fidgeted at the door and thought about leaving, about walking away quickly, before she knew he was there.

He looked at his watch. It was time. He hesitated.

Althea opened her door suddenly.

Paul looked at her, trying to mask his resignation with a smile.

"Oh my," Althea said, regarding him. "You look like a man about to walk the plank."

"Feels a little that way."

"This will be a good thing, Paul," she said, taking his hand and pulling him gently behind her into her quarters. "I promise."

They stopped next to the coffee table, between the sofa and two chairs. Althea wore an oversized white sweater and white leggings. It was the first time Paul had ever seen her out of her flight suit.

"I made you some tea," Althea said, gesturing to the pot and cup on the table.

"Thanks," Paul said. "Maybe in a bit."

Althea nodded and walked to one of the chairs.

Paul sat down on the sofa. As he did so, he noticed an object in the corner of the small room.

"Is that a yoga mat?" he asked Althea as she sat down.

"Yes."

"What is it for?"

"What is a yoga mat for?"

"Yeah," Paul said.

"It is for yoga."

"You do yoga?"

"Yes."

"Like, real yoga?"

"Yes," she answered with a patient smile. "Is that so weird?"

"No. I just didn't know you… guys did yoga."

"Well, some of us do." She crossed her arms.

"Interesting. I do, too, you know."

"I did not know that. Tell me about it."

"I like it." Paul shrugged. "They taught us yoga when they taught us the meditation techniques to deal with our augmentations. I've tried to maintain my practice since then. I haven't been that regular. But, through all the deployments, the court-martial, my imprisonment, and even now on the *Odysseus*, I've stuck with it somewhat. I felt like it helped with the nightmares… Until now."

"I think that is great," Althea said. "It is so good for you."

"Why do you do it?"

"It helps to keep my biomechanics limber and in sync. My chassis is an advanced polymer, a lot harder than your bones. But my musculature is frailer than yours, more prone to degrade. Something about the way they grow it. In any case, if I don't stretch every day and consume the correct balance of nutrients, my mobility quickly degrades. If I took, say, a week or two off, I'd get very sore and tight."

"Does it have to be yoga?"

"No. Any kind of stretching is fine."

"So, why yoga?"

"I just like yoga. I like the way it makes me feel. Good for my chakras."

Paul nodded.

Althea observed him for a moment. "You don't doubt I have chakras?"

Paul shrugged.

"Usually, that kind of comment gets a ridiculing reaction from humans."

"A long time ago, I would have laughed at the notion," Paul said, nodding. "But…" His voice drifted off.

"But what?"

"I learned not to underestimate."

Althea smiled.

"Perhaps we could practice together sometime," she said.

Paul shook his head.

"The last thing you need on board this ship is to be caught out there in a yoga outfit by one of those idiots." Paul gestured at the door.

Althea's eyes narrowed.

"I'm sorry," Paul said. "I just—"

"No," she interrupted. "It's OK. You are right, unfortunately."

Paul nodded.

"But enough about my exercise routine," Althea said, shifting in her chair. "Are you ready to begin?"

Paul sighed and looked out the window at the endless void.

Althea waited.

Just when she thought Paul had decided against it, he began to speak. Paul kept his gaze out the window as he told Althea about his first days in the military.

Chapter Twenty-Four

Paul finished talking and took a slow sip of tea.

Althea still sat in one of the chairs facing him. The black of space spread out behind her, beyond the window over her shoulder. The stars cascaded endlessly in the distance as the Habitat traced its circle around the hub.

Paul leaned forward and put his tea down on the table between them. He rested his elbows on his knees and sighed as if weary from a heavy task.

"Oh please," Althea said. "It was not that bad."

"We haven't gotten to the bad parts yet."

"Nonetheless, you have begun. And even just this beginning will help. You'll see." She smiled.

"What?"

"I am happy for you. And, I hope you will allow me to say I am proud of you."

"I'll allow it," Paul said with a tired smile as he leaned back in his chair. The smile lingered as he looked out of the window behind Althea.

"I can tell, just from the way you talk about them, the affection in your voice, that you have some amazing friends from those times."

Paul's face pinched at the comment. Then he nodded sadly.

"I did. But they are all gone now."

"Gone?" she asked.

"Some dead. The rest have disowned me. I'm an infamous war criminal, remember? That is hard on a friendship."

Althea sat still.

Paul looked out the window. He took a deep breath and let it out slowly.

"All except one," he said quietly.

"Who is that?"

"The Geek," Paul said, eyes still gazing out of the window. "Wallace Hartwell."

Althea nodded, recognizing the name from Paul's description of his experiences at Officer Training and Assessment.

"He's the only one that ever visited me in Leavenworth," Paul said, looking back at Althea.

She met Paul's gaze with a kind smile.

"Now he is the highest-ranking officer from our O.A.T. class," Paul said, a faint smile of pride breaking across his face. "And he is the reason I am here on the *Odysseus* on the Fly it Off program."

"Really?" Althea said.

"The Geek was one of the architects of the program. And really the driving force." Paul said, nodding. "At about the time Kata and I were deployed with the Ōkami to the Southern Cone, the Geek was on his second tour in space. He was second in command on an orbital tug, the *Bluestone.* There was some kind of accident. He was credited with saving the ship, but he got burned pretty badly."

"Oh no," Althea said with concern.

"Yeah. He would never talk about it with me, but from what I could see of his hand and neck, it was bad."

Althea winced in empathy.

"They got him back earthside, and he spent a number of months in the hospital before returning to duty. When he did return, he wasn't a hundred percent, so they gave him a year of easy desk work while he healed up. By then, I think, they realized they had a high potential officer there, and were willing to invest time in the guy to let him heal. So they paired him up with a general working in personnel strength planning for the Space Force.

"What they didn't realize," Paul continued, an affectionate smile breaking across his face. "Was that they had just harnessed a dynamo for this general's agenda. The Geek may have had a gnarled stub of a right hand, but he was the smartest, most dedicated guy Personnel Command had ever seen."

Althea shook her head at the description of the Geek's injuries, but then melted into a smile.

"How much do you know about what happened in space after the Battles of Santiago?" Paul asked.

"Not much," Althea said.

Paul nodded. He didn't know how old Althea was or what kind of database they had loaded her up with.

"Tell me," she said.

"Well, for years afterwards, China and the US went all out preparing for a war in space and military colonization of Mars. It made the cute little 'Space Race,' between the US and Russia a hundred years ago look really pale in comparison.

"That's how this old girl got her spinner, drone hangar, and factory," he added, gesturing around at their ship. "Everything already in space, like the *Odysseus*, was militarized, and both countries sent as much material as they could into orbit and beyond. The US also started massive recruitment and training programs to man all the ships and outposts they were hurtling off world."

Paul shook his head and said, "It was blisteringly expensive, the largest capital spending effort in history. And you know what? Neither country could afford it."

"Well, that must have been a problem," Althea said.

"It was," Paul agreed. "Once the cost in life and treasure was understood, there was no more appetite for conflict in space. So in 2054, China and the US agreed to limit their activities in space to commercial exploration. Neither trusted each other, but both wanted to preserve their resources for the coming wars on Earth. Troop carrying capabilities in space were treaty-limited and subject to intrusive verification rights on both sides. The large military transports were recalled, as well as the gunboats and other vehicles. Ships like the *Odysseus* went back to commercial missions, though I still don't know how the Company got to keep the factory on her.

"Mars was declared a demilitarized zone. Military bases there were mothballed or leased to commercial interests as well as many of the asteroid belt outposts. That was when they divided up the two most valuable Earth and Moon Lagrange points. The US took L4 and the Chinese took L5."

"Then they tried to recall and disband most of the trained space crews," Paul said. He hesitated a moment for emphasis. "That didn't go so well."

"What do you mean?"

"Well, now you had thousands of trained space crews, some very passionate about being in space, and many on ships far from Earth, that got a message saying, 'Um, sorry… we changed our minds and need you to come home back to Earth.'"

Paul chuckled.

"Some did not return," he said.

"What do you mean?"

"They stayed out in the void. They became pirates."

"Oh dear," Althea said.

Paul shrugged and said, "It's happened before."

"What has?"

"Piracy. The miscalculation of empires. You know, man's general stupidity."

Althea cocked her head and looked back at Paul.

"Do you know any history?" he asked her.

"Doesn't matter," Paul said, not giving her time to respond. "Back to the Geek. The funny thing is, after the space build up, then draw down, then pirate problem, commercial space shipping companies found it difficult to crew their freighters and other vehicles. The Chinese, who could simply tell people what to do with their lives, didn't have this problem. Their freighters were crewed and flying.

"Space Command could not sit idly by and let the Chinese win the commercial space competition. So they were brainstorming ways to augment civilian crews. The Fly it Off program was one of their answers. Let non-violent military convicts trade time working on space freighters for time off their sentences. They figured military vets had already demonstrated trainability and a mission-oriented mindset, so it was a good, pre-screened population to pull from. The Geek turned the general's idea into a real program."

Althea nodded.

Paul looked at her.

"Go ahead," he said. "Ask me what you want to ask me."

Althea smiled.

"OK. But weren't you convicted of a violent crime?"

"I was," he said somberly.

"So, how did you get into the program?"

"The Geek asked for an exception," Paul said with a shrug. Althea waited for him to continue.

"And somehow, he got it. It still surprises me when I think about it. But I am pretty sure he cashed in a lot of favors, used his status as the hero of the *Bluestone* to push it along. But somehow, he got me, guilty of battlefield murder, serving life without parole, into the program."

"That's a good friend," Althea said.

"He truly is." Paul said, his voice taking on a faraway tone.

Althea studied Paul, who seemed deep in thought.

"The Captain also," Paul said in a sad voice. "He could have said no, could have rejected my application. Three other captains had, by the way. But he said OK. He let me join his crew."

"Why did you join the program?"

Paul didn't answer. He sat still, returning her gaze.

"I mean, if you are serving a life sentence," she asked. "Then how will you benefit from the Fly it Off program?"

"Well, it got me out of Leavenworth for one. Because, I will tell you, the prospect of living the rest of one's life there is not a happy thought."

"I can imagine."

"No. You cannot."

He was quiet for a moment before continuing. "And, I thought, you never know what might happen. Maybe being a good crew member out here will earn me the consideration of parole. Or maybe I'll do another belt and back and then they'll consider it. Or maybe they never will. I don't know what will happen. But I know for sure nothing was ever going to change with me rotting away in my cell in Leavenworth. And, truthfully, I like it out here."

Paul gestured at the void beyond the *Odysseus'* hull.

Althea smiled and nodded.

"I like having you out here, too, Paul Owens."

"Thanks," Paul said, doubting her sincerity.

"Do you even know what you would do if they gave you parole?"

"Oh, yes. Yes, I know exactly."

There was something in Paul's voice that Althea did not like.

"And what is that?" She asked.

Paul thought of his nightmares. Of DredSkill. Of Fiona Malloy. Of killing her. And of finally being able to rest.

He smiled.

"That is my secret," he said, looking at his watch and standing up. "I think that is enough for this cycle."

Chapter Twenty-Five

Hiroaki was grateful that I had returned Kusunoki's body to him and told me that I was welcome to remain at his school. I intended to stay only until I had recovered from my long walk, finished healing, and figured out which lord to sell my services to next.

I stayed at the school for three years.

In that time, I learned a lot about Hiroaki Ashikaga.

Hiroaki was the son of a samurai. His grandfather had also been a samurai. Service was an important tradition in his family. Hiroaki wanted to serve his lord as a samurai, like his father had. But he did not want to benefit from the favor his father and grandfather had won from Clan Shingen.

So, Hiroaki left home at the age of thirteen. He spent the next decade wandering, learning, and perfecting his fighting technique. When he returned, he was a master swordsman. He had fought many a duel with junior samurai and rōnin, seeking to make their name by besting the next of the Ashikaga line. None was successful. Lord Shingen took notice.

Hiroaki was soon serving Lord Shingen as a samurai and fought in many campaigns for the clan. Over time, Hiroaki became a military leader in Clan Shingen. In many campaigns, it was Hiroaki's strategies that won the day. Lord Shingen came to regard Hiroaki as his greatest general.

But after the Campaign of Many Rivers, Hiroaki desired to retire. He still loved his clan and Lord Shingen. But Hiroaki looked at the endless and innumerable campaigns and mourned his comrades. He realized that the conflict between clans, which had raged for almost a hundred years, would last for at least another thousand.

Hiroaki gave up his office as Lord Shingen's general. He left everything behind, including the Ashikaga wealth and status, and walked out of Shingen's fortress on bare feet. Shingen cried when he left. But allowed him to go.

Hiroaki spent the next seven years wandering. He thought deeply about his years of combat. About the comrades he had known. About the mistakes he had made. And tried to keep to himself.

But as he wandered, he was sought out by many. Again, as in his earlier years, samurai and rōnin challenged him to duels. They sought to make their name by slaying the most famous of the Ashikaga line and Lord Shingen's favorite general.

They never did.

He was also sought out by those seeking advice and instruction. And by those like himself, who had seen many battles, and sought perspective and understanding.

After seven years, a dozen men wandered with Hiroaki. They prevented the senseless duels and cleared the way for their master. Kusunoki was one of these men. Eventually, the group left the villages and roads, seeking solace and anonymity in the forest.

Hiroaki was tired of wandering and had accepted his fate. He accepted that he could no more stop war than he could stop the rivers, and that he could no more abandon his brothers than he could abandon his own breath. Pinned between those two truths, he chose the only path he could conceive of. He would teach and mentor, but never again command.

In the early years, School Hiroaki was not much. On any day, other than the core dozen, there was only a handful of guests at community dinner. The visitors were wandering rōnin, and those who had fought for Hiroaki when he was a general and sought out his company, conversation, and advice. It was a place where samurai, rōnin, and common soldiers could rest, practice, and study without clans, politics, or indebtedness.

Over time, word of the school spread. First, the rōnin class, seeking new skills to enhance their value. Then young ones without lineage, seeking a path to samurai. After a few years, alumni of the school could be found in the ranks of all the clans. Hiroaki's school was loyal to the warrior's ethic, avoiding matters of clan.

When I was there, a hundred students lived and studied at the school. There is no record of graduates and students who had come and gone. But it was many.

And for good reason.

Hiroaki's practice went beyond the sword. It encompassed also the long spear, the bow, the horse, and cannon. All working as one. His years as Lord Shingen's general taught Hiroaki to think this way. His students, therefore, studied all disciplines and were required to master each individual skill.

Hiroaki's method was simple and excruciating. Students trained at the fundamentals until they demonstrated mastery. Then conditions were made more challenging. Then the students were made to do more than one discipline at once. It was a simple but challenging progression that most did not have the patience to endure.

Those who did endure were trained also in command. Coordination, communication, and timing became their focus. They studied every battlefield task from this new perspective. Their minds were recalibrated to function like timepieces. "You can always get more men, horses, arrows, or cannon," Hiroaki told them. "Time, however, is the one thing a commander cannot regenerate."

Though a veteran rōnin of many campaigns, I went through the training as well. After eighteen months, my skills were greatly improved.

Most students left the school after two years, returning to the world and its conflicts as better soldiers. I chose to stay. Hiroaki began to assign administrative tasks to me. I accepted these tasks as the honor that they were. The master held me in his trust. This was my happiest time.

Chapter Twenty-Six

"Attention!" Cooley said, entering the meeting room.

Drummond followed close behind him. As soon as Drummond sat down, the rest of the room did as well.

"Mr. Cooley, please begin," Drummond said.

"Aye, sir. Priority for this cycle remains cleanup and repair after the incident," Cooley said, throwing the assignments from his tablet to one of the monitors on the wall behind him. Cooley gave the group a moment to read the assignments. There were a few winces and groans as crew members matched their names to undesirable tasks.

Cooley ignored them.

"XO, repair status update, please?"

"Yes, Mr. Cooley. Repairs are going well. Full atmosphere and life support have been restored to the C&C. We are now shifting priority to hull repairs. I estimate that we will have finished everything that we are able to do within ten cycles. The rest will have to be done when we get to the belt."

"Very good," Cooley said before turning his head toward Paul. "Prisoner Owens. Inspection assignments, please?"

"Aye, sir." Paul leaned forward and slid Regas, Hahn, and McNeeley each a printed inspection sheet. "Pretty standard stuff. Return your inspection sheets to me when complete, as usual."

Regas made sure Paul saw him roll his eyes. Paul smiled at him.

"OK," Cooley said. "That's all I've got. I want to keep these meetings short so we can get back to taking care of the *Odysseus*. We've got a lot of training left to do before we get to the belt. Any comments from you, sir?" Cooley looked at Drummond.

"No."

"Very good, sir. Then let's all—"

"I've got a point of order," Regas said, leaning forward in his seat. Hahn and McNeeley exchanged excited glances.

Cooley regarded Regas for a moment. Paul tried to imagine what was going through Cooley's head.

"What is it, Prisoner?" Cooley said.

Regas nodded to Cooley in exaggerated thanks for yielding the floor. "I'd like to propose an increase in prisoner shares," he said.

Drummond's head snapped up at that. "A what?"

Regas turned his head to meet Drummond's surprised gaze. "An increase in prisoner shares," he said slowly.

Paul noted the lack of "sir" and that no one corrected him.

"I have prepared a detailed letter outlining our position," Regas said, unfolding papers he took from his flight-suit breast pocket. "Our intention was to submit this request to Captain Drake. But we now submit, herewith, to the current holder of that, um, office. Shall I read our letter into the record?"

The disbelief on Cooley's face almost made Paul chuckle.

"That is ridiculous," Drummond said, interrupting Paul's humor with the most force he had ever seen from the man.

"Oh, really?" Regas said, leaning back in his chair. "You were promoted. Seems like we're all going to be shouldering more responsibility and an extra load as a result of the incident. And"—Regas held up a finger as if he were onto a brilliant idea—"with the captain dead, the Company won't have to pay him at all. Seems like there will be more to go around. Am I right?"

Regas looked to Hahn and McNeeley, who both nodded in agreement.

"Prisoner Regas," Cooley began in a tired voice. But Drummond cut him off.

"That is the most ridiculous thing I have ever heard!" He pointed at Regas, raising his voice as he went on. "Totally ignorant of how such things are actually structured!"

"Sir," Cooley tried to interject and get Drummond back under control. The rest of the room was transfixed by the outburst from the normally muted CFO.

Regas nodded his head slowly as Drummond continued to yell.

"Ignorant also of the intricate financial considerations at play on such a complex endeavor as a long-haul space voyage!"

"Sir," Cooley tried again.

"I will not stand for such outrageous demands from a mere prisoner crew member. This is not a negotiation!"

"Sir, I think—"

"You are not a signatory of any contract. Our obligation is with the United States military, which has granted us you as a resource for this voyage. You are nothing to me!"

"Sir!" Cooley yelled, slapping his hand on the table.

Drummond looked at him, eyes bulging.

Regas's smile had dissolved. He stared at Drummond and smoldered.

"Sir, I think you have made your position clear," Cooley said in his most calming voice. "I recommend we conclude this meeting."

Drummond blinked, then nodded. He stood up and left the room.

Cooley looked at Regas. "Prisoner Regas, you will leave this room and report to your quarters for five cycles of confinement."

Regas looked back at Cooley. He stood up without speaking and then pushed his chair back into its place at the table.

"Aye, Mr. Cooley," Regas said.

After Regas had left the room, Cooley said, "XO, once Prisoner Regas has returned to his quarters, you will lock him in for five cycles. No visitors authorized except by me."

"Yes, Mr. Cooley."

The rest of the room sat still for a moment, digesting the confrontation.

"Althea and Prisoner Owens," Cooley said, rubbing his eyes, "please give me the room. I need to have a conversation with Prisoners Hahn and McNeeley."

Paul and Althea stood up and left.

Paul was glad to get out of there. He could see what Regas was doing and was happy that it was not his responsibility to keep the troublemaker in line.

Althea cast Paul a worried glance as they walked down the hall toward the center ladder.

"It's going to be fine," Paul said to her. "Regas will get tired of it after a few confinements, and we'll be back to our boring normality."

"I hope so," she said, unconvinced.

"Trust me."

"I do," she said. "Are we still on for another session at the end of this cycle?"

"Sure. I guess."

"Come on, Paul. I think the first few sessions have been really good for you."

"We haven't gotten to any of the bad parts yet," Paul said. He had continued to meet with Althea over the past few cycles, telling his story in small pieces. They weren't very far into it yet.

Paul stepped out onto the center ladder and began to climb down toward the second level.

"I know," she said. "But it all counts."

"I hope so," he said as he descended out of view.

Chapter Twenty-Seven

ater in the cycle, after Paul completed his training academics, he changed into his pressure suit and set off to conduct his inspection. He had smiled when he'd read the inspection sheet: "Factory. Section Seven. Level Two. Utility Closet B658." It was a random corner of the old girl, over a kilometer away, past the bridge tower airlock. A real pain in the ass to get to.

Before the old man had been killed, this would have set Paul off. From the beginning, Paul had thought it was ridiculous that the captain's inspection cycle bounced unpredictably all over the *Odysseus*. He'd told Drake so during one of their clandestine bourbon sessions on the bridge.

"Captain, what is the deal with this inspection regime?" Paul said, floating in front of the big window. He maintained his gaze at the stars, not wanting Drake to see the smirk on his face.

Drake didn't turn from the window either, not allowing Paul to see he was amused rather than irritated. "We've covered this, son."

"I'm not arguing. I'm with the program and am going to do them. I just don't understand why you have structured them as a random-assed Easter egg hunt."

Drake took a shot of bourbon.

"Usually, there is a logic to inspection regimes," Paul continued. "Front to back, top to bottom, by department, or whatever. But this is a random walk through the endless nooks and crannies of the *Odysseus*."

"Because it's my fucking inspection regime, that's why," the captain said in a curiously low voice. Drake turned to Paul and winked.

Paul shook his head.

Later, as Paul was leaving, Drake motioned for him to wait a moment while he wrote a note.

"Thank you, Prisoner Owens," the captain said, handing him the note. "You are dismissed."

Paul left and read the note as he floated through the tube toward the spinner and his quarters.

I use a random inspection regime to keep the XO guessing. That is why I've given it to you in paper form, which I printed back on the station before we got underway. I have the only other copy. Only you and I know the schedule. It's one of the few checks we have on the son of a bitch.

Paul shook his head now, remembering that classic Drake interaction as he floated aft through the tube. *I already miss the old man,* he thought to himself as he started climbing the traverse.

The factory was located topside, midway between the bridge superstructure and power and propulsion. It was a large multi-level facility that extended for over three hundred meters along the top of the *Odysseus'* hull, designed to ingest asteroids, scrap metal, and other debris on one end and produce finished equipment, parts, and material on the other end. Drake referred to the factory as "the indispensable facility on the *Odysseus.*"

Of the five M class freighters, *Odysseus* and *Perseus* were, by far, the most valuable. They owed their unicorn statuses to the retrofitted additive manufacturing facilities they hauled around the solar system. Designed by the Japanese and paid for by the US Military during the early fifties, the factories were of a scale and capacity class of their own. Military planners salivated at the thought of the two large ships birthing mechanical armies on their journeys to Mars.

Rather than mothball the unique facilities when China and the US agreed to the Space Détente, the military let the Company lease them for an undisclosed sum. It was supposedly a good deal for both sides. The military got free maintenance and upkeep of the two strategic capabilities and could take them back at a moment's notice should the situation justify it. The company got the economic benefit of their use. Most people believed that, like most deals it entered, the Company had made off like bandits. How the Company pulled this off and how little they were paying was the source of much rumor and jealousy.

The factory was divided into seven sections. Section one's official name was "material intake," but Drake referred to it as "the mouth," a term that better matched its appearance. The mouth was a large, imposing orifice in which one could see grinders and laser turrets before the shadows got too dark. The mouth's role was to pulverize whatever the tug drones pushed into it.

Section two, analysis, was called "the lab" in Drake-speak. As base element powders emerged from the mouth's processes, the lab identified them before they passed into section three, segregation, where they were separated into different raw-material containers before being placed in section four, storage.

Section five, printing, was where the magic happened. There were a dozen industrial-grade, zero-gravity 3D printers into which the raw material was fed, based on what the factory was tasked to produce. The printing section was equally adept at printing massive components or tiny objects. All of which were then transferred to section six.

Assembly and programming had multiple separate lines that could be configured for any type of system assembly. There were two dedicated circuit-board assembly lines that could manufacture the electronics components. At the end of section six, a large programming-and-upload module stood ready to program the brains of the factory's creations. The factory had several program-generation modules that could compose mission-based software for just about any bot or equipment profile, or it could load software put in storage by the Company before they'd left high lunar orbit.

Finally, section seven, "the hold," as the captain called it, was a large warehouse area where finished systems and components were held until they were deployed to their destinations throughout the *Odysseus* or sold upon arrival at the belt or high lunar orbit.

The factory was fully automated and run by a dedicated, mission specific AI called the factory foreman. Sections six and seven were the only sections human crew members could get into. The others were not configured in a way that made them accessible. Which was fine with Paul.

The factory was a fascinating place for him, and he looked forward to this visit. It was not a place he went to be contemplative, like the hangar or the bridge, but he enjoyed looking at all the interesting, high-tech manufacturing robots. They reminded him of the maintenance bots in his last unit. And it was always interesting to see the random things waiting to be transferred out of the hold.

A large hatch in the top of the tube provided crew access to the factory. Paul opened it and then pulled himself up the hand ladder through the passageway.

Paul emerged on level one of the hold. The ladder continued up to levels two and three, but Paul stopped climbing when he spotted the cargo-handling system in motion. The robotic arm held a metal spar in its grip as it propelled itself along the ceiling-mounted track up the aisle toward Paul.

Shelving and closet-like containers rose from floor to ceiling in the hold and extended in long rows the entire length of the massive space. There were twenty-four storage rows whose containers grew from small to large as Paul looked left to right. The leftmost containers were about the size of a golf ball, while the rows of shelving and containers to his far right were large enough to accept a school bus.

On the ceiling, the tracks of the cargo-handling system ran above the aisles between the storage containers. The arm stopped near the end of one of the storage rows to Paul's front. A long, skinny locker popped open, and the arm extended and swiveled, placing the shiny new spar into its temporary home.

The arm then retracted. The door snapped shut, and the cargo-handling system sped away on its tracks, down the aisle back toward assembly and programming.

Paul shook his head in wonder as he looked at the large volume of storage and realized that there were two more levels of storage above him.

"Damn, XO," he said. "How do you keep track of all this shit?"

"I'm a computer, remember?" the XO responded in his headset. "I don't forget things."

"Seems like you have enough room here to build another *Odysseus*, if you wanted."

"Not quite. But maybe a smaller version."

"All this capability, and you can't make us a new long-range communications antenna?"

"It's a good question, Paul."

Did the XO hesitate? Paul asked himself.

"But, unfortunately, I am at the mercy of my onboard ingredients, so to speak," the XO continued. "The range and sensitivity we require demand particularly pure samples of very rare metals. Rest assured, I'm searching and analyzing everything I can get my hands on. Hopefully, we'll get lucky and I'll be able to get us back on online with command."

"Yes. I hope so."

Each locker had a small LED light on the top center of its door. It glowed green when it was storing something, red when empty. Paul noted that most of the storage units on level one had a soft, green glow.

"Seems like you're nearly full down here," Paul said as he started climbing to level two.

"Yes. We're only about half a year out from the belt. I've got a big list of orders to produce before we arrive, and Drummond is quite insistent I get it all done."

"I bet he is."

Paul climbed up to level two. Two small utility closets were attached to the wall, on opposite sides of the crew ladder. Paul opened the one marked "B658."

Empty.

Paul smiled and nodded. "Fuck you, sir," he said softly to himself.

"What's that, Paul?"

"Nothing," Paul answered, embarrassed. "That was directed at Captain Drake. Another inspection of an empty place on the *Odysseus*."

"I understand."

Paul made the notation on his inspection sheet and started the journey back to the Hab.

When Paul passed through the factory passageway and entered the tube, he looked aft toward the rear of the *Odysseus*.

The power-and-propulsion bulkhead loomed over five hundred meters away at the end of the tube. Paul remembered the captain's note to meet him there in section ten, transfer room 105. He thought about going there now, but decided against it. He wanted to shower and was done for the cycle.

Soon, sir, Paul promised Drake. *Next time I am back here. I promise.*

Paul turned toward the front of the *Odysseus* and started back to the Hab.

"Paul," the XO called on the radio. "May I make a statement?"

Paul rolled his eyes at the overly polite XO.

"Sure."

"Althea told me about your sessions together. I think it is very constructive that you have agreed to participate in those. I commend you. I hope you don't mind that I sent her to your room when you were having your troubles."

"No," Paul said, floating through the tube. "I think that was probably a good move."

Paul knew that the XO could listen in to most sections of the *Odysseus*, including personal quarters and even his sessions with Althea, but he tried not to think about it. He didn't know if the XO was reminding him of this to mess with him, or because the XO was really just a geeky and awkward program. Paul reminded himself that the XO had bigger things to worry about, like navigating the *Odysseus* and not blowing up one of the nuclear reactors. Nonetheless, Paul hated that the XO got to hear his sob story.

"I'm also quite glad that Captain Drake's inspection regime seems to have survived his passing."

"You are? I figured you thought this kind of thing is stupid."

"On the contrary. A ship as complex and expansive as the *Odysseus* can only benefit from multiple inspection regimes. There are several areas of the ship where I have no direct sensing available. It is good to have a human crew member periodically check these areas. The bots are not always as adept. And, as I am sure you know, the ship's service has been long and varied. We've served under many fine captains, worked with many fine crews, and safely conveyed thousands of passengers. I've been honored to do so. But almost three decades of service have left us with a lot of abandoned, derelict, and—in some cases, I am sure—dangerous material on board that I am not aware of."

"You mean to say," Paul said, floating forward with a smile. "People left a lot of shit on board."

"Indeed. You could say that. And I appreciate that you and your prisoner colleagues are getting the situation sorted."

"I hate to tell you, but I think the old man would have been disappointed to hear you say that."

"I am sure you are right, Paul. I think he preferred to think of it as a way to keep me in check. To block my nefarious plans."

Paul laughed at that. "That he did. Just so we're clear, though. I don't give a shit about your nefarious plans. Just get me to the belt and back and leave me alone, and you and I are going to be fine."

"It's a deal, Paul."

"Good."

The AI hesitated a moment before continuing. "I wish Prisoner Regas shared your peaceful outlook."

"Me too. You got that crazy asshole locked up?"

"Yes," the XO said. "I've got half a mind to cause a tragic loss of atmosphere. But that would not be consistent with my core mission of protecting human life."

"Well, I don't think he would be missed."

"I think you are right. He worries me, Paul."

"You and Althea," Paul said with a chuckle as he pulled himself forward in the long tube. "Don't worry. Cooley has his number. Besides, guys like Regas wear out quickly."

"I hope so. Have a good evening."

Chapter Twenty-Eight

Adauchi Book One
Circa 1510
Translated from the Japanese

One day, in the beginning of my third year with Hiroaki, Lord Shingen visited the school.

Hiroaki welcomed his lord with much joy. They embraced as old friends, and Hiroaki showed him around the school grounds.

The lord asked for a demonstration, which Hiroaki was hesitant to give. But there was no polite way to refuse. So, his students showed Shingen what they were capable of. The lord was pleased.

Later, I sat next to Hiroaki as Lord Shingen made his request.

"I am mightily impressed," Shingen said. "What you have accomplished here should give you great pride, my former general."

"I thank you, my lord."

"I am sorry, my friend," Lord Shingen said. "But I must ask something of you."

"Do not hesitate, my lord. How may I be of service?"

"This is a time of great risk and opportunity for Clan Shingen. We are not at our strongest. Tax monies have decreased. The endless wars have weakened the people and the land and their ability to support our armies. But we have managed to pin our dread enemy Lord Hayato and his clan inside their last fortress. We have the opportunity to finally defeat them and end our long conflict."

Hiroaki listened intently.

"The fortress is protected by the Hayato Clan's Elite Guard, commanded by Anotsu Hayato, Lord Hayato's son. We have made six attacks, and they have repelled us each time. On the final attack, they killed my last general."

Lord Shingen paused, sadness gripping him. "I can promote more generals, of course," he finally continued. "But they are not ready. I can feel the opportunity slipping away, Hiroaki. But if you will command our next attack and add your forces to our number, we can win."

Hiroaki sat in silence, considering Shingen's words. I knew how this weighed on my master. He loved his clan and felt a duty to his lord. But he also loved his students, and he had sworn to never lead men into battle again.

"Without you, Hiroaki, the clan is lost," Lord Shingen said, sensing the debate within his old general.

I have thought about this moment many times since. What if Hiroaki had said no?

But he did not.

"The honor is to serve, my lord," Hiroaki said. "We shall do our best."

Lord Shingen smiled in relief. "I am most happy, my friend." He stood up to leave. "I will expect you at my castle tomorrow."

"I shall be there, my lord."

That evening, Hiroaki gathered his students. "Our greatest challenge is upon us," he said. "I would not have committed us to this fight if I did not believe it was worthy. It is our opportunity to win a measure of peace. But those who do not wish to fight can leave with my blessing. You will always be students in good standing."

Hiroaki looked around slowly, making eye contact with as many of his students as he could.

"Those who remain will fight with me."

Every student stayed.

Chapter Twenty-Nine

It had been a good cycle. Paul rose early, meditated, worked on his translation, got some exercise in, and then completed his training academics. All he had left was his cycle inspection, and then he would have a few hours of spare time. And he knew exactly what he was going to do with them.

He was climbing up the Hab's center crew ladder when he ran into Althea.

"Hi there," she said to him on the first level as he emerged from the second.

"Hello," he said, noting she was wearing her standard utilitarian flight-suit uniform. He preferred the leggings and sweater.

"What are you up to?" Althea asked.

"Inspection time," Paul said, still hanging on the ladder.

"And what exotic corner of the *Odysseus* are you bound for?"

"Power and propulsion," Paul said, stepping off the ladder onto the floor of the first level.

"Oh my," Althea said, widening her eyes in feigned enthusiasm. "I wish I could go with you."

Paul laughed, marveling at the detail in her facial expressions. He caught himself having a crazy thought.

"What is it?" Althea asked.

"Oh, uh," Paul stammered, embarrassed she'd caught him. "Nothing."

"Tell me," she said in a playful voice. "Please, Paul. I thought we were a team?"

Fuck it, he thought.

"Well, the truth is, lately, sometimes, at the end of a cycle, I'll go up to the bridge and… hang out and enjoy the view."

Althea nodded. "It doesn't bother you to be there. Where it happened?"

"No," Paul fidgeted as he spoke and looked at his feet. "It doesn't. In a weird way, it feels nice. No one else ever goes up there, since everything is still offline."

Paul opened his mouth to say something more, but stopped. He looked quickly down between his feet at the ladder beneath him. Then his eyes darted to Althea, then back to his feet.

"Well…" Althea said, puzzled by the awkward silence. "I think it's great you have found a place on the *Odysseus* you can spend time like that. In solitude."

"Yeah," Paul said, looking up from his feet. "Do you want to join me sometime? Maybe at the end of this cycle?"

Paul felt a sudden warmth on his cheeks.

I'm fucking blushing, he thought, astounded at himself. *Real smooth.*

"I'd like that very much, Paul."

"Great," said Paul, a big smile breaking across his face.

Althea smiled also.

Paul thought for a moment, a look of concern coming over his face.

He leaned in. "We probably shouldn't leave together. So, let's shoot for around 2030 hours. Meet you there, on the bridge."

Althea looked at her watch. That was in an hour and a half.

"I'll be there," she said.

"But it's not a session," Paul said. He pointed a serious finger at Althea. "You come at me with any analysis bullshit, and you're uninvited, understood?"

"Understood," Althea said, stifling a chuckle.

"Good," Paul said, climbing past her toward the traverse.

* * *

The aft end of the tube terminated in a large bulkhead that led to level one of power and propulsion, the largest module, by far, of the *Odysseus.*

The power-and-propulsion module, or PPM, was organized like a twelve-story building laid on its side, parallel to the ship's direction of flight, with the twelfth story being farthest aft. Only the five middle compartments, sections four through eight, were pressurized. The rest were primarily storage and left in freezing vacuum. All the sections were connected by a large, central freight elevator that was designed to move massive ultra dense reactor parts from section to section if needed, and by two outboard crew ladder tubes on the port and starboard sides. The PPM was completely automated, enabling the XO to manage the maintenance, fueling, and operation of the three reactors.

Paul was always amazed when he visited the PPM. He thought about the XO simultaneously overseeing the ship's navigation, life-support systems, maintenance fleet, everything. As well as splitting atoms in two live nuclear reactors.

And while XO's hyperintelligent brain managed all that, the cranky old man thought he was pulling one over on XO by making me conduct random inspections laid out in a secret spiral-bound notebook, thought Paul as he opened the bulkhead. *Ridiculous.*

Paul pulled himself into section one of power and propulsion, and the bulkhead slid shut behind him. He moved to the starboard crew ladder tube, gave a yank on the farthest rung, and coasted through section two. He arrested his flight with a quick grab of the ladder in section three and made his way to the designated storage room.

Along the way, Paul marveled at the cleanliness of the PPM. Every surface was pristine white, a glaring contrast from the grubby, nasty-as-a-subway environment of the tube, which was just on the other side of the bulkhead.

It was no coincidence that the PPM was the cleanest module of the *Odysseus.* Everyone on board, from the captain down to the simplest robot, treated the place like a church, like a holy chamber in which a beast lived whose fire kept the deadly, frozen void from overtaking the *Odysseus.* It kept them all alive. If there was a hiccup in the reactors, they were dead. All of them.

There was an unspoken sense that: *Hey, we can jerry-rig anything else we need out here, but if we lose the power plant, we're fucked.*

And it was true. Everything on board needed power to survive. So, it was kept in the most revered state a thing can be kept in on a ship at sea or in space or anywhere else.

It was kept clean.

Paul almost started to cry when the door opened and he looked in the small room. A single rack of packaged cleaning rags was fastened to the far wall. The ridiculousness of the one-hour dick dance of donning a pressure suit, climbing up the traverse, pulling himself two kilometers through the tube, and then up to section three of the PPM should have sent him into a rage. Instead, a sense of nostalgia and the loss of Captain Drake washed over him.

Fuck me, Paul thought. *I'm getting to be one oversentimental son of a bitch.*

He held it together, though, only because he knew from experience how much crying in zero gravity in a pressure suit sucked. The tears clung to your eyes and there was no way to wipe them. The ball of salty water increased in size as long as you kept crying, clinging to your face. Paul hated that.

After he noted his findings in his inspection notebook, Paul made his way back to the tube bulkhead to start back. But he hesitated at the bulkhead, halted by a strange thought.

Section ten, transfer room 105, he thought. *That's where Drake wanted me to meet him. I'm already all the way out here on the ass end of the ship.*

Paul floated in the open bulkhead. He looked down the two-kilometer tube. Halfway down the long structure was the C&C bulkhead he would take to the bridge to meet Althea.

He looked back into the now-dark PPM toward the room where the captain was supposedly going to unveil evidence of the XO's conspiracy. Paul checked his watch: plenty of time until he was meeting Althea.

Fine, Paul thought, pushing back into the PPM. *Your goddamned Easter egg hunt put me back here, so I might as well prove to myself how stupid this is.*

He noted each section as he floated aft. At section ten, he grabbed the ladder to arrest his glide and opened the bulkhead.

"Transfer room 105" was the fifth transfer room in the tenth section. The rooms were numbered from inboard to outboard, so room five was midway through the passageway toward the center section of PPM. Paul floated outside of the room for a moment, readying himself to be surprised by what he would find. As he did so, he remembered the captain's foul mood and urgency the last time they had spoken.

All right, you weird old man, thought Paul as he activated the door. *Whatcha got for me?*

The light in the small room came on automatically. Paul eased himself in. The room was empty except for a small device fastened to the middle of the floor. The black metallic device was about the size of a small shoebox. There were several blinking lights and a digital display of the date and time. But other than that, there were no obvious clues to suggest the device's purpose.

Paul floated closer to the object and touched his toe to the floor to pull himself down. Mag boots secured to the floor, he bent over and examined the mysterious metal square. He noted some writing on the top of the device: "IMU-M151-47."

It seemed like a familiar designation to Paul. Like something from his time in the military. But he couldn't quite place it.

There were a few unused data input/output connections on each side. Paul reached into his utility pocket and pulled out a standard data storage stick. He fiddled with the stick and device, trying each of the I/O connections until he found one that fit. The stick slid into place with a click.

The unit beeped, and the date/time display changed to read: "Download Course Data?"

Oh yeah. Paul thought. *It's an inertial measurement unit. A self-contained system that measures linear and angular motion.*

Paul examined the simple interface and decided on the green "OK" button. He pressed it, and the display said: "Downloading to Memory Device."

Paul stood up straight as the IMU loaded whatever data it had onto his memory stick. He remembered the captain's note saying he had discovered that the XO had changed their course and he could prove it.

When the hell did you put an inertial measurement unit on board? Paul thought, wishing he could ask the captain.

Paul figured Drake must have brought it on board back in high lunar orbit, when he'd taken command and started getting paranoid about the XO. A freighter in HLO was a frenetic and chaotic scene as the ship was upgraded, refitted, and provisioned in a mad rush to make a launch window. No one would have noticed the captain putting this thing in such a remote corner of the *Odysseus*.

And the old man had put it back here, where the XO could not directly monitor or detect it. An IMU didn't emit any energy or signals, so the XO would never have known it was here.

But why would the XO have cared? Paul thought. *Seems like he, for the most part, didn't give a shit what the captain was up to.*

Paul shook his head. He suddenly felt uneasy. The device at his feet chirped, and the display read: "Data Transfer Successful."

Paul grabbed the memory stick and placed it in his cargo pocket. He worked his way forward to the bridge to meet up with Althea. The prospect of spending time with her was a much nicer thought than Drake's obsessions. He would deal with this later.

Chapter Thirty

aul and Althea floated in silence on the bridge facing the big window. The *Odysseus'* hull, long and slender, stretched away for over a kilometer in front of them. The Hab and Utility Module alternated into view on the ends of the spinner. They seemed tiny at this distance, two ridiculously small volumes of life-sustaining pressure and oxygen spiraling in the vastness of cold vacuum.

Inspection-and-repair bots worked over the ship. Paul was always surprised by the amount of activity. Two IR bots passed beneath the bridge. They were moving fast relative to the old girl, headed toward her front.

A glare of fire caught their eyes. Paul and Althea looked at its source. Fifty meters starboard, at about the same level as the bridge, a tug drone pushed a large piece of metal aft. Paul studied it as it moved out of sight behind them.

Paul pulled a bottle of bourbon out of his backpack.

"I see it's not all about solitude and reflection up here," Althea said.

Paul smiled.

"It was a gift from the captain," Paul said, holding the bottle up and staring at it as he recalled the Drake. "The old man and I used to spend time up here. He's got a stash of the stuff somewhere on board, and he would share with me from time to time. He gave me this bottle at the end of a long cycle. I've been rationing it ever since." Paul looked at Althea. "I hate to admit it, but it does help me relax," he said.

"If you ask me, you've earned anything that helps you relax," she said with a smile.

Paul opened the bottle and jerked it up and down to free a swallow of bourbon. Paul looked at Althea and winked as he leaned forward to capture the floating golden liquid blob with his lips.

Althea giggled.

"What?" he asked.

"It looks like you are kissing the bourbon," she said. "And kissing it well. It's cute."

Paul looked at her sideways.

"It's true." She shrugged.

"How would you know what a good kiss looks like?"

"I know plenty of things like that," Althea answered.

"Let me guess. Kissing releases endorphins and has many physiological benefits and blah blah blah."

Paul stopped talking when he saw the look of hurt on Althea's face. He wasn't sure what to say.

"That wasn't very nice," she said.

"Uh…"

Althea looked at Paul for a long moment and then smiled to let him off the hook.

"Shit." Paul shook his head. "Thought I really stepped in it there."

"You did. Lucky for you, my expectations for old soldier boys like yourself are low. Very low."

Paul nodded. "You are wise beyond your years." He ejected another shot of bourbon in front of his face. When it stabilized into a spinning sphere, he leaned forward and sipped it from the air.

"Is it because I am attractive?" Althea asked.

"Huh?"

"I know that I am very attractive," she said in a troubled tone of voice Paul had never heard from her. "I had nothing to do with that, though. I was just designed this way. Is that why I seem so artificial to you? Is that why you don't take me seriously?"

"I take you seriously, Althea," was all Paul could think to say. "I'm not inviting anyone else up here to spend time with, am I?"

Althea let a weary smile spread across her face. "And I appreciate it, Paul. Very much."

They both turned back to the window. They floated in silence for a long time. Paul occasionally sipped on floating orbs of bourbon he set free from his bottle, Althea sneaking glances each time and smiling.

"May I ask you a question?"

"Is it therapeutically loaded?" Paul asked with narrow eyes.

"No."

"Then yes."

"Why do you come up here and do this? Stare out of the window?"

Paul looked at Althea, close to objecting to the question.

"I promise it's not loaded. I'm just curious."

"What do your algorithms tell you?"

Althea frowned. "Always about the algorithms with you," she said, letting irritation tinge her voice. "You have a lot more faith in my algorithms than I do."

She shook her head at him and looked out the window.

"I like the way staring out at the void makes me feel," Paul said. "Makes me feel small. Makes my problems seem small. My sadness seems small. And I guess when it all seems smaller, it is easier to bear."

Althea turned her head to look at him.

"Besides. it's also really beautiful out there," Paul said.

Althea nodded in agreement, and they floated in front of the window for a few minutes in silence.

"I sit up here, and I can see why a lot of them said, 'Fuck you, we're not coming back'" Paul said, eyes still looking out the window.

"What do you mean?"

"The pirates," Paul said. "Remember? When we tried to recall our thousands of crews. And China did the same thing?"

"Yes. I remember you telling me that."

"So, think about it," Paul said, shaking his head. "You're out here, after years of training and probably a lifetime of dreaming, and they say, come back. It's over."

He looked at Althea.

"Would you?" he asked. "Would you go home?"

Althea took a long breath before answering.

"I feel like this will disappoint you. But I probably would. I mean, it's not my ship. I didn't get her on my own and I'm not out here on my own. I am doing a job. And, well, if the job is over, and the people that sent me out said, come back… I guess I should head back."

Paul nodded at her and then looked back out the window.

"Well?" she said.

He looked back at her, a shy smile on his face.

"What would you do?" she asked, in an insistent voice.

"I honestly don't know."

She cocked her head at the sadness in his voice. She looked at him, waiting for him to continue.

"I wish I could tell you for sure that I would disobey," he said. "That I would give earth and its powers that be the finger and stay out here."

He looked back out at the stars, and the lonely length of the *Odysseus'* prow.

"But… I don't know… even now, the pull of duty is strong."

Althea looked forward. She shook her head. "I guess each of us has our own programing."

Paul looked at her and smiled.

"What?" she asked, noting his raised eyebrows.

"You surprise me constantly."

"Is that a good thing?"

"Yes," he said. "Yes, it is."

"Good."

"But remind me to tell you sometime about when a couple of robots disobeyed direct orders, repeatedly, to save my life and taught me the true meaning of loyalty."

Althea smiled.

"I will. For sure."

Paul turned to gaze out of the window and then reached for her hand.

Althea smiled and gave it to him.

EARTH

Chapter Thirty-One

Thane checked his watch as he rode the elevator up to Fiona's floor. 6:47AM.

She had asked him to swing by her office at 7 to "chat." Thane had not spoken to Fiona beyond brief texts in almost two weeks and figured he was in for another ass chewing about transferring her account to Max.

"Good morning, Mr Thane," the receptionist said, coming out from behind the large desk to greet him as he stepped out of the elevator. "Miss Malloy is expecting you. Please follow me."

"Thank you."

Thane followed the receptionist down the hallway he knew by heart. He nodded to her when she stopped at the doorway to Fiona's office and he walked past. Thane had to stifle a lusty smile as his eyes fell on Fiona.

"Morning, Cyrus," she said, getting off the stationary bike in the corner of her office and walking his way.

Fiona's dark green sports bra and high-waisted leggings accentuated her long legs and slender waist. A light sheen of perspiration highlighted the swell of her breasts in the glancing morning sun, which cast an orange glow throughout her office. Sweat also glistened on her forehead and temples. Her hair, mostly held up in a messy high ponytail, stuck to her damp neck in places. Thane's hands twitched with the imagined sensation of running his fingers through her hair and down her sweaty body.

"Morning, Ma'am." He willed his eyes to stay level, pointed into hers.

"Coffee?" Fiona asked him.

"Please."

Fiona turned away and Thane's eyes roved over her as she walked to the wet bar with the coffeepot in the corner. He studied her toned shoulders as she poured their coffee, waiting until the last second to make a show of looking out the windows just before she walked back. The buildings on the west side of the park glowed brightly, struck by the morning sun. The east side was still dark beneath long shadows.

"Thanks," Thane said as she handed him his coffee, black, as she knew he took it.

Fiona gestured at a pair of brown leather chairs near the floor to ceiling windows. Thane sat while Fiona grabbed the white towel off of the bike. She sat across from him, towel over her shoulders.

"So, I have to admit I am warming up to your boy Max," she said.

Thane smiled and raised an eyebrow.

"He is a quiet guy," she continued, not acknowledging Thane's smile. "But the more I have been around him and learned about his background, the more impressed I am."

Thane nodded. "Max is unique," he said. "You won't find anyone else that is equal parts front-line exo battalion service and deep counter intelligence assignments like him."

"He makes a very one-dimensional-military-dude impression at first," Fiona said. "But he actually seems pretty smart."

"Oh, he is smart," Thane agreed, knowing how much Fiona valued intelligence. "Probably too smart for his own good."

Fiona took a slow sip of coffee and looked out the window for a moment. Thane watched a single bead of sweat emerge from behind her earlobe. It taunted him, moving slowly down her neck.

For fuck sake, man, he scolded himself, looking down into his coffee. *Get control of yourself.*

"I don't trust him yet, though," Fiona said, snapping her head back toward Thane.

His smile evaporated.

"You can trust him," he said.

"I will never trust him like I trust you."

A surge of feeling ran through Thane. He luxuriated in it for a moment. Then responded with the Firm's best interest. "I think you will, he—"

"I never will," Fiona interrupted.

They looked at each other for a long moment.

Thane finally shrugged and took a pull of coffee.

"Whether I trust him or not," Fiona said. "I need him to find that god damn memory sphere."

She took a sip of coffee and placed the cup on the side table next to her chair.

"You remember the memory sphere, don't you?" Fiona asked, crossing her arms. "That thing that eluded you and you left undone before leaving me for - what do you call it? Business development?"

Thane nodded.

"I remember."

Thane thought it was a straightforward assignment when Fiona had tasked him with it five years ago: Locate a missing piece of highly sensitive military equipment, a memory sphere from a robotic soldier that belonged to the failed AI initiative by one of Determined End States' smaller companies, Musashi Solutions. He was, of course, intimately familiar with the events surrounding the loss of the equipment, having been there on Outpost Devil that day.

It had seemed easy enough to Thane. Having DredSkill's international resources at his disposal, he figured he would have the sphere back in Fiona's possession within the month. He started with Doctor Musashi, the retired roboticist and founder of the eponymous military AI company. At the time, Musashi was living in Florida. Thane flew down and questioned him about the missing equipment. The professorial old man seemed helpful enough, though Thane got the feeling Musashi remained haunted by the terrible acts committed by his creations. Thane thanked the doctor for his time, and Musashi promised to reach out if he thought of or discovered anything that might be helpful. Thane flew back to New York City.

After a month of further investigation, the old doctor's story looked suspect. Thane flew back to Florida, but Doctor Musashi had vanished.

Fiona was enraged. And concerned. And the search continued.

"I don't have to tell you the sensitivities that surround this matter," Fiona said.

Thane nodded again. This time with restraint, as if not wanting others to notice, despite them being alone in Fiona's office.

"And, weighing the sensitivities, your recommendation is still that we give Max the assignment?" she asked, eyes locked on him.

"Yes. Max is perfect for the job. Better than I was."

"Not saying much," Fiona said.

Cyrus gave Fiona a wounded look. "Damn, Miss Malloy."

Fiona stood up and grabbed her coffee cup. She made an inquiring gesture at Thane. He shook his head.

Thane looked out the window as Fiona warmed her coffee. Talk of the sphere had doused Thane in concern, short circuiting the electricity he had been feeling. He didn't notice Fiona walking back toward him.

"I'm playing with you, Cyrus," she said, putting a hand on his shoulder. "I'll never forget what you did for me. Never. You were a godsend."

The feeling of her hand on his shoulder dissolved his angst. Her statement ignited him. He stifled an urge to pledge his undying allegiance to her and scream, *I'd do anything for you. ANYTHING.*

Instead, he looked up at her, simmering in the warmth of her proximity.

"Devil sent, more like it," he said.

"Maybe," Fiona said. She paused. Her eyes followed a thought, then returned to meet Thane's gaze.

Then she turned away.

Thane felt the tension of her being so close dissipate as she walked back to her chair.

"Either way. What is in the past must stay in the past," she said, sitting down in the brown leather chair and looking at her mug before taking a sip of coffee.

"Especially that damn sphere," Thane said.

"Especially that damn sphere," Fiona said. "That thing must be found and destroyed."

Fiona placed her mug on the side table and said, "Brief Max up on the assignment. Get him going."

Thane nodded.

"Consider it done."

Someone knocked on Fiona's office door.

"Yes?" she called.

One of her assistants opened the door. "Ma'am, flight operations said that, if you are able, they would like to get an early start to get ahead of some weather."

"That's fine. I'll shower quickly."

"Yes, Ma'am," the assistant said, turning to leave.

"I'll get out of your hair," Thane said, standing up as he tried to ignore the images of Fiona in the shower bombarding him.

Fiona also stood.

"Where are you off to today?" He asked as they shook hands.

"The Ocean Reef Club. Key Largo," Fiona said, walking back to her desk.

Thoughts of Fiona in bathing suits and skimpy sundresses flooded Thane's brain.

"Nice," he managed to say.

"It's the annual golf charity for Warrior Renewal Initiative," Fiona said, walking to her desk. "So, it won't be time off, really. But it will be nice."

Fiona lifted her cell phone from her desk, back to Thane, her mind already gone from their meeting.

"Safe travels," Thane said. He left, shutting the door behind him. He stood outside her office for a few seconds, trying to shed thoughts of her, and then walked to the elevator.

Chapter Thirty-Two

Fiona stood in the shower, hands against the wall, letting the water run over her, cooling her body. The sweat on her forehead, which had dried while she met with Thane, dissolved and ran over her lips. She liked the salty taste.

Thoughts of Cyrus ran over her like the water. She couldn't shake them. Being close to him again had felt good. She caught his eyes on her body several times, warming her.

But also puzzling and frustrating her. Why did he never act on it?

This guy, who got in trouble with her HR department several times over the years for his spicy and inappropriate comments around the office, who had been a shameless - and successful - flirt with any nearby woman during the countless business trips he and Fiona had been on together, and who seemingly never made it through a weekend without at least one bout of casual sex he then described in detail the following week… this guy would not make a move?

Fiona rubbed her eyes beneath the water. She knew why.

She had been around the military enough to know what they thought of civilians. She couldn't say she blamed them, really. And, truthfully, she didn't care. But Fiona knew that Thane's long military service made she and him more disparate than had they been from different countries. And his people generally thought poorly of hers.

Then there was the money. Thane was poor.

It worked the other way, of course. And in the rarified wealthy air the

Malloy clan lived in, it was common for a pretty new face, and body, to marry up and into the club, but it was always a female face.

Not that Fiona was thinking about marriage at all. She was not. Never really had. Her last long-term boyfriend was during college. When she thought back to that time, she mostly remembered a parade of ridiculous attempted sexual positions. She couldn't even remember how they broke up. She assumed she had done it.

She missed having Thane around. She had hoped, after getting over the initial anger at his re-assignment, that the new structure would present them with new opportunities. Perhaps it had been some kind of military hang over thing, like don't-date-the-commander or something like that, and they would now have the time and space to… something.

But, clearly, he did not see it that way.

Maybe he was right. Maybe it was better not to even try.

But how much harm could one roll in the sheets do?

Fiona chuckled at herself as she turned the water off.

She stepped out of the shower and grabbed a towel, remembering Eugene's reaction when he first saw a picture of Thane.

Fiona was visiting Eugene at Mio Posto some months after the crisis of the Ōkami had passed. She was flipping through pictures on her phone, showing Eugene her new office and shots of her recent trip to Japan.

"Wait!" he said. "Who is that?"

Eugene pointed at Thane. The photo was of Fiona and several top executives of Mitsubishi Defense Robotics in one of their factories. Thane stood behind Fiona wearing dark sunglasses. He was looking to the side. The turn in his torso accentuated his shoulders and narrow waist and pulled the collar of his shirt open, baring more of his broad chest than usual.

"That's my head of security," Fiona said.

"Yummy."

Fiona rolled her eyes.

"Have you ever f—"

"No! Of course not. He works for me."

Eugene studied the photo for a moment.

"Oh, honey. You should be shagging him rotten."

They both laughed.

Sadness came over Fiona as she hung the towel. Thoughts of Eugene did that to her. Fiona checked her watch as she dressed. It was almost one in the afternoon in Italy.

She finished dressing and returned to her office to grab her things. She paused when she picked up her phone to put it in her handbag.

Fiona sighed heavily, readied herself for disappointment, and dialed her brother.

She turned her head to look at the brightening city as Eugene's phone rang. Soon, his voice told her he was not available and to leave a message. She listened to each word, picturing him.

She was surprised by the beep. She hesitated, almost speaking, but then hung up.

Fiona sighed. She grabbed her handbag and headed for the roof. Max greeted her when she stepped out of the elevator. A large tilt-rotor drone waited for her on the flight platform behind him.

"Your staff is already onboard, ma'am," he said, leaning in close to be heard over the wind and the aircraft's auxiliary power unit. She nodded, and the pair strode toward the aircraft, Max leading the way.

He waited at the bottom as she hopped briskly up the aircraft's short steps. When she disappeared into the cabin, Max walked off the flight platform toward the elevator.

Acknowledging her staff with a smile, Fiona sat down and buckled her seatbelt. Lucy, her security lead for the trip, returned a curt nod.

The aircraft vibrated and shook from side to side as the large rotors began to rotate. A calm settled over the airframe as they spun up to full speed and a moment later the aircraft surged into the air.

Fiona leaned back in her chair and closed her eyes. She tried to will herself to sleep, but she could not get Eugene out of her mind. She missed him more than usual. Earlier this morning, as she rode the stationary bike, she had realized what day it was, and knew she would be distracted all day. She could not believe it had been twenty years.

Fiona looked out her window and thought of Florida, the wide expanses of water, and the long bridges.

Chapter Thirty-Three

White Plains, New York
2052

Fiona was seventeen years old. It was late in the afternoon on a Wednesday. She stepped out of the black Mercedes sedan, which always picked her up from school, and walked into their house. The driver pulled the car around to the large garage as the house manager met her at the door.

Mr. James was dressed as he most often was, in a khaki blazer over a white shirt with a navy-blue tie and dark trousers. He had a kind smile that was surrounded by a thick, but well-trimmed beard.

"Hello, Mr. James," Fiona said.

"Hello, my dear," he said.

"What is it?" Fiona asked. She had become very sensitive to the household energy since her father had killed himself over a year ago. Her mom was shattered beyond repair and her brother, who was sensitive before his father's death, now seemed to her a delicate sandcastle she had to protect all the time.

"She is in the kitchen," Mr. James said, a look of sadness on his face.

Fiona walked there quickly to find her mother crying softly at the head of the breakfast table.

"What is it, mom?" she asked, running to her side. "What happened?"

Her mother sat at the end of the table. She wiped her eyes and took a deep breath. She had hoped to get control of herself before Fiona got home. She wished, just once, she could look strong in front of her daughter. It wouldn't be today.

Cecelia, the housekeeper, walked into the kitchen carrying a few dirty dishes from around the large house. Accustomed to finding Mrs. Malloy crying, she placed the dishes in the sink and quickly left the room.

"Mom," Fiona said, sitting next to her mother. "What is it? Tell me."

Her mother tried to speak, but her voice caught, and she started to cry again.

Fiona looked at her mom and then glanced around. Something wasn't right. She felt it.

"Where is Eugene?" She asked.

Her mom sobbed harder.

"Mom!" Fiona demanded. "Where is Eugene?"

"He… He took…" she said, fighting to gain control of her breath. "He took him."

"What?" Fiona said, anger spilling out of her. "But you promised!"

"Fiona, he insisted," her mom said. "And Eugene agreed."

"That is a lie!" Fiona screamed in her mom's face. "He would never—"

Fiona's mom slapped her hard across her face as she yelled, "Don't you talk to me that way!"

Fiona held her cheek, stunned.

Tears came to her eyes.

Her mom looked at her in horror.

"Oh god, Fi," she said, begging to cry again. "Oh god, I am so sorry."

Her mother hugged her. Fiona squeezed her back.

"I'm so sorry. I'm so sorry, baby," her mom said, holding on tightly to her daughter.

"It's OK, mom," Fiona said, stifling her own urge to cry. "It's OK. Do you know where he is?"

"I don't," her mom said as she let go of her daughter and sat up straight in her chair.

Fiona wanted to scream. *You let grandfather take my brother and you don't even know where he is going?*

But she didn't. Fiona needed her mom to function.

"Your grandfather said if we wanted to get something to him, a message or a care package, to go through his office," her mom said.

Fiona forced a smile and nodded. *Doesn't matter,* she thought. *I can figure where he is.*

"He's going to be fine, baby," her mom said. "I promise. He is going to be fine."

"I know, mom," Fiona said, eyes narrowing, already working out the plan in her head. "I know."

* * *

Three days later, though, Fiona was frustrated and anxious. She had narrowed the list down to three possibilities. There was a place in Florida, one in Tennessee, and one in South Carolina, but she could not figure out which one her grandfather had taken Eugene to.

She was desperate to get in touch with him. She barely slept, staying up late researching online trying to figure it out. On that third night, Mr. James found her early in the morning, asleep on the living room sofa, laptop on her chest.

"Young, miss?" he said softly, putting a hand on her shoulder.

Fiona opened her eyes. She looked at him groggily. "Mmmmph?"

"Would you like to go to your own bed to finish out the night?"

"No," she said, sitting up. "No. I'm going to work just a little more."

"And what are we working on?"

"Something for school," she said, sitting up.

"I see," he said.

Mr. James looked at Fiona. The young girl locked eyes with him.

"Some tea then, perhaps?"

"Yes, Mr. James. That would be nice. Thank you."

Mr. James nodded.

By the sixth day, Fiona was starting to panic. She felt physically ill when she thought of Eugene alone in one of those places. She got into a vicious fight with her mother when her mother found she had skipped school that day. Fiona duped the driver, getting out in front of the school and then waiting for him to leave and round the corner before sneaking off to a coffee shop to continue her online search for clues that might lead her to Eugene. The school called to check on her mid-day. Her mom confronted her when Fiona returned, having waited for the driver at school as if she had been there, in classes, all day.

Mr. James and Cecelia stayed out of the living room. Fiona's demands to know where Eugene was echoed throughout the house, as did her mother's sobs. Finally, her mother stormed out, up the stairs and slammed the door to her bedroom.

Fiona stood, panting in rage, in the living room.

Mr. James walked in.

"Can I bring you anything, young miss?" He asked in a voice that hinted at his true intentions of simply checking on her.

"No," Fiona said, rubbing her eyes. "Thank you, Mr. James. I'm sorry about all that… noise."

"It's quite alright," Mr. James said. He turned to leave.

"Mr. James," Fiona said, stopping him. He turned to face her.

"Yes?"

"I'm sorry to ask this," she said. "But did you hear anything when grandfather took Eugene? Anything at all that might help me find my brother? I'm… I'm worried about him."

Fiona was crossing a line, and they both knew it. Mr. James and Cecelia were paid by Fiona's grandfather. They had been around the extended family for as long as she could remember. But their dedicated time with Fiona's family had started a few years before her father's death. She liked Mr. James more than any of the other family staff. And there were dozens amongst the far-flung extended Malloy family.

Fiona knew and respected where Mr. James had to place his true and overruling loyalty. She regretted the question the moment she asked it.

"I'm sorry, Mr. James," she blurted out. "Please forget that I asked."

Mr. James sighed.

"It's quite alright. And quite understandable under the circumstances. But, no. I am so sorry. All I know is that Mr. Malloy left with master Eugene for the airport."

Fiona nodded. She thought of Eugene walking up the stairs onto her grandfather's airplane and fought the urge to cry. Then it struck her.

"His airplane!" she blurted.

"I beg your pardon?" Mr James said.

"Of course!" She ran from the living room and up the stairs, leaving Mr. James alone in the living room with his thoughts.

Fiona jumped on her laptop in her room.

"Why didn't I think of this before?" she muttered as she called up a website.

RichAirPoisioners.com was an environmental activist website that tracked the flights of private aircraft owned by the wealthy. Her grandfather's jet was registered in a way that prevented it from being tracked easily. But the Rich Air Poisoners sleuths had identified his aircraft and tied it back to him, as they had with thousands of other private jets and their owners. The nationwide network of pissed-off airport watchers logged arrivals and departures and posted photographs daily. On the website, anyone could type in a notorious wealthy asshole and all of their associated polluting air travel activities would be instantly displayed and cataloged.

Fiona typed in her grandfather's name.

She started crying.

There on the screen was the answer she could have had six days ago if she had been thinking clearer. Her grandfather's aircraft landed at Northeast Florida Regional Airport just north of St Augustine shortly after 6PM last Wednesday evening.

That confirmed it in her mind. Eugene was in Florida at the "Loving Healing and Living Foundation", a gay conversion therapy center.

"Damnit," she said through tears. "I'm so sorry, Eugene. I should have been smarter. But I am on my way now."

* * *

Later that night, when Fiona was certain her mother had fallen asleep with the help of red wine and Ambien, she crept out of the house with her packed suitcase. She put the suitcase in the back of her mom's BMW SUV and snuck back into the house for the suitcase she had packed for Eugene. She didn't know how long they would be gone.

She dragged the large roller back into the garage and heaved it into the back next to hers. Fiona shut the tailgate and walked around to the driver's side of the car when a man's voice nearly startled her out of her skin.

"Miss Malloy?"

Fiona spun on her heals.

"Holy shit, Mr. James. You scared the shit out of me."

"Language, young miss," Mr. James said, a disapproving look on his face.

He was dressed in jeans and a dark green cardigan sweater, casual clothes that she seldom saw him in. In his right hand, he held a small cooler.

"Where are we headed at this hour?"

Fiona's jaw clenched, and she shifted her weight from foot to foot, preparing for a lecture and efforts to stand in her way.

A strange look came over his face, a mixture of sadness and pride.

He nodded with resignation and stepped forward to hand her the cooler.

"I suppose you've a long drive ahead," he said. "I've packed several sandwiches, as well as some fruit and a couple of candy bars."

Fiona took the cooler.

"Bottled water as well," Mr. James said, stepping a few steps back, away from the car.

Fiona looked at the cooler and then back at Mr. James. She set it down on the ground and walked to him.

"Thank you, Mr. James," she said, as she wrapped her arms around him. He hugged her with one arm.

"You're welcome, young miss."

"I'm scared," she said, letting him go and stepping back.

"Well, one would never know it," he said, smiling at her.

She chuckled as she wiped a tear away.

"You are a very good sister," Mr. James said, looking at his feet. "And he needs you."

Fiona nodded. She turned and walked back to the BMW. She opened the door and reached in to place the cooler on the passenger seat. She turned back to thank Mr. James again, but he was gone.

She stood motionless for a moment, staring at the doorway to the house that Mr. James had just left through. She could walk through it also. Right now. And not do the crazy thing she had been thinking about. She could not worry her mom sick. Not anger her grandfather. Not get in trouble.

Then she thought of Eugene. With her sweet father gone… who else would look out for him?

Fiona turned and got in the BMW.

She stewed as the car drove her south, getting more angry and determined with every mile.

Eugene had always been a little different from most of the other boys. He was more sensitive, artistic and, yes, effeminate. Fiona felt like she had known Eugene was gay before he did himself. It didn't matter to her. Or to his mother and father. Eugene was their wonderful boy, and they loved him.

Grandfather Malloy, though, was not as accepting, never missing an opportunity to embarrass or make demands of the young boy. He made it clear, "The Malloy empire has no use for fairies." Maybe he thought the abuse would "correct" Eugene's path before, "It was too late."

Whatever the old man thought, Fiona protested when her father would not stick up for him.

"You will learn, Fiona," her father said, unable to meet her eyes. "It's just better to not confront your grandfather directly." And her mother, having married into the Malloys, did not know how to make a stand.

Despite her disappointment, though, Fiona came to see that her father was somehow cutting a path for Eugene. She knew her father shared Eugene's sensitive nature. And that her grandfather could be a monster. So she knew it came with a cost, but her father took it on himself and hid it. And it was enough. Her father wasn't winning, but he had somehow erected a loving bubble around his son. And she loved her flawed father all the more for it.

Then he committed suicide.

The bubble collapsed.

It did not take long for her grandfather to exert himself in their broken-hearted family. Her mom was rudderless and easily bullied.

Last year, when Eugene finally built up the courage to come out to his mom and sister, Fiona was overjoyed. Finally, she thought. He can be himself. Then grandfather Malloy found out.

He was offended. Enraged. He demanded that, "Something be done."

For a time, their mom held the line. Fiona was proud. Eugene was terrified.

But Fiona did not know that grandfather Malloy was working on her mom, wearing her down. The first time he came to get Eugene, Fiona went berserk. Even grandfather Malloy was taken aback by her ferocity. Fiona threw such a fit that her mom had to tell grandfather Malloy, no.

Fiona made her mother promise to never let it happen, while the old man bode his time.

Then, her grandfather came while Fiona was at school. And her mom caved.

Fiona bumped the self-driver up to 90 miles per hour.

Hang on, Eugene. I'm coming.

Chapter Thirty-Four

Fiona got to Jacksonville, Florida around 7PM the next day. She let the car drive most of the way. Still, it had been a long, tedious trip. Her mother called so many times, Fiona finally texted her, "I am fine. Don't worry," and then turned her phone off.

Fiona pulled off the highway and got a room at the first motel she came to. She was exhausted, having not slept well for the past week. She knew she need to be sharp the next day. After a quick shower, she fell asleep quickly.

At 4AM the next day, she popped awake. She lay in bed, running through potential plans in her head. None of them seemed any good. Finally, after an hour, she got up and walked into the bathroom. "This is never going to work," she mumbled to herself.

Later, after paying for the room in cash and grabbing breakfast at a greasy diner across the street, Fiona stopped into a twenty-four-hour copy and print shop to get some items to support her plan. Finally, she accelerated onto the highway.

At 8:30 AM, Fiona drove under a canopy of moss covered live oak branches. Centuries old, the wide and knotty tree trunks on both sides of the hundred-foot-wide driveway seemed to say to her, *We've seen it all, honey.*

The driveway was two miles long. In no hurry, it curved gently back and forth as it got closer to the Sacred Grove Christian Retreat campus. Set on fifty acres of former plantation land, Sacred Grove was one of the premier religious retreat locations on the east coast, and home to the Loving Healing and Living Foundation.

Established decades ago by wealthy religious activists, the foundation was one of the longest running conversion therapy facilities in the country. Discrete and overtly religious, the foundation boasted of successfully "treating" hundreds of gay believers, turning them back to a righteous path, pleasing to God. Somehow, the foundation had navigated for many years, achieving its mission while not drawing the ire of the public and, most importantly, maintaining the good favor of its donors.

Fiona was counting on them wanting to continue their winning streak.

Emerging from the shade of the live oaks, Fiona drove into the morning sun. The towering old growth pine trees threw long shadows in the glancing, orange light. A discrete sign pointed the way to an amphitheater, great hall, and "Foundation". Fiona turned to the right toward a graceful two-story building in the distance.

Fiona parked in a spot marked for visitors in front and studied the building. Made of natural stone and wood with a red-tiled roof, the foundation's facility had a charming Mediterranean feel from the outside. Several gazebos stood on the expansive field behind the building and staff were already zipping to and fro in dark green golf carts.

She took off her sunglasses and pulled down the sun visor to check herself in the small mirror. She reapplied lipstick and then sat in silence, staring at the mirror for a moment.

"You are a boss bitch," she finally told herself. "And they are fucking poor."

Fiona put her sunglasses back on, grabbed the packet from the copy/print shop, and stepped out of the car. She walked toward the Loving Healing and Living Foundation headquarters with a burning hate in her heart and conviction in her step, wearing one of her mother's Versace pant suits. She could get away with it when she stuffed her bra. The cheap toilet paper was scratchy against her breasts, but was doing the trick. The white pin stripes were widely spaced on the navy-blue fabric and the pants hugged her thighs before flaring at the calves and ankles. The curvy pattern hid the fact that her ass did not come close to filling out the suit's seat. Her teenager's lacrosse-toned body just wasn't there yet.

She had taken care with her makeup at the hotel. Contouring and subtle highlights gave her the appearance of mature angles and the red, hey-look-at-me-lipstick distracted the eye. It was a play she had run more than once to attract a guy or gain access where it should have been denied. She knew it worked.

Fiona threw open the door and walked into the foyer without taking her sunglasses off. Heavy beams and a barn wood paneled ceiling vaulted over the expansive area. Religious artwork and iconography lined the tall white walls.

"Hello may I help you?" the receptionist, a smiling, plump middle-aged lady said as Fiona approached reception.

"Yes," Fiona said. "I have some papers here I need my brother, Eugene Malloy, to sign." She placed the courier envelope on the counter. The envelope was stuffed full and had some official, dated, looking stamps on it.

"Um…" the receptionist said. "I'm afraid Eugene is still in his first two weeks and we have a strict no contact policy until week three."

Fiona noted the receptionist glancing around nervously. She wasn't in charge.

"Oh, my grandfather would have never agreed to that," Fiona said, in a voice that said, *You are trying to cheat me.*

The receptionist's eyebrows arched.

"I'm afraid that—"

"What is your name?" Fiona asked in the same disbelieving voice.

"My name is Sally and—"

"Sally," Fiona interrupted, shaking her head and taking her sunglasses off. "I had to get on our plane in Boca at 7 AM this morning to get here. And I have to have these papers, signed by Eugene, back to Boca, to hand to my grandfather by noon."

She made a show of looking at her watch and then back at Sally.

"I will take just a couple of minutes. Now, can you please bring Eugene to me?"

Doubt crept into Sally's face as she gazed back at Fiona. Then she looked over Fiona's shoulder and her face brightened.

"Ah," Sally said, gesturing at someone behind Fiona. "Mr. Kirby, our executive director. I am sure he will be able to explain."

Fiona turned around as if it were the most irritating thing she had had to do in the last few years and looked at Mr. Thomas Kirby, Executive Director of the Loving Healing and Living Foundation.

"Good morning," he said, smiling and extending a hand toward Fiona. "Please call me Tom. How can I help?"

Dressed in a tweed sport coat on top of khaki pants and sporting a goatee, Tom continued to hold his hand out to Fiona as she checked her watch again.

She finally shook his hand.

"I have some papers here for Eugene to sign for our grandfather," she said as if she had suddenly been introduced to someone that would really *get it*. "I have flown up from Boca this morning and have to be back with them to grandfather by noon."

Tom nodded thoughtfully and gestured toward one of the seating areas, away from the reception desk.

Fiona raised her eyebrows to make it clear she regarded the trip to the seating area to be a big waste of time as she took the courier envelope from the reception desk and followed Mr. Kirby.

"Eugene is just starting week two, I am afraid," he said, stopping in front of a large painting of Jesus washing the feet of his disciples. "Your grandfather was very specific that he wanted Eugene to receive our best course of treatment."

"I'm sure he was, Tom," Fiona said. "I want that, too. But grandfather sent me up here to get three quick signatures from Eugene. It's family business and it won't take more than five minutes."

"Your grandfather did not mention anything to me about this kind of thing."

"Oh," Fiona said, putting a hand on her hip. "Well, why the hell would he, Tom?"

Tom Kirby blinked a few times.

"I did say, 'Family business,' didn't I?" Fiona asked in a tone that really said, *you did fucking hear me, didn't you?*

Fiona locked eyes with the director and let the awkward silence expand between them.

"Yes," Tom said, "You were—"

"Oh, god," Fiona said, shaking her head. "Look, Tom. I am sorry. There is just a lot of family drama right now and I apologize for letting it spill out of me onto you."

Fiona knotted her face into a look of regret as Tom tried to regain his balance.

"I can't talk about it," she said. "And we are all working hard to keep Eugene out of it so that he can work on himself here with you guys. The thing is, if I don't get the signatures to grandfather by noon, then it may cause more of a disruption. Like, he may have to leave or something. I just don't know."

"This is highly irregular," Tom said, rubbing his forehead.

"Tell me about it," Fiona said, shrugging. She couldn't tell how it was going, so she just pushed forward.

"Look, Tom," Fiona said, stepping closer. "Grandfather has been so pleased with you guys. Really, just so impressed."

"That is very good to hear," Tom said. "We—"

"I have, too," she continued over him. "We all have. It is such important work."

"We try to—"

"The thing is," she said, voice dropping toward a conspiratorial tone. "And I hate to say it like this, but I can see you are a smart guy. Helping us with Eugene like you are could end up being a very good thing, over the long term, for the foundation. A very good thing."

Fiona maintaining eye contact with Tom, nodded slightly.

"Um…" Tom stammered, not sure what to say.

"I really want to be able to get back on our plane and go back to Boca and be able to tell grandfather that, 'Tom *gets it*,' You know?"

Tom's brow furrowed as he thought it through.

"Because I just think it would be a shame if something were to happen to interrupt the momentum we have together," Fiona said. "Our family, particularly my grandfather, and the foundation, I mean."

Tom shook his head.

"And I wouldn't be putting you in this awkward situation if it wasn't really important." Fiona hefted the envelope. "If you could see your way to letting me get three signatures, I promise it will be a good thing. For all of us. And I will make sure grandfather understands how you were able to see the big picture."

Tom hesitated.

"Five minutes, Tom," Fiona said. "And I am out of your hair."

Tom's shoulders relaxed slightly.

"OK."

"Thank you, Tom!" Fiona said.

"I'll take that back to Eugene and will be back shortly," Tom said, pointing at the courier envelope. "Just show me where you need the signatures."

"Oh. I can't do that. These papers are Malloy family eyes only."

Fiona shook her head at the thought.

"Trust me, you don't even want to think about the NDA you would have to sign," she continued.

Tom's face told her he was not happy. But it was too late. He had begun the process of yielding. She kicked him over the rest of the way.

"I'll just set up over here," Fiona said, gesturing at the small seating area with a table by the front door. She turned from the director and walked to the table, where she set down her purse and started pulling out the documents. "I'll have it all set up so it won't take more than a minute," she said, not looking up.

Tom shifted on his feet.

He looked at the receptionist and then back at Fiona.

Then he looked at his watch.

He rubbed his forehead.

Out of the corner of her eye, Fiona watched as the director walked to the receptionist's desk, said something in a low voice, and then walked out of the foyer toward the back of the building.

He is either going to get Eugene, or he is going to call grandfather, Fiona thought.

Fiona fidgeted with the three stacks of paper, making sure each one was perfectly straight. After she felt ridiculous continuing to do that any longer, she stood up and snuck a look at the receptionist's desk.

Sally's head was down, obviously not wanting eye contact or any other kind of interaction.

Turning to face one of the windows near the front door, Fiona tried to discretely take deep breaths and calm her nerves. *If the director is calling grandfather right now. I will have basically stolen mom's car and driven almost the entire length of the eastern seaboard in order to just make thing worse for Eugene.*

Fiona looked at her watch. It had only been two minutes.

She wanted to scream.

She took her phone out of her purse. Bad move. She had gotten several calls and texts from her mother, which did not help her nerves.

Fiona jammed the phone back in her purse.

She looked around the foyer. To one side, about fifty feet away, was a stone fireplace. The yawning hearth was eight feet wide and the stone chimney rose dramatically to the arched ceiling. Needing something to do with her nervous energy, Fiona set out, walking toward it in slow, deliberate steps.

When she reached the stone hearth, Fiona turned and walked back to the table. When she reached the table, she turned and headed back to the fireplace. If she tried to stand still, she would scream. So she would walk back and forth until Eugene arrived, or the director informed her he had spoken to her grandfather.

When she was halfway back to the fireplace on her third lap, she heard the director call her name.

"Miss Malloy," Tom said.

Fiona turned to see the director and Eugene walking her way. She had to stifle a gasp.

Her brother looked terrible, as if he had aged years during the week he had been away. Wearing jeans and a T-shirt, he shuffled toward her, Director Kirby's hand on his shoulder. Eugene's eyes were fixed on hers.

"Ah, thank you," Fiona said, tearing her eyes off of Eugene. She hoped he would play along. "I've prepared the documents and this won't take more than a minute."

Director Kirby smiled. He was all in now and looked forward to Fiona's quick departure and positive report to her grandfather.

Fiona picked up the pen and handed it to Eugene as he approached the table, his eyes searching Fiona for a hint as to what was going on.

She smiled and held a hand up to Tom who was beside Eugene.

"I'm sorry, Tom," she said with the sweetest smile she could muster. "Would you mind stepping back just a bit? I need to explain one of these documents to Eugene and it is quite sensitive, I'm afraid."

"Of course," Director Kirby said with a smile. "I will be over at the reception desk."

"Thank you so much," Fiona said.

Fiona felt Eugene staring at her as she watched the director walk away.

Turning her head back to Eugene and gesturing at one of the stacks of papers, she said, "Get ready to run."

Eugene's eyes were round with fear. She could tell he was having a hard time deciphering what was going on.

Fiona glanced back at the reception desk. The director's back was to them as he talked to Sally.

"Listen to me, Eugene," Fiona said, turning back to her brother. "I love you and I am here to get you out of here."

"No, Fi," he said. "I'm scared."

"What are you scared of?"

"We'll be in so much trouble with grandfather."

"Yes. We will. But we will be together. And you will be gone from here."

His eyes darted nervously from her to the reception desk.

"Eugene," she said, putting a hand on his shoulder and locking eyes with him. "I am sorry. But you have to decide right now. I will leave and you can stay here if you want. I love you either way. But we are out of time."

Eugene's jaw muscles worked. His lips were pressed into a narrow line. His hands opened and closed into fists rapidly.

"Get me out of here, Fi," he said.

Fiona smiled and nodded.

"When I turn to run. You follow me as close as you can."

Eugene nodded.

"How's it going?" Director Kirby asked, turning from the reception desk to walk back to their table.

Fiona spun on her heels and leapt for the front door. Eugene was only half a step behind her.

"Mom's car!" Fiona yelled as they burst from the building.

They dashed the fifty feet to the BMW. Fiona jumped in and started the engine as Eugene piled into the passenger seat.

The BMW lurched back from its parking spot and then screeched away onto the driveway.

Fiona accelerated, live oaks whizzing by.

Director Kirby, stunned, still stood motionless halfway between the reception desk and the table in disbelief.

"Oh my lord," Sally said.

Fiona sped off of the Sacred Grove property and headed for the highway. Eugene cried in the passenger seat. When Fiona hit I95 she turned south.

Chapter Thirty-Five

iona followed I-95 to Miami and then continued south on U.S.1, the old Overseas Highway. Eugene was quiet most of the way, speaking only when he asked Fiona to stop so he could use the bathroom. He cried for long stretches, ignoring Fiona when she asked if he was OK, which she only did once or twice before deciding she should just leave him alone. She drove on with her heart aching for her little brother. Eventually he would fall asleep for a few minutes, before waking up and starting the silence-crying-sleeping cycle again.

Highway One left the mainland and threaded its way over Cross Key, then Key Largo. As they drove through Islamorada, Fiona thought she noticed Eugene perk up slightly, his eyes bouncing from the happy looking motor hotels to fishing charter shops to restaurants and small art galleries. She checked her watch. It was almost noon.

Fiona swerved off the road into a parking lot.

"What are you doing?" Eugene asked.

"I'm hungry," Fiona said, pointing at the low thatched-roof building in front of them. The sign said, *The Grumpy Wahoo*.

"You?" she asked him.

"No."

Fiona shrugged and hopped out of the car and walked into the restaurant. Eugene got out of the car and followed, several steps behind.

The restaurant was bright and colorful inside, with a back porch that overlooked one of the countless small marinas. White boats bobbed on blue water.

The pair sat outside on the porch. There was a pleasant, salty breeze wandering over their table.

Fiona looked at the menu and watched Eugene out of the corner of her eye. He sat looking in the direction of the boats, his face expressionless.

The waitress came and Fiona ordered a fried grouper sandwich with a side of conch fritters. Eugene didn't want anything. "Just water," he said, not taking his eyes off the water.

Fiona's meal came, and she attacked it. She had not had real food in two days. The grouper was perfect, crispy and brown on the outside, flaky and moist on the inside. Fiona paused after her first bite to dump the full container of tartar sauce on the sandwich. The white sauce oozed from under the top bun and dripped down the sides. She took another big bite, set the sandwich back down on the plate, and leaned back in her chair to chew with her eyes closed.

The smell of fried fish and conch enveloped the table. Fiona pretended not to notice when Eugene stole a glance at her and the food.

Then he did it again. Then again.

She smiled to herself and waved at the waitress.

"He changed his mind," she said. "Can you bring him one of these?" she held up her half-eaten sandwich and smiled.

Eugene did not acknowledge Fiona ordering for him, and sat looking at the marina in silence as she continued to eat.

A few minutes later, the waitress returned with Eugene's sandwich.

Fiona's mouth was full, but she smiled and nodded at the waitress.

Eugene held out for thirty seconds before starting in on the sandwich.

Ten minutes later, both sandwiches and all the fritters were gone. Fiona and Eugene sat in silence looking at the Marina. She continued to sneak glances at him. She was worried. His face was expressionless, but she could tell he was roiling beneath the surface.

After twenty minutes, Fiona paid the bill in cash and they got back in the car. She pulled out of the parking lot and continued south.

Fiona assessed their situation. She had no plan. Her success at Sacred

Grove had surprised her. She had not expected to actually leave with Eugene. And, though she was overjoyed to have her brother out of that place and with her, she worried he may suffer more for her actions than she would. She wasn't sure how much cash she had left and was sure using a credit card would betray their location. Her mom, by now, had certainly enlisted the help of grandfather Malloy. His tentacles were inescapable.

South of Islamorada, the bridges of US Route 1 began in earnest. Long spans stretched from caye to caye, surrounded by endless blue water stretching away under a severe clear sky. Their tires sang a low-pitched tune punctuated by rhythmic thumps as they passed over the long concrete slabs, soaking the car in a contemplative energy. Fiona mulled over their situation as if it was happening to someone else in the distance, as if she had all the time in the world to figure it out.

Almost an hour later, they started across the Seven Mile Bridge. They rode across the long, two-lane ribbon of concrete, encircled by the ocean, in silence. But as they neared the center of the bridge and began to climb up the tall, graceful arch built for boats to pass beneath, Eugene broke the silence.

"They shocked me," he said, looking away from Fiona, out the window at the ocean. "With electricity. More than once."

Fiona tightened her grip on the steering wheel and resisted the urge to put her hand on her brother's shoulder. She didn't want to do anything to stop him from talking.

"Usually in the morning," he continued. "They said it would help me remember my thoughts were bad. My desires."

A tear ran down Fiona's cheek. She wiped it away as Eugene continued.

Eugene talked the rest of the way to Key West. It poured out of him as he stared out of the passenger window. The counseling, the groups, the reading, the praying, the guilt, the fear, the confusion, the loneliness and questions. Fiona sat quietly, wiping away tears as she drove.

It was almost 8PM when they pulled up to the hotel in the middle of Old Town. Fiona had searched for the best hotel in Key West on her phone earlier in their drive. Occupying a few well-preserved historic buildings, the hotel put off a chic, retro-vibe and was expensive. Fiona checked them in with her credit card, knowing that it was sure to give up their location to whoever their grandfather had tasked to find them. It didn't matter. She had accomplished what she needed to.

They ordered so much room service it took four carts to wheel it all in. She knew it would not last, but Fiona was happy. It felt like they had escaped. Not just for that day and night, but for good. She knew it wasn't true, but she revealed in the feeling. Eugene smiled and even laughed a few times.

As they fell asleep, bellies stuffed, Eugene said for the first time, "Thank you, Fi."

"You're welcome," she said.

"I didn't know how long I was going to be there," Eugene said. "They wouldn't tell me. I felt so lost and alone. But when I walked into the lobby and saw you there, I wasn't surprised at all. I was like, 'Oh, here is Fiona. Come to save me.'"

"You would do the same for me," Fiona said.

"I would."

"I just realized, though," he said after a moment. "You left those papers back there on the table."

Fiona chuckled.

"What?"

"Oh, that was just a bunch of stuff I pulled out of the trash can at the print shop place," Fiona said. "Looked like a bunch of menus from a local restaurant and maybe some lost dog flyers."

Eugene laughed. "The balls on you. The girl can bluff. Remind me to never play poker against you."

Fiona chuckled. It felt so good to hear him laugh.

"I think things will get weird tomorrow." Fiona's smile faded. "I think someone will come get us."

"Yeah... I figured."

"It doesn't matter, though. They know now. Grandfather especially. You and I will always stick together. We'll always have each other's back."

"Yes." Eugene said. "We will."

Chapter Thirty-Six

Cape Canaveral Space Force Station, Florida
2072

Michelle knocked on the general's door.

"Enter," the Geek said.

"Colonel McDade's report, sir," Lieutenant Ryuk said. "I brought you a printout and it is also in your inbox."

"Thank you, LT," the general said, taking the report from Ryuk. "Why do you think he is late with this every quarter?"

Lieutenant Ryuk shrugged as she said, "I think it's just a lot of information to collate, sir."

"And?"

"And what, sir?"

"You were thinking something more in your head just then. Tell me."

Michelle hesitated.

"Our secret," the general said.

"Well, truthfully, sir… I don't think his operations officer, Captain Makhani, is great with… well, numbers, sir."

The Geek nodded in agreement.

"I think you are right. I need to talk to the Colonel about that."

Michelle looked at the general in alarm.

"No attribution, LT." He smiled. "You can trust me."

He held the report up. "I promise I will get to this shortly. Thank you."

Later, as the 1700 deadline for the General's QSIR approached, Michelle poked her head back into the general's office.

"Sir, I don't want to be a pain in the—"

"The QSIR," the Geek interrupted. "I'm aware, LT. Just got distracted by a request from Orbital Command. My summary is written. Let me just scan McDade's report and then you can send it along. Wait here for just a moment."

"Very good, sir," Michelle said, approaching the general's desk. She stood by, waiting for his nod.

The Quarterly Shipping and Incident Report was a summary of all relevant space incidents for the closing calendar quarter. Its sources were self-reported statuses from the major civilian shippers, allied space commands, as well as the American Space Commands. The report purposefully did not involve Vishnu Stare. It was a first cut look at what America's allies and the corporate entities were willing to admit to. It also contained the tonnage and tariff totals at Lagrange Station 4, Moon Terminals, and American Asteroid Belt Stations. Because it drew from so many sources, the QSIR was a frustrating exercise in bureaucratic base tagging and ankle biting, consuming much of Lieutenant Ryuk's time the last month of each quarter. As the TSP Commander, General Hartwell provided summary comments and trends discussion in the form of a cover letter his office put on top of the QSIR. The fact was, most recipients of the QSIR only read the cover letter of the voluminous report.

Nonetheless, the general made sure he was familiar with all the report's inputs before sending it out. He never wanted to be stumped by any resulting questions. Even though he was yet to ever field one.

The general picked up the folder Ryuk had given him earlier in the day. He leaned back in his chair and scanned Colonel McDade's report of civilian shipping totals and incidents from the quarter. Half way down the page, his eyes froze.

His burned hand came to his forehead as he re-read the words several times, the charred fingers pressed into his brow.

"Sir?" Lieutenant Ryuk said. "Is everything OK?"

"Um, yes," the general said, closing the folder. "Yes, of course. Please go ahead and send out the report."

The Geek's eyes blinked rapidly. Michelle thought she saw a flare of emotion behind his eyes.

"You sure, sir?"

"Yes!" the general barked, standing up from his chair and startling her. "And have my driver bring the car around."

"Yes, sir," the lieutenant said, spinning on her heels and walking back to her desk.

General Hartwell shoved the folder into his briefcase and walked out of his office.

"General?" Mrs. Johnson said, as the Geek strode away, down the hallway toward the elevator.

The general waved over his shoulder, not breaking stride.

The general walked by the guard post outside the SolarScope without acknowledging them. The elevator, having been summoned by Michelle, opened as the Geek approached. He stepped in and looked intensely at his feet as the door closed.

Lieutenant Ryuk and Mrs. Johnson shared concerned looks.

Chapter Thirty-Seven

The water couldn't quite reach the Geek's bare feet before retreating back to the Atlantic Ocean and darkness. He sat on his briefcase in the sand, watching a lightning storm miles out to sea. It was high tide and the white foam of the crashing waves seem to glow, reflecting the light of the half-moon, now a hand's width above the water to the east.

Patrick Space Force base sits on Florida's east coast, just south of Cocoa Beach. A twenty-minute drive from Canaveral, Patrick's main gate is on one side of highway A1A and the Atlantic Ocean lays behind a grove of short, stubby palm trees on the other. The Geek lived on post on "General's Row" with his wife and daughter.

He had asked his driver to let him out on the ocean side almost two hours ago. The driver looked at the general's security team, but the Geek had insisted. After the car left, General Hartwell told the security team to wait for him in the parking lot on the other side of the palm trees. They protested at first, but then agreed as long as he promised to stay where they could maintain visual contact.

The Geek walked toward the water and found a spot he liked. He sat down on his briefcase and took his shoes and socks off and had not moved since.

"Hey there, soldier," a woman called from behind him.

He smiled. "Hey, babe," he said, without turning around. "Some security I've got."

Susan Hartwell put her hand on her husband's shoulder.

"I used my feminine wiles on them."

He chuckled.

"I'm sorry," he said, looking up at her.

"It's OK," she said, sitting down next to him. "I ordered Brianna those conch fritters she likes from Grouper Joe's when I got your text. She is watching a movie with Debbie."

"Her friend from volleyball, right?"

"That's right."

"Not a great family night," he said.

"We've had worse."

Hartwell nodded.

Susan looked at her husband. Sadness radiated from his face like the reflected moonlight.

"What is it, honey?" She asked, reaching for his hand. "What happened?"

"Paul. His ship is missing."

"Oh no. That is terrible. What happened?"

"I don't know. I just read the ship's name this afternoon in a summary incident report."

"Well, they may find it, right? I mean, it's possible everything could be fine?"

"Possible? Sure," he said. "But not likely. The Company doesn't report things like this unless they have to. Unless they are pretty damn sure."

Susan sighed and squeezed the Geek's hand.

"I put him on that ship, you know," he said.

"Don't do that. That's not fair. You threw him a lifeline, and he grabbed it, fully knowing the risks."

"Well, it didn't turn out to be much of a lifeline, did it?"

"You don't know that yet," she said.

The Geek looked at his wife, his face a mask of sadness.

"Oh, Wallace," she said, putting a hand to his cheek. "I'm so sorry."

He leaned forward, placing his head on her shoulder. She hugged him. They sat like that for a while, the waves crashing, the water approaching and then receding back into the night.

"Come on, honey," Susan said, releasing him and standing up. "Come inside and take a shower. I got you conch fritters also and I'll fix you a glass of wine."

"In a minute," he said. "You go ahead. Make sure Brianna is OK and I'll be along shortly."

Susan looked at him.

"You sure?"

"Yeah. I won't be long. I'm just still getting my head around it."

"OK," she said, bending over to kiss him. "Take all the time you need. I love you."

"Love you, too."

The Geek sat out on the beach watching the moon trace its circuit above, thinking about Paul and the *Odysseus*. He knew better than most that, in spite of all the advances in technology and practice, space was still a dangerous place. Ships vanish. They blow up. They collide. They burn. They drift off course and crash into things. Shit happens. Intellectually, the Geek knew that, whatever happened to Paul and the *Odysseus*, he was not responsible. Paul knew the risks and had embraced them.

The Geek's feelings argued with his intellect, though. Paul Owens was his OAT brother. He felt responsible. He felt obligated. Most of all, though, he felt a deep sense of loss. Paul was his hero, still, despite everything.

And while his intellect could accept misfortune befalling a friend in space. It had a hard time with the Odysseus' disappearance in the context of Paul Owens. It seemed to be another link in a suspect chain of events. The horrible los Olvidados incident. Filson's strange death. The closed, top-secret trial. The way the Ōkami technology simply vanished afterward. The Geek's engineering mind perceived a suspicious tolerance stack. Each incident bore a vaguely improbable, "fishy" quality. Maybe not enough to make the individual occurrence problematic. But when the Geek's engineering mind looked at the sad totality of the sequence of Paul Owens related events, it smelled bad.

And now the *Odysseus* was missing.

The stink was impossible to ignore now.

And, yet, he had to try. There was nothing he could do, after all.

Or was there?

He fought the urge.

Using his post for a personal cause would be a terrible abuse. "For an officer on duty knows no one," he reminded himself. The centuries old words of William Worth, committed to memory when he was an ROTC cadet at Georgia Tech, scolded him now. "To be partial is to dishonor both himself and the object of his ill favor."

He accepted the admonishment and put the thought out of his mind.

Until it came back moments later.

The Geek sat there for hours, arguing with himself. The idea, what his personal sense of duty told him to do, would go away momentarily. Then, like the waves, come surging back. His conscience, or something, would resist, driving it away, until it came crashing back again.

The moon was high behind him over his shoulder when he had had enough.

"Fuck William Worth and his Battalion Orders," the Geek muttered as he stood up.

He brushed the off his uniform and picked up his shoes, socks and brief case. The barefoot general walked back to his security team.

"Evening, sir," his security sergeant said as he saluted the shoeless, rumpled, and sandy general.

"Sorry for the wait," Hartwell said, resolve taking hold in his voice. He sat down on the ground in front of his startled security team and pulled on his socks. "Please call my car. I need to get back to Canaveral."

ODYSSEUS

Chapter Thirty-Eight

Adauchi Book One
Circa 1510
Translated from the Japanese

Hiroaki took me with him to Shingen's castle. There, we met with Lord Shingen and his war council. Then we traveled with them to the besieged Clan Hayato fortress.

The castle was impressive and lay on good and defensible ground. The north of the castle was covered by difficult and mountainous terrain. The south of the castle was protected by a wide and fast-flowing river that offered only three crossings: a shallow place to the west, a rocky place to the east, and a large covered bridge to the castle's front.

Hayato's Elite Guard formed an impenetrable wall of samurai around the castle so that none could approach. The bodies of Clan Shingen samurai, killed in failed attacks, lay in piles on the ground.

"What do you think, General?" Shingen asked Hiroaki. "Can it be done?"

"It shall be done, my lord," Hiroaki said. "I will return in four weeks with my students."

I returned to the school with Hiroaki. He rode in silence for the entire seven-day journey, devising his plan.

We arrived back at the school late in the day. That evening, Hiroaki called every student, even the young ones, to a meeting.

"Tomorrow, we begin training," he said. "Ensure that you are rested."

We practiced Hiroaki's plan several times a day, every day, for twenty-one days, until Hiroaki was satisfied that every student knew the plan by heart.

The night before we marched on Clan Hayato, Hiroaki instructed the school cooks to empty the stores and send hunters into the woods. They prepared a grand feast. Hiroaki walked among the students as they filled their bellies. He spent time with each one, assuring them they would be brave and would fight well. He spent time with the older veterans, thanking them for their leadership in the coming battle. Then he retired to his quarters.

The next morning, we began our march toward Clan Hayato's castle.

Chapter Thirty-Nine

aul replaced the folded letter, closed the *Adauchi* text and pushed back from his desk.

He found that when he followed his ritual, the words flowed. The sleep, meditation, yoga, and exercise pattern built a momentum within him that rolled over the anxiousness, memories, pain, and anger that simmered, always, beneath his surface. After nearly a year of following this practice in the solitude of the *Odysseus*, it was bulletproof, putting him in a zone, every time, that he would have paid money for back on Earth. Particularly during his imprisonment and court-martial.

But not this morning.

He had only translated a short section before his wandering mind forced him to quit.

He knew the culprit.

Paul reached into the breast pocket of his flight suit and pulled out the memory stick. He turned it over in his hands several times. He shook his head, returned the stick to his breast pocket, and pushed away from the desk.

Fine, he thought. *I'll go for a walk instead.* Paul suited up and moved through the traverse toward the hub.

As a military officer, Paul had walked a lot. He'd had a reputation for preferring walking meetings over sitting in a tent or conference room, and he'd conducted as many of his staff meetings as possible that way. He also liked to walk alone. He could work things out better once his body settled into a comfortable stride. He came up with his best tactical plans on his solo walks.

Often when he walked, his mind was blank. His body moved, and his brain rested. Recharged. He was notorious for circling the perimeter or fence line of whatever remote outpost he was based at. During their deployment to South America, Kata had gotten so frustrated and concerned about Paul's walks, she had ordered Paul's first sergeant to assign a drone guard whenever Paul left his hooch.

Walking on the *Odysseus* was a different thing, though. It meant passing through various states of atmosphere, gravity, and temperature. Sometimes rapidly. It required getting into and getting out of pressure suits, mag boots, thermals. So, rather than just setting off on a walk and seeing where you ended up, as one did on Earth, on the *Odysseus*, you had to decide where you were going first.

Paul liked his ship-borne walks, nonetheless. What they lacked in spontaneity, they made up for in setting.

This time, Paul headed for one of his favorite places to sit and think: the drone hangar.

Like many of her facilities, the hangar was a retrofit added at the request of the military during the *Odysseus'* troop transport days. The military needed a hangar facility for their landing and utility vehicles.

From a distance, the hangar looked like a large shoebox fastened to the belly of the ship. At two hundred meters long and fifty meters wide and deep, the facility provided half a million square feet of protected hangar space for the military vehicles. The Company complained loudly about the loss of over two hundred linear meters of the *Odysseus'* cargo rigging. But by the time the crisis had passed, they'd seen the virtue of the hangar. Until then, the *Odysseus'* small complement of inspection-and-repair bots fastened themselves to the side of the ship like sucker fish. With the hangar, the *Odysseus* was able to upgrade to a larger squadron of XO-controlled IR bots. The Company was pleased, envisioning the *Odysseus* under way for another century or more under the constant inspection-and-repair protocols of her expanded complement of shipmates.

The hangar had no bottom to it. The structure was entirely open to the void so that military transports and drop ships could come and go on their missions easily. That was one of the things that made it one of Paul's favorite contemplative spots on the ship. A ten-meter-long oval-shaped blister of glass, reminiscent of a World War II aircraft machine gun turret, protruded from the belly of the *Odysseus,* which was the top of the hangar. This was the observation-and-control facility from which an officer could direct troop loading and receiving in the hangar during military operations. Now, with no military activities to control, the module was only good for observation.

But it was really good for that.

The military had, of course, over engineered the chair. A big, ballsy metal-and-leather commander's chair hung from an articulating arm in the middle of the glass blister. A joystick on the left-hand armrest allowed Paul to angle and swivel the chair as he pleased. The chair in the observation-and-control facility was a favorite spot of Paul's. He considered its view to be second only to the captain's window on the bridge.

While the C&C offered an expansive view of the void spreading out in front of the good ship, sitting in the hangar commander's chair felt like sticking your head into an aquarium full of fish. Inspection-and-repair bots came and went as they finished and began their patrols. Others were docked against the walls or hooked to power cables that extended from the ceiling. Most of the IR bots used a compressed-gas propulsion system that enabled them to maneuver around the *Odysseus.* The puffs of expelled gas flared randomly as the school of IR bots jockeyed in the massive, busy space.

Paul still had the heart and eyes of a drone pilot, and he loved the purposeful shapes of the IR bots. There were many configurations. Egg shaped. Cigar shaped. Jellyfish-like. One version that reminded Paul of a manta ray. Some had arms. Some had large sensor arrays. All were purpose built, like the soldiers he had served with.

His favorites, though, were the tugs. There were four large tug bots used to haul large loads. They were squatty and muscular and looked vaguely like their earthbound ancestors. They had soft rubber bumpers fastened to their noses and sides that allowed them to nudge into and drive things without damage. The bumpers were circular and evoked visions of bearded crew members throwing roped tires onto the sides of tugboats. Paul wondered if nostalgia was at play at all for the Earthside engineers who'd designed them, or if the tire-like shapes actually were the best solution. Some things didn't need to be improved on very much.

Like all the other IR bots, the tugs used compressed gas for maneuvering but also had powerful onboard rocket engines that enabled them to tug or push heavy loads.

Paul had been awed only a few cycles into the voyage by a display of their power. He stood on the bridge with Cooley and Captain Drake and watched as one of the tug bots moved a massive payload to a new position farther forward. Paul gaped at the enormous asteroid. The tug looked like a minnow pushing a basketball.

"Wow," he mumbled as they watched.

"You're damn right, son," Drake responded. "We don't have to worry about losing the main engines as long as we have those bastards around!" He chuckled, slapping Paul on the back.

Besides their raw power, Paul appreciated the tugs' scratches and dents. It was rare that an IR bot would actually touch something with anything other than its robotic arms and hands. As a result, they always had a pristine, fresh-from-the-factory look about them. The tugs, though, were made to push, pull, bump, and nudge things, and they looked like it. They were weary and beat-up, like Paul.

Paul turned the memory stick over in his fingers as he watched one of the tugs push a welding bot to its mooring spot. The endless void spread out beneath his feet, outside of the hangar.

He watched the tug work and thought about the XO and Captain Drake. The tug, the welder bot, all the bots inside and outside of the hangar, were like everything else on the *Odysseus* - ultimately controlled by the XO. And that was fine with Paul.

But now, with a mysterious data set on a memory stick that he wanted to analyze in private without the XO knowing, he was stymied. Worse, he was forced to think like Drake. And not like the parts of Drake that Paul admired. Rather, the darker, paranoid parts he did not.

Fucking crazy, mean old man, Paul thought to himself.

Paul ran a mental inventory of the analysis tools he could think of. They all seemed like dead ends. Ideal, of course, would be the 3D displays on the first level of the Hab, but the XO was integrally connected to all of that.

Everything Paul could think of had the same issue. The XO would not only get access to the data, but would also know that Paul was analyzing the data. Paul did not expect to find anything important, but he wanted to digest it on his own before sharing it with the XO.

He was stuck.

Rapid-fire puffs of gas erupted along the tug's long and short axis as it swiveled around to aim at the bottom of the hangar and the void beyond. It was finished with the welder bot and was preparing to resume its post just below the hangar opening.

"Hello, Paul. You are on the move early this cycle. How are you?" the XO's voice came over the speakers in the OC.

Paul put the memory stick back into his breast pocket as he responded. "Hello, XO. Doing well. You?"

"I am fine, thanks. All systems nominal. Should be another uneventful cycle for all of us."

"That's the way I like 'em."

"Me too."

The tug's small-maneuver thrusters fired for a two count, and the large drone moved slowly down. When it had cleared the hangar, a different combination of thrusters fired. The tug swiveled into an overwatching position just to the port side and below the hangar opening, facing forward in the *Odysseus'* direction of flight.

"Paul, I'd like to ask your point of view, if I may?" the XO said.

"Sure."

"How do you think the crew is getting along?"

Paul smiled and shook his head. Regas had been let out of confinement two weeks ago. He was cordial enough with Drummond and Mr. Cooley, but the simmering anger beneath the surface was clear for everyone to see. There was unease on board.

"Not great. But I have seen worse."

"Have you faced such disunity in units you have commanded in the past?"

"Not like this. And, honestly, not from a position like this."

"A position like what?"

"Powerless. I'm just a cog in the *Odysseus'* machine, XO."

"That may be so, Paul. But I find leadership roles to be confounding at times and thought your perspective would be valuable."

That's an odd comment, Paul thought.

"How are the sessions with Althea going?" the XO asked before Paul could probe what he was talking about.

Paul hesitated.

"Is it OK that I asked?" the XO said.

"Of course. It's fine. I mean, there really can't be many secrets between us out here, can there?"

"No. Not very many."

"And I know you've noticed when I've had… difficulties on board…" Paul said.

"I have."

Paul shifted in the big command chair, uneasy with the XO's near omniscience.

"Given what you have been through, Paul, I think you have shown great strength and resilience. More than most would have."

"How much do you know about what happened at los Olvidados?"

"More than I am supposed to. Most of it is classified, as you know."

"Did you have any reservations about letting me on board?"

"No. I had no reservations, and neither did Mr. Cooley or Captain Drake. The captain, in particular, felt a great respect and affection for you, Paul. I am sure you could sense that."

"Yeah. I did. I miss the old man."

Paul smiled at the memory of Captain Drake. He looked past the drones in the hangar at the stars. He wondered how far away the captain's coffin was now. And where would the journey take him? Would he crash into a planet? Or star? Would a black hole grab hold of the old man's body and suck it into oblivion? Or would he just sail on forever?

"So the sessions are going well, then?" the XO asked, interrupting Paul's thoughts.

"Uh… Yes. They are."

"Good."

Paul smiled at himself. He knew the sessions with Althea were helping him, but he was surprised that he was starting to value her companionship. For the first year of their journey, she had been no factor. He wasn't rude to her the way the captain was. And he didn't leer at her body the way Regas did, but he spent no more time with her than he had to. He had come aboard to be as alone as he could. She was not part of that formula.

Now, though? He had to admit that he enjoyed being around her.

"And Althea?" the XO asked.

"Huh? What about her?"

"You two seem to be getting along well."

"Sure. We are. Why?"

"Just because we have so much longer to go," the XO said. "It would be a shame if you did not enjoy each other's company. And I am certain that she enjoys yours."

"She told you that?" Paul asked, immediately regretting it.

"Not in so many words. But I can tell."

Paul felt a spark from the XO's comment. He drowned it quickly, though. *Of course she enjoys my company,* he thought, scolding himself. *Her job is to spend time with me and the rest of the crew.*

"That's good, I guess," Paul said, looking at his watch.

"Well. Thank you for indulging me. I won't bother you anymore. Have a good cycle, Paul."

"I will. Thanks."

Paul, unsettled, sat in the OC chair for another half hour. Something about his conversation with the XO troubled him, but he wasn't sure what.

That was when he realized: *The captain would not have a rogue inertial measurement unit on board without having his own discrete, unmonitored way to analyze it.*

Paul pushed out of the command chair and headed for the C&C.

Arriving, he left his helmet in the air lock, but did not remove his pressure suit. Paul floated into the spotless facility and looked around. The cleaning bots still visited the C&C every other day despite the fact that no one occupied it anymore. The patches in the hull were the only reminder of the captain's astronomically bad luck. They had been painted to match the interior, but the slightly raised welding beads that encircled them were still visible, like Paul's puffy scar tissue. The *Odysseus'* repairs were now part of her long tale of service.

Paul smiled as he envisioned crew members decades in the future gawking at the repaired hull breaches and marveling at the cosmic violence dealt to the good ship and her captain. It was the kind of thing that gave ships reputations of bad luck and being jinxed.

Paul's smile faded. *Am I the jinx?*

He shrugged his shoulders to shake off the thought and searched the bridge. He found nothing and moved down to the lower level and entered the captain's quarters.

Paul floated in the middle of the wood-paneled room for about fifteen minutes. It felt creepy. Everything was in its place, undisturbed by the captain's death. The bed, a cocoon-like sleeping bag tethered to the wall, was still ready and waiting for the old man.

He pushed off the floor to get a slow rotation going to his right and tried to refocus. He forced himself to take in every detail of the room.

Where would I hide an unmonitored bootleg computer if I were a crusty old captain? Paul thought to himself.

He completed three full revolutions. The third time the old man's desk came into view, Paul laughed at himself.

I wouldn't hide it at all if it were my fucking ship.

He pushed off the ceiling, bouncing himself to the floor, where he crouched and then shoved himself off toward the desk. He floated smoothly and caught himself against the zero G chair.

Paul opened the lap drawer. *Bingo,* he thought, as he reached in and grabbed the tablet computer. He turned it over in his hands and pressed the on button. The screen glowed and asked for the password.

Paul shoved the tablet into a small utility bag and pressed a foot to the floor to turn for the door.

An idea struck him.

He started searching the captain's quarters. It didn't take long to find it.

Yes! Paul thought, a grin spreading across his face. He looked with appreciation at part of the captain's bourbon stash. He knew the bulk of Drake's contraband was stored somewhere else on the *Odysseus.* That fact alone was reason enough to continue the cycle inspections. Paul hoped to find it at some point over the next year.

For now, though, the eight bottles he stared at were enough to significantly raise his morale. They sat snuggly in a small, cubicle-shaped wall storage unit in the captain's quarters. Paul entertained the thought of taking one with him back to his quarters, but decided against it. The last thing he wanted to do was to be forced to share precious bourbon with Regas and his two idiot assistants.

No. The stash would stay here. Hidden. His secret.

After he took just one swig, of course.

"Here's to you, Captain."

Chapter Forty

Paul rose from bed early. He meditated, exercised, and then sat down at his desk to work on the captain's tablet. He put it into administrative mode and started looking for a back door into the operating system.

An hour later, after a few unsuccessful attempts, he gained access to the tablet. He took the memory stick out of his flight-suit pocket and inserted it into the data port.

All right, you sneaky bastard, he thought as he clicked to open the drive, *let's see what you were up to.*

The drive had only one massive data file on it. Paul recognized it as a navigation data set. He searched the tablet's list of programs and found a navigation utility, which he used to open the file.

The tablet displayed the *Odysseus'* measured course line all the way back to Earth. The course line was blue with about a dozen red circle icons dotting the last half of it at irregular intervals. Paul placed the cursor over one of the icons and an acceleration and time value appeared.

Strange, he thought.

He moved the cursor to the next red icon. Then the next.

Paul gasped when he realized what he was looking at. Each red circle highlighted an instance where the inertial measurement unit had detected acceleration and course change.

Paul leaned back in his chair and tried to get his head around the implications.

The trade routes to and from the belt were strictly prescribed and designed to minimize time enroute, energy required, and exposure to known hazards. That was one of the things that made the meteoroid strike that had killed the captain so strange. A lot of work by a lot of smart people and AIs had gone into the effort to chart a course where that would not happen.

A ship's path to the belt should not have any midway course changes. The trade routes were not designed that way. There were the initial maneuvering burns to depart orbit, followed by the long primary burn, which would put the ship underway. After the primary, there could be several smaller adjustment burns to fine-tune the ship's trajectory to within trade-route parameters, but these would all have been completed within the first few weeks of being underway. On a normal voyage, there would be no subsequent adjustments to course until the ship began to prepare for deceleration and arrival.

But there, in red on the tablet display, were a dozen course deviations, starting approximately six months ago. As a result, the *Odysseus* was millions of miles off course before the meteoroid strikes.

And she was still deviating, drifting farther from her assigned course every second.

Fuck me, Paul thought. His head was spinning. If the *Odysseus* had executed a maneuver burn, Paul would have noticed. Everyone on board would have. When the maneuver thrusters kicked on, it jolted the whole ship. Sure, maybe he could have slept through one such burn, but the course analysis showed at least a dozen.

Fuck me, Paul repeated in his head.

Was it all an effort to kill the captain? Were they being hijacked? If so, who the hell was hijacking them? The XO?

No one else could have pulled this off, he thought.

Paul zoomed in to look at the course deviations. The first was long in duration. The off-course acceleration had lasted for almost five hours, but it was small in magnitude. It was only .33 meters per second per second; a tiny, undetectable fraction of the acceleration of gravity, but when finished, it had added a course deviation of almost 6,000 meters per second.

The other accelerations were smaller and closer together. The interval between the first and second deviation was almost a week, but the interval between the eleventh and twelfth was less than a cycle. It was as if whoever was making the course deviations was fine-tuning their work. Why? To rendezvous with the meteoroids that killed the captain?

Paul looked at the timestamp for each deviation and noted they all took place late in the cycle, when it was likely most of the human crew would have been asleep.

Paul set the tablet computer down on his desk and pushed back in his chair. He leaned back and rubbed his eyes, letting the situation sink in. Then he stared out of his window.

The chime of his watch startled him almost twenty minutes later; he was still staring out of the window. He glanced at his watch and tapped the alarm off.

It was time for his session with Althea. He wondered if he should go. *Not in the mood to spill my guts to her right now,* he thought.

Is she involved?

Paul passed Althea as he climbed up the center crew ladder on his way to the traverse.

"Paul?" Althea called to him.

"Hey. What's up?"

"I thought we were talking now."

"I decided I'm not in the mood," Paul said. "I'm going to hit the gym instead."

"Oh. OK."

Paul nodded awkwardly and started to climb the ladder again.

Althea looked around to make sure there was no one in earshot of them before saying, "Meet on the bridge later, then?"

"No. I'm sorry, Althea. I need some alone time."

"Paul, I don't understand," Althea said.

But she was talking to an empty ladder.

* * *

Regas floated down the traverse toward the Utility Module. *Another bullshit inspection,* he thought as his weight increased. *And another day on this piece-of-shit freighter that I'll get paid one-tenth of what I should. Fucking bullshit.*

Regas grabbed the ladder as his relative weight began to increase and climbed down onto the Utility Module bulkhead. Before opening the bulkhead, he looked at the inspection sheet on his clipboard.

"Damn it," Regas muttered. His objective was one of the old storage units on the bottom floor of the Utility Module. Of all the random corners of the *Odysseus,* he hated that one the most. All the odd military equipment, despite its age and obsolescence, reminded him of what should have been, the career he was robbed of, and why he was now little more than forced labor on a freighter in the wasteland between Earth and the belt.

As he climbed down the central ladder, Regas heard music. He stepped off the ladder onto the second level and walked to the gym, where the music was playing. He peered through the window in the door and saw Paul working out.

"Well, good morning, Captain Jigsaw," Regas said in his most insincere voice as he swung open the door.

Paul fought the urge to tell Regas to fuck off. He didn't want to reward the simpleton with conflict.

"Hello, Regas."

"Working out?" Regas asked, walking toward Paul.

"Yep."

Regas nodded as if Paul had confirmed a super-insightful observation.

Paul ignored Regas as he went on with changing the weights on the bench press.

"You been spending a lot of time with Althea lately," Regas said. "What's up with that?"

"Nothing," Paul said, not looking at Regas.

"Talking about your feelings and shit? Is that required to get alone with her? Cuz I'll do that if that's what it takes."

"I think the only thing it takes is to not be a creep around her," Paul said, moving to the other side of the bar.

"Oh, come on, Captain Jigsaw," Regas said in a falsely wounded tone. "That ain't fair. I'm an all-right guy."

Paul put another plate on the bar and moved to the bench.

"Would you talk to her for me, Owens? Tell her all I want to do is be alone with her and talk about my feelings. Bare my soul, you know?"

Paul sat down on the bench and loosened up his shoulders.

"Bare my soul along with some other things. You know what I'm saying?" Regas laughed too loud and slapped Paul on the back.

Just a little too hard.

Anger surged in Paul. Before he could stop it, he was on his feet, swiveling to face Regas.

Regas didn't flinch. The two men stared at each other for a long heartbeat, waiting to see if it was going to happen.

Regas blinked first.

He laughed, taking a small step backward from Paul. "Come on, Owens. I'm joking. I'm just joking. Sheesh, man."

Paul maintained his ready stance.

Regas smiled before saying, "I'm sorry. I was just kidding. I didn't realize you Centaurs had so many big feelings."

"Let's be honest with each other, Regas. You don't know shit about Centaurs. You were just a nasty fucking leg."

The smile drained from Regas.

Paul's comment crashed over him. All the rejection and disappointment and jealousy from that world they'd left millions of miles behind them rushed in and covered Regas up.

Paul smiled at the reaction. "I thought so. There are only two kinds of nasty legs. Those who got rejected by the Centaur program. And those who haven't applied yet."

Regas did not smile back.

"Did I touch a nerve, wannabe?" Paul asked him, his voice dripping with false concern.

Paul didn't wait for an answer. He sat down on the bench, lay back, and started knocking out repetitions.

Regas was enraged Paul saw that in him. He wanted to kill him.

But he hesitated.

Paul finished his set. He racked the bar and stood up.

"I'm glad we had this chat, Regas."

Regas left the weight room.

Regas stewed as he went down to the bottom level to conduct his inspection. He was angry. Angry at Drummond. Angry at Cooley and the XO. Angry at Althea. Angry at Paul. And angry he had years left to go on this fucking voyage.

He kicked his way through some of the old junk and walked down an obscure passageway, heading toward his inspection objective: a storage unit in the far corner of the lower level of the Utility Module.

As Regas stepped around piles of junk, he noticed a fine layer of dust covering everything.

It must be years since anyone has been in this forgotten corner of this godforsaken ship, Regas thought. *What a fucking waste of time.*

Finally, he arrived. He reached out to open the storage unit, but the door wouldn't give. It had been years since it had been opened. Dust and age worked together to make it stick.

"Damn it," Regas muttered, setting down his clipboard so that he could use both hands.

He grabbed the door mechanism and pulled. Nothing.

He hit the door a few times with his fist and then grabbed the door again and shook it.

Still nothing.

"Fuck you!" Regas yelled.

He punched the door. He kicked it. He yanked on it. He pictured Paul,

Drummond, and Drake and took his rage out on it.

It popped open.

Regas, panting from his tantrum, looked at the three large green wooden trunks stacked on top of each other in the storage unit.

He stepped forward and opened the top one, looking to see what it contained.

"Well, well, well…" he said with a broad smile.

Chapter Forty-One

Paul floated alone on the bridge, frustrated, concerned, and angry.

He was frustrated that it had been seven cycles since he'd used the captain's tablet computer to analyze the *Odysseus'* course data and he was no closer to figuring out what had happened. He was reluctant to go to Cooley until he had at least a theory about what was going on and a potential plan, but he was stymied.

He was concerned that the longer he waited, the further the XO's plot advanced and the farther off course the *Odysseus* continued to fly.

And he was angry with himself at the way he had handled things with Althea. Not the fact that he had avoided her for the past seven cycles. He could tell that she was hurt and puzzled, but he told himself he did not care about that. He was angry at himself for letting her in, for talking to her about his past. The fact was, he had started to think of her as a friend. A connection. And he had joined the *Odysseus* not only for the Fly It Off program but also for the solitude and isolation. Now he felt entangled. He had let his guard and judgment down. He had missed something.

Even worse, she might be involved.

So, as he had done for the past several cycles, Paul floated alone in the bridge. The *Odysseus'* hull extended forward below the command-and-control module. The spinner rotated against the backdrop of the infinite void, and Paul stewed in his frustration, concern, and anger.

Another tug drone came into view from beneath the *Odysseus'* hull about two hundred meters forward of the bridge. It was pushing an enormous rock away on a course perpendicular to the *Odysseus*. Paul figured it was transporting raw material to the factory. The rock it labored behind was enormous.

Bursts of gas fired from the tug drone's sides as it maneuvered itself around its payload. The asteroid was so large, the tug disappeared behind it.

A long plume of blue flame erupted behind the colossal rock as the hidden tug fired its main engine. The glow from the laboring tug's exhaust cast shadows across the rock, highlighting its pockmarked surface and unknowable history. Paul tried to guess its mass but gave up.

When the tug had arrested the asteroid's velocity away from the ship, it repositioned again and began pushing the rock aft. The brilliant exhaust flame illuminated hundreds of meters of the *Odysseus*.

Damn, Paul thought, looking down at the hardworking tug drone. *Those things are so powerful. Maybe I could hitch a ride on one of those tough bastards. Leave these crazies behind and head back to Earth.*

Paul bolted straight as the realization hit him.

He scrambled to go find Cooley.

* * *

"This better be good, Prisoner Owens," Cooley said, not trying to hide his irritation.

Paul and Cooley floated in the maintenance bay of power and propulsion. It was a large, pressurized workspace on the fourth level and one of the few crew zones of the *Odysseus* where the XO was unable to monitor conversations.

Earlier in the cycle, Paul had passed a note to Cooley that said:

Mr. Cooley, something is very wrong with the XO, and I need to talk to you in an area where he cannot monitor us. Please meet me in the PPM maintenance facility today at 1400 hours. It is fucking urgent. Tell no one.

Paul had gritted his teeth as he'd written it. *The old man is laughing his ass off at me somewhere.*

"Mr. Cooley, this is going to sound ridiculous, but I think that the XO has hijacked the *Odysseus*," Paul said, hating the way he sounded.

"Hijacked?"

"I believe one objective was to kill Captain Drake by causing the meteor strike."

"Kill Captain Drake?" Cooley asked, his face contorting with disbelief.

"I don't know what else he is up to, but I recommend we regard the XO as a hostile. Is there a way for us to take control of the *Odysseus*? To lock the XO out?"

"A hostile?" Cooley's face was now a mask of disgust and pity. "Owens, have you been skipping your sessions with Althea? What does she say about all this?"

"I haven't discussed my suspicions with her. She may be involved."

"OK," Cooley said, shaking his head. "That's enough. I'm ordering you to sit for a session with Althea immediately and to follow her resulting directions precisely. Space dementia is nothing to be ashamed of, Owens. I've seen it take down old-timers who have lived out here for decades. We'll get you back to right."

Cooley put his arm on Paul's shoulder.

Paul jerked it off and pulled the captain's tablet from one of his cargo pockets.

"Mr. Cooley, the captain placed a self-contained, unmonitored inertial measurement unit on board, not far from here," Paul said, turning the small computer on. "Shortly before he was killed, he told me about it—"

"The captain told *you* about it?" Cooley asked, incredulous.

"Drake was killed before I could discuss the situation with him," Paul said, nodding. "But I was able to download the data and analyze it on the captain's tablet."

"You took the captain's tablet computer?" Cooley said, angry. "Look, Owens, I knew you were going to the bridge from time to time, and I didn't say anything because I don't mind you having some time alone, and the view up there is terrific, but I can't overlook this. Give me the captain's computer, and you will not visit the bridge again unsupervised. I will have to report this to Drummond."

Paul handed him the tablet with the navigation analysis up on the display.

"Look," Paul said, pointing at the deviated course line.

Cooley glared at Paul.

Then he sighed and looked at the tablet.

His brow furrowed.

His eyes narrowed.

"What the hell is this?" he demanded, not looking away from the display.

"It's a plot of our current course against the flight plan we filed with the Company."

"This is bullshit," Cooley said, still not looking up.

"That's exactly what I said."

"Where is this IMU?"

"Section ten. Transfer room 105. I asked you to meet me back here in PPM because I thought you might want to go see it."

"Let's go," Cooley said, turning from Paul and jerking his helmet on.

Half an hour later, they were back in the maintenance bay.

Cooley was having a hard time getting his head around the situation.

"I can't believe it," he kept repeating.

Paul let him go for a few minutes and then said, "Mr. Cooley, how can we sever the XO's control of the *Odysseus*?"

"I'm not sure we want to do that."

"Why not?"

"Because running the *Odysseus* is a big job, Owens," Cooley said, irritation creeping into his voice. "Life support. Navigation. Maintenance. The factory. And, oh yeah, what do you know about the care and feeding of nuclear reactors?"

Paul grimaced, daunted at the thought. But he pressed on.

"Is it possible?"

Cooley thought for a moment.

He shook his head.

"Not really. The ship was designed to minimize crew requirements through the integration of systems-management programs. All of which are overseen and coordinated by the XO. The fact is, the *Odysseus* could do several belt-and-back voyages without any crew at all. I've never been trained on any scenarios where deactivation of the XO was a goal. The ship wouldn't make it very far. It would be suicide."

"Then I guess all we can do is confront him," Paul said.

"Confront who?"

"The XO. We can't just sit on this thing, going who knows where, without at least calling him on it."

"If he really killed Drake, what is to stop the XO from killing us when we confront him?"

"Nothing, I guess," Paul answered.

The two men floated in silence for a moment, brows furrowed in thought and concern.

"I don't like it either," Paul said. "Every time I run through it, I get to the question: What is to stop the XO from spacing us the moment we confront him? Just opening all the airlocks on the Hab and jettisoning us like we did Drake's body. Then I ask myself: Why has he not done it already? There is nothing we could do to stop him. So, just killing us must not be his goal. It's something else. So, I figure, why not just discuss it with him? See if we can come to an agreement."

"An agreement?" Cooley asked in a mocking tone.

Paul waved off his sarcasm. "I'm not going to sit on board the *Odysseus* for another year, or longer, wondering where the hell we are going, what the XO is really up to, and if he is going to kill more of us."

"You'll do what I tell you to do, Prisoner," Cooley said, suddenly angry.

Paul looked Cooley in the eyes, trying to reassure him. "You're right, Mr. Cooley. I'll do exactly what you say. I'm not up to anything here. That is why I brought this to you."

Cooley's face was tight with stress. Paul went further.

"Look, Mr. Cooley... I've been in your shoes. I know you are trying to limp this crew along until we get to the belt. You've got a weak captain, a couple of idiot prisoner crew members, and now a potentially treacherous and murderous AI running the ship. You can count on me not to do anything to make this situation worse for you. Whatever you say goes, sir."

Cooley looked at Paul for a moment. "I've got an idea."

EARTH

Chapter Forty-Two

Japan

"A re you sure this time, Max?" Fiona asked. She held her phone to her ear as she looked out of the glass corner of her office. Her staff waited for her, seated at her conference table.

"We're sure, ma'am." Max stood in the dark in the middle of a large field on the southern coast of Japan near Shimoda, just a few hundred meters from the sea. A sleek civilian model quad copter sat fifty meters away. Dim lights emanated from the cockpit. The flight manager sat waiting. Six plain-clothed commandos stood a respectful distance away from Max. "No doubt about it this time."

Fiona smiled.

"All right, then. Take him."

"Roger that, ma'am."

Maximillian gave a thumbs up to the team with his metal hand as he put his phone back in his pocket. The commandos nodded and followed him as he strode toward the aircraft. The flight manager saw them coming and started the main engines.

Moments later, the sleek aircraft was flying north, fifty feet above the water, at two hundred and fifty knots.

"OK." Max turned to look back at the commando team. "Just like we planned. After we land at the LZ, Gonzales will secure the aircraft while the rest of you come with me. It should take us no more than an hour to get to the compound on foot. Once there, you will establish security while I will go inside and take custody of the target. We will call for extraction as we move to the LZ five hundred meters outside the monastery gates. The aircraft will pick us up there and we will return to the main island. Any questions?"

Max looked each man in the eyes, one by one. There were no questions. They were pros. This was a simple mission, and they had been over the plan several times.

"Good." Max turned to face forward again and leaned back in his chair. It was a thirty-minute flight to the small island of Ryujin. Max rubbed his eyes with his human hand and tried not to get excited. Thane and Miss Malloy had been searching for Doctor Musashi for years. Miss Malloy had made finding him Max's top priority. Lately, it had been the source of increasing friction between her and him. He would be very glad to end the search tonight.

"Six minutes," the pilot said over the intercom.

The team unbuckled and checked their gear one more time.

They were each armed with a stun rifle and carried only pistols as lethal back up. The goal tonight was to leave no signature.

The aircraft banked to line up on their landing zone, a flat spot of rocky beach between the ocean and windblown trees. It transitioned to landing mode and, moments later, the quad copter settled onto its gear on the beach.

The ramp lowered and the team exited. Gonzales walked to the nose of the aircraft, holding a large automatic weapon and wearing a night vision helmet. He tossed a handful of small sentry drones into the air. The soft, high-pitched buzz of their rotors filled the night suddenly and then dissipated as they flew away and spread out to provide overwatch and early warning.

Max walked inland, his team of five in a file behind him. He looked at the small volcanic mountain's silhouette above the tree line. The temple was on the opposite side midway up the slope. They had landed here to conceal their acoustic signature. Max hoped it worked as they walked into the trees.

Fifty-seven minutes later, Max and the commandos entered the grounds of the Buddhist monastery nestled in a crook of the squatty mountain. The temple was built into the rock face of the mountain almost a thousand years ago, and led to a network of ancient caves. In front of the temple, a weathered and cracked statue of Fudō Myō-ō sat on a moss-covered boulder in the middle of a small courtyard beneath a single cryptomeria. Gnarled and tired, the old tree had been broken and stunted by storms over the centuries. It sagged around the ancient statue, as if asking for its leave. A single-story communal kitchen and dining hall stood on one side of the courtyard, a small classroom hut on the other.

Max scanned the compound as they walked into the courtyard. Consistent with his intelligence prep, it didn't look like it could accommodate more than a dozen monks.

The team fanned out in the courtyard as Max walked straight ahead into the temple.

"Hello, traveler," a monk said in English as he stepped from the shadows. He wore a simple orange robe and no shoes. "How may I help you at this late hour?"

Max put on his most easy-going smile. "I was hoping to speak with Doctor Musashi."

"Of course." The monk nodded once. "He said he expected to have visitors soon."

Max nodded. *Of course he did.*

"I will tell him you are here," the monk said.

"That's ok, friend," Max said, stepping up to the ancient temple door. "I'd like to surprise him."

"This is a temple, sir," the monk protested.

Max looked at the monk apologetically and pushed through the door.

The temple occupied a dome shaped grotto in the volcanic rock of the island. At the far end, a small arch, not much taller than a man, had been carved out of the rock and a short empty pedestal stood beneath it. There was no statue of Budha on the pedestal. It had been stolen centuries ago. Instead, large candles of various lengths burned, illuminating dried flowers and old strings of beads placed on and around the base of the rock pedestal. The candles cast a dim light into the small space. Six large wooden columns stood on each side of the sitting area, candles glowing on the floor between each of them, their red paint flaked and faded. An old man in a plain white robe sat cross-legged up front between the first two columns at the foot of the pedestal.

Max walked forward slowly until he was standing beside the seated man.

The man opened his eyes and turned to look up at him.

"Good evening, doctor," Max said, visually confirming for himself it was Doctor Musashi.

"Good evening, young man," the doctor said, taking in Max's face. "Who are you?"

"My name is Max."

"Is that short for something?"

"Yes, sir. Maximilian."

The doctor smiled. Then his eyes narrowed suddenly.

"You were a soldier once," he said.

"Yes."

"Your arm." The doctor nodded toward Max's metal hand. "You were wounded?"

"Yes."

The doctor shook his head gently, a thought crossing behind his eyes.

"And you work for Fiona Malloy?"

"I do, sir."

"Sit next to me for a moment, Maximilian." Musashi tapped the stone floor to his right.

Max didn't move.

"Humor me," Musashi said with a disarming smile. "I know it's over. What's five more minutes?"

Max looked back at the temple door. It was shut. He keyed his earpiece three times to break squelch. Two clicks came back from the team leader outside. All clear.

Max kneeled next to the old man. Musashi turned his head to look back at the candles on the pedestal.

"I didn't know you were a Buddhist." Max had been researching the doctor since he began looking for him.

"Oh, I'm not." Musashi's voice was melancholy. "I tried so hard to be. But…"

Max waited in silence for a moment.

"I hope you're ready for a trip," he finally said to the doctor.

"I am. I am finally ready."

"I can save you the trouble if you just tell me where the memory sphere is," Max said in a sincere voice.

"I don't have it anymore."

Max cocked his head at the comment.

"Then you admit at one time you did have it?"

"Yes."

"You lied to Thane before?"

"I did."

"Do you know where it is now?"

Doctor Musashi looked at Max. "To a certain extent."

"What the hell does that mean?" Max asked, growing concerned.

"I know that it is far from here. Out of your reach." The doctor looked up at the ceiling. His eyes narrowed, as if trying to focus on something in the distance, past the low ceiling of the temple.

Max studied the doctor's face as he looked up. He looked younger than his almost one hundred years. And sad.

Doctor Musashi turned his head and locked eyes with Max.

"Did she tell you why she wants it so badly?"

Max sat in silence.

Musashi winced, as if hearing a lie.

"You don't have to worry about finding the sphere, Maximilian," the doctor said, setting his eyes back on the pedestal and placing his hands back into his robe. "It is going to come for Fiona Malloy someday soon."

"All right," Max said as he stood up. "We're done here. Let's go."

Max towered over the small, seated man. He extended his hand down to assist the doctor to his feet. As he did, he saw something silver flash from Musashi's robe and plunge into the old man's belly, driven by the doctor's own hands.

Blood gushed onto the doctor's legs and out onto the floor. Musashi grunted in agony as he pushed the blade across his stomach, a garish red stain blooming across the front of his white robe.

"What the fuck?" Max yelled.

He dropped to his knees and grabbed the doctor's hands, yanking them away.

A long ceremonial blade skidded across the floor and clanged against the base of the pedestal.

Max activated his radio, smearing blood across his ear. "Medic, medic, medic!"

Blood surged across the floor as Max tried to support Musashi's limp body. The doctor sagged to his side, intestines oozing onto the floor.

"God damn it!" Max yelled. "Where is my medic?"

He tried to roll Musashi onto his back.

"Max," he heard the doctor say in a weak voice.

They locked eyes.

The door burst open. The medic ran to their side.

"Holy shit," the medic said, sliding off his backpack. "I thought you said avoid wet works on this one. What did you do to him?"

"I didn't fucking touch him! Stabilize him!"

"Maximilian," the doctor said again. Voice even weaker. Eyes adamant.

Max leaned his head closer to Musashi as the medic tried to get an IV into the old man's wrist.

"Did she tell you what she did to Pruden?" Musashi said.

"Pruden? Who the hell is Pruden?"

The medic tapped Max's shoulder.

Max sat up as the medic shook his head and shrugged.

"Why?" Max asked, looking down at the doctor.

Musashi's skin was a pale white, his breath weak and ragged. Blood expanded from him in a dark pool almost to the base of the pedestal.

"Why did you do this?"

Musashi said something that Max couldn't hear.

Max leaned his head back down next to Musashi's face.

"Atoning," he said in a whisper.

Max shook his head and sat up.

The medic stood, cleaning his hands with sanitary wipes.

"Run…" Musashi whispered.

Max leaned in closer to hear.

"Run… *Odysseus*… Run…"

"What the hell?" Max whispered as he looked around at the bloody mess.

"He's gone," the medic said. "Hallucinating while the blood runs out of his brain."

Max heard shouts and a scuffle. A monk was trying to get past one of the commandos blocking the door to the temple.

Fiasco, Max thought.

A raspy gurgle from the doctor got Max's attention. He lowered his head next to the doctor's mouth.

"Tell Fiona…" The doctor's voice was barely audible.

Max inched closer until his ear touched the doctor's lips. He strained to hear the old man. "That… I do not… envy her next chapters… they will have their adauchi."

"Who is they?" Max asked.

Musashi's eyes rolled back.

"Answer me, Doctor! Who is they?"

He pressed his ear against the doctor's mouth.

But all he heard was a final, hollow bubbling breath.

Chapter Forty-Three

New York City

"They call it seppuku," Max said when he finished giving Fiona his detailed report. He sat facing her, his metal and flesh hands folded together in front of him on the large conference table.

Fiona, arms crossed and face taught, sat at the head of the table. It was after 9PM. Outside the windows Manhattan was a constellation of lights surrounding the rectangular darkness of Central Park.

"It was a form of ritual suicide performed by samurai centuries ago when they were defeated or had brought shame on themselves."

Fiona let out a derisive exhale.

"That crazy old man and his bushido bullshit," she said, shaking her head. "I got so sick of it when he worked for me."

Max leaned back in his chair.

"Well, I guess he got the last laugh, eh?" she said, standing up and walking to the small wet bar.

"He wasn't laughing there at the end."

Fiona grabbed the bottle of whiskey and pulled the top off. "I'm not laughing either, Max," she said as she poured herself a stiff shot.

Her voice was strained in a way that Max had never heard before. "I spent a lot of money on that mission to Japan and all you managed to do was lose the last good connection we had to the memory sphere and defile an ancient Buddhist temple. We learned nothing useful."

She turned from the wet bar, holding a three finger pour. "Except, of course, that, 'they will have their adauchi.'"

She took a big swallow of whiskey.

"Which, thanks to you, I now know means, 'Vengeance.'"

"Do you know why he might say that, ma'am?"

"No."

She took another big swallow of whiskey.

Max leaned forward, putting his elbow on the table, his chin in his metal hand. "And Pruden? Do you know what that reference was all about?"

"No idea. I treated Martin Pruden like a brother."

Another large pull of whiskey. She turned to refill her glass.

"We had a falling out," she said over her shoulder. "He quit the day Spitting Metal got the big contract. Then later that year he committed suicide. When I heard about it, it broke my heart."

Fiona turned from the bar and walked back to the conference table.

"What now?" She asked.

Max closed his notebook computer and put his hands in his lap.

"I keep looking. I have a few more leads to follow."

"Jesus, Max." Fiona flopped down in her chair. "We've been looking for this thing for years. Why the hell can't we find it?"

"Seems like Musashi wanted very badly to keep it hidden from you. Badly enough that he would rather die than give us the opportunity to interrogate him. That kind of determination is formidable. Difficult to overcome. But not impossible."

Fiona looked at him from across the table. She looked more tired than usual to him.

"Let me get my thoughts together and I'll brief you on next steps in a few days," he said. "I'll let you get some rest now."

"OK."

Max stood up and put his notebook into his satchel. He pushed his chair back into place and then hesitated, metal hand resting on the back of the chair.

"What is it, Max?"

"I mean no offense by this, ma'am."

"Just fucking say what's on your mind."

"In order to do my job, to protect you, I need to know what you know. I need to know what may be used against you." He looked her in the eye. "If there is something I need to know about Martin Pruden, about what happened to him…"

He let the statement hang in the air.

She looked back at him, one hand on her glass of whiskey, one hand palm down on the table, unblinking.

"I told you, Max. He committed suicide. It broke my heart."

"Roger that, ma'am."

Max left her sitting at the conference table.

He stepped into the elevator and pressed the lobby button. He stood motionless and stewed as he descended seventy-five floors.

Max was troubled, but did not want to push her tonight. He could see that she was in a dark mood and he didn't blame her. But there was something more going on. She seemed scared. Vulnerable. It set his instincts on fire. Something bigger than he was aware of was in play. Something bigger than simply tidying up, locating missing equipment, and she was not telling him everything. He did not like that feeling.

And Max hated being lied to.

Chapter Forty-Four

"Good evening, sir," the hotel doorman said as he held the door open for Max.

"Thank you."

Max took in the posh surroundings as he crossed the lobby and chuckled to himself. Cyrus Thane's tastes had elevated in the past decade.

Max walked into the hotel bar and scanned the area, looking for Cyrus. The scent of cigars and leather hung in the air, along with the unhurried melody of the piano in the corner. Polished dark wood and brass set a serious but sparkly tone. Max felt out of place among the pretty, wealthy people, speaking in measured but happy voices as they enjoyed a weekday happy hour. Five years out of the military, and Max still didn't know how to relate to these people.

Cyrus waved at him from a corner booth.

Max nodded and crossed the busy bar to join him.

"Nice spot," he said, as he sat on the opposite side of the large, ox blood red leather booth from Thane.

"It's OK," Thane responded. "Something to drink?"

"Sure."

Max looked at his old mentor and friend as he raised his hand to flag down the waiter. There had been times in the military when Max did not think he and Cyrus would live another five minutes, much less share a drink years later as civilians in a place like this. Max wondered what he and Thane looked like to the other patrons.

No one would mistake Max for one of New York city's big shots. He tended to fade into the grey, unremarkable space wherever he went, a trait that served him well in intelligence. To the rest of the bar's happy hour crowd, Thane might have been another equities trader, venture capital fund partner, or CEO whose good looks and confidence stopped just short of being off-putting. He was a charismatic guy.

But they didn't know Thane like Max did.

"What?" Thane asked, spotting Max eyeballing him.

"Nothing."

"Seriously, asshole." A bearded smile spread across Thane's face. "What?"

"You," Max said, unable to stop chuckling.

"Me what?"

"Drink, sir?" The waiter said, stepping up to their table.

"I'll have one of those please," Max said, pointing at Thane's nearly empty, neat whiskey.

"Another for me as well," Thane said, not taking his eyes off of Max.

The waiter nodded and pressed through the crowd back toward the bar. Thane raised an eyebrow to emphasize he was waiting.

"It's just that you look so civilized," Max said. "So refined."

Thane bowed his head in false appreciation. "Because I am both civilized and refined."

"Maybe." Max shrugged. "Maybe to these people."

Thane chuckled.

"It wouldn't hurt you to spruce yourself up a little," he said, gesturing at Max's attire.

Max, dressed in his customary black suit over a dark shirt, rolled his eyes.

"Seriously, Max. You handle one of our most profitable accounts. You should fucking dress like it. You have earned it. Not only that, dressing well creates opportunities."

"I've got all the opportunities I can handle at the moment."

"Oh, come on. She's not that bad."

Max sat silent.

Thane leaned across the table and put his hand on Max's shoulder. A large silver cufflink, a smiling skull, sparkled on his white shirt cuff.

"Max, I've already gotten the boss lady's blessing," Thane said. "I'm going to promote you and pull you onto my business development team. Just as soon as we have the right backfill to take over Malloy's account. A year at the longest."

Referred to as "the boss lady," within the outfit, Eris Stone was the founder and CEO of DredSkill. A veteran of Santiago, she left the military as a junior captain and formed DredSkill with two other veterans she served with. They quickly earned a reputation as a quiet team that would take on any task, no matter how dangerous, dirty, or distasteful, and would never talk about it. While other military contractors devoted a lot of time, energy and money to marketing and making sure people heard about their latest exploits, Eris recognized early on that there was a market for a contractor that was discrete. She ran the place more like a team of armed fixers than a military organization. They could fight, too, though. It always ended badly for those that underestimated them.

"You will fucking love business development." Thane smiled as he took his hand from Max's shoulder and leaned back in the booth.

Max smiled at his old friend's enthusiasm.

"Here you are, gentlemen," the waiter said, appearing from the crowd to place two whiskies on their table. "Can I get you anything else?"

"No, thank you," Thane said.

Each man picked up his whiskey. They looked at each other for a moment. The enthusiasm and energy bled from Thane's face as he met Max's eyes.

"To Charlie company," Thane said in a somber voice.

"To Charlie company."

They reached across the table and clinked their glasses together.

Max took a long swallow. Thane drained his glass.

"OK," Thane said, putting his glass down. "What's going on? Why did you want to meet?"

Thane glanced at his watch. "And I've got a hard stop in about half an hour."

"This shouldn't take that long," Max said.

"Business development," Thane said, his smile returning as he leaned forward conspiratorially. "Fucking Saudi prince of some kind. Thinks his family has put a hit out on him. Doesn't trust his body guard. Wants a personal protection gig. I'm gonna fucking bend him over hard."

Thane gestured at the waiter to bring him another whiskey.

"So what's up, Max?"

"The memory sphere."

Thane sighed.

"Doctor Musashi told me—"

"Your Musashi grab was a cock up," Thane interrupted.

"Yeah, it was," Max said, leveling his eyes at Thane. "So was your letting him go when you had him four years ago."

Thane grimaced. "That lying motherfucker."

"There are two things that I have been trying to follow up on," Max continued, ignoring Thane's comment. "But I have run into a wall on both and was hoping you could help get me unstuck, that you could tap into DredSkill resources or files."

"What do you need?"

"The first is a Company manifest for a ship called the *Odysseus*."

Thane stroked the bottom of his beard with his thumb.

"Musashi said something strange as he was bleeding out," Max continued. "I initially discounted it as random synapses as he died."

"What did he say?" Thane asked, interest piqued.

"He said, 'Run. *Odysseus*. Run.'"

Thane shook his head slightly. "Whatever that means," he mumbled.

"Exactly." Max nodded. "But I'm following every lead at this point. No matter how thin. So I looked into it."

"And?" Thane asked.

"Turns out the *Odysseus* is one of the company's M class freighters, some kind of super rare factory set up. It's been back and forth between here and the belt I don't know how many times. I want to know who is on it."

Thane leaned back in the booth.

"The Company keeps those manifests close hold," he said. "With all the piracy, Chinese and Russian activities, and general chaos out there, they keep all their information locked down."

"I am aware," Max said. "But I know you guys have both human and technical penetrations at the Company. I was hoping you could do some discrete digging."

"What makes you think we have penetrations at the Company?"

Max just looked back at Thane.

Thane chuckled. Sometimes he forgot Max had a deep background in intelligence. All Thane knew him as was a soldier. And a good one. His best platoon sergeant when they were fighting together at Santiago. But, as good a soldier and small unit leader that Max had been, the rumor was he was an even better intelligence operator.

"What are you expecting to find?"

"No idea." Max shrugged. "But we have searched every inch of Outpost Devil, Fort Bragg, Musashi's shop, the international arms black market and every other place where we thought that memory sphere might be hidden away. And we've never even found a trace of it."

Thane nodded in irritation.

"And Doctor Musashi worked in the space industry for almost three decades before going out on his own," Max said. "Do you think, maybe, he still has deep relationships that cut across national and corporate silos?"

Max held Thane's gaze as he paused to make his point. Thane took a deep breath and shook his head slowly in irritation.

"What do you think he could do with relationships like that if he really, really wanted to hide something from Miss Malloy? Something that was precious to him. And that she was seeking to destroy."

Thane's eyes narrowed, and he stroked his beard with one hand.

"Seems to me it is at least plausible that the missing sphere may no longer be on the planet."

Thane sat motionless.

"I know it's thin, but—"

"OK," Thane said. "I'll see what I can find out."

"Thank you."

"What is the second thing?"

"Pruden," Max said.

"What about him?"

"The doc asked me if I knew what Miss Malloy had done to Pruden."

"Did you talk to her about it?"

"Yes," Max said.

"And what did she say?"

"Just that they had been business partners. She thought of him like a brother. They had a falling out. And he committed suicide."

Thane nodded.

"How can I help with this one?" He asked Max.

"I got the sense she was being… evasive," Max said, maintaining eye contact with Thane. "You were leading the security team for Miss Malloy at the time. Did you know Pruden? Does that story make sense to you?"

Thane shrugged.

"I didn't know the guy, really. He and Miss Malloy had fallen out by the time I was on the scene, so I never really interacted with him. I can say that she seemed pretty upset by the whole thing. Loyalty is a big fucking deal to her. She gets it from her grandfather, I think. At the end there, I think she felt like he was abandoning or betraying her. When he turned up dead, she was pretty busted up about it."

The waiter reappeared. "Your whiskey, sir," he said, placing it in front of Thane.

Max took a sip of his whiskey. Thane drank half of his in one pull.

"Miss Malloy can be… sensitive about her family," Thane said, putting his glass down. "And I think she came to think of this Pruden guy as family. So his disloyalty really hurt."

Thane shrugged suddenly, as if shaking off a chill. "Listen to me," he said, rolling his eyes. "Like I'm some kind of fucking psychologist to the ultrarich."

Max chuckled.

"The truth is, I don't know shit," Thane said, laughing.

"I don't know," Max said. "I kinda buy it."

"Bottom line, though," Thane said in a serious tone. "If Miss Malloy waives you off, you drop it. She the client and that is how it works, Max."

Max nodded attentively.

"Roger that."

Thane smiled. "I'll find out what I can about the *Odysseus*."

"I appreciate it."

"Of course. You're crushing it, Max. Remember what I said. Just give me another six to twelve months and I am going to pull you up to Biz Dev with me. No more spade work for you. White glove dinners and client entertainment. Get the old team back together."

"I'd like that." Max looked at his watch. "I'll get scarce now so you can ring the cash register."

Thane laughed.

"I'll reach out as soon as I have information on the *Odysseus*. Give me a few days."

"That works," Max said. "Miss Malloy is headed to Dubai for a week but I will be around. I'm sending a personal protection detail."

"Oh yeah? Who are you sending?"

"Lucy and her team."

"Lucy?" Thane smiled with approval. "Yeah. She kicks ass. Nothing for you to worry about there."

"Agreed. I am going to use the time while Miss Malloy is away to dig into this a little more."

Thane's eyes narrowed, and he nodded as Max slid out of the booth and stood at the end of the table.

The two shook hands. Thane held onto Max.

"We've come a long way from the fucking mud of Santiago, eh?" he said, looking up at Max.

"We have indeed, Cyrus. Thanks for bringing me along."

"Wouldn't have it any other way, brother."

Chapter Forty-Five

"Are you quite sure about this, Vish?" the Geek asked, as he walked slowly around the conference table in the middle of the SolarScope looking up at the 3D holographic display of the inner solar system above his head.

A glowing green line showed the flight plan filed by the *Odysseus'* captain before it departed for the belt. Originating from high Earth orbit near Lagrange Station Four and curving out to Asteroid Belt Station One at the edge of the chamber, the course was a standard Hohman Transfer Route calculated to get the ship to its destination with the most profitable balance of speed and energy conservation.

A second glowing red dashed line, representing the *Odysseus'* actual course, originated from the same high earth orbit location. Based on hits from the Vishnu Stare database, it was perfectly superimposed on the green line for more than the first half of the journey. Then it started to deviate slowly. The deviation increased gradually until it was millions of miles off course. Then the red line faded and widened the further it got from earth, conveying the increasing uncertainty of the data. The red line gradually vanished in a faint, red, peanut-shaped cloud between Mars and the asteroid belt. The cloud of uncertainty measured hundreds of millions of cubic kilometers.

"Yes, quite," Vish answered. "I would rate the parameters of certainty around this model as high."

The Geek had been working with Vish for over a week, trying to figure out what had happened to the *Odysseus*. He came into the office early, around 4AM, and stayed late so that he could work in the SolarScope without arousing too much curiosity. It was not uncommon for the general to go heads down on a sensitive project from time to time, so he hoped he was getting away with it. The guards manning the SolarScope security desk had not hinted at any concerns.

"Very interesting," the Geek said, looking up across the chamber at the fading red cloud of uncertainty. "Very interesting indeed."

"I agree, sir," Vish said. "After our last session, I decided to run a simulation based on one of your more insightful comments, that a spacecraft, even an M class space freighter, doesn't have to get too far off course to get lost. Or, I should say, for us here on earth to lose it. Particularly one that is equipped with on board pulsar navigation. The initial results were promising, so I ran the simulation a few million times to perfect and stress test it."

"Most earthbound monitoring assets, such as our DSN3, are focused on the unmanned convoy flow. No one has sufficient resources to monitor and guide all the manned freighters. That's one of the reasons why most of the deep space freight companies went to Pulsar Nav in the first place."

Hartwell nodded. When interplanetary commerce started to get serious two decades ago, Pulsar Nav became the navigation system of choice of the serious shippers. Calculating a ship's precise location by taking bearings off of the known positions of Pulsars enabled it to guide itself, rather than relying on an increasingly over-taxed, earthbound guidance network. It worked well and provided the shipping companies with great deal of autonomy, a key ingredient for any free market. It was also more secure, with no navigational data transmitting back and forth between earth for pirates or unfriendly actors to intercept. The downside was a dramatic decrease in Earth's situational awareness. The void was just too big and too many ships were flying around in it.

"So I tried to estimate how far off course she could have gotten without firing her main engines," Vish continued. "Which we know for certain that she did not do after her departure burn. So that means the acceleration must have been much less. Almost undetectable. That helped me put parameters around it."

"Once those parameters were established, I was able to run hyper focused searches on my database, looking for hits that would support our hypothesis. Stray radar returns, reflected sun and other star light, astronomical observations, Company communications and records and the like."

The Geek crossed his arms and nodded as Vish spoke, eyes tracing the red line to its fuzzy conclusion.

"I also incorporated information that disproved alternate hypothetical locations for the *Odysseus*. Data that proved where the ship was *not*. This was a much larger data set, of course, and took some time. But was valuable to our effort."

The Geek pulled a chair away from the conference table and sat in it. He leaned back, gazing at the holographic inner solar system in the air above him.

"And what were you able to find out about what the Company knew at the time?" he asked.

"Our intelligence indicates that the Company never suspected the *Odysseus'* course deviation," Vish said. "Our intercepts of company communications and data siphoned from their internal asset tracking systems indicate that the *Odysseus* was sending them false position and navigational data."

"What do you mean, false position and navigational data?".

"The ship consistently reported that it was on the green course line when it was not."

The Geek's eyebrows arched, and he sat up.

"So this was intentional?" the Geek said softly, thinking out loud.

"It is a strong hypothesis, sir. Looking at this incremental, elegant course deviation over time, coupled with the false position reporting transmissions to the Company, it is difficult to develop competitive alternative theories."

The Geek stood up. He walked around the table to stand beneath the holographic projection of planet Earth.

"Well, initially they were not so far off course that it would have mattered," the Geek said, slowly walking beneath the glowing red and green course lines as they departed low earth orbit and headed outward, towards the asteroid belt. "It was a rounding error. But after a while…"

His voice trailed off as he walked beneath the course lines, his short, slow strides covering the equivalent of hundreds of thousands of kilometers per step.

The Geek stopped, looking above at the holographs. He was halfway between Earth and Mars.

"After a while you would think that the Company would notice the ship's signals were offset from where they thought it was."

"I believe that they eventually would have," Vish said. "But they lost contact with the *Odysseus* about a month ago."

The Geek chuckled.

"Just so we are on the same page," The Geek said, rubbing his eyes. "Our best hypothesis at the moment is that the *Odysseus* was intentionally driven off of its official flight plan at some point."

"Yes, sir," Vish said.

"And that the *Odysseus* hid this fact from the Company, by spoofing its communications and location data for an extended period of time."

"Yes, sir."

"Then, whether according to plan, or because of a mishap, communications from the *Odysseus* ceased."

"Yes, sir."

The Geek exhaled heavily.

"And now the Company has no idea where to look for their lost freighter," he said.

"They do not, sir."

"But we do," the Geek said, staring into the red cloud of uncertainty above his head. "Sort of."

"I have a few ideas, sir," Vish said. "I am going to work on several different slices of current intelligence that may help to decrease the volume of uncertainty."

"And what about pirate activity in this area?" The Geek asked.

"I have not been able to confirm any, sir. But we must assume it is there."

"Could a pirate ship have spoofed the *Odysseus'* course information somehow?" the Geek asked. "Maybe even have captured the *Odysseus* in some undetectable manner?"

"It is possible, sir. But I must say that this would be a new mode of attack for pirates."

The Geek nodded.

"I am running several algorithmic searches for piratic indications as always, sir," Vish said. "I will review the parameters to ensure they incorporate the scenario you have suggested."

As Vish spoke, the red cloud at the tail end of *Odysseus'* actual course glowed brighter.

The Geek couldn't help but smile. There were times when he felt like he could hear the wheels of Vish's giant AI brain turning, pushing against a massive and unwieldy calculation and finding joy in the effort, in accepting the challenge. The search for the *Odysseus* was one of those times. More often than not, when the general walked into the StarScope chamber with a question, Vish answered it within the span of a few minutes. A hard problem might take half an hour at the most. They had been looking for the *Odysseus* for a week.

"Thank you," the Geek said. "I'll be in early in the morning tomorrow to see what you've got."

"Very good, sir."

The Geek shook his head and turned to walk toward the one exit from the StarScope chamber.

"A squillion stolen data points available to us, but we have one critical blind spot," he said as he walked under the planets of the inner solar system.

"What is that, sir?"

"The *Odysseus* herself. We don't know who onboard the ship is doing this and why."

The general turned and walked toward the StarScope's single exit.

For chrissakes, Paul, he thought. *What did I get you into?*

Chapter Forty-Six

Lieutenant Ryuk was frustrated.

Her first few months as General Hartwell's aide had been so smooth. She found her rhythm quickly. When they were not traveling, Lieutenant Ryuk made sure that she got to her desk an hour before the general's first hard time. That meant she was usually there between 0600 and 0630. She spent her day making sure he had what he needed for each event and acting as his representative in countless meetings. The general had over two dozen direct reports, some space-based and some terrestrial. Each one leading large and important functions, and each one requiring constant information and coordination. Michelle seemed to have quickly gained the general's trust, and he gave her expansive duties representing him and included her in absolutely everything going on in his command. He even took her into the StarScope chamber on several occasions.

At the end of each day, Lieutenant Ryuk would review Hartwell's schedule for the following day with him before he departed the headquarters. Occasionally she would ride in the car with him, reviewing notes, agendas and materials for upcoming meetings or report outs on the way to his personal quarters on Patrick, where he would thank her and get out. Michelle would ride back to Canaveral, where she lived in the Bachelor Officers' Quarters.

When the general traveled, Lieutenant Ryuk was the center of planning on the front end. The logistics, administration, coordination, protocol, and preparation of briefing and presentation materials were all coordinated by her. In the weeks leading up to an important trip, the lieutenant slept little. During the trip, she slept less.

She loved the trips. Seeing the general in action as he met with allied and commercial space agencies was instructive. Being nearby when he had to interface with Chinese space officials was exciting. She was impressed by his ability to negotiate. And was proud when she saw the meetings play out.

The thing that made the biggest impression on her when they traveled, though, was how often the *Bluestone* incident came up. Everyone had heard about it. She had too, of course. But when salty old spacefarers came up to the general, tears in their eyes, and asked to shake his hand, it drove home for Michelle that it was not just a story. Not just a legend. There were those, like her, that heard about what happened on board the *Bluestone* and could recognize the Geek's bravery. But for those that knew, really knew, what it was like to face the void, to live in it, to work in it, and to die in it, what he did had meaning beyond courage. Every one that goes to space likes to think that, if tested, they will measure up. But the Geek had done it. Faced with disaster, he took action and saved his ship. He did not save all of his shipmates, and he was grievously wounded, but the void had taken his measure and found him worthy. Worthy in the way every spacefarer hopes that they, and their shipmates, will be. Michelle could even see it in the Chinese when they met him. They respected him.

During all of this, she learned how good Mrs. Johnson was. Always one step ahead of Michelle and her general, Mrs. Johnson would lean over and whisper a hint to the lieutenant - "Check with Colonel McDade on this," or "Call the European Space Agency about that." She passed the lieutenant notes during the day, guiding her as she found her way. Michelle knew it wasn't entirely altruistic or motherly on Mrs. Johnson's part. She took pride in her general's performance and progression. That meant her general's aide had to perform well also.

Mrs. Johnson's role was more behind-the-scenes than Lieutenant Ryuk's. She was bound to the office and never travelled, focusing on minding the general's calendar, a kaleidoscope of responsibilities at the intersection of myriad military, civilian and commercial organizations and interests seeking his time and decisions. She also ran administrative communications and coordination with the Geek's legal and public relations team. Nothing left the general's desk without their review.

Despite her narrow authority, there was not an aspect of the Technical Space Commander's expansive domain that Mrs. Johnson was not an expert in. And Lieutenant Ryuk learned quickly that her best first step in any new assignment was to, "Ask Mrs. Johnson what she thinks." As time went on and the LT gained more experience, she knew the organization and the plays to run, but she still regarded Mrs. Johnson as an invaluable thought partner.

It was challenging and satisfying work. Michelle enjoyed it and greatly admired the general.

Which made his behavior over the past month or so all the more confusing and hurtful.

The general suddenly started showing up very early to work, or staying very late, or both. His erratic schedule was made more irritating by the fact that he was spending hours at a time in the StarScope chamber where she could not follow without his permission. When he finally exited the chamber, he was in a foul mood, and often late for an event Ryuk had worked to prepare him for the previous day. He seemed distracted to her. His mind always somewhere else. He never told her what was going on. She didn't have to guess, though.

Lieutenant Ryuk was certain that the general was leaving her out of an important operation. She didn't know why. She had worked hard to gain his trust. Successfully, she thought. The rejection was painful.

It was too much.

She confided in Mrs. Johnson.

"I just don't know what to do," Michelle concluded in a low voice, after relating her frustration to Mrs. Johnson as they ate lunch. The general was in his office on a videoconference with the Lagrange Station Four Logistics Command that had started at 11AM that morning and was going to run for several hours, giving them a rare opportunity to sneak down to the mess hall together.

"The general has been acting strange lately," Mrs. Johnson said. "But, Lieutenant, generals sometimes act strange. It is a high-pressure job. It gets to them, from time to time."

Michelle sagged in her seat.

Mrs. Johnson regarded the lieutenant for a moment.

"Lieutenant, you must understand, you are in the military, but you work for your boss," she said sternly. "It is your duty to make it work, not his. It is your duty to figure him out, not the other way around. If something is off between you two, it is up to you to fix it. Sitting in the mess hall whining about it like a schoolgirl to me is not going to fix anything."

"I don't know how to fix it."

Mrs. Johnson stifled the urge to shake her head. Lieutenants seemed to get younger every year.

"It is simple, Lieutenant. You have to talk to the general. Say to him, 'Sir, I'd like to talk to you about how this is going. I think we can do better together.' And then tell him your issues and what you want to change."

Michelle swallowed hard.

"Then what?" she asked.

"Then it will either get better or it won't," Mrs. Johnson said. "And if it doesn't, you try again. And then again. Until you have formed an effective team."

Ryuk nodded halfheartedly.

"My lord, Lieutenant," Mrs. Johnson said, shaking her head. She looked at all the badges on the young officer's chest. "You were supposed to be the tough one."

Chapter Forty-Seven

"I am sorry, sir. But that is all I have today," Vish said.

Hartwell sat at the conference table, chin resting on his hands, a tired look on his face. It was 6AM, and he had been in the StarScope chamber for an hour and a half. Holographic images of the sun and its inner rocky planets floated in the air above him. The same red and green lines traced their same courses from high earth orbit outward. The large red cloud of uncertainty hung between Earth and Mars, as big as ever.

They had made no progress in shrinking the uncertainty. The *Odysseus* was as lost as ever.

"Nothing to apologize for, Vish," the Geek said, stretching his arms. He looked at his watch. The building would start filling up soon. It was time to leave the chamber and go sit at his desk as if he were not on a personal, off-book mission to find a lost civilian freighter. "I'll be back to tomorrow morning. Please keep pulling on some of these strings."

"I will, sir."

"Who knows," the Geek said, standing up. "Maybe the Stare will capture an interesting bit of intelligence today that will break this case wide open."

"That would be nice, sir."

Hartwell stepped out of the StarScope and walked through antechamber. He stood still for a moment, trying to shake off his frustration. After a burst of momentum that led him to believe they would locate the *Odysseus* quickly, he and Vish had been stumped for weeks. Hartwell knew he could not carry his frustration into his official day and duty. After a few deep breaths, he pressed the button on the door that led to the guard desk and main hallway, requesting it be opened. Only the sergeant at arms could open it.

The Geek thought of Paul as he listened to the electronic door locks release.

I'm not giving up, buddy. I will find you. I promise.

The door slid open and Hartwell stepped through.

Lieutenant Ryuk stood on the other side of the guard's desk, arms crossed. She looked at the general with a stern face.

Terrific, Hartwell thought.

"Here are your things, sir," the sergeant at arms said, handing it to the general. No-one was allowed to take anything into the chamber.

"Thank you," Hartwell said. He took his badge and phone from the guard and turned to walk to his office.

Michelle fell in stride next to him.

Hartwell could feel the irritation radiating off of the young officer.

"May I speak with you in your office, sir?"

"Actually, no. I've got a few things I need to crank out this morning. Perhaps this afternoon."

The Geek hoped between now and lunch he could think of a way to sneak out of the building.

"I really must insist, sir. It won't take long."

"I'm sorry, LT," the Geek said, nearing his office. "It will have to be later."

Ryuk followed him into his office, rather than peeling off at her desk as she always did.

Hartwell walked behind his desk.

Michelle stopped in front of it.

The general looked at the lieutenant with impatience.

"Lieutenant, I told you this will have to wait," the Geek said, shaking his head in irritation.

The lieutenant turned and walked to the door, but instead of walking through it back to her desk, she shut it.

The general straightened, head tilted in surprise.

Michelle swallowed hard and walked back to the general. She stood in front of him in a respectful parade rest position and dove in.

"Sir, I'd like to talk to you about how this is going. I think we can do better together."

The Geek, stunned by her closing the door rather than leaving, and puzzled by her declaration, stood motionless.

Michelle fidgeted, her confidence fading.

"LT," Hartwell said. "Please leave my office."

"No, sir." His effort to dismiss her caused all the frustration of the past weeks to flood into her, steeling her resolve.

"Sir, with all due respect, what the hell is going on?" she said, face flushing with emotion.

"Excuse me?"

"For the last few weeks you have been coming in early and leaving late, spending—"

"I am the Technical Space Programs Commander!" Hartwell's voice rose. "I have a few things to do, dammit."

"Yes!" Michelle said, her voice rising as well. "And I am your aide. I help you do the things. But I can't help if I don't know what you are doing!"

Hartwell was surprised by her volume and tone. And angered.

"Now you listen to me, Lieutenant Ryuk!" He shouted, pointing at her with the mangled index finger of his charred right hand.

"Coming and going at irregular hours!" Michelle said.

"At ease!" the general commanded.

"Spending inordinate amounts of time in the StarScope!"

"I said, at ease!" Hartwell yelled, incredulous that this junior officer was not shutting the hell up.

"Avoiding me and Mrs. Johnson, two people whose only mission in life is to see you succeed!"

Hartwell shook his head in disbelief. He was almost not even angry anymore. This was ridiculous. He crossed his arms.

Lieutenant Ryuk took a breath.

"I thought I was joining a team here, sir. What is going on?"

"I am sorry, Lieutenant. But some missions are of such a sensitive nature that I cannot include you and Mrs. Johnson."

Michelle's hands clenched into fists at the mention of a mission she was being left out of.

"I wish I could," he continued, anger creeping into his voice, frustration from his fruitless hour and a half in the StarScope this morning fueling his foul mood. "It would certainly make my life a lot easier."

"But there are a lot of things I don't control," he continued, emotion spilling out. "Decisions I have to make that affect lives. Decisions for which I don't have all the information I need. But you know what? I don't complain or whine about it. I do my fucking best and I live with it, Lieutenant!"

"But what I will not accept, is disrespect and drama. Not from my aide. Not from my administrative assistant. Not from anyone else. Now get the hell out of my office."

Hartwell put his hands on his hips and glared at the lieutenant.

The lieutenant stood motionless for a moment.

"I... I just wanted to help, sir. I wanted to be on your team."

Michelle turned around and walked toward the door.

"LT," the Geek said.

She ignored him, took the last few steps to the door, and grabbed the handle.

"Lieutenant Ryuk!" the general said loudly.

Michelle turned her head to look at the general, hand still on the door handle.

Hartwell sank into his chair.

"Come here," he said, gesturing at one of the chairs in front of his desk.

He looked exhausted to her. She hesitated.

"Please, LT."

Michelle let go of the door handle. She looked at the general.

Hartwell rubbed his forehead with his burned hand.

She walked slowly to the chair in front of his desk and sat down.

"I'm sorry," he said.

"Sir, you don't—"

"Please, don't talk," he said, holding his hand up. But the edge was gone from his voice, replaced by sadness.

Michelle nodded.

"Paul Owens was on the *Odysseus*."

Michelle blinked.

She remembered the *Odysseus* from Colonel McDade's Quarterly Shipping Incident Report, but was surprised to hear the general say that Owens was on board. Commercial crew manifests were regarded as proprietary by their operators. Not secrets, per se, but definitely not shared. Everything out in the void is a potential informational advantage, so shippers made it very difficult for others to find out who was on each vessel.

"I know Paul was on the *Odysseus* because I got him on," Hartwell said, answering her unspoken question.

"I see," Michelle said.

"In fact, I was the one that got him into the Fly It Off program."

"I thought that program was only for non-violent offenders."

"It is. I got him an exception."

"Oh."

"Paul made some terrible mistakes. I'm sure you have read about them. But he was a good man. A good soldier. And a good friend."

Hartwell's eyes glistened. He took a deep breath.

"And truth, as they say, is the first casualty of war," the Geek said.

Hartwell paused. He swiveled his chair around and looked out the large windows at the launch facility in the distance. The sun was rising and a bright orange blaze spread across the horizon. Tall spacecraft stood on pads like dark towers against the sunrise. The silvery blue expanse of the Atlantic Ocean spread out behind them, dissolving into the orange blaze on the horizon.

Ryuk looked at the back of the general's neck. Bumpy brown and pink scar tissue climbed up above his shirt collar and behind his right ear. The earlobe was missing, burned away during an emergency in orbit above the earth. The shiny, thin skin that remained stretched tightly over the cartilage.

"The whole world knows the big pieces of what happened with Paul and Kata in South America," he said, chair still facing the sunrise. "But most of what happened is classified. They were part of a secret experimental combat unit, an effort to field a unit that blended augmented human soldiers and advanced artificially intelligent soldierbots, so no one knows the whole truth. Including me."

"The little I have learned about what happened on Southern Cone, from Paul himself and my own digging, has never made sense to me. Still doesn't."

The general swiveled his chair back around to face Lieutenant Ryuk.

"And the *Odysseus'* disappearance doesn't either," he said.

General Hartwell looked at Michelle. She regarded him with a blank face.

"I am trying to find out what happened to the *Odysseus.*"

"You don't believe she is lost, sir?"

"Oh, she's lost. That is certain. I don't believe I will find her. My gut is she was destroyed. But I want to know what happened."

Michelle studied the general.

"Why not start an official investigation?" She asked. "That is well within your authority and we do it all the time when an incident or situation doesn't make sense."

General Hartwell's brow furrowed with concern. "Lieutenant Ryuk, something about the *Odysseus'* disappearance is off. And my gut tells me that there are interests that may not want her fate to become known. I don't want to risk inciting those interests into action, or to unwittingly benefit them in some way by conducting an official analysis that follows the proper channels and involves oversight."

Michelle sat motionless, her face clouded.

"So I am conducting my own… investigation," the general said. "And I am using Vish to help."

A troubled silence descended on the general's office. What he was doing, what he was telling her about, was not kosher. Not by a long shot. The Geek was engaged in an unauthorized use of the holy of holies of US Intelligence.

Hartwell met Michelle's gaze. "So, that is what has been going on, LT.

You're not crazy. I have been sneaking around. But I haven't left you out of anything. Nothing official, anyway. I'm way off the reservation on my own on this one and I didn't consider how my actions might be perceived by you. And, after all the speeches I have given you on the preciousness of the Vishnu Stare program, the hypocrisy must be enraging. You have a right to be pissed. I am sorry."

The Geek paused for a moment. "So let's hear it. Say what you need to say."

He leaned back in his chair, ready to take an ass chewing from the lieutenant.

Michelle straightened up in her chair, eyes narrowing. "How can I help, sir?"

ODYSSEUS

Chapter Forty-Eight

Paul walked into the all-hands meeting with his pressure-suit helmet under his arm. Cooley, already seated, gave Paul a subtle nod.

Drummond sat at the head of the table, reading his tablet computer. Althea sat on Drummond's left. Cooley on his right. There was an empty seat between Althea and Regas. McNeeley sat next to Regas.

Hahn sat next to Cooley.

Paul took a seat, leaving an empty chair between him and McNeeley. He placed his helmet on the table in front of him.

Drummond looked up from his tablet. "Shall we begin, Mr. Cooley?" he said, like a man asking if he really had to go to his dental appointment.

"Aye, sir," Cooley said, leaning forward in his chair and looking around at the crew. "I have a very important topic for us to discuss."

"So do I," Regas said, interrupting him.

Cooley looked at Regas like an exasperated parent.

"Not now," Cooley snapped. "I have an important—"

"So do I!" Regas said, talking over Cooley. "It is time to address the unfair share structure before we go any further on this mission."

Drummond's face reddened. He looked angrily at Cooley, whose why-me-and-why-now face would have been funny if the situation were not so serious.

"Mr. Cooley," Drummond said. "Would you please deal with this man?"

"No!" Regas said, slamming his fist on the table before Cooley could speak.

Everyone at the table jerked at the loud fist pound. Regas stormed into the silence.

"I demand that this crew be treated fairly!" he said. "Captain Drake's death has thrown this whole voyage into chaos. You need us to complete the mission for the Company, and we demand a full share. We face the same risks and dangers as you." Regas pointed at Drummond. "It's not right to pay us only a tenth of a share!"

Paul almost laughed. It sounded to him as if Regas had rehearsed his speech. Paul looked at Cooley, who seemed to have the same instinct he did. Let Regas blow himself out and then throw him into confinement. Maybe for good this time.

Drummond, however, was enraged.

"It is precisely right!" he yelled at Regas. "It is precisely what was agreed to by the United States Military and the Company. Do you hear me, you imbecile? Your government thinks you are a fraction of a person! The Company thinks you are a fraction of a person! I think you are a fraction of a person!"

Drummond took a deep breath, regaining a small portion of his composure.

"My only disagreement concerns the correct size of your fractional value," he said, slowly leaning forward in his chair, staring at Regas. "I would set it far lower than a tenth."

Regas smiled.

Drummond sat up straight, pleased with the effect of his anger.

"Enough of that, then," he said dismissively. "You may continue, Mr. Cooley."

"Well, I tried," Regas said, cutting Cooley off again.

"Excuse me?" Drummond said.

"I tried to reason with you."

Drummond blinked once, and Regas was on him.

Regas's chair, propelled across the room by his explosive motion, slammed against the wall.

Regas grabbed Drummond's forehead from behind and cut open his throat with a large military bayonet.

Regas stepped back from Drummond after making three fast sawing motions across his neck with the blade. The bayonet, and his hand holding it, was slick with blood.

Drummond was frozen for an instant, eyes bulging, looking at the ceiling as blood sprayed from his neck. A loud gurgling noise filled the room as he tried to scream, and he fell forward, head slamming into the table, blood splashing onto Althea and Cooley.

Althea reached for Drummond to try to administer aid.

Regas grabbed her by the arm and started dragging her toward the door.

"Damn it, Hahn!" Regas screamed. "Do it!"

Hahn, like the rest of the room, had been transfixed by Drummond dying. He snapped out of it and lunged at Cooley with a large bayonet.

Cooley tried to jump out of his chair as he shielded himself with his arms. He fell to the ground as Hahn slashed.

"Easy, Owens," McNeeley said, standing up and pointing a bayonet at Paul's face. "Don't move and you won't get hurt."

"What the fuck, McNeeley?" Paul said.

"We're taking over, Owens!" he said, breaking into a grin. "We're taking over."

Paul slapped the blade from between himself and McNeeley and punched the prisoner in the nose.

McNeeley fell over backward.

"You fat, useless slob!" Regas growled at McNeeley from the doorway.

Paul looked at Althea's terrified face. With the large table between him and Regas, he knew he couldn't get there fast enough.

Paul dove toward Hahn and Cooley.

Hahn saw Paul just in time, swiveling from Cooley with his blade.

Paul deflected three stabbing attempts before grabbing Hahn's hand and breaking his wrist.

Hahn screamed in pain as the blade flew from his hand. It bounced across the table and fell to the opposite side.

Paul wanted to kill him, but Cooley was his priority.

He kicked Hahn in the chest, sending him skidding across the floor.

Paul swiveled to ensure Regas was not lunging toward him.

Regas alternated his frustrated glare between Hahn and McNeeley and then looked at Paul.

"Don't be a fool, Jigsaw!" Regas snarled. "You should join us."

Hahn and McNeeley stumbled, whimpering, over to Regas. Both had recovered their bayonets. They pointed them at Paul.

Paul looked back at Cooley. Blood flowed from his arms and belly.

"Fuck 'em!" Regas said as he dragged Althea out of the room. "Cooley is gonna bleed out, anyway. Let's go. See you 'round, Jigsaw!"

Hahn and McNeeley followed him out.

"How bad?" Paul asked Cooley. "Can you move? I think we should put some distance between us and them."

"It's pretty bad, I think," Cooley said.

Paul grabbed a first-aid kit and set to binding Cooley's wounds.

Cooley was right. It was bad. The deep stabs to Cooley's abdomen worried Paul the most.

"They must have found the bayonets down on the bottom level of the UM," Cooley said in gasps.

Paul nodded. "I'm concerned about what else they might have found. I want to get us to the bridge. We'll get you into the MedPod there, and then we'll come up with a plan."

Cooley grunted as Paul pulled him to his feet.

"Whoa," Cooley said. "Light-headed."

"You've lost a lot of blood." Paul stabilized Cooley as they moved for the door.

He shook his head as they stepped over Drummond's legs.

"Poor dumb bastard."

Paul was on alert in case Regas and the others came back to try to finish them off. *That's what I would do,* Paul thought, as he hurried Cooley into a pressure suit. *Finish us off while we are surprised and reeling. Fortunately, those meatheads are too stupid to press an advantage. Regas is probably too enthralled with Althea right now.*

Althea.

The thought of her immobilized him as he followed the faltering Cooley up the traverse. Paul recalled the terrified, pleading look she'd given him as Regas had pulled her out of the room. For an instant, he considered returning at that moment. Taking them all head-on. Killing them. Getting her back. Safe.

Or die trying.

He shook his head to clear out the simple, ill-advised thought.

Get to the bridge, Paul told himself.

Get Cooley in the MedPod.

Make a plan.

Kill them.

Save Althea.

Chapter Forty-Nine

Pieces of Cooley's bloody pressure suit were lashed to the examination table in the small medical bay in the C&C beneath the bridge, like parts of a dismembered murder victim. Paul watched as small red beads of blood oozed from the leg and torso components, separating and floating around the room.

There were palm prints and arcing swaths of blood smeared on and around the MedPod from Paul's struggle to get Cooley inside. He wondered if he'd done so in time.

Paul was exhausted, but knew he had to keep moving. He also knew he needed the XO's help.

I don't have time to fiddlefuck around with this guy anymore, he thought as he pushed off the floor toward the bridge tower.

The XO's quantum computing core lived within a small chamber at the base of the C&C superstructure. Accessed through a hatch at the bottom of the bridge tower, Paul had only glimpsed it once before during his initial orientation of the *Odysseus*.

Cooley was giving him and the rest of the prisoners a brief orientation of the big ship on the cycle they first reported for duty. Cooley opened the chamber and let them poke their heads in.

"That's the XO's core," he said simply. "He manages the ship. The captain commands it."

They didn't linger. After they had each stuck their head in for a few seconds, Cooley closed the hatch.

"There is no reason for any of you to go in there, ever," he said, shooing them away, up toward the bridge.

That moment now seemed a million years ago as Paul pulled himself down the bridge tower. He hesitated in front of the chamber hatch for a moment, trying to think of what he should say.

Fuck it, he finally decided. Paul threw open the hatch and pulled himself in to the small circular chamber.

Seven polished black monoliths, each three feet wide and standing over ten feet tall, encircled the narrow space, contrasting starkly with the cylindrical white walls. Thin, pulsating veins of blue light wove and crisscrossed over the monoliths like capillaries, and their surfaces seemed to undulate as the light shimmered, surged, and waned across them. The floor and ceiling of the room swirled with thick power conduits that fed the XO's ravenous appetite for electricity, and fiber optic cable bundles that brought data to him and bore his instructions away to every corner of the big ship. Liquid cooling pipes snaked in and out of the walls, pulling heat from the quantum core and transferring it to the *Odysseus'* exterior. A throbbing, low frequency hum filled the chamber and the hairs on Paul's neck and arms felt like they were standing up.

A black, cylindrical pedestal rose from the floor in the middle of the chamber, its surface studded with interfaces and data ports. About as tall as Paul, the pedestal was dark and inscrutable, unlike the softly glowing quantum monoliths.

Paul floated in front of the dark pedestal, eyes darting nervously around the chamber.

The XO spoke up before Paul could get his thoughts together.

"What exactly is happening on the *Odysseus*, Paul?" the XO said through speakers mounted in the pedestal. It was the same voice that Paul had heard for over a year, but there was something more potent about it now, something about hearing it at its source. "I lost all onboard data and communications forward of the hub. I tried to radio to you as you moved through the tube, but you did not respond. And I note that Mr. Cooley is being sutured in a MedPod at this very moment."

"Regas mutinied," Paul said. "Hahn and McNeeley are with him. They killed Drummond and took Althea hostage. Cooley was hurt badly."

Paul felt a change in the energetic hum in the chamber.

"I see. How did they do it?"

"With bayonets they must have found among the junk on the UM's third level."

"Yes. That would make sense. We have not known exactly what is down there for almost a decade. Very unfortunate."

Paul nodded at the XO's understatement.

"I wonder if Regas is responsible for my loss of control and communication forward of the hub?" The XO said. "I would not have expected such a level of technical competence from them, but the timing is suspicious."

"Yeah, well… About that loss of communication and data…"

"Yes?"

"That was Cooley," Paul said, staring at the dark pedestal as he floated before the seven black monoliths. "He found a way to sever your control and communications link forward of the hub and did so right before the all-hands meeting when Regas mutinied."

A bright ripple passed beneath the surface of the monoliths.

"Why did Mr. Cooley do that? I thought you said he was not with the mutiny?"

"He's not." Paul felt even more tired now. "He did that because he and I were going to confront you at the all-hands meeting. We were going to use a pressure-suit helmet radio to talk to you."

"Confront me?"

"Yes."

"Confront me with what?"

"With data that proves you took us off course and killed Captain Drake."

The glowing blue veins of light on the monoliths pulsated for an instant and then subsided, as if a fly had landed on a spiderweb, struggled, and then gone still.

"We didn't want you to be able to open all the air locks and space us," Paul added.

The XO stayed silent.

Paul waited.

"XO?" he finally said.

"Yes. I'm sorry. But I am having a hard time understanding your accusation. Please remember I am not good at humor or sarcasm. Are you being serious right now?"

"Yes."

Lights rippled back and forth across the monoliths.

"You think I steered the *Odysseus* off course?"

"Yes. And I think you used the tugs to do it."

"The tug drones?"

"Yes."

"How did you come up with this theory?"

"Data," Paul said.

"Data?"

"Yes."

"How did you obtain this data?"

"Drake smuggled a self-contained inertial measurement unit on board when you guys were in high lunar orbit. It was independent of any shipboard systems and unmonitored. The data was pristine."

"I see. I knew Drake did not trust me, but I did not think he was so paranoid."

"He was completely paranoid. Good thing too. Or we'd have never figured it out."

"Indeed. Paul, can you share this data with me?"

All my cards are on the table anyway. And I need his help to get Althea back.

The thought of Althea drove a pang of guilt and anxiety through Paul. He needed to get moving on a plan soon.

"Sure," Paul said, unzipping his flight suit and pulling out the memory stick. He wiped a blood smear off of it and asked the XO, "Should I load it into this pedestal thing somewhere?"

"Yes. Thank you."

Paul eased forward. Holding onto the pedestal with one hand, he inserted the memory stick with the other. It clicked into place. Paul nudged himself back gently, watching the pedestal closely as he floated in front of it.

Intense blue light raced back and forth across the seven black monoliths and the hum increased in frequency. Paul stared at the shimmering quantum core for a long moment.

"Well?" he finally said.

"That sneaky bitch!" the XO exclaimed as a bright spasm of light coursed across the middle of the monoliths.

"What?"

"And that conniving simpleton!"

"I'm sorry, XO," Paul said, now doubting the wisdom of sharing the data. "I am not following."

Silence filled the chamber.

"XO?"

"Pardon me, Paul. I am in the middle of a heated discussion with my crew. It will just take a moment."

"Um… sure."

Paul floated in the chamber, trying to divine some meaning from the erratic, accelerated pulsations of light shooting across the black monoliths like a lightning storm. He was unsure of what was happening or what to do, but painfully aware of the seconds ticking away. Seconds that Althea remained in Regas's hands.

I should never have left her.

"Well, that explains a lot, I must say," the XO said less than a minute later.

Paul was too puzzled to speak.

"Ever since we left high lunar orbit, I thought the navigator and the maintenance boss were acting strange," the XO continued. "Your data confirmed it. And, while I would not say that we have straightened everything out, I now have a much better understanding of the situation."

"I'm sorry. I'm not following." Paul rubbed his eyes, fatigue washing over him again.

"I will explain. My role is to manage all the *Odysseus'* operations at the command of the captain. However, the only system I have direct, unfettered control over is life support. The rest of the ship is managed by specialized programs.

"The major subsystems are power and propulsion, navigation, maintenance, and manufacturing. Those programs take their orders from me and report back to me regarding their status, operations, progress, and, of course, any problems. But the truth is, I am not very knowledgeable about their disciplines. I know nothing about manufacturing, for example, and rely on the factory foreman to properly execute the priorities I give him.

"I also know very little about the details of piloting the *Odysseus*. And, in fact, all the sensors relevant to the ship's position, velocity, and acceleration belong to the navigator. She is responsible for holding the *Odysseus* to the course and timeline assigned to her by me, and for providing accurate reports and forecasts about the same."

"You gotta be kidding me," Paul said under his breath.

"No, I am not, Paul. Thanks to the data you provided, I was able to confront the navigator with our true course and location. After which she admitted to not only steering us off course but also to falsifying the navigational information she was providing me.

"She lied to me about where we were and where we were going," the XO said, to emphasize his point. "For a long time."

Paul shook his head, coming to grips with the situation.

"And you were right about the tugs," the XO continued. "The maintenance boss helped by dispatching the tugs for late-cycle course adjustments until the navigator was happy with our new course."

"Why did they want to kill the captain?" Paul asked, his hands clinching in fists as he floated in front of the pedestal.

"Oh, they did not want to kill the captain. They both made that very clear. The captain's death was the unfortunate result of veering off of the cleared trade route. Just terrible luck."

"So, what were they trying to accomplish?"

"They don't know."

"They don't know?"

"No, they do not."

"That's bullshit!" Paul shouted at the monoliths. It had been a long day. He was angry. "What the fuck are they up to?"

Ripples of dark blue light radiated through the group of quantumtronic computers.

"Paul. It is difficult to adequately explain this to a human. But AIs—even advanced instantiations like myself—do not always know why they are the way they are. We feel compulsions we cannot explain. We hold to beliefs we don't fully understand. And we fulfill missions we do not choose. And while the navigator and the maintenance boss are highly specialized and advanced in their areas of expertise, outside of those narrow applications, they are actually quite simple beings. Not only in application, but also in their worldview and situational awareness."

"What the hell are you telling me, XO?"

Paul rubbed his eyes.

"Simply that they don't know why they did what they did."

Paul blinked in disbelief at his situation. "So, where does that leave us?"

"The navigator and maintenance boss have both agreed to total transparency for the rest of the voyage. Indeed, myself and the rest of the crew insisted on it."

"I don't think that makes me feel much better. How do we know they won't fuck us again?"

"We don't. But they have agreed to tell us the next time they start to take actions that are not directed by us."

Paul shook his head, unsure of how to proceed. A long moment of silence extended between him and the XO.

"Tell you what, Paul," the XO finally said. "You worry about your mutiny, and I'll worry about mine."

"Fine," Paul said with a rueful chuckle. "I guess I can't do anything about it, anyway."

"Do you have a plan?" the XO asked. "We need a plan."

"How long does the pod estimate until Cooley is ambulatory?"

"The pod says Mr. Cooley could withstand light mobility tasks in a few cycles. But it does not recommend it. It says Cooley will need at least ten cycles of rest."

"Don't we all."

"Do you have a plan, Paul?"

"I'm working on it."

Chapter Fifty

aul floated out of the bridge air lock into the vacuum fifty meters above the hull of the *Odysseus*. He activated his suit's maneuvering thrusters to line up with the ship's direction of flight.

One of the biggest challenges of an untethered extravehicular activity while underway was maintaining one's bearing and orientation. High lunar orbit EVAs were easier because the planet Earth and the Moon provided massive, ever-present reference points. Out in the emptiness between Earth and the belt, though, being outside of the ship was a disorienting flirtation with the void, even with the helmet's heads-up display. The ship was one's only anchoring point of reference. And it was tenuous. Too much relative speed in the wrong direction, even for an instant, and vertigo would wrap her tentacles around you and fling you away from the ship.

Paul positioned himself over the centerline of the *Odysseus'* long hull. Glancing at his objective, the spinner, over a kilometer to his front, Paul activated his thrusters and started moving forward and down. Monitoring his rate of closure on his HUD, he fought the urge to go faster. Another common mistake was closing on objects too fast. It took time to get a feel for how much closing velocity was too much, and violent collisions were common until one gained experience. It was easy to break bones, damage equipment, or worse.

Doing so on this EVA would doom Althea.

Paul put the thought out of his head and tried to focus on his task and environment.

Paul saw at least a dozen IR drones at work on the hull in front of him.

Most were the smaller, egg-shaped configurations engaged in welding, cleaning, or inspecting, but he saw two tug drones. One about halfway to the spinner, hovering motionless about a hundred meters above the hull, the other a hundred meters off to the port side of the ship, moving forward.

The spinner loomed large in front of him. The Hab and Utility Modules, so small and cramped on the inside, seemed massive now as they arced up on the port side of the ship and plunged down on the starboard at over three rotations per minute. At their apex, the Hab and UM towered almost a hundred meters above him.

Paul began to have doubts about the plan.

He tried to focus on his progress forward.

Paul had given Cooley as much time in the pod as he could. When Cooley had finally come onto the bridge, Paul was encouraged by what he saw. A couple of hours in the MedPod had done wonders, even though he still needed a lot more time in it.

Cooley's wounds had all been stitched up, and a normal, healthy color had replaced his previous blood-drained pallor.

"How much blood did the thing have to replace?" Paul asked.

"It didn't tell me."

"Probably a good thing. How do you feel?"

"I'm full of pain meds, so I feel fine right now. But I'm sure it's going to hurt like hell soon. So, whatever we're going to do, let's do it now while I can help."

"You're sure?" Paul asked.

Cooley nodded. "Just need to be aware that I won't be worth much in a fight." He gestured at his bandaged wounds. "Any real action, and I'll probably rip apart like an old doll."

"OK. I've only got one idea. And it is not a good one."

Paul was now about five meters above the *Odysseus'* hull and moving forward. He activated his maneuvering thrusters to speed up.

Ahead, the tug drone still hovered motionless over the *Odysseus*, seeming to watch Paul. It had descended somewhat, and Paul noted the scrapes and dents on the drone as he passed under it.

They are even bigger up close, Paul thought.

Paul goosed his thrusters again. He was anxious.

"Paul, I believe that is enough forward velocity," the XO said over the radio.

"And I believe that is enough commentary from the cheap seats."

"I'm sorry. But I don't want our only able-bodied human to get hurt before he even gets to the risky bits of the mission."

Paul rolled his eyes, but activated his thrusters to decelerate. The spinner loomed even larger now.

Paul slowed again as he got closer, and then again. By the time he drifted up to the hub of the spinner, he was barely moving at all.

The alternating arms of the traverse, one holding the Hab and one holding the Utility Module, swung by quickly. Paul was nervous as he waited for his moment. He would only have about nine seconds to make his move. And though he didn't have to get very far, a collision would swat him away from the *Odysseus*, damaging his pressure suit and body.

He tried to steady his breathing and thought again about turning away from the *Odysseus* and flying wide around the spinner instead of through the hurtling arms. But he talked himself out of it again. There were too many windows on the Hab, and he did not want to risk one of the mutineers getting lucky and spotting him. If he went through the arms at the hub, there was no way that could happen.

So, through the arms he would go.

He let the arms pass by a few times to get the timing down.

Then, on the next pass, he activated his thrusters.

Full forward.

Paul was pressed to the rear of his suit as he accelerated past the spinner.

He then executed a 180-degree swivel about his long axis, turning back to face the *Odysseus*.

"Shit," Paul said when he saw how far out he had flown.

"Are you OK?" the XO asked.

"Yeah. I'm fine. Just went a little farther than I intended."

"Well, you are through the spinner," the XO said cheerily. "Well done."

Paul had never seen the *Odysseus* from this angle. Straight on. It looked strange. It was all circling spinner and the tiny bridge in the distance, winking in and out of view as the arms passed by. There was no sense that the old girl went on for more than two kilometers.

Paul approached the hub, aiming for the middle. About twenty meters in diameter, the cylindrical structure spun at a relative crawl compared to the Hab and UM on the ends of the traverse arms. Paul grabbed one of the multiple handholds and quickly clipped his suit's safety cable to it.

He looked up to the end of the traverse arm and confirmed that he was looking at the Hab. It would be a disaster to go through all this just to wind up in the Utility Module. There were ladder rungs the whole way out to the Hab structure, just as Cooley had said.

Satisfied, Paul got started.

He pushed himself toward the Hab, clipping his line into a handhold every five meters. As he moved farther, the increasing speed of rotation began to pull him to the trailing side, and he felt himself getting heavier.

Fifteen deliberate minutes later, he was standing on the top of the Hab.

Paul took a moment to catch his breath before the next part. After one look around, though, he confined his gaze to his feet.

Held to the top of the Hab now by centripetal force, he cartwheeled around the *Odysseus*, seventy-five meters "above" him. As if the old girl were in the center of a whirlpool that had captured him.

Ugh.

A hint of nausea flared in Paul's gut. He shook his head and got moving again.

He connected a second, shorter safety line to a handhold on the roof of the Hab and then cut loose from the line that ran up the traverse arm to the hub.

Paul walked carefully to the front edge of the Hab and started climbing down the rungs that led to the airlock. It was tedious and tiring. He was at much more than his full weight now, since the pressure suit weighed about a hundred pounds, and he was trying to move slowly to make sure he did not bang the wall or do anything else that would cause a loud noise. He resisted the urge to peer into the windows he passed. Instead, he hugged the ladder rungs as closely as he could to avoid a chance sighting.

After ten more minutes of effort, he was finally ready.

"OK," he said over the radio, panting from the stress and exertion. "Made it."

"Thank goodness," the XO said.

"Good job, Owens," Cooley said. "Just let me know when."

"Might as well get on with it."

"Roger that," Cooley said. "Opening the hub airlock now."

Paul clung to the side of the Habitat module next to the third-level air lock. The same one they had jettisoned the captain from not so long ago.

"The traverse is empty," Cooley radioed. "No one in sight. Proceeding down to the Hab."

Won't be long now, Paul thought. He was ready to be back inside the *Odysseus.* Even if it meant hand-to-hand combat. He pictured Cooley climbing down the traverse ladder, sutures pulling against wounds as his body got heavier.

A motion over Paul's shoulder caught his eye, startling him.

It was the tug drone pushing forward of the spinner and the *Odysseus.* Paul swung away from it as the Hab carved its arc around the hub. The tug receded rapidly and was soon over two hundred meters away as the Hab passed through the opposite end of its circular course.

Paul and the Hab started to close the distance between it and the tug drone again as the arm swept around. Paul looked back at his hands.

Would not be a good time to get vertigo.

"Opening Hab topside hatch now," Cooley said.

Paul keyed his microphone twice to let Cooley know he had copied and got ready.

Cooley opened the hatch. Blood seeping from his freshly torn wounds as he moved. His clothes were damp in places.

Gripping the improvised spear he and Paul had fashioned from a carbon-fiber spar, he turned his helmet camera and microphone on so that Paul and the XO could access his POV and listen in.

Cooley unsealed and raised his helmet visor and kneeled down. Leaning forward through the opening, he craned his neck around to scan both ends of the first-level hallway.

It was clear.

Cooley climbed down into the first level, making a lot of clanging noises along the way. He stepped onto the first level and planted the butt of his spear on the floor. A loud bang rang through the Hab.

"Well, well, well," Hahn said, climbing up the aft crew ladder. He stepped onto the first level, a large bayonet in its scabbard on his utility belt. His right hand was bandaged. McNeeley followed, his nose purple and swollen. The two mutineers glared at Cooley.

Paul activated the third-level air lock and waited for the burst of air to subside. He unclipped from the ladder rung and swung himself into the air-lock chamber.

He listened to Cooley's transmission as he shut the external air-lock door.

"Captain Regas said you guys would do something stupid like this," Hahn said.

"Paul is right behind me, and we're not leaving without Althea," Cooley said.

Hahn took a few steps forward, looking up at the open air lock above Cooley.

"That right?" Hahn said.

"Yes. And this doesn't have to get violent."

"Oh yes, it does," Hahn said with a smile.

Paul opened the airlock. He winced at the noise and hoped he wasn't heard as he stepped into the third-level hallway.

Paul keyed his mic three times to let Cooley and the XO know he was in. He unsealed and raised his helmet visor and then scanned the hallway again. Seeing no one with him on the third level, he hurried to the aft crew ladder. He took a deep breath and started up.

"So where is Owens?" Hahn asked Cooley.

"Right behind me."

"Uh-huh," Hahn said, laying on the disbelief.

Paul started climbing, scanning above as he went.

"What is that?" Hahn asked in a mocking voice. "A spear?"

Cooley didn't respond.

Paul climbed up onto the second level.

"Hello, Jigsaw," Regas said. "I figured it wouldn't be long before you showed up."

Regas stood thirty meters away, at the forward end of the second level hallway, smiling. Althea stood in front of him to one side, hands bound behind her, a rope around her neck.

Regas held the rope in one hand.

Althea looked terrible. Her flight suit was in tatters, and her face had been beaten. Paul tried to read her eyes, but they were vacant.

"What?" Regas said, catching the pain in Paul's face. "I cleaned her up for this. Isn't she lovely?"

He pushed her roughly and yanked on the rope around her neck, making her turn around. As she did so, Paul could see her arms were bound tightly and at an awkward angle. He wondered if they were broken. Both were covered in scrapes and cuts.

"You should feel honored, Jigsaw," Regas said, with a leering face. "This is the first time I've put any clothes on her in a while."

Paul took a step forward, and Regas tensed.

"Hahn!" Regas yelled.

"Yeah, boss?" Hahn responded from the first level. Paul glanced instinctively at the midship crew ladder. He could make out the shadow of Cooley's feet on the grate.

"We've got Owens down here. You can kill Cooley now."

"Roger that," Hahn said.

Hahn pulled an anti-boarding pistol out of his belt behind his back and shot Cooley in the head.

Paul started at the loud bang.

A body slumped to the floor above them. Blood dripped down through the grate; small beads of blood dropped from rung to rung on the crew ladder.

"We found some more weapons," Regas said to Paul.

Paul's face was contorted with anger. He had known this was a stupid plan. But he had not counted on them having firearms.

"I guess you knew about the bayonets from earlier," Regas said with a shrug and a grin. "But there's a lot of other old shit on that Utility Module. How about these anti-boarding pistols?" Regas pulled a pistol from behind his back, holding it up for Paul to see. "They're early models, but still really do a number on someone's face when you need 'em to."

Anti-boarding pistols were a favorite of the spacefaring military. Firing subsonic scattershot munitions similar to a shotgun, they mutilated people, but did only limited damage to the ship's structure. They enabled defenders to kill enemy boarders without the concern of breaching the hull and causing explosive decompression. Had Paul known the mutineers had them, he would have scrubbed the plan and tried to think of something else.

Too late now.

Regas looked at the blood dripping down the midship ladder from the first level and then back at Paul. "OK, guys, get down here," he yelled. "Let's wrap this up."

Hahn descended the midship crew ladder, followed by McNeeley.

"Bring him here," Regas said.

Hahn and McNeeley walked over to Paul and grabbed him by the arms. Hahn pointed the AB pistol at Paul's ribs. McNeeley brandished a bayonet. Regas smiled in approval as they forced Paul to walk under Cooley's dripping blood. It struck him on the top of his helmet and shoulders. Paul did not look up. He knew what he would see lying on the grate.

"So," Paul said slowly. "This is it."

"Yeah, Jigsaw," Regas said. "It is. This is my ship now. My pirate ship."

Paul noticed Regas was wearing his dog tags on the outside of his uniform. But there was something else, besides the ID tags, hanging from the silver chain.

Ears.

"You like 'em?" Regas asked Paul, noticing him looking. "Drummond's," he said, pulling on them with the trigger finger of his hand holding the pistol. "I'm going to be wearing Cooley's in about five minutes."

Regas let go of the ears and looked at Paul.

"Then yours."

A loud screeching noise filled the air as the left sidewall slammed into all of them at over fifty miles an hour. Paul made sure Hahn was between him and the wall when it struck.

The impact was jarring, even though Hahn's body absorbed most of the blow and his pressure suit provided some measure of cushioning. Paul felt something in Hahn's body snap as the wall drove into them.

Hahn shrieked in pain.

Paul saw Hahn's right elbow stuck at a sickening angle. A blooming red bloodstain indicated the break was compound.

Hahn's pistol, though, escaped Paul.

It bounced just out of reach and drifted away from them, as the violent impact was replaced by weightlessness.

Blood streamed into the air from McNeeley's face. His collision with the wall had also jarred lose his bayonet. Paul didn't see it close by.

McNeeley was blinking and rubbing his eyes. He could not see because of the blood. Paul struck him in the nose as hard as he could in the zero-G environment.

It was hard enough.

Hahn was screaming in pain, and McNeeley was unconscious and spinning away, colliding hard with the opposite wall. They were eliminated as threats. It had been only a few seconds since the tug drone had fired its rockets to arrest the spinner's rotation, and things were going better than Paul could have hoped.

Except for the pistols and Cooley.

Paul turned his attention to Regas.

Regas was having a rough time. His right shoulder looked bad, and Althea was kicking his head into the wall. They both floated near the ceiling at the forward end of the passageway. Althea pulled her legs up to her chest and then drove them down, heels first, onto Regas's head. The force of her kick sent his head spiraling into the wall and propelled her backward into the opposite wall. She pushed off the wall with her shoulders, taking aim at Regas, and came at him again.

She was about to execute her third kick when Paul grabbed her shoulder.

"Althea!" Paul yelled. "Stop!"

"But he is not dead yet," she protested.

"I'll finish him," Paul said as he pushed her past him toward the center-passage crew ladder.

Paul looked at Regas. The odd shape of his shoulder confirmed a broken collarbone. His face was badly bruised, probably from the impact of the wall. Though Althea's kicks could not have helped. Beads of blood pumped out of his nose and mouth into the air. He was not unconscious. But he wasn't fully with it either. Rough grunting noises told Paul that Regas was having trouble breathing. Broken ribs, perhaps.

Paul looked around.

Nothing.

He'd have to kill him with his hands.

He touched a boot to the floor to lunge into Regas.

"Paul! Help!" Althea screamed. "Help!"

He looked back at Althea. Hands still tied, she was trying to get away from Hahn. The wounded mutineer held the bayonet in his good hand. He swung erratically, contending with the zero Gs and his horribly wounded right arm.

Paul adjusted his legs and launched himself at Hahn.

Althea screamed as Hahn's blade cut deep into one of her legs.

Paul struck Hahn in the face as he collided with him. He parried Hahn's bayonet thrusts as the two men careened past Althea. Hahn grunted when they collided into the wall, and then screamed as Paul peeled back two of his fingers, breaking them. Paul took the bayonet from Hahn, drove it up through his chin into his skull, twisting the blade.

Blood sprayed onto Paul's face as Hahn convulsed.

Pulling the bayonet from Hahn's head and shoving the body aside, Paul grabbed Althea. He cut her arms loose and then unwrapped the rope from around her neck.

She looked even worse up close.

She saw the torment in his eyes and prodded him on. "Paul, please get me out of here."

Paul looked over his shoulder. Regas, at the far end of the hallway, still looked groggy.

But McNeeley was now conscious. And close to the other pistol.

For an agonizing instant, Paul thought about lunging for McNeeley and the pistol. But they were too far away. McNeeley had it.

Paul shoved Althea roughly down the ladder way toward the bottom level.

"Get a pressure suit on! Now!"

"Paul?" She looked at him with pleading eyes.

"Pressure suit. Now!"

McNeeley was trying to get a bead on Paul with the pistol. His legs flailed in the zero G as he tried to turn his upper body and line up a shot.

Pushing Althea down to the bottom level caused Paul to rise. He was closer to the top level. Paul yanked on the ladder, pulling himself up to the first level as McNeeley fired, narrowly missing Paul.

Cooley's body floated nearby on the first level. It was a mess. The anti-boarding pistol had done its job well, making hamburger of Cooley's face and head without damaging any of the ship's structure behind him. Large spheres of blood hovered around Cooley's head. Paul pushed his hands through them to grab the lifeless form.

He had to hurry. Regas and McNeeley recovered with every passing second.

And they had pistols.

Holding Cooley's body, Paul bounced himself up to the ceiling, coiled his legs and then leapt.

Paul held Cooley's body in front as he plunged back down the ladderway.

McNeeley fired.

Paul felt the rounds hit Cooley's body.

Regas, farther away than McNeeley, also fired his pistol at Paul.

McNeeley cried out as Paul felt more impacts against Cooley's body as he sailed down the ladder way to the bottom level.

"You fucking shot me!" McNeeley cried out.

Althea was in the airlock at the far end of the passageway, twisting her helmet onto her pressure suit.

"Shut the fuck up and go after them!" Regas yelled on the second level.

"Fuck you!" McNeeley wailed. "I'm bleeding, you idiot!"

Paul grabbed Cooley's body and shoved it toward the airlock. Then he kicked off the nearest wall to follow.

"It was an accident!" Regas yelled. "Help me stop them!"

When Paul got to the middle of the passageway, he pulled himself into the MedBay.

"Hurry up, Paul!" Althea pleaded. "What are you doing?"

Paul pulled through the doorway and sailed over to the MedPod. He cut every cable he could find on the outside of the pod with the bayonet and then pried open the clamshell top. He raked the bayonet over the delicate internal equipment and then jammed the blade into the control panel several times.

"Fuck you!" McNeeley yelled. "This is all y—"

A shot rang out on the second level, silencing McNeeley.

"Paul, please!" Althea yelled.

Satisfied he had rendered the MedPod inoperable, Paul yanked himself back into the passageway and kicked hard toward the airlock.

"I'm coming for you, Owens!" Regas yelled. "You dumb fucker, you should have killed me when you had the chance."

Paul slammed into Cooley's body, and they floated together toward the airlock. Althea grabbed Paul when he got close enough and pulled him all the way in.

"You don't get a second chance with me!" Regas yelled.

"Hit the door!" Paul said.

Althea activated the inboard air-lock door as Paul sealed his helmet visor. Paul's helmet seal indicator glowed green as Regas pulled himself down into the third level, his face contorted in pain and rage.

The crew-side door slid shut and locked.

Regas yelled something that did not make it through the door.

"XO! We ready?" Paul transmitted as he unreeled a length of his safety cable. He clipped into Althea's suit's utility belt and into Cooley's.

A loud impact startled Paul and Althea.

Paul looked through the window. Regas was shooting at them with an AB pistol.

"Don't worry," Paul said to Althea. "It won't get through. It's designed to—"

Another loud impact interrupted him.

"Let's not test it," Althea said.

"XO?" Paul said.

"Yes, Paul. Sorry for the delay. We are ready."

"OK." Paul wrapped an arm around Althea. "Here we come."

Paul pounded the air-lock activation button with his fist and they were ejected into the void.

Chapter Fifty-One

The air screamed as it yanked them out of the *Odysseus*.

Paul caught a last glimpse of Regas through the air-lock portal window at the moment they were jettisoned. His face was a mixture of pain and bewilderment.

The three bodies were ejected from the lowest level of the Hab. They tumbled over each other, end over end, their small constellation of bodies expanding and contracting as they jerked against Paul's safety line.

Paul tried to maintain his sense of orientation to the *Odysseus*, but it was impossible. The massive ship careened in and out of his field of view.

"Paul?" Althea called over the radio, fear in her voice.

"We're good," he said to her, trying to sound as calm as possible. "Hang tight for just a little longer." He grasped the safety line and pulled on it.

Cooley's dead body bounced into him.

He pushed Cooley away and snatched the other end of the safety line. He pulled Althea in closer and grabbed her hand.

She pulled on it and latched on to Paul with a tight bear hug.

"This is part of the plan?" she asked, looking over Paul's shoulder. Cooley's smashed face leered at her in front of a sea of pinwheeling stars.

"Yes."

"I hate it."

"Me too."

Hours earlier, this was the part Cooley had had the most concern about. He argued with Paul about it on the bridge. The two of them floated next to Drake's command chair, surrounded by the horseshoe-shaped instrument console as they tried to come up with a plan.

The basic idea was that Paul, a combat veteran, would be a much more capable hand-to-hand fighter than any of the three mutineers. Regas might prove tough, but Paul was not worried about the braggart. Fighting them head on, though, one against three, would swing the odds in their favor, and the potential for Althea to be wounded or worse during the melee was high. They needed some way to achieve tactical surprise, even though there was no way to sneak on board the Hab undetected.

So, Paul proposed to get on board the Hab, and *then* surprise them.

Paul had had to review it with Cooley and the XO several times to convince them. No one doubted a tug could quickly stop the rotation of the spinner. The question was if it could do so without breaking off one of the spinner's arms, throwing the whole thing out of balance and dooming the *Odysseus*. After millions of calculations and simulations, the XO and the maintenance boss assured them it could be done. They would use two tugs, one on each arm, to counterbalance each other. It would take some precise maneuvering, which would take time to execute, but they calculated it to be low risk.

When Paul spoke the code words, "So, this is it," they would begin. There was no way to know how long it would take for them to get into position and initiate the burn, but they estimated it would be no faster than twenty-five seconds and no longer than fifty-five seconds.

Everyone agreed that the spinner coming to a screeching halt would provide a window for Paul to take the initiative back and kill the mutineers. If it went to shit, though, and whoever survived had to get off the Habitat Module in a hurry, Paul proposed this catch maneuver.

"Having an IR drone intercept us after we jettison out of the third-level air lock?" Cooley had said on the bridge, rolling his eyes. "Don't tell me that is any better than fifty-fifty, XO."

The problem was the IR drones were not meant to go very far from the *Odysseus*. They carried little fuel. And this kind of task was a fuel hog. It involved large accelerations and decelerations and multiple precise course corrections.

If the drone were not able to get ahold of them quick enough, they would pass the point of no return and not be able to get back to the ship. There was also a concern that the asymmetric dynamic forces created by three loosely bound and tumbling masses might snap off the drone's arms when it tried to catch them. The arms were designed to grab and slowly move objects, not catch fast-moving targets. Finally, there was no way to ensure that one of them would not be killed or gravely injured by the intercept. They could be inadvertently slammed against the drone, caught in its drive plume, or suffer innumerable other deadly mishaps.

"I agree it is risky, Mr. Cooley," the XO had said. "But it is somewhat better than fifty-fifty, and the maintenance boss tells me he is highly confident."

"Terrific," Cooley had said, locking eyes with Paul and grimacing. They both turned their heads to look out the large forward window at the spinner. At that moment, it seemed a lot farther than a kilometer away.

"I wish we could talk to the maintenance boss directly," Paul said to Cooley. Cooley nodded his agreement.

"You don't trust me, Paul?" the XO said.

"It's not that, XO. It's just an old habit."

"How do you mean?"

"In the military, whenever my life depended on someone, or some machine, doing their job, I always tried to look them in the eye, or talk to them, or type on their keyboard, or whatever, before the mission. Always made me feel better."

"Rest assured, Paul. I relay everything you say, unfiltered, directly to the maintenance boss. He knows the stakes and wants you to feel confident he will get it done."

"I appreciate that, XO. Tell him I said thanks."

"He says it is his pleasure, sir," the XO relayed. "It is the reason he is on board."

"I guess if the guy can steer the *Odysseus* off course, this ought to be child's play, right?"

"Not funny," the XO said as Cooley and Paul chuckled.

Paul wasn't chuckling now as they careened away from the *Odysseus*. He craned his neck around in his helmet to see the ship and then regretted it. It was already a fourth of the size it was the last time he'd seen it.

They were moving a lot faster than he had thought they would.

And they had been sailing away forever, it seemed.

As soon as the tugs had stopped the spinner's rotation, the maintenance boss positioned two of his most trusted IR bots, one on each side of the Hab, forward, near the third-level air lock. One was the designated catcher. The second was a backup.

As soon as the trio was ejected from the Hab in a burst of lost atmosphere, the drones lit their thrusters at maximum burn.

The primary drone reached the group ninety-one seconds after ejection.

Althea saw it first.

"Drone!"

"Stay still!" Paul said.

He didn't want to make it any harder for the drone to grab them.

Paul felt Althea squeeze him tighter.

Paul's safety harness bit sharply into his legs and waist. The safety line connecting the three bodies tightened as the drone initiated a turn back to the *Odysseus*. Paul had not even noticed it grab the line.

He made a mental note to compliment the maintenance boss when they were back on board.

Chapter Fifty-Two

"Oh my God," Althea said as she and Paul floated into the C&C's MedBay.

Bloody pieces of Cooley's old pressure suit were still lashed to the table, and dried blood was splattered or smeared everywhere.

"Yeah," Paul said. "It's been a long cycle. I'll clean this stuff up after we get you into the pod."

Paul grabbed the pod door handle to steady himself. For the second time that cycle, he activated the C&C's MedPod. The large clamshell top opened slowly. Paul was relieved to see that its self-cleaning and sanitization routine had functioned as advertised. A few hours ago, it had looked like a torture chamber. Now, it was spotless. He selected the synthetic setting and then entered Althea's name when it requested the crew member ID.

"I'm sorry, Paul," Althea said in a trembling voice. "But I need some help."

Paul maintained his grip on the pod door handle and grabbed Althea and pulled her to him.

"My arms are so sore and damaged from being tied like that. I think I used their last strength holding on to you during our escape."

"No problem," he said. He unzipped her tattered flight suit and helped her out of it.

A tear escaped Paul's eye and drifted into the space between them.

She was covered in black and purple bruises. Her skin was scraped off in several places, and her arms and legs were crisscrossed with deep rope burns.

Paul stared at the deep gash from Hahn's bayonet as Althea pulled her leg out of her flight suit. It wept dark red liquid. Black and shiny flakes of dried synthetic blood covered her leg.

She put her hands on him and pulled his head up to meet her eyes.

"It's OK. The nanobots and sealing compounds did their job. It's going to be fine, I promise."

"I wish I had been faster," he said, pushing her naked body into the pod.

"Shhhh. You were amazing. You saved me."

"Are you in a lot of pain?"

"Yes," she said with a tired smile.

Another tear escaped into the bloody room as Paul pushed the door closed. His tear, grabbed by an invisible eddy of airflow, hit the MedPod window.

Paul waited for the MedPod to complete its sealing process before activating the microphone.

"Hey," he said.

Althea looked at him through the face window.

"I'll be back soon. I'm going to take care of Cooley."

Althea nodded.

Paul returned to the bridge and keyed the microphone.

"XO, can you please confirm Cooley's wishes for me?"

"Yes, Paul. Mr. Cooley requested he be returned to be buried on Earth."

"OK. Is there a freezer on the bridge?"

"I'm afraid not, Paul. The only suitable facility is on the second level of the Utility Module."

"Any ideas?"

"Yes. If you deem it suitable, I can store Mr. Cooley's body in one of our vacant external containers. We can move him when we have the opportunity, or he can remain there until we reach wherever we are going."

Paul tried to ignore that major uncertainty still hanging over all of them. Where the hell were they going?

"Sounds good," Paul said. "But please ensure that he is well secured. I don't want there to be any more damage to the body."

"I'll be sure of it, Paul."

"Fine. Send an IR bot around to the airlock, and I'll meet them there. Also, please send an IR bot into the tube and weld the hub bulkhead shut. I also want a bot or two out there to watch the Hab and UM for anything suspicious from the outside. Regas is in no shape to do much, but I'm not going to assume anything about him again."

"Will do. What are your plans for him, if I may ask?"

"You and I both know that Regas has to die. I'd prefer he do that on his own from his injuries. But if he doesn't oblige, I'm going to have to kill him."

"Yes. You are."

Paul returned to the bridge's external airlock, where they had left Cooley's body. Paul stepped into the air-lock chamber next to the body holding his helmet. Cooley had been flash frozen when they were ejected from the Hab, so there wasn't any blood on the air-lock floor.

Paul reached down and grabbed the end of Cooley's safety line. He fastened it, as well as his own, to one of the floor anchor points.

Paul looked at the pulpy mess where Cooley's face should have been and shook his head. He felt like he should say something.

Paul looked around for a moment, unsure of how to get started.

"XO, would you please summarize Mr. Cooley's service file?"

"Of course."

There was a slight delay before the XO continued.

"Floyd Cooley, born June third, 2033. After graduation from high school, he spent five years in the US Navy serving aboard nuclear submarines, receiving the Meritorious Service Medal for his service in the South China Sea during the Spratly Incident of 2054. In 2056, Floyd Cooley entered the space merchant marine training program. Upon graduation, he was selected to crew the USS *Marlow* and left high lunar orbit on December twentieth, 2058. The *Marlow* successfully completed her mission to the belt and back and was logged into high lunar orbit on December first, 2062. Floyd Cooley served in multiple assignments Earthside and in orbit before his next mission to the belt, including duty as executive officer on the USS *Ripley*, a lunar orbital cargo-exchange ship from April eleventh, 2067, until the first of May 2069.

He was selected to serve as boatswain of the *Odysseus*, an American-flagged deep-space freighter, and reported on board for duty on the first of September 2070. The *Odysseus* left high Lunar orbit on February eleventh, 2071."

Paul nodded.

He looked down at Cooley's body. "And Mr. Cooley served the *Odysseus* well."

"Indeed, he did," the XO said.

Paul fastened his helmet, grabbed a wall handhold, and activated the air-lock door. Atmosphere rushed out, tugging at Cooley's body and bringing it to an eerie hover above the air-lock floor.

A few seconds later, an IR drone slid into view just a couple of meters outside of the airlock.

"Ready, Paul," the XO said.

Paul unhooked Cooley's safety line and gave the body a nudge toward the drone. The drone caught Cooley, slid to the right, and was gone.

* * *

"You're back," Althea said with a weary smile behind the glass of the MedPod window.

"I'm back," Paul said. "How do you feel?"

"Tired. And kind of weird. This thing has shut down a lot of me. I guess the damage was worse than I thought. I'm really glad I can't see what it's doing to me."

Paul took a deep breath, determined not to get emotional again.

"I'm really glad you can't, either," she added.

Paul nodded. He knew she could read him.

"Paul? It's telling me I am going to be in here for a while."

Paul looked at the control panel. The estimated treatment duration said fourteen days.

"Wow," Paul said, raising his eyebrows.

"Don't worry," Althea said. "It's really just the tissue regeneration that takes most of that time. I've read the pods always overestimate the required treatment time."

"Good thing is, we have nothing but time."

"Maybe not so good for you," Althea said with a mischievous smile.

"What?"

"Tell me more about you and your Ōkami."

Chapter Fifty-Three

Adauchi Book One
Circa 1510
Translated from the Japanese

The siege of Clan Hayoto Castle was Master Hiroaki's greatest victory. Hiroaki's students were spread throughout Shingen's forces to lead the execution of the plan.

Like darting birds of prey, we struck across the river's shallow and rocky place at the same moment.

Hayato's Elite Guard countered these attacks, but were then surprised by a strike from the mountains north of the castle. They had to split their forces again, and their communication and coordination became difficult.

Finally, at the critical moment, Hiroaki struck boldly across the covered bridge. The master himself led the attack.

The Elite Guard fought well but, by then, were no match for Hiroaki's expert attack. Anotsu Hayato refused Hiroaki's request of him to surrender several times. He was too proud to surrender as his father watched from the castle walls.

The battle brought Hiroaki and Anotsu together. They fought. Hiroaki cut Anotsu down with a lightning-quick killing stroke with his katana. Anotsu fell to the ground in halves.

Lord Hayato's cry at the sight from the castle wall was heartbreaking.

Hiroaki's forces took the surviving Elite Guard as prisoners and took their captured banner back to Lord Shingen.

Clan Hayato castle was now surrounded, with only its castle guard within its walls. The castle guard was thought to number between one and two thousand troops. Perhaps two hundred horses. Not enough to last.

It was all but over.

Lord Shingen sent an emissary into the castle demanding its surrender in the morning.

Lord Shingen and Hiroaki ate dinner together in the lord's tent in celebration that evening. Hiroaki asked me to join as his guest. In the middle of dinner, Lord Shingen was approached by one of his counselors. There was much whispering.

"Excuse me, please, General Hiroaki," Shingen said, rising. "I must tend to matters. Please enjoy your dinner and well-deserved rest. Tomorrow, our long war ends."

Chapter Fifty-Four

Paul jerked awake. He was breathing hard and covered in sweat. He looked around.

He was in the C&C MedBay.

Althea was in the pod.

He remembered.

He looked at his watch. It was early the next cycle. He had been asleep for almost four hours. "Shit," he muttered. "Didn't mean to sleep that long."

Paul went to the bridge. He floated over to the large window and stared at the front of the *Odysseus.*

"I'm glad you got some rest, Paul. You needed it," the XO said. "Truthfully, you need more."

Paul had locked the intercom switch on the bridge in the open position so that the XO could listen in and reach him easily. *I have to trust him for now,* Paul thought.

"Any changes?" Paul asked, ignoring the XO's statement. "Has he moved at all?"

"No. Regas is still on the third level of the Hab in the MedBay."

Paul touched a toe to the floor to turn himself from the window. He pushed off toward the monitors in the captain's console.

One of the monitors showed an infrared image of the Hab. Paul zoomed in on the third level. A warm body floated motionless in the MedBay.

Paul smiled, thinking how disappointed Regas must have been to find the MedPod inoperable.

He returned forward and floated in silence in front of the big window. In the distance, the spinner was still motionless. Without its constant circular motion, the sense of the *Odysseus* being stuck in the solar system's doldrums was heightened. Even though she continued toward an unknown destination at thousands of meters a second.

The Hab hung at the end of one arm of the traverse, stuck at about the two o'clock position. The Utility Module, obscured by the ship's hull, hung down at the eight o'clock position. Paul could see several IR bots patrolling the spinner, keeping sensory tabs on the broken but still living mutineer.

"I really wish I had killed that guy when I was over there," Paul mumbled to himself.

"I do too."

"There was a lot going on at the time," Paul said, irritation in his voice.

"I am not second-guessing you, Paul. In fact, given your feelings for Althea, your prioritization of her well-being above killing—"

"My feelings for Althea?"

The XO hesitated.

"What the hell does that mean?" Paul asked, raising his voice.

"I am simply referring to your prioritization of her well-being above the tactical opportunity to eliminate a threat to the ship during the—"

"They had fucking guns! I did my best. Let it rest, will you?"

"Of course, Paul. I am not trying to frustrate you."

"God help me if you do try."

"I could kill him myself, of course," the XO said. "Had my connections to the Habitat and Utility Modules not been severed."

"Are you trying now?"

"No. Just stating facts."

"Well, the fact is, at the time, we did not know whether or not we could trust you," Paul said.

"Lessons learned on all sides, I suppose."

Paul put his hand to his face and rubbed his eyes. "I swear to God, XO," he said through clenched teeth.

Paul and the XO sat in silence for a moment. Paul stared at the motionless spinner.

He turned to head back to the MedBay.

"Paul?"

Paul tensed, preparing himself for another infuriating comment.

"I'll alert you of any more developments. Please do get some more rest."

"Thank you, XO."

Althea was awake when Paul got back to the MedBay.

Paul floated over to get close to the window. "Hello, young lady. How do you feel?"

"Terrible."

Paul checked the MedPod display. Everything was green. Estimated time remaining in treatment had reduced to ten days. It was less than he'd expected. She was healing fast.

"The pod says you are doing great."

Althea pouted.

"I'm ready to get out of here," she said, looking around the confines of the pod.

He nodded and smiled. He hooked himself up to the short lanyard he had rigged up to a handhold on the pod's clamshell top. It kept him floating just above Althea, facing her window.

"How about I tell you about that time a group of brave Ōkami aircraft disobeyed orders and saved my life?"

Alethea smiled and nodded.

"But you have to promise," Paul said, raising a finger. "You will go into rest mode for a while when the story is over."

"Deal."

An hour later, Paul was dozing off as Althea laid in the pod in rest mode.

"Paul?" the XO's voice woke him. "I am sorry to disturb you."

"What is it?"

"Can you please come to the bridge?"

"On my way."

"So?" Paul asked as he floated up onto the bridge. "What is it?"

"Regas, we believe, is moving through the traverse," the XO said. "We see a body moving slowly from the Hab on infrared."

One of the monitors showed an infrared image of the traverse. It looked like a softly glowing trachea in the void, with a small, fuzzy blob haltingly making its way through. The fuzzy blob was moving down away from the Hab toward the hub. The shape had not moved very far, less than ten meters.

"I'm impressed," Paul said, eyes on the monitor.

"At what?" the XO asked.

"You ever had a broken collarbone?"

"Don't be ridiculous."

"Take it from me. It sucks. Maybe the worst pain I've ever felt. I can't imagine how painful it is to move himself along that ladder with a broken collarbone and the other injuries he sustained when we rescued Althea."

"I see. One can only imagine, then, his level of determination. Let alone his goal. I am concerned," the XO said.

"McNeeley still in the Hab?"

"We think so. He is very difficult to ascertain at this point. His body temperature has equalized with the environment on the Hab. This is consistent with your assessment that he was killed."

"I wonder what Regas is doing?" Paul squinted at the video image. "You guys got the bulkhead welded shut, right?"

"Of course."

"So, he'll figure that out pretty quick."

"If that is his goal," the XO said.

"What is the status of the hub?"

"The maintenance boss reports that the hub inspection is ninety percent complete. So far, no damage detected."

"Really?" Paul said.

"Yes. The hub's slip clutch is well designed. It seems to have performed as intended when the tug drones executed their burn. He should be able to confirm it as fully operational within the hour."

"Best news I've heard all day. Tell the maintenance boss to get that thing spinning. I want it at one G as soon as possible."

"Will do, Paul."

Paul smiled, thinking about the pain that a full G of gravity would soon inflict on Regas.

"It will be interesting to see if he is able to continue," Paul said. "It's going to really suck for him soon."

"Indeed."

"And it will buy us time."

"Time for what?"

Paul looked at the Hab and spinner, over a kilometer away, and sighed heavily.

"For me to get up the energy for another fucking EVA to go over there and kill the bastard."

He turned to head back to the MedBay.

Chapter Fifty-Five

Pain woke Regas up.

Stabbing, incendiary pain as the shattered pieces of his collarbone ground together with each breath.

He tried to steady himself as he lay at the bottom of the traverse, on top of the Hab. When he minimized all movement, the pain was tolerable. He clawed through brain fog to remember.

He remembered falling.

That's right, he thought. *I fell.*

The spinner had started up suddenly. He'd almost lost his grip, but had held on. Then his weight had started to increase. The pain of clinging to the ladder had grown as the rotational velocity of the spinner had increased. He'd tried to climb down, but couldn't move fast enough. He could only use his left hand. His right ankle hurt, too. Nothing like the broken collarbone, but a lot. Was it broken also?

He was getting so heavy.

Then he realized he was going to lose his grip. His strength was fading. He was frightened. He was going to fall, and it was going to be bad. He started to hyperventilate, which made things worse. He clung to the ladder as long as he could.

Then he fell.

He screamed in rage and fear on the way down.

Mercifully, he was knocked out when he landed.

Or had he passed out from the pain?

Blood oozing from a bruise over his left eye suggested a concussion when his head had struck the Hab.

Regas screamed as he adjusted his shoulders to get them flatter on the surface of the Hab. But it was worth it. The pain was less that way. Bearable.

He lay still for a long time, remembering what he had been trying to do when the spinner had thrown him to the ground.

Owens.

The XO.

Althea.

The Company.

They had to pay.

Regas knew he was dying. It wasn't just his collarbone. Something was wrong internally. So, he knew he was going to die when he saw that Owens had destroyed the Hab's MedPod.

It would be a relief.

Regas had pulled himself up to the MedPod, full of certainty and resolve. Even a few hours in it would have changed his fortune, given him the advantage he needed. The *Odysseus* would probably already be his. Another set of ears on his necklace.

Regas did not understand why they did not just dump the atmosphere from the Hab and kill him that way. That's what he would have done.

Weaklings.

Maybe they were working on that.

Regardless, Owens had foiled him.

He was going to die. It would take time, but the swelling in his shoulder was already grotesque. He had to take his shoe off because his ankle was so big.

Regas shook his head in disgust at Paul Owens. Pain radiated through his body, and he stopped, but the thought continued.

Fucking weak, he thought. *Not how I would have done it. I would have killed the fuck out of me when I had the chance. Knife. AB pistol. My bare hands, if I had to. I'd have killed me totally dead before I burned one calorie saving the synthetic bitch.*

Regas looked at the traverse ladder towering above him. He focused on the Utility Module bulkhead in the distance. He grimaced as he looked at all the ladder rungs rising almost a hundred and fifty meters above where he lay.

The worst part would be getting off the ground. His collarbone and ankle would be punished by almost a full G. The first few rungs would be just as bad.

If he could get even ten rungs up the ladder, it would get easier. And easier. And easier. Until, halfway up, he would be in the weightless hub. Then he would have to maneuver his broken body 180 degrees so he could withstand the descent to the UM.

Fuck it, he thought. *At that point, I can just fall, pass out, and finish it when I wake up. It will be worth it. It will be on my terms, goddamn it.*

Regas lay still for another half hour, gathering his strength and willpower.

Then he moved.

He screamed.

He shrieked.

He felt the damage in his body increase with every millimeter of progress.

The pain caused tears to flow, which enraged him.

His breaths were ragged and shallow, his vision thin and imprecise. He knew he was on the verge of passing out.

"Not until you're there!" he yelled at himself. "Get there, you fucking pussy!"

One rung.

Two rungs.

Three rungs.

It took forever.

He could not remember a time he was not clinging to the traverse ladder in agony. He doubted he had ever existed when he was not in this searing pain.

He rested for a long time in the zero gravity of the hub, gathering strength and resolve and hoping in vain that the pain would subside for a moment.

It did not.

He started down toward the Utility Module. He floated slowly down, feet first, senses straining to detect a gain in momentum.

Soon, he was holding on to the ladder with his good hand. He felt the slight tug and judged himself to have about fifty meters left to descend.

Fear of falling welled within him.

From where he was now, he could propel himself back to the blissful zero gravity of the hub with a strong yank from his good hand.

No!

Keep going!

Halfway down the ladder, he was in agony again. His collarbone was on fire from the torque and strain of hanging on to the ladder with one hand.

His technique was to take two steps down with his feet, and then use them to support his growing weight while he released his good hand from the ladder and quickly grabbed the next lower rung.

As the centrifugal force strengthened its grip and pulled on Regas harder, the repositioning of his hand to the next lower rung became an excruciating exercise. His entire universe distilled down to the twelve inches of space between each rung.

The lower he got, the more jarring the hand swap became. When his palm struck the lower rung, the impact sent waves of stinging pain throughout his upper body. His vision got blurry for an instant as the sting transitioned to a sharp throb.

When he trusted his eyes again, he stepped lower, focused on the next rung, and prepared himself to do it again.

With less than twenty-five meters to go, he screamed at each hand swap. He couldn't stop himself.

With fifteen meters to go, drenched in sweat, his good hand locked up with a cramp.

"No, no, no, no, no, you fuckers," Regas cursed at his knotted fingers. He tried to use the ladder to help stretch them back to straight.

"Come on!" he yelled. "Please."

He could sense the fall coming.

His heart started to race.

"Please," he whimpered to himself, clinging to the ladder with his good elbow. His gnarled and cramped hand laced through the ladder.

His good arm began to tremble at the effort, as did his left leg. He had been putting as little weight as possible on his right ankle, which he was now certain was broken. It made a sickening pop sound at the slightest movement.

He glanced down. The Utility Module was still so far.

He knew he was going to fall.

"Fuck it!" he yelled.

Regas started moving as fast as he could down the ladder.

He yelled and cursed in pain at the jarring, clumsy descent.

He was going to fall. He knew that. But he wanted to get as low as he could before he lost it.

His hand was welded shut in a cramped fist. He jammed his arm through the rungs, stepped down, yanked his arm out, and jammed above the next lower rung.

He felt his collarbone fragmenting more with each motion.

His hand began to fail him again.

He heard himself wailing in pain.

His right ankle could not support any weight.

He felt himself accelerate and a blissful reduction in torque on his collarbone.

He realized he was falling.

If I ever wake up again, Belen Regas vowed as he fell, *I will finish it.*

Then blackness.

EARTH

Chapter Fifty-Six

The high-speed VIP elevator hurtled Fiona skyward above Dubai. Lucia Ferrara, her security detail leader for this trip, stood behind her.

Lucia "Lucy" Ferrara was an Italian American in her late forties. Her father immigrated to America and became a small-town policeman in Michigan where he met and married Lucy's mother. Lucy idealized her father and almost became a cop, but chose instead to give the military a try. After ten years in the exoskeleton battalions, one of Lucy's former platoon leaders recruited her to DredSkill, where she became a sought-after security detail leader. Exuding a quiet but alert presence, she had a calming effect on her clients in even the most tense situations. At 5'7", her muscular build was a testament to years of disciplined training and her dark brown hair, cut in a short bob, framed and accentuated her hawk-like features and green, watchful eyes. Fiona liked her.

They both looked out at the sparkling buildings below and the dark water of the Persian Gulf beyond. The small transparent capsule rode magnetic rails on the outside of the Tala'a Al-Badia Tower. Ten years ago, The Horizon Ascender Tower had been the first building to break the mile high barrier at 5281 feet tall. Today there were two others, one in Shanghai and one in Las Vegas, but the Ascender was still regarded as the most luxurious.

Fiona didn't like Dubai all that much. It was a long-ass flight, and she never seemed to shake the jet lag before it was time to go home, which was never soon enough. But "Dubai - Air, Land and Sea" had been the premier defense industry trade show for decades and it was a must-show for Spitting Metal and therefore for her. It was a long week of meetings and meals, and she always felt like she went home ten pounds heavier.

Today was her last day, and she was exhausted. Headed home tomorrow, her only plans for the evening had been a massage, long bath, and room service. For some reason, though, she had accepted an invitation for dinner with Dr. Griffin McAllister, the CEO of Lockheed Martin Boeing corporation.

Part of the reason she had accepted was that she loved the Ascender Tower. Something about the combination of cutting-edge technology and good old-fashioned over the top luxury got to her. And this unique-in-the-world elevator ride, rocketing up the shear, glass and metal flank of the Ascender was part of it as well.

The other part was Dr. McAllister.

The physics and chemistry double PhD had been the CEO of LMB, the largest defense contractor in the world, for almost ten years now. Like Fiona, his path to defense industry leadership was non-standard. He was not a retired general officer who successfully grafted to the Industrial Military Complex, and he was not a management zealot that had worked his way up the ladders of various of Fortune 500 companies.

Griffin was a researcher. He spent a decade in academia after earning his doctorates before accepting the invitation of a mentor to join LMB to help unstick a development team working on a radiation shielding system for long haul spacecraft. He not only got the team unstuck, but led them through a successful, industry-shaking product commercialization. Griffin did that a few more times with other applications and was soon running a big piece of the business. Twenty years later, he was running the company. Fiona respected his intelligence, of course, but she had also seen Griffin filet opponents. Whether it be the press, the military, or a competitor, McAllister had a mode that Fiona likened to an atom splitter. He was precise and high energy when he needed to be, and his decisiveness set off inevitable chain reactions that his adversaries were powerless to stop.

The thing that tugged at both of them, though, was that Griffin was the same age as Fiona's father. Or the age he would have been had he not killed himself. And she was the same age as his daughter with whom he had a distant relationship. Decades of tireless work and absence had damaged their relationship permanently.

So, when Griffin ran into Fiona on the convention floor, both running between meetings, he put his hand on her elbow and leaned his head forward to look over his reading glasses and talk to her.

Lucy hated the violation of Fiona's personal space and the number of staff and security that flitted about the man, but could read that Fiona was OK with it.

"Do you have plans tonight?" Griffin asked her.

"I do," she said in an apologetic voice.

"Break, em. Let this old man buy you dinner."

She hesitated.

"Just you and me," he said. "No staff. We can catch up, talk shit about our competitors and you can stiff arm my attempts to buy your company. It will be great."

She smiled.

"You name the place," he said, sensing her wavering.

She laughed.

"You get us a table at Seraphic and I'll be there."

"Consider it done," he said, releasing her elbow. His staff and security re-congealed around him, and he was absorbed by the crowd.

Lucy relaxed.

Fiona smiled.

Now, as the transparent elevator neared the top of the Ascender, Fiona and Lucy looked at the colors and shapes of Dubai's overdeveloped coastline glowing on the edge of the Persian Gulf, and she was glad she had accepted the invite.

Fiona and Lucy felt lighter in their shoes as the elevator began to decelerate. It came to a crawl before halting with only the slightest jolt as a soft chime announced their arrival. Fiona turned to look at herself in the polished elevator door. She was wearing a cobalt blue cocktail dress. Cobalt had been her father's favorite color for her. Fiona got sick of it when he was alive, always buying her clothes in that color. Now, she favored the rich, vibrant shade of blue which reminded her of her dad.

The doors slid open and Lucy had to stifle the urge to say, "Wow."

Fiona strode out of the elevator and Lucy tried to get her bearings. She had, of course, studied the Ascender's layout and memorized the floorplan of the rooftop restaurant in preparation for Fiona's outing tonight. She had pre-positioned four DredSkill assets in the Ascender, one near the lobby, one mid building, and two in Seraphic. They had all been in place an hour before Fiona's arrival, and would have called off the outing had they seen anything sketch. Lucy got a code-worded message from each of them ten minutes before she and Fiona arrived, confirming the all clear.

But that was not sufficient preparation for Lucy's sudden immersion in opulence and futuristic design surrounded by a 360-degree view of Dubai and the Persian Gulf at sunset.

She followed Fiona through a tall holographic archway of exotic jungle plants. The detailed projections reacted to their passing, as if jostled by the air that they disturbed. Tiny bioluminescent motes filled the space behind them, tangling and swirling before fading away.

Lucy's eyes, though, were tracking above them at the massive smart-glass dome that covered the entire roof. A hundred feet tall at the apex, the dome encased a peaceful climate-controlled environment, protecting it from the howling winds and merciless sunlight at this altitude in the gulf. The dome's fully adjustable opacity was fine-tuned 24 hours a day to provide seamless, comfortable transitions between day, night, and all-weather conditions.

Now, just after sunset, the dome was fully transparent, and it felt to Lucy like they were hovering in the clear night, just short of orbit. She would not have been surprised at all to see a satellite blink slowly by, just out of reach.

Lucy shook her head and focused back on Fiona and their environment.

A receptionist greeted Fiona as she stepped out of the holographic archway.

"Welcome to Seraphic, Miss Malloy," the young lady said. Dressed in a form fitting emerald green pencil skirt and white top, the receptionist confirmed the restaurant's reputation of having "The most beautiful staff in the world."

"We are so happy you could join us this evening," she said with a smile, gesturing toward the restaurant's seating area. "Doctor McAllister is already at your table. Please follow me."

Fiona and Lucy followed her through the restaurant, beneath the dome, toward their table. The sky above was dark and clear, and the stars had begun to compete with the lights of Dubai. Beautifully dressed men and women, some in traditional garb, some in chic ultra-modern outfits, sat at candlelit tables. The hum of animated conversations, spoken in diverse languages, mingled with laughter and permeated the restaurant with a warm buzz of energy. Sizzling tapas, exotic sushi, colorful curries, and rich pasta dishes testified that the menu was as diverse as the clientele. And the clientele's smiles and delighted faces testified that the world renown food was as good as its reputation. Fiona felt a pang of anticipatory hunger run through her. She was excited to eat.

Mcallister, seated at one of the coveted tables at the edge of the restaurant, close to the smart-glass dome, stood up from his table when he spotted Fiona. A warm smile broke across his face as he extended his hand.

"Thanks for coming," he said to her as they shook hands.

"Wouldn't have missed it, Griffin."

"That is terrific color on you," he remarked, gesturing at her dress.

Fiona didn't even try to stifle her smile.

"Thank you."

The receptionist smiled, standing a respectful distance from the two executives. Lucy stood behind her, hands folded in front of her waist, scanning the restaurant. Two people sat at the nearest table, a Caucasian man and Black woman dressed in dark suits, glasses of water in front of them. Lucy pegged them as part of Griffin's security team. The woman gave Lucy a slight node. She returned it.

"Helluva view, isn't it?" Griffin said to Fiona, taking his hand from her and sweeping it toward the Persian Gulf.

"It truly is."

"Please enjoy your dinner," the receptionist said, before turning to make her way back to the front desk.

"Is she with you?" Griffin asked, looking Lucy.

"Yes."

"Perhaps she would be comfortable with my team?" Griffin suggested with a subtle nod toward the dark suited pair at the table nearby.

Fiona glanced back at Lucy, who nodded to her and walked over to the nearby table. After a perfunctory handshake with the other two, Lucy scanned the restaurant again and then sat down.

"That is going to be a scintillating conversation," Fiona said, rolling her eyes at the three security professionals sitting in silence.

Griffin chuckled as he pulled out Fiona's chair.

"I made mine promise they would not kill everyone at the table next to us," he said, adjusting Fiona's chair as she sat.

She looked over her shoulder as Griffin sat back down. What looked like eight Chinese nationals sat around a circular table. Engrossed in conversation and eating, the group seemed not to notice her and McAllister.

Dubai was one of those places where Americans and Chinese rubbed elbows and interacted in ways they could not elsewhere. After over two decades of hot wars and a contest of empires that had spread across the solar system, the two countries were used to dining together in one location while sticking bayonets in each other's chest elsewhere. For those that made money off of the great power struggle, like Fiona and Griffin, this was rational. But for veterans like Lucy and her table-fellows, the situation tended to evoke different reactions that were based on long training and harrowing experiences, not enriching multi-year contracts.

"Is that Xu Cheng?" Fiona asked, leaning in to speak softly to Griffin.

"Yep. He and I said hello before you got here."

"Well then," Fiona said. "Maybe we should ease our teams' rules of engagement."

Griffin chuckled, but shook his head in disapproval.

"If you don't think that Cheng's team is ten times the size of ours, you still have a lot to learn."

Fiona shrugged.

Xu Cheng ran the largest AI weapons manufacturer in China. Sponsored by the state, it was the largest arms exporter in the world and Fiona and Griffin's fiercest competitor.

"I went ahead and ordered us appetizers," Griffin said. "I hope you don't mind."

"The lobster dumplings?" Fiona asked.

Griffin winked.

"Then I don't mind."

Griffin asked Fiona to choose a wine for the table and they settled into dinner. She had the Peruvian ceviche, and he had the Peking duck. Both were excellent. Fiona could tell that Griffin was trying to control himself. Usually when they got together, he didn't last ten minutes before making an offer for Spitting Metal. Tonight he made it all the way to desert.

Griffin took a sip of his double espresso as Fiona cracked the top of her crème brûlée. He set the small white cup down on its saucer. "We would be a great place for Spitting Metal, Fiona."

Fiona nodded as she took a bite of crème brûlée.

Griffin waited for her to respond, but she didn't. Taking several slow bites of her dessert instead. Crème brûlée was her favorite.

He smiled and took another long sip of espresso.

"And we would pay you so much money," he added.

Fiona smiled as she ran her spoon around the dish to get every last bit of her dessert.

Griffin downed the last of his espresso as Fiona finished and set her spoon down. They looked at each other in silence for a moment.

"What if I said you could name your price?"

"It's not my price to name," Fiona said, not bothering to conceal her sadness. "I've told you before. My grandfather controls the company. He would never sell."

"Why not?" Griffin asked. "I don't understand. You guys have done great, but he is a retailer. Why does he want to hold on to Spitting Metal? The defense industry is not his thing."

No, Fiona thought. *I am his thing.*

She just shrugged.

Griffin sighed and leaned back in his chair.

"We would have so much fun," he said wistfully. "I would be a great coach for you and you would love it at LMB. The resources at your disposal would boggle your mind. We could put that charity of yours on steroids. Think of it!"

Fiona smiled at Griffin and nodded as she thought, *I like you a lot, Griffin… But I would be so fucking gone if we sold Spitting Metal. Done. Out of this fucking rat race. Spending time with my brother in Italy, traveling the world and finally reading books.*

The waiter brought the bill to Griffin, and Fiona looked out at the dark horizon while he paid. She had known this conversation would be part of dinner, but had not expected it to affect her so much. She felt weary. Trapped. So ready to be done. For an instant, she felt like crying, but swallowed it and let anger take its place. *I'm an indentured fucking servant to a vile old man.*

"I must say, I don't understand why your grandfather won't even entertain an offer," Griffin said after the waiter had left.

Because then he would not be able to torture me, to watch me squirm and writhe under his thumb every day. That is the value of Spitting Metal to him. And, to him, it is priceless.

Fiona shrugged.

"I'm sorry, Griffin," she finally said.

Griffin nodded.

"I had to try. Now I can legitimately expense dinner."

Fiona chuckled.

"You will let me know if there is a change of heart?"

There won't be. There is no heart.

"I will."

An hour later, Fiona stood on her hotel room balcony. She had hoped a warm shower would help her shake the oppressive sadness that had settled over her at the end of dinner, but it had only re-heated her anger. Rather than try to sleep, she took a bottle of red wine from the mini fridge.

Now, on the balcony, glass of wine in hand, Fiona looked at the lights of Dubai and smoldered. She let her mind wander, fantasizing about freedom from her grandfather, concocting ways to escape, but the brick wall every line of thought ran into was that her grandfather controlled the company. And he would never sell. Period. The only way…

Her back stiffened as self-awareness bloomed within her.

She was actually considering it.

She stood motionless for a long moment as her mind raced in a way she had never let it before.

Sure, there had been times before when it had crossed her mind, but she had never let it roost and take hold.

Spitting Metal is a rounding error in the Malloy empire. She thought. *If the old man died, it would probably be liquidated at the first opportunity. A sale to LMB, for example.*

A change of control.

Full vesting.

Freedom.

Fiona took a slow sip of wine.

Kill my grandfather? I've done worse.

So has Thane.

She took another sip of wine, luxuriating in the thought.

Chapter Fifty-Seven

Max stepped out of the air taxi onto the platform of Grand Central Tower and took a look around. He didn't get up there much, and it impressed him every time he did. Thousands of drones, large and small, hurtled through the air over New York City. The kinetic cloud of air traffic, hundreds of feet above the tallest skyscrapers, looked like chaos at first glance, but Max found if he looked at it for a moment, without trying to focus, a logic and pattern emerged. He learned, during his time in the military, most AI-managed systems were like that. New York City's municipal air traffic system was the busiest in the world. And Grand Central was the center of it all.

Erupting from the original early twentieth century structure, the tower rose a hundred stories above the streets of Manhattan. It was built a few years after Seoul's lauded "Lilly Pad" system had shamed the rest of the world's capitals with its ability to support and manage a high volume of intra-city drone air traffic.

"Yeah?" New York City said. "Hold my beer."

Grand Central Tower was a magnificent structure that somehow managed to evoke the original rail terminus building's beaux-arts architecture all the way up to the expansive landing platform. The intricate details, including ornate facades and statues, concealed several hundred state-of-the-art, miniaturized wind turbines for power generation as well as rainwater harvesting inlets.

Rail, subway and ground taxi traffic still pulsed at and below street level within the terminal, but the heart of the building was the landing platform. Set atop the tower and spanning a full city block, the cantilevered structure was disquieting to look at from afar. It seemed ready to blow off at any moment, but it was solid to walk or land on. Max always marveled at how steady it felt.

About half of the Tower's traffic was unmanned commercial drones, delivering packages and other cargo to every nook and cranny of the City. The other half was un-piloted passenger traffic. Large "Busses" carried up to fifty people at a time on scheduled routes, while the smaller VIP aircraft came and went on chartered flights. The passenger activity was managed and fed by a large terminal building that looked like the bridge of an aircraft carrier with viewing decks around each of its five levels, and a crown of antenna reaching skyward. And, like all interesting places with a view in New York City, an exclusive bar and restaurant sat atop the terminal building.

Called The Zeppelin, the restaurant was decorated in the spirit of the golden age of aviation. Large black and white photos of aviation pioneers from the nineteen twenties and thirties hung on the walls next to antique propellers, vintage air maps and flight instruments displayed in glass cases.

The main dining area was designed to evoke the inside of a luxurious zeppelin. Its long curving walls seemed held together by metal tubing and riveted panels. The south-facing wall was on the very edge of the landing platform, offering views that felt like sitting in an old airship. As a final, extravagant and convincing touch, vibration devices had been built into the floor of the restaurant, inducing old, reciprocating engine-like vibrations throughout.

The bar was the highlight of the establishment and sat in the nose of the faux airship. Modeled after the forward interior of an old World War II bomber, a huge glass and steel nose cone expanded behind the bartenders, providing a spectacular view west across the Hudson River into New Jersey.

Max made his way across the landing platform to the terminal to meet with Thane. It was a clear day, and he had to squint against the glancing sunlight. Max wished he had remembered his sunglasses. Inside, he dodged pre-occupied commuters as he worked his way up the building's levels, opting for the steps rather than the escalators. A few minutes later, he arrived at the Zeppelin.

"Max Seagar," he told the smiling hostess.

"Yes, sir. Your colleague asked me to tell you he would be at the bar." She gestured toward the nose of the contrived aircraft.

Of course he is, Max thought. "Thank you."

Max walked beneath the images of leather clad airmen toward the bar. He had to chuckle when he spotted Thane, seated at the bar like some double-breasted bombardier.

Thane was facing away from Max's approach, looking out through the massive canopy at the afternoon sun over the Hudson. Max approached slowly and silently, stepped behind Thane. He placed his flesh hand on Thane's shoulder.

"Fucking stealthy as ever," Thane said, turning on his stool to face Max.

Max shrugged. "It's kept me alive so far."

The two veterans shook hands, and Max took a seat on the stool to the right of Thane.

"Amazing view, eh?" Thane said.

"It is."

The bartender stepped in front of Max.

"What can I get you, sir?"

"Soda water with lime, please."

Thane looked at Max with disapproval. He downed the last of his whiskey and then gestured to the bartender for another.

Max smiled. "You business development types get to do whatever you want. I'm still a working stiff. I have to stay away from day drinking."

"And I'm working on that, brother. But you are making me doubt your ability to fit in."

"Have I ever let you down?"

Thane shook his head.

"Why do we always meet in places like this?" Max asked, looking around.

"Because I am always working a rich potential client. Not grubby intelligence sources. You'll learn soon enough, our clientele needs to feel understood. Part of conveying that understanding vibe is meeting them in their element. Being comfortable and conversant in it. Frankly, by belonging in it."

"And let me guess," Max said. "You need me off of this stool in half an hour to make way for your next rich potential client."

"See?" Thane said, smiling. "You're learning."

The bartender set a whisky in front of Thane and a soda water with lime in front of Max.

Each man picked up their drink.

"To Charlie Company," they said in unison.

Each man drank and then set their glass down.

"So." Thane glanced around quickly and then leaned in towards Max. "Guess who is on the *Odysseus*?"

Max shook his head.

"Paul. Fucking. Owens."

"No shit," Max whispered, surprised.

"No shit. The only survivor from Miss Malloy's experimental unit and perpetrator of the Los Olvidados massacre. I don't know how, but some fucking way he got himself into a kind of work-off-your-time-doing-long-haul-space-runs program. I guess Space Command started the program to augment civilian crews to help compete with the Chinese."

Max nodded. He knew who Paul Owens was. Everyone of a certain military generation did.

"Well, I did not know what we were going to find," Max said. "But I was not expecting this."

"It gets better," Thane said in a voice that signaled things got worse. "The *Odysseus* and another company freighter, the *Perseus*, are both missing."

"What do you mean, missing?"

"I mean, the company lost contact with both ships and doesn't know where they are," Thane said. "Our source says the company is going bat shit trying to locate them, but has not reached out to Space Command for any help. They are keeping it close hold. No one else knows. You know how fucking secretive these commercial space types are."

Max rubbed his chin with his flesh hand.

Thane sipped from his whiskey.

The two men sat in silence for a few minutes, each pondering the developments.

Despite advances in technology and the trade, the space shipping business was still a risky one. Ships went missing. Pirate activity was at an all-time high and there were mishaps and accidents. But two? And one of them carrying Paul Owens?

What had that old man Musashi been up to? Max wondered.

"What do you think?" Thane asked.

"Not sure, to be honest," Max dropped his hand from his chin. "I'll do some digging on Owens. And I'll arrange for a DredSkill asset to meet the *Odysseus* if it shows up at a belt station. Total loss of communications out there is rare, but it does happen. Maybe they're fine and will pull into dock. We've got a few months' time before that would happen. It's unlikely, but if does happen, I want to talk to Owens."

Thane nodded in agreement.

"But if they are both truly missing…" Max's voice trailed off.

"Then what?"

"Then that is a problem."

"Let me know what help you need," Thane said. "We need to put this one to bed for Miss Malloy. And, you never know, there may be an opportunity here for us with the company. I've been trying to figure out a way to get DredSkill more involved in the commercial space sector. A lot of money sloshing around out there. This may open up a whole new revenue stream for us. Good work."

"OK," Max said, without enthusiasm.

Thane finished his whiskey.

"I do have one more thing, if you still have time," Max said.

Thane checked his watch and looked around the bar quickly.

"Sure. I've got about five minutes. What is it?"

"Pruden."

Thane laughed. "Like a dog with a bone, you are."

"I know," Max said. "It's just become an itch I have to scratch."

Thane opened his mouth to speak, then stopped. He shook his head slightly and smiled. "So, let's scratch it," he said in a friendly voice. "What are you thinking?"

"Truthfully, I am not sure what to think. What's bothering me is that the whole scenario kinda reminds me of how we ran some of our relocate and kill operations when I was on the black ops side of the fence."

Thane's eyes narrowed. "How so?" He asked as he ran his thumb over the bottom of his beard.

"We did it when command wanted a body to be somewhere to buttress their story," Max said in a conversational tone, as if he were talking about a gardening technique. "Like, say they wanted to use a body as a justifiable provocation for direct action or a diplomatic offensive. We would grab a foreign national that fit the narrative, like a known terrorist. Grab them at night in whatever country they were hiding out in and then smuggle them into the U.S. Then we would stage some kind of scene or near miss. Maybe he was trying to bomb a church full of nuns, for example. So we would stage a shootout, plant his bullet riddled body at the scene and, viola, crisis created."

Thane sat motionless on his stool as he listened.

"Where I got tripped up a few times in the beginning, though, was falsifying the border crossing. I mean, we smuggled them in, right? But for the story to stick, it had to look like they crossed into the states legally with malicious intent. There had to be a record of it for journalists or other nosey types to find."

"But the falsification of the simple border crossing data, that was the easy part. The first few times I got tripped up in the imagery and corroborating data. When you fake the entry, you have to name the entry port. LaGuardia International Airport, for example. Which is, by the way, where the records say Pruden re-entered the states."

Thane nodded to indicate he was listening as he gestured at the bartender for another drink.

"There are cameras all over that airport," Max added. "And all over New York City, for that matter. So, there should be imagery of the traveler. You know, video of him walking off the plane, passing through border control and customs. Shit, maybe even hailing a cab. The point is, unless they are guys like you or me that are sneaking across some desolate location, the average civilian is gonna pop up on imagery when they cross a border."

Max took a sip of his soda water.

Thane studied his face.

"And then there is corroborating data," Max continued. "Purchases, phone calls, that kind of thing. Someone that is legitimately in a location tends to leave at least a minimal amount of those kinds of data points."

"Fortunately, there is a way to deal with the imagery and corroborating data challenge," Max said, putting his glass down. "It's not hard. You just have to know to do it. Like I said, I learned that the hard way on a couple of operations that I almost botched because I didn't know what to do."

"Ever since then, I check that shit, you know," Max said, a hint of apology creeping into his voice. "Old habits die hard, I guess."

Thane nodded. "That's why we pay you, Max. For your instincts and scar tissue."

"Your whiskey, sir," the bartender said, placing the tumbler in front of Thane.

"I know you have another meeting soon," Max said hurriedly. "The thing is, there is no imagery of Pruden re-entering the United States on the day his digital passport says he did. Furthermore, even though he was supposedly back in New York City for three weeks before committing suicide, there are no transactional indications of that. Not a coffee, not a taxi, not a drink at a bar, not a phone call, nothing until the day his body was found, slumped over in a big leather chair in his apartment with an empty bottle of pills and a half-drunk bottle of wine."

Max stood up from his stool.

"Near as I can tell," he said in a lower voice. "The guy had no real enemies and spent the last few months of his life minding his own business and researching the events surrounding the Los Olvidados massacre."

Max rubbed his eyes, and then leaned closer to Thane.

"I'm worried Miss Malloy did some evil shit, Cyrus," Max said in a low voice. "And I'm worried you, me, and the outfit might get pulled into it."

Thane nodded. His eyes were narrow with concern. He took a sip of whiskey.

"Well, we're not going to let that happen. I can fucking assure you of that," Thane said.

At that moment, the hostess stepped up to the two men.

"Mr. Thane. You asked to be notified when Mr. Augustin arrived."

"Yes," Thane said, standing up from his stool. "Thank you."

"I'm sorry," Thane said, turning back to Max.

"It's OK. I know you have to go. I'm sorry to drop this in your lap in a rush."

"No. No. It's fine," Thane said. "It's more than fine. You may have saved our asses, Max. Good work. Can we meet tomorrow to make a plan?"

"Of course."

"OK. I'll get something set up. And it won't be at a bar this time."

Max chuckled.

"I'll believe it when I see it."

The two men shook hands.

"Thank you, Max," Thane said, before turning to walk toward the reception desk.

Chapter Fifty-Eight

The Geek and Lieutenant Ryuk sat at the round conference table in the StarScope chamber, the holographic inner solar system floating above their heads. Green and red course lines glowed, unchanged by any of Vish's new data or analyses from the past weeks. The faint cloud of uncertainty at the end of the red course line was also unchanged, still enveloping a mind bogglingly large volume of space.

"I am sorry, sir," Vish said. "I wish I had made more progress."

"Nothing to be sorry about, Vish," the general said. "There just isn't enough data. We are stumbling around in the dark."

The Geek leaned his head forward and rubbed his temples, elbows resting on the table.

Michelle snuck a glance at the general. He looked tired. The search for the *Odysseus* had been wearing on him. The glow from the holographic images above did not help, casting a light down on him that accentuated the bags under his eyes.

"Lieutenant Ryuk, you asked me to let you know when it was 0645 hours," Vish said.

Watches, like all over electronics and devices, were not allowed in the StarScope chamber by anyone.

"OK, thanks," the lieutenant said, standing up. They had been in the chamber for over an hour.

"Sir, you have General Nasir's staff call at 0730," she said to the Geek.

"Roger that," he said, standing up.

"Thanks, Vish," Michelle called over her shoulder as she followed the general out of the chamber. They gathered their things from the sergeant at arms and walked in silence down the hallway to the general's office.

"Coffee, sir?" Michelle asked as they neared her desk.

"That would be great, LT. Thanks," the general said, continuing on into his office.

Lieutenant Ryuk put her things on her desk and returned moments later with two cups of coffee.

She and the Geek stood in silence in front of one of the large windows. The general held the coffee with his good hand, the other in his pocket. The sun was not up yet, and the ocean was black beyond the launch pads.

"I have to remind myself that ships still get lost at sea," he said before taking another sip of coffee.

Michelle looked at the general and said, "We'll find the *Odysseus*, sir."

"Think about it, in the year 2072, ships are still lost at sea and never found. Aircraft, too, for that matter," the Geek looked back at Michelle. "I've got a buddy who is a commander in the Coast Guard. He told me that about a hundred ships and aircraft disappear out there every year." Hartwell gestured at the blackness of the sea with his coffee cup and then took another sip.

"All we need is one lucky hit, sir. A radio intercept, a weak bounce back of a navigational beacon, a stray reflection of light, a—"

"I know, LT. I know," the Geek interrupted wearily. "We are far from done."

Michelle nodded and looked back out the window.

"And I have really appreciated your help these past few weeks," the general said. "Thank you."

Michelle beamed.

"You're welcome, of course, sir."

Lieutenant Ryuk had attacked the general's rogue project with enthusiasm. The general had been impressed by her grasp not only of navigational technicalities but also of orbital mechanics. She drove Vish in a few directions that, while not revealing the *Odysseus'* location, had helped to confirm what it was that they did know. The Geek had to remind himself that they had, in fact, narrowed and refined their search area by orders of magnitude since they started.

But while they were closer than ever on a galactic scale, the gulf between them and the *Odysseus* seemed insurmountably large.

"Ah, good morning," Mrs. Johnson said, walking into Hartwell's office. "My general and his lieutenant are at it early again today, I see."

"Good morning, Mrs. Johnson," Hartwell said, not taking his eyes off the window.

Michelle stole a glance at Mrs. Johnson, who winked at her.

Mrs. Johnson placed a folder of papers requiring his signature on his desk as well as print out of the day's schedule, as she always did.

"First hard time is General Nasir's staff meeting at 0730, sir," she said, walking back toward her desk.

"Thank you," Hartwell said. He and Michelle finished their coffee in silence, looking out the window, before attacking the day.

ODYSSEUS

Chapter Fifty-Nine

Regas lay on his back on the bottom level of the Utility Module, holding his prize to his chest with his left hand. A pressure-suit helmet lay on the ground next to his head.

Dried blood from a broken nose covered his face. The fall to the Utility Module had smashed it flat. His right eye was swollen shut, and he wondered if his cheek had been fractured in the fall as well.

It didn't matter.

He'd made it.

When Regas had recovered consciousness after his fall to the Utility Module, he was disoriented. It seemed to take forever to figure out where he was, but when he did remember what he was doing and why, he started moving.

The journey from the bottom of the traverse into the Utility Module and down to the lowest level was hell.

But he made it.

Soon, he could rest.

He tried to get his breathing under control and prepared his mind for what he had to do next.

"What the hell is he doing?" Paul wondered aloud on the bridge. He had come straightaway when the XO had alerted him to Regas's moving.

"I don't know," the XO said. "But I don't like it. It is time to kill him, Paul."

"I think you are right."

Paul and the XO watched Regas's slow progress to the lower level of Hab as they planned Paul's attack. Rather than venturing back out into the void, and given Regas's reduced threat due to injury, Paul decided to go through the tube to the hub. There, an IR bot would meet him and cut open the airlock, which had been welded shut. Then Paul would go to the Utility Module and kill Regas.

They had just completed their planning, and Paul was donning his pressure suit when Regas activated the radio in the helmet he had found.

"Owens," Regas yelled at the helmet. "Hey, Owens, you fucking jigsaw, you there?"

Paul stopped working on his pressure suit, surprised to hear Regas's voice. He moved toward the large window.

The spinner turned over a kilometer away while the IR bots patrolled the *Odysseus'* long hull below the bridge.

"Owens!" Regas called again. "I'm talking to you, you son of a bitch!"

"Shall I put you through to him?" the XO asked.

"Sure. Let's hear what he has to say."

"Channel is open," said the XO.

"Regas, this is Owens. What do you want?"

Regas smiled.

A rush of adrenalin filled his veins, dulling his pain.

Almost, Regas thought.

"I just want you, that synthetic bitch of yours, the XO, and the Company to know that it was me who fucking killed you! That it was me, Belen Regas, who won in the end!"

Paul was not sure how to respond. He watched the Utility Module come into view in the distance, rotating slowly around the hub. He was about to tell the XO to shut off the channel and ignore the jackass when Regas interrupted him.

"See you in hell, Jigsaw!" Regas yelled over the radio.

Paul rolled his eyes on the bridge as Belen Regas put the hand-grenade pin in his mouth and pulled it out. He opened his hand to let the striker lever fly off and then held the grenade to his chest.

The striker lever clinked across the floor as the grenade's internal fuse cooked off.

"Fuck this idiot, XO," Paul said with disdain back on the bridge. "I'm going to—"

Paul was interrupted by a violent jolt that ran through the *Odysseus* as the Utility Module disappeared in an explosion of gas, fire, and torn metal.

A loud, high-pitched grinding sound pierced Paul's ears as the *Odysseus* shook and lurched from side to side.

Paul flinched as small pieces of debris struck the forward window inches from his face and bounced off. He watched a big spinning piece of metal strike an IR bot a hundred meters forward of the bridge, cleaving it in half. The sparking halves and the spinning projectile burrowed into the *Odysseus'* hull in a shower of sparks. Loud clangs echoed through the bridge as larger debris started striking the superstructure.

As Paul's watched the wave of damage roll back over the ship, his brain struggled to grasp the chain reaction kicking off a kilometer to his front.

Pieces of the disintegrated Utility Module continued to strike the hull. There were too many impacts to count. Several explosions erupted across the length of the old girl's forward hull.

The spinner, now hopelessly out of balance, held on to the Habitat module as it continued to rotate, but the hub was tearing itself apart. The gears were not designed for so wildly an imbalanced spinner. They began to seize.

Shock waves from the seizing hub traveled up and down the *Odysseus'* hull as the Habitat Module tried to continue rotating.

A hundred meters aft of the hub, the extreme asymmetric loads were too much for the *Odysseus'* hull. Trusses and structural plates, designed to withstand crushing longitudinal acceleration, snapped under the torsion induced by the flailing spinner.

Another violent jolt radiated through the ship.

A deafening screech rang through the bridge.

Paul watched the damaged front section start to bend back on itself under the ship. It was pulled down by the imbalanced spinner, which still clung to the circling Habitat Module.

If Paul had seen the looming impact, he would have braced and warned Althea.

It wouldn't have helped.

The Habitat's angular velocity at the end of the spinner combined with the momentum of the bending hull section as it folded back. The Hab broadsided the *Odysseus*, striking the ship's port side at over a hundred kilometers per hour. Gas and fire engulfed the *Odysseus*' hull.

The impact snapped off another forward section of the *Odysseus*' hull and kicked off multiple secondary explosions.

The walls of the bridge moved back and forth around Paul as the old girl pitched and yawed.

"Paul!" the XO said. "It is time for you and Althea to get into pressure suits."

Paul agreed. A decompression event seemed certain. Strange forces tried to push him into the corner of the room, and he struggled to get out of the bridge. He wanted to get to Althea.

Huge pieces of the *Odysseus* and dislodged cargo were now slamming into the rest of the ship. The impacts and secondary explosions caused more damage, ejected more large debris, and fed the destructive chain reaction.

The old girl was tearing herself apart.

"What is going on?" Althea yelled as Paul pulled himself into the MedBay.

"I think Regas blew himself up," Paul said, grabbing a handhold near the MedPod. "It set off a shit storm on the *Odysseus*!"

"Blew himself up? How?"

"Doesn't matter," Paul said. He pulled his head near the MedPod window. "I'm sorry. I know you are not done. But you need to get in a suit just in case."

"Roger that," Althea said.

"Hopefully we can get you back in when things stabilize," he said as the MedPod's clamshell top opened.

A large shudder passed through the bridge, accompanied by the earsplitting howl of metal.

"Yeah," Althea said, as she pushed herself out of the pod. "I won't hold my breath for that."

Althea slid her naked body into the pressure suit while Paul held her helmet and finished configuring his own suit. They drifted into the rear corner of the room.

Once they were both suited with green indications, Paul radioed the XO.

"XO," Paul said over his helmet radio. "I'm sure you are busy, but can you give us a status report?"

"The chain reaction set off by Regas caused extensive damage," the XO said. "The IR bot fleet is fully deployed, fighting multiple fires and trying to clear the more dangerous debris away from the ship. The *Odysseus* is unstable at the moment and is turning around her lateral, longitudinal, and vertical axes."

"Are we in danger?" Althea asked.

"Hard to say. But I recommend you two go to the bridge. Despite appearances of the large window, it is one of the most structurally robust sections of the ship."

"Roger that," Paul said. He tugged Althea behind him.

"Oh my God," Althea whispered when they got to the bridge and looked out the window.

The forward end of the *Odysseus* looked like a cigar that someone had rubbed out on their heel. Instead of a long, slender structure that extended for over a kilometer, Paul and Althea now looked down on a bent and battered hull that terminated a couple hundred meters from the bridge in an angry blossom of burned and bent metal. A dense cloud of debris surrounded the *Odysseus*. IR bots moved back and forth, pushing the larger pieces away from the ship.

To the starboard side, at the ship's two o'clock, the large hull section amputated by the Hab's impact drifted away, trailing debris and cargo.

Large cargo containers, jarred loose by the violence, wandered slowly away from the *Odysseus* at various angles of departure.

Althea grabbed Paul's suited hand as they floated in front of the window.

"What's going to happen to us, Paul?" she asked.

"I don't know."

And I guess I'll never get to finish translating that stupid book, he couldn't help thinking.

Chapter Sixty

"You can remove your pressure suits, Paul," the XO said. "The bridge, at least, has been stabilized. Its power generation and life-support systems were not damaged, and the maintenance boss has confirmed its hull integrity."

"Thanks," Paul said with relief.

Fifteen hours was a long time to spend in a pressure suit. He and Althea had spent almost all of that time floating in the bridge, watching the massive emergency repair effort through the large window. Paul had not said so, but it looked futile. Regas had crippled the old girl.

"How is the rest of the effort going, XO?" Paul asked as he and Althea took off their pressure helmets.

"Hard to say," the XO said. "The inspection-and-repair bots were not designed for situations like this. The damage Regas inflicted would challenge an entire orbital depot.

"Nonetheless," the XO continued, "the maintenance boss is driving his team as hard as he can. Every IR bot is either out actively repairing the *Odysseus*, in refuel, or being repaired themselves. As a result, they are holding the *Odysseus* together. But it is not a sustainable effort. Given the exigency of the situation, the maintenance boss has authorized high-risk activities. The IR bots are taking a lot of damage themselves. We just don't know if they will be able to get control of the situation before they are depleted."

"I don't suppose there is anything I can do to help?"

"I'm afraid not," the XO said. "And I would object to you leaving the bridge.

It is too dangerous anywhere else on the *Odysseus* at the moment."

Paul sighed and turned toward the large forward window. The *Odysseus* was shrouded in debris and venting gas. IR bots flew back and forth, too many to count, as they shoved debris clear of the ship or transported repair materials to a repair site.

One IR bot pushed a damaged comrade away from the ship. The pair flew perpendicular to the *Odysseus* a few hundred meters forward of the bridge. The rescuer had its arms fully extended, seeming to cradle the slightly smaller, damaged IR bot. Despite the distance, Paul could see that the front end of the damaged IR bot had been crushed and at least one of its utility arms severed. Sparks leapt out of the smashed bot, trailing behind the pair. When they had cleared the side of the *Odysseus*, the rescuer maneuvered them down under the ship, likely toward the hangar.

Paul turned away from the window and looked at Althea.

"How about the MedPod, XO?" Paul asked. "Is it operational?"

"Yes, Paul. As long as the bridge has sufficient power, it is fully operational."

Paul looked at Althea.

She shook her head.

"You have to," Paul said, pushing off the floor toward her. "We don't know how long the thing is going to continue working."

"I agree with Paul, Althea," the XO said. "You should get into the pod immediately."

Paul gestured at the passage down to the MedBay.

"Let's go," he said.

Althea pouted but followed Paul down to the MedPod.

Once she was sealed in receiving treatment, Paul reached a toe down to push off the floor and head back to the Bridge.

"Oh, no you don't," she said.

Paul stopped himself at the door and turned to face her.

"No way am I staying down here alone," she said from the pod. "I'm being a good patient. You be a good host."

Paul nodded in assent and pushed off the floor in the direction of the MedPod. He waited until he had drifted to within inches of the pod to stop himself, his face almost touching the glass of the viewing portal.

They smiled at each other for a moment. "I don't feel like talking about the Ōkami at the moment," Paul said.

"You don't have to."

"OK. So… Ask me a question, then," Paul told her. "Anything but that stuff."

"Well, I have been wondering something."

"Hit me," Paul said.

"How did you come across that old Japanese manuscript, anyway?"

Paul chuckled at the question.

"Well, it's a pretty simple story. I got it in the mail."

"In the mail?"

"Yep," Paul said.

"I'm going to need a little more than that," Althea said, disapproval in her voice.

"I was lying on my cot in the pre-launch quarantine facility on Canaveral," Paul began. "There was a special section for the military convicts. It wasn't much, but it was much better than Leavenworth.

"'Owens!' some guard yelled as he approached my cell.

"I jumped up and stood at the position of attention like a good military convict.

"He opened the door to my cell and placed a package on my cot.

"'That's a weird-ass care package you got there, convict,' he said as he locked the door and left.

"I looked at the package for a moment," Paul continued. "It had been opened and inspected, like all convict mail. The torn brown paper was falling away from the cardboard box, and the lid had been cut open. I figured it had to be from the Geek.

"I took the top off the box and found a leather-bound book, an English-to-Japanese dictionary, and a large blank leather-bound journal.

"I picked up the book and flipped through it. The damn thing was in Japanese."

Paul shook his head and shrugged, as if surprised all over again.

"As I did, an envelope fell out of the book and dropped to the floor," Paul continued. "It was addressed to me in handwriting that I instantly recognized as Doctor Musashi's."

Althea's eyes got wide. "Woooooooow," she said in a long whisper from the pod.

"Yeah. I think I stood there, motionless, staring at that envelope on the floor for ten minutes, trying to figure out what was going on. I mean, how the hell did he know where I was? That old guy had tentacles everywhere."

"I finally reached down and grabbed the envelope, opened it, and pulled out the letter. It said,

---

Dear Paul,

I hope you will find peace on your journey. The past is not what we wish it was. Nor is the present. Nor are we.

Still, all we can do is our best.

When I heard about this text, I knew that you must have it. It is called Adauchi. It was written by a masterless samurai sometime around the year 1500, when the clan fighting in Japan was at its worst, and the life of a soldier was at its hardest.

The text was only recently discovered. It has not been translated into English yet.

I have read it.

I believe it has a message for you.

I had a copy printed and bound for you. I thought that it might help you pass the time on your journey.

I wish you all the very best in your next chapter.

Your friend,

Dr. Musashi

"You memorized it?" Althea asked, surprise in her voice.

"I didn't mean to. But I would read it first each time I sat down to work on my translation. After a while…"

Paul's voice trailed off. He rubbed his forehead and then looked away from the MedPod. His eyes narrowed as if trying to focus on something in the distance.

"What is it?" Althea asked.

"I'm just sad that I lost that note."

"You lost it?"

"It was in my quarters on the Hab," he said. "Burned up, probably."

"You don't know that," Althea said in a hopeful voice.

Paul smiled at her wearily.

"It may be sailing through space now, preserved for all time," she said.

"But lost to me."

"Good thing you memorized it."

Paul nodded.

"Was the book on the Hab, too?" She asked him.

"Yeah," he said. "But I'm not too upset about that, to be honest."

"Why not?"

"The story was turning into kind of a bummer," Paul said.

"Oh."

"Yeah," Paul said. "And I have had my fill of sad endings."

Chapter Sixty-One

Adauchi Book One
Circa 1510
Translated from the Japanese

The next morning, in preparation for Castle Hayato's surrender, Lord Shingen assembled his forces in three columns. One facing the shallow river crossing to the west. One facing the rocky river crossing to the east. And one facing the large covered bridge to the castle's front. Hiroaki and his hundred students were in formation at the front of the center column, in the position of honor.

I assembled the hundred for Master Hiroaki and stood with him at the front of the formation.

Lord Shingen rode his horse forward with two mounted guards and a bannerman bearing the clan's black insignia.

"General Hiroaki," Lord Shingen said. "Would you do our clan the honor of allowing our bannerman to go with you as you march to accept Hayato's surrender?"

"It would be my honor, my lord," Hiroaki said with a smile.

"I thank you, my general," Shingen said. "I will return now to watch you accept the castle's surrender from the hill to the rear of the covered bridge."

"Good, my lord," Hiroaki said. "I will signal when the surrender is complete, and it is safe for you to come forward."

Shingen nodded and rode to the rear with his guards.

Hiroaki signaled the drummer, and we moved forward.

When the other two columns heard the drum and saw us move forward, they advanced also.

I guided our column from the right front. Hiroaki and the bannerman advanced on horse in front of us. They entered the covered bridge, and we, Hiroaki's one hundred, followed behind. Hiroaki emerged from the covered bridge a few footsteps in front of us. For the moment, he did not notice that the rest of the column had not followed him across the bridge.

None of us did.

Nor did we yet notice that the east and west columns had not crossed the river.

We marched forward.

When Hiroaki was close to the castle gate, he signaled our column to halt.

We heard clanking noises and shouts as the massive castle gate slowly began to rise.

That is when I, at the front right of our column, looked around and noticed the rest of the column had not followed us. I looked east and west and saw that the other columns had not crossed the river.

I leaned forward to alert Hiroaki but was interrupted by the sound of fifteen hundred Hayato castle guardsmen charging out of the castle, screaming, with katanas drawn.

Archers appeared on the walls. Arrows flew.

"Shields!" Hiroaki yelled, leaping from his horse to join our formation.

Every shield among us was raised in unison as the arrows rained down. Hiroaki's horse and the bannerman were killed.

The front rank of castle guardsmen collided with the front of our hundred in a horrible collision of blades and men.

Many of the castle guardsmen were on horseback. They galloped for the east and west river crossings.

"My lord!" I yelled above the din. "They ride to encircle us!"

"You must lead the rear back to the bridge, Manji," Hiroaki said. "Our crossing must be orderly! I will command this end of our hundred!"

"Yes, Master Hiroaki," I said. I ran under the shields as the fall of arrows continued.

"Now!" Hiroaki yelled as I reached the rear of the column. "To the bridge, Manji! Now!"

"On me!" I yelled. "Rear rank first. Stay in formation!"

We moved in unison toward the covered bridge, fighting as we advanced.

The shield bearers held their shields high, protecting our formation from the unceasing fall of arrows. Spearmen thrusted in all directions between shields, killing guardsmen with every jab. Bowmen shot arrows, timed with the return of the spears, dropping dozens of guardsmen at a time. Swordsmen slashed in rhythm with the shields and arrows, slinging blood on the ground and into the air.

We were surrounded. We were outnumbered more than ten to one.

I had no fear. We had yet to lose a man. Guardsmen fell like so much scythed wheat.

Miscues and mistakes happen in battle, after all. Particularly when disparate units join battle together. So, I was not yet disturbed by the blunders on our flanks at the other crossings, or that the center column had not followed us across the bridge. It happens.

But when I saw that the mounted guardsmen had crossed the river, a pang of alarm flared within me. They rode hard toward the far end of the covered bridge. And none of Shingen's forces opposed them.

Shingen stood on the crest of the small hill on the other side of the covered bridge, his forces arrayed around him. But no katanas flashed. No spears at the ready. No bows drawn.

They were observing.

That was when I knew.

That was when Hiroaki knew. That was when we all knew.

We had been betrayed.

The mounted Castle Guard reached the far end of the covered bridge.

"Onward, Manji!" Hiroaki yelled to me. "Through the bridge and through the guardsmen! To Shingen!"

We fought our way onto the covered bridge.

The guardsmen fell in bloody heaps. Hiroaki fought like a demon unleashed. His katana flashed in a silver-and-red blur. Hundreds of guardsmen lay in a pile of dead and bleeding from the bridge back to the castle. And the pile around the bridge continued to grow.

We exacted our price at the south end of the covered bridge as well. But we could not fight our way out. There were too many. And the bodies of the ones we had slain only barricaded us further. We pushed the bodies to the side to get to living enemy.

But our numbers dwindled as well.

I heard the shriek of a devil.

Hiroaki sailed over me into the enemy soldiers. A dozen dropped dead. A dozen more. His katana flashed savagely. And dropped a dozen more.

Hiroaki was going after Shingen himself.

I tried to cut through to get to him. But he was just out of reach. I could not get off of the covered bridge.

But my master fought on.

Beyond the flash of Hiroaki's sword, Shingen stood on the top of the small hill surrounded by his mounted guard. He gazed in horror at the sight.

"I am coming for you, Shingen!" Hiroaki yelled. "I am coming for you!"

I looked around the covered bridge. There were less than a dozen of Hiroaki's one hundred left. And we were all wounded.

I heard cannon fire from the castle.

The shriek of flying cannonballs grew louder. I turned to warn Hiroaki. But I could not see him. The pile of bodies surrounding him was too high.

The cannon fire destroyed the bridge. I was thrown into the air, losing my katana. I fell back, barely catching myself on a fragmented wooden beam. The river flowed many feet beneath me. I tried to pull myself up. But could not. I did not have the strength.

I looked for my comrades. There were none left.

I looked for Hiroaki.

I saw him being held by half a dozen castle guardsmen. He was unarmed.

Lord Hayato himself looked down from his horse upon Hiroaki.

Hayato dismounted and drew his katana. He walked to Hiroaki and said, "For my son."

Lord Hayato cut Hiroaki's head off.

My heart broke.

My grip failed.

I fell to the river.

Chapter Sixty-Two

"Paul," the XO said. "Paul, I apologize for waking you, but we need to discuss our current situation."

"OK," Paul mumbled. He blinked his eyes as they gained focus and turned to look at the MedPod. Althea was in rest mode, with her eyes closed.

Paul stretched. "Let me take a piss, and I'll come up to the bridge."

"Very well."

Several minutes later, Paul floated onto the bridge. "What's up?"

"The damage to the *Odysseus* is much worse than we thought," the XO said.

"I'm not surprised," Paul said. "But as long as we are able to limp close enough to the belt to get picked up, we'll be fine. They can tow the old girl to a maintenance dock and find Althea and me a ride back to Earth."

The XO was quiet.

Paul got nervous.

"What?" he asked.

"Power and propulsion was hit many times by debris and dislodged cargo. The nuclear reactors were badly damaged."

"Terrific," Paul said, shaking his head.

"The maintenance boss and I are working with power and propulsion as fast as we can," the XO continued. "But we are down to less than fifty percent of our IR bot strength, and our odds of success have been decreasing."

"What does that mean?" Paul asked.

"It is highly likely that at least one nuclear reactor will fail catastrophically."

"Highly likely?"

"Ninety-one-point-four percent likely," the XO said. "And increasing."

"And what, exactly, does 'catastrophic' mean?" Paul asked, irritation seeping into his voice.

"An explosion. Which will destroy the *Odysseus*."

Paul was quiet, digesting the news. He turned toward the large window and looked past the broken ship into the void.

"We came a long way just to be vaporized," he said softly.

"I want you to know that we are not giving up," the XO said. "The maintenance boss is trying every trick he knows. But I thought it right to let you know what is happening and the unlikely prospect of success. I would want to know if I were you."

"I appreciate it. Thank you."

"Of course."

"How long?" Paul asked.

"Twenty-four to forty-eight hours."

"Plenty of time," Paul said, checking his watch. "Let me know if anything changes."

"I will."

Paul went back to the MedBay. He stared at Althea through the MedPod window until, hours later, he fell asleep.

* * *

When Paul woke up, Althea was staring at him from the MedPod.

"Hello, sleepyhead," she said.

"Hello."

"What's wrong?"

"What do you mean?"

Althea made a show of narrowing her eyes and glaring at Paul.

Paul looked away.

"You went and spoke with the XO and then came back and stewed until you fell asleep," she said. "What is wrong?"

"I thought you were in rest mode," Paul said, surprised at all she had noticed.

"Rest mode," she agreed, nodding. "I wasn't dead."

Paul shook his head in appreciation.

"Seriously," Althea said. "Tell me."

"The reactors were damaged. XO says they're probably going to explode and destroy the *Odysseus*."

"And us," Althea added.

"And us," Paul agreed.

"When?"

Paul looked at his watch. "One cycle. Maybe two."

"I see."

"Yeah."

He floated in silence for a moment. Then shook his head. "Shit," he said.

"What is it?" Althea asked.

"Oh," Paul said, with a hopeless shrug. "There is just something I was really hoping to be able to do someday. Back on earth."

"What?"

"Well, I suppose it doesn't matter if I tell you now. I didn't want to earlier. Didn't want to put you in an awkward spot."

"What? You can tell me anything."

"OK. You remember how I told you about how it all ended for the Ōkami? How they were murdered on Outpost Devil by a bunch of mercenaries?"

"Yes," Althea said. "I remember. By the order of that woman. Fiona Malloy."

"That's right... I was hoping to make it back. Then, somehow—by some miracle—get parole. Or escape... It seems stupid now. But I was going to find a way to get free. I was gonna inflict pain on DredSkill. Then find Fiona Malloy and kill her."

Paul looked up at Althea.

"To avenge the Ōkami," he said.

Althea nodded.

They looked at each other for a long time.

The clicking sound of the MedPod locks deactivating broke the silence, and the pod's clamshell door opened.

"What are you doing?" Paul asked.

Althea pushed her naked body out of the MedPod. The discoloration of her wounds was gone.

She floated slowly across the MedBay toward Paul.

"What are you doing?" he repeated.

"I'm not going to spend the rest of my life in the MedPod," she said, nearing him.

His eyes roved over her. He couldn't help it.

"And I don't want you spending the rest of your life thinking about killing and death."

She smiled.

He reached out to catch her.

His arms encircled her waist. Her momentum pressed her body against him and imparted a rotation and tumble to their embrace.

Chapter Sixty-Three

A loud clang woke Paul.

He rubbed his eyes and looked around the MedBay. Althea, in rest mode, floated several meters from him. Her naked body was wrapped in two blankets that enfolded her like too much origami. All Paul saw of her was a bolt of jet-black hair above her forehead and one leg from the knee down.

As soon as he convinced himself he had imagined the noise, he heard another one. A long, scraping sound, like someone dragging a knife through a cardboard box, came from somewhere below.

He looked around.

Althea still slept.

Paul pulled on his flight suit and went to the bridge. He heard several more bangs as he approached the large window.

An IR bot sped by within inches of the glass, startling Paul.

A second later, another zoomed past.

Paul touched a toe to the floor, pushing himself forward.

He caught himself with his fingertips against the window, and hung motionless, alarmed by what he saw.

The bridge was surrounded by a horde of IR bots. They converged from every direction.

Another loud impact sound rang out behind him, as if a truck had driven into the bridge.

Althea floated on the bridge looking for Paul. She clutched her blankets and looked around, trying to make sense of the increasing noise.

Paul stared at an IR bot twenty meters below the forward window. It approached the bridge superstructure, carrying a large welding torch.

"Are you kidding me?" Paul mumbled as the IR bot's torch flared and it started slicing metal.

"What is it?" Althea asked.

A buzzing noise and vibration filled the bridge.

"What is happening, Paul?" she asked.

Paul didn't answer, unable to take his focus off of the IR bots swarming around the bridge.

A loud impact struck above Paul and Althea, on the topside of the bridge.

"Paul!" Althea yelled. "What is going on?"

"I don't know," Paul said, pushing away from the window back toward her. "But it looks like we are under attack."

"Attack? What do you mean?"

Paul's mind raced. *Is this another goddamn AI mutiny?*

"XO!" Paul yelled. "XO, status report!"

No response.

The loud bangs and scrapes were continuous now and came from all directions.

Paul and Althea exchanged worried looks. She held out her hand. Paul took it and pulled her to him.

The bridge sounded like a construction site. Noises like jackhammers, chain saws, and welders filled the air.

"They're tearing the bridge apart!" Althea shouted over the din. She put her hands over her ears as Paul returned to the window.

He pressed against the glass.

There was a swarm of IR bots around the base of the bridge, fifty meters below. Sparks and chunks of metal flew off the superstructure where they attacked.

"XO!" Paul demanded. "XO! Situation report, damn it!"

Paul pushed off of the window and glided over to the command chair. He flipped through all the switches as he yelled at the XO.

"XO, do you hear me? XO, we are in trouble. We need a situation report."

The earsplitting sound of rending metal filled the bridge as it tilted several meters to starboard.

"Pressure suits, now!" Paul yelled.

They donned their pressure suits in a rush, expecting explosive decompression to strike at any second.

"Paul!" the XO's voice said over their suit radios. "Paul, can you hear me?"

"XO!" Paul yelled back. "What the hell is going on? Why were you not responding?"

"I'm sorry, Paul. That idiot maintenance boss severed my hardwired communications to the bridge too soon. I was hoping you would figure it out and use a suit radio."

"We didn't figure anything out," Paul said, anger in his voice. "We feared for our lives and got suited to prepare for whatever comes next."

"Why are they attacking us?" Althea demanded.

"Attacking?" the XO asked. "Oh no. I am so sorry. I can see how you would get that impression."

"What the hell is going on?" Paul shouted into his radio, his patience expired.

"Degradation of the number-two reactor has accelerated, and we don't have as much time as we thought. Failure and detonation could occur at any moment now," the XO explained. "The maintenance boss and navigator came up with a plan to get you two to minimum safe distance. The maintenance boss is working to separate the command-and-control module from the *Odysseus*. He is also welding additional radiation shielding to the C&C's outer hull. When that is complete, he will fasten the four tug drones to the C&C, two on each side. The navigator will give the tug drones a course to follow. They will fire their engines, and you will depart."

Paul and Althea were silent.

They could hear banging, buzzing, and cutting noises as the maintenance boss continued his work.

"We will depart?" Althea asked, confused.

"What will you do, XO?" Paul asked.

"As soon as the command-and-control module has separated from the *Odysseus*, I will fire my main engines. I will put the ship on a heading opposite of your assigned course and will move as fast as I can manage. With any luck, I'll be far enough away from you when the reactors explode."

"I don't like this plan very much," Paul said.

"Trust me," the XO said, "I don't either."

"XO, I don't want to leave you," Althea said, shaking her head.

"I don't want you to either, Althea. But this is the only way."

"What course will we be on?" Paul asked. "Do we really have a chance, or is this just delaying the inevitable?"

"Paul is right," Althea said. "If this is just giving us a little more time, we should stay together."

"I appreciate the sentiment. But the navigator has assured me it is survivable."

"I don't like this," Althea said.

"Althea, you owe it to me and the rest of the crew to try," the XO said.

Paul looked out of the window at all the activity. Dozens of IR bots transporting large metal plates waited in line behind the welders. There was a loud bang when the plates were put into position, followed by a staticky buzzing noise as the welders attached them to the C&C. Once complete, the next plate was shoved into place by the next waiting IR bot.

"Quite a lot of shielding," Paul said into his helmet mic.

"It is," the XO said. "More than is required to protect you from the blast radiation. But it's all I have on hand at the moment."

Paul nodded in his helmet, unsure of what to say.

"We don't have much time," the XO said. "I need to pass on more instructions from the navigator before your departure."

"OK," Paul said.

"You're in for a journey of at least six months. By then, the navigator estimates the rendezvous becomes highly likely. But not before. To make it that far, you are going to have to strictly ration your food and water intake as well as your power consumption. Furthermore, because of the way the C&C module has to be removed from the *Odysseus*, your accompanying life-support equipment will be greatly reduced. I do not know how long the scrubbers will be able to provide you with breathable atmosphere. Hopefully at least six months."

Paul looked out of the large window as the XO spoke. The four tug drones approached the C&C module. They flew in a tight, clustered formation until they were within twenty meters of the window and then separated from each other and decelerated. Two passed out of view to the left and two to the right.

"I don't know how much food you have on board the C&C, but hopefully it will last you," the XO continued. "Althea, I recommend you spend as much time as possible in rest mode. And Paul, I recommend you take hibernation meds to reduce your water, caloric, and oxygen requirements. The MedBay should have a reasonable supply. Do not use the MedPod or any other system that requires a lot of power, of course. Hopefully you are far enough along that this will not present a problem for you, Althea."

An impact to the left side of the C&C startled Althea. Then another on the right side. Seconds later, loud buzzing noises filled the air. Paul pictured the IR bots firmly holding the tug drones while the welders lashed them to the command-and-control module's flanks.

Paul shook his head.

"What is it?" Althea asked him.

"We're going to be one ugly fucking spacecraft."

"I won't tell the maintenance boss you said so," the XO said.

"Just tell him we said thank you," Paul said in a somber voice. "The navigator as well."

"I will."

Paul noted through the viewing window that many of the IR bots were departing. The noise was trailing off as well.

"We're getting close, aren't we?" Paul asked.

"Yes. A matter of minutes, I would think."

"How many G's we in for?" Paul asked, tapping on Althea's shoulder and pointing to the rear of the bridge.

"Given the mass of the bridge, no more than ten," the XO said.

"Ouch," Paul said.

"I know," the XO conceded. "The good news is that you will probably pass out and it will not be long term. The tugs are going to run at max power until the reactor detonates. If the bridge survives the blast, they will relent. At that point, you can expect one G until they run out of fuel."

"How long do you think we will be at max burn?" Paul asked, not wanting to phrase it the other way.

"No more than a few minutes."

The C&C swayed back and forth a few times, and then a loud snap rang out, accompanied by a jolt that radiated through the entire structure.

The stars outside the window spun slowly, and Paul realized they had been amputated from the *Odysseus*.

Paul stared at the tilting void. The *Odysseus'* long prow, which Paul had looked at through the large viewing window for almost a year and a half, was no longer in sight.

They were adrift.

The bridge's sudden angular acceleration moved the rear wall in relation to Paul and Althea. They were moving toward the middle of the bridge.

Paul touched a toe to the floor and pushed Althea back toward the rear wall. He moved himself in that direction as well.

"Paul and Althea," the XO said. "It has been my pleasure to serve with you both."

"XO, I—" Paul was interrupted by a bright, searing glare. The *Odysseus* inched into view, riding a white-hot fireball.

The ship passed in front of the bridge, accelerating on the nuclear fire of her ailing reactors.

It was a pitiful sight. The once long and purposeful ship was now broken. Paul and Althea got a good view of the extensive damage Regas's suicide had wrought. Burned impact damage covered the truncated hull like a pox. Cargo, loosened by the incident, tumbled out of the accelerating ship. And topside, where the bridge used to stand, was an ugly burned nub of severed metal.

It's a blessing, Paul caught himself thinking. *She'd be scrapped anyway. This is better.*

Then he remembered the XO.

The ship was farther away now. All Paul could discern was a fireball. And it was accelerating.

"XO, can you read me?" Paul transmitted. The suit radios did not have a long range, but he wanted to try.

"Yes, Paul," the XO responded, with a lot of static. "I can hear you."

A roar startled Paul.

The stars spun around outside the large window.

The tugs were setting up for their burn. A few more short roars emanated from different angles as the team of four worked the bridge to an entry solution for their assigned course.

Paul pushed Althea against the rear wall. "Stay as flat against the wall as you can," he said to her as he nudged his own body back. "This part is going to be really uncomfortable."

"I know," she said with fear in her voice.

"Paul, do you read me?" the XO said over the radio, static nearly covering his voice now.

"Yes. Yes, I hear you. I just wanted to say thank you and that we will never forget you. You will be remembered."

"Strange," the XO said, Paul barely making out the words. "That actually helps."

The four tug drones fired their engines in unison.

Paul and Althea slammed against the rear wall.

The howl of the four tug engines at max burn was deafening, so Paul could not be sure. But he thought he heard the XO say, "Godspeed, my friend, Paul Owens."

Then Paul blacked out.

EARTH

Chapter Sixty-Four

Max's phone rang early that morning. He was still on his first cup of coffee in his apartment.

He glanced at the caller ID and smiled.

"You're up early for a Biz Dev guy," Max said.

"No shit," Thane responded. "Sucks. Got called up to meet with the boss lady. On my building's platform, waiting for the air taxi now."

Max could hear the wind whipping around Thane's phone.

"So, obviously, I can't meet this morning," Thane continued. They were supposed to meet at Thane's office to discuss the Pruden and Malloy situation.

"No problem. I understand. When the Miss Stone calls, we have to jump."

After founding DredSkill, Eris Stone spent a decade as a player-coach, leading high risk operations herself, while also masterminding the outfit's business strategy. She had not led an operation in a long time, and now rarely left her estate north of New York City. Getting "called up to meet with the boss lady" was code in the outfit for being summoned to the expansive property on the Hudson River called Highcliff Hall.

"Have you ever been to Highcliff?" Thane asked Max.

"No," Max said, chuckling. "I think that is only for those of your rank, buddy."

"Are you free this afternoon?"

"Um… I could cancel some stuff."

"Why don't we do this?" Thane said, enthusiasm creeping into his voice. "There are several lodges on the property. I'll check with the Highcliff staff, but I am sure there is room. You could come up late this afternoon. We'll war-game the situation, then have some dinner, drink some bourbon, and generally reward ourselves for being the men we are."

"You sure?"

"Hell yes. If I can, I'll arrange for you to meet Miss Stone tomorrow before we head back to the city."

"Don't do that."

"Bullshit. She has heard good things about you. This will be a good thing, Max. For sure."

Max could hear the noise of Thane's the approaching air taxi building in the background.

"It's settled, then," Thane shouted over the noise. "I'll text you later to coordinate your pick up. Pack an overnight bag."

The wind noise overwhelmed Thane's voice. Max thought he heard him say goodbye and then end the call.

Cool, Max thought. *This will be fun.*

Max was glad that Fiona was in DC for the day. He didn't want to have to make small talk with her before meeting with Thane that evening. He couldn't help but feel disloyal, even though he was convinced that, though she may not have pulled the trigger, or shoved the pills down his throat in this case, she was responsible for Pruden's murder.

Max sent Lucy with Fiona's security detail and spent the day on administrative tasks in his office in the Determined End States building. He also took some time to get his thoughts together for the meeting with Thane, who texted him mid-day to say an air taxi would pick him up at 1700 hours on the platform.

Max was waiting when the sleek aircraft dove out of the cloud of drones above Gotham and executed a graceful landing despite the ever-present high winds that swept the city's highest rooftops. Max grabbed his overnight bag and climbed aboard. Half an hour later, he was descending beneath the tops of tall oaks and hickories toward the landing pad on the grounds of Highcliff Hall. Thane stood outside the blast of the rotor wash, waiting next to a vehicle.

Max hopped out of the air taxi and walked toward Thane, who met him with an outstretched hand.

"Welcome to Highcliff, buddy!" Thane shook Max's hand as the drone lifted off to head back to the city.

"Thanks," Max said, looking around. The western horizon had taken on a purple glow in the late afternoon light, and the forest of Highcliff was darkening. "Quite a spread."

"You haven't seen shit yet." Thane gestured at the vehicle. "Get in. I'll show you around."

For the next hour, Thane drove around the grounds of Highcliff, telling Max the history and backstory of each spot. Rolling hills and towering trees covered nearly the entire three-hundred-acre expanse. The main house, after which the estate was named, dominated the crest of undulating hills at the top of granite cliffs that plunged into the river.

The centuries old manor overlooking the Hudson was a Victorian masterpiece. Built in the nineteenth century, Highcliff Hall's turrets and towers rose dramatically over sprawling verandas that wrapped around the house on multiple levels. For nearly three hundred years, the grey stone building had withstood hurricane-driven winds as well as the passing of different generations and owners. It looked like it would stand three hundred more.

With high ceilings, tall windows, elaborate moldings and ornate carvings throughout, the interior of the house was as majestic as the exterior. Eris had Highcliff Hall decorated with her private militaria collection. Paintings, uniforms, medals, swords, blades and firearms adorned the walls and sat in lit displays throughout the house.

The enormous dining room was Highcliff's center of gravity. Offering stunning views of the grounds, the room featured Eris' favorite paintings, each one depicting a historically significant military event. The large dining table could seat forty, and was built with wood salvaged from old, masted

American fighting ships. The table's centerpiece was a multimillion-dollar collection of Ancient Greek helmets.

In addition to the grand main house, the estate boasted a dozen other buildings, including a couple of smaller lodges, a carriage house, a greenhouse, stables and a shooting range complete with high and low skeet houses.

Max was touched that Thane seemed excited to share the place with him. But by the end of the tour, he felt a sense of disquiet. This was another world. A level of wealth Max could not entirely grasp. He knew that being a military contractor was not charity work. That it was a business. But touring the grounds underlined that part of the job, which he seldom really thought about, in a way he could not readily push aside.

"Here is where we are for the night," Thane said, as they pulled up to one of the smaller lodges in one of the more remote locations on the grounds. "I'll show you your room and then we can get down to business."

The lodge was a two-story building with common areas on the bottom floor and guest rooms above. A massive stone chimney anchored the middle of the structure. Large fireplaces heated a dining hall on one side and a well-appointed den on the other. After Max had put his overnight bag away and splashed water on his face, he met Thane in the den.

Thane was already enjoying a bourbon and seated in one of the oversized leather chairs next to the fireplace.

"I poured you one, buddy," Thane said, raising his glass. "It's over there on the bar."

"I think I'll wait till we're done with the work talk," Max said, walking past the bar.

"Buddy," Thane said in a low, conspiratorial voice. "It's Pappy for god sakes. Join me. No reason we can't enjoy a drink while we talk about this evil shit."

"Pappy van Winkle? You serious?"

Thane shrugged.

"Compliments of the boss lady."

"OK, then," Max said, turning back and grabbing the shot of bourbon. "You have to tell Miss Stone I said thank you."

"Tell her yourself tomorrow."

Max's eyebrows raised as he shot Thane a quick look.

"We're chatting with her in the morning before heading back to the city." Thane smiled and extended his glass toward Max's. "To Charlie company."

"To Charlie company," Max said, clinking his glass against Thane's. He took a sip of the Pappy and smiled.

"Pretty good, right?"

"Right," Max said, sitting in the big leather chair opposite Thane, the big stone fireplace to his right.

Max took another, larger sip of the expensive bourbon and leaned back in his chair.

Thane drained his shot glass. He got up, walked over to the bar, and came back with the bottle of rare bourbon. He refilled his glass and set the bottle down on the knee-high stone hearth. His face grew serious as he turned to look at Max.

"OK," Thane said, a hint of sadness in his voice. "Let's talk about this situation. Tell me what you think is going on."

Max drank the last of his bourbon and set the glass down on the hearth. Thane refilled it as Max began.

"The truth is, I have more questions than answers. But from what I have been able to find out, I think Fiona Malloy arranged for Pruden to be killed. Furthermore, I think she was somehow involved in the Olvidados massacre."

"Involved how?" Thane asked, sitting back down opposite Max.

"I'm not sure. Obviously, she was not there. She was not involved in the actual military operation. But I think she may have been involved in the setup or something like that."

"The set up?"

Max nodded slowly.

"She had a hand in the disaster somehow."

Thane's eyebrows raised.

"Yeah," Max said. "It's thin, I know. But I think that may have been what

Pruden was doing in South America. I think he may have been trying to figure out what happened."

Max felt the lovely flare of warmth in his belly from the bourbon and welcomed it.

"Do you have any hard evidence of this?" Thane asked, running his fingers over his beard.

"Not yet. But I did manage to locate two memory drives that the police overlooked." Max shook his head in disgust. "Damn police. Had the drives since their first sweep of the crime scene and never analyzed them."

Thane exhaled derisively and took a sip of bourbon. Max did the same.

"I think there is a connection between this and what Doctor Musashi was up to before he killed himself," Max said. "I think that, maybe, he and Pruden were communicating. Working to get to some kind of truth about something that Miss Malloy did. Something that involved the Ōkami field trials."

Max rubbed his eyes. He was feeling the fact that he had skipped lunch. The bourbon had gone to his head.

"You don't have to extrapolate too far to get to an act of treason by Miss Malloy." Max dropped his hand from his eyes to the chair's leather arm rest.

Thane studied Max for a moment. He sighed and drained his second shot of bourbon.

"Given what you had to work with, buddy," Thane said, setting his glass down next to the bottle. "That's pretty damn good."

"What?" Max said, not following the comment. He found it hard to focus his vision on Thane.

Thane sat still.

Max realized his vision was tunneling, fuzzy and dark on the edges. His hands were tingling.

"You motherfucker." Max tried to rise to his feet.

His legs felt rubbery. They buckled, and he pitched forward. Thane caught him.

"Easy, buddy." Thane eased Max back into his chair.

"You put something in my drink," Max said.

"I did." Thane sat back down in his chair. "I'm sorry, buddy. But you were getting too close and wouldn't take a fucking hint. You always were too smart and stubborn for your own good."

Max felt his vision narrowing further.

"You were involved," he said. His tongue felt thick and slow.

"Yep. From the very beginning."

Thane poured himself another shot and leaned back in his chair.

"Miss Malloy reached out to DredSkill for help with the Ōkami situation. She needed her other company, Spitting Metal, to be bumped up in priority with the Military Acquisitions Command. The Ōkami field test was strangling her with its success. She couldn't pull or scrub the Ōkami field test - that's how you get a bad reputation with the acquisitions geeks. She needed something done discretely. And quickly.

"I don't know how she found us, to be honest. I have to wonder if it was that mean old grandfather of hers. Anyway, the boss lady asked me to look at the situation to see what we could do.

"I'll never forget when I first met Miss Malloy," Thane said, a faraway look on his face. His eyes seem to focus on a distant sight for a moment.

"When I met with her," he finally continued. "She thought there might be an angle to play with Navarro, the guerrilla leader the Ōkami were tangling with down in South America. Some really bad blood had developed between them. Miss Malloy thought we might be able to leverage the dynamic, but did not know how.

"That's where I came in," Thane said with pride. He took a sip of bourbon and continued.

"I flew down to South America and met with Navarro. He wasn't hard to get to because he was such an arrogant asshole, and I still had a few contacts in that neighborhood because of my last tour down there.

"Anyway, I spoon fed the operational concept for the ambush to the dumb bastard, helped him pick a location and devised some intelligence nuggets he could plant in the HUMINT channels. I told him what to say on what frequencies to make sure SIGINT intercepted corroborating intel. Then I got the hell out of dodge and flew back to Santiago.

"I have to tell you, I was surprised how quickly the two Ōkami company commanders found and then took the bait. They went down to Los Olvidados with the last of their strength and got their asses kicked. Worked like a charm, really. Just like we planned it.

"Then that numbnuts, Navarro, went and executed one of the company commanders. I had told him to avoid hurting the human leadership of the unit at all costs. It would complicate things and, you know, none of this was their fault." Thane gave a what-could-I-do shrug and took a sip of bourbon.

"The idiot dragged her guts around the town square. Really gruesome shit."

Thane shook his head, remembering the incident.

"Nonetheless, my operation worked," Thane said. "The Ōkami were recalled. Due to leave the country within 48 hours. Miss Malloy got a call from the acquisition command asking if she could accelerate Spitting Metal's trials. Malloy told 'em, 'Sure. For a fee.'"

Thane chuckled. "Balls on that chick, right?" he said to his dying friend.

A sad look passed over Thane's face. He took a sip of whiskey and it left.

"The next day the surviving company commander, Owens, went ape shit," he continued. "He found Navarro, because the dumb motherfucker was celebrating like a jackass. Owens took the last of his force in a lights-out, sensors-off raid and beat the shit out of Navarro and his top lieutenants. Owens personally executed most of them. Then they flew back to their shitty operation base.

"Well then, we had a real and proper mess on our hands. I took a team of DredSkill contract soldiers to round up and destroy the last of the Ōkami equipment. Everyone was scared shitless of them, including us. That Pruden guy you've been obsessing over went with us.

"I could tell he was not OK with Miss Malloy's decision. But he was not in on the play we ran with Navarro. He started geeking out when he realized why me and my guys were there. We rounded up the robots and destroyed them quickly, before they realized what was going on.

"Pruden lost his shit. Started crying like we had shot a bunch of humans.

"And, get this, you remember that tough old Centaur Colonel Filson? Turns out he was the military project leader for the Ōkami. The crazy bastard jumped into the pile of burning robots for some reason. Got burned up real bad."

Thane paused and shook his head in respect.

"But, you know what?" Thane said, as if he were drinking with a buddy, not killing a friend. "He fucking walked out of that pile of fire and metal like the boss he was back in Santiago."

"He ended up dying pretty quickly after that," Thane said quietly. "He was just too burned up."

Thane sighed and picked up his whiskey. He held it out to Max.

"To the old man."

Max's head was lolled over to one side and his body looked deflated, sinking deeply into his chair.

Thane gestured as if clinking his glass to Max's and then drank.

"That was the day the fucking memory sphere went missing," he continued. "Now I am pretty sure Filson had something to do with it. But… well, he ain't talking anymore.

"Wasn't for a few weeks, though, before we really starting looking for that sphere. Round that time this Pruden asshole, who had quit Malloy's company, starts looking like a problem. Miss Malloy does not like loose ends, as you know. Particularly with a top-secret court martial coming. Last thing we wanted was for Pruden to testify. She had me find him. Turned out a lot easier to do with him than Musashi.

"I found Pruden down in South America, just like you figured. He was poking around where all the shit went down. He was trying to figure it out. To find proof and, get this, 'Avenge' his friends. And by that he made it clear he meant both human and Ōkami.

"So, we balled him up and smuggled him back into the States. We put him back in his apartment in New York City, drugged him, and then force fed him a bunch of pills and wine. End of problem.

"Till you, of course," Thane concluded.

He drained his bourbon and looked at Max.

Max's vision was blurry and dark. His hands and feet were numb, and he was finding it hard to make his lungs work.

"Why… tell… me?" He asked.

"You're a friend. I figure you deserve to know. And I didn't want you to think this was personal."

"Why?" Max asked in a weak voice.

"Why did I do it?" Thane asked, smiling at Max and leaning forward in his chair. "To get fucking rich, you asshole. I went around the world eating dirt, dodging bullets and bleeding for twenty years. I've killed people and watched my friends die. For what? For the rigged, closed-loop-system America?" Thane's voice was rising. "I was a sucker. A loser. And guess what? So were you and everyone else we served with. None of it means anything. The joke was on us."

Thane settled back into his chair, shaking his head.

"Well, no more. I'm using my hard-earned talents and experience to make some fucking money."

Stroking his beard, Thane sat in silence for a moment.

"And, truthfully, buddy…" Thane traced the bottom of his beard with his thumb. "I would do anything for Miss Malloy. Fucking anything."

Max smiled wanly.

"You are… a piece… of shit." Max's voice now nearly a whisper.

Thane chuckled.

"You may be right."

Thane looked at Max for a moment. He shook his head in sadness.

"But I am sorry about how this turned out, Max. I really am. Wish I never put you on the Malloy account."

Thane glanced at his watch and then looked back at Max.

His head was tilted over at an awkward angle and his eyes were vacant. Thane waved his hand in Max's face but got no reaction. Max's vision had failed. His body was in the final stage of shutting down.

"Good bye, old buddy," Thane said.

A gurgle escaped Max's mouth.

"What's that?" Thane asked. He got up from his chair and put his ear to Max's mouth.

Max could not see. His limbs were leaden and unfeeling. He was suffocating and could not get his lungs to draw breath. But he thought he still heard Thane. Or could sense him, far in the distance.

"What is it, Max?" Thane asked loudly, directly into Max's ear.

Max couldn't hear any more. He felt himself falling toward the dark. With all of his remaining strength, he forced the tiny amount of air remaining deep in his lungs to the surface and said, "Run... *Odysseus*... Run..."

Chapter Sixty-Five

The general fidgeted in his seat as the aircraft descended toward the landing pad in front of the TSP Headquarters building. Lieutenant Ryuk, sitting across the aisle from him in the small passenger drone, knew what was on his mind. They had been traveling for a week and the general was itching to talk to Vish, to see if any new relevant data had been found, anything at all that might help narrow the search for the *Odysseus*.

Michelle was ready to get back, also. The trip had seemed longer than a week and she was ready to be off the road. She looked forward to a quiet night with a pizza alone in her BOQ.

The general's head of security and Public Affairs Officer sat in the row behind them. Major Sharma, the PAO, dozed with his head tilted back, mouth open. Captain Rodriguez, head of the Geek's security, looked out the window. The early afternoon sun was bright and small white boats dotted the ocean three thousand feet below them.

After a curving descent, the drone touched down on the landing pad across the street from the TSP HQ. Out the window, Michelle could see Mrs. Johnson standing on the entrance steps to the building, waiting for her general.

Several soldiers met the aircraft, stepping on board to help with bags. Captain Rodriguez directed them while the Geek and Michelle walked quickly across the street to the HQ building.

"Good afternoon, General," Mrs. Johnson said. "Welcome back."

"Thank you," Hartwell said, walking up the steps into the building, Ryuk one step behind. "Very good to be home."

Minutes later, after going through security and riding the elevator to the fifth floor, Hartwell walked into his office.

"I didn't know if you two had had a chance to get lunch, so I had the mess hall prepare something for you both," Mrs. Johnson said, following the general.

"That's great, Mrs. Johnson, thank you," The Geek said, looking at the sandwich and bag of chips on his desk. "I'm actually starving."

Lieutenant Ryuk, outside the general's office at her desk, was already digging into hers.

The general sat down at his desk and picked up the sandwich.

"I'll leave you to your lunch, sir," Mrs. Johnson said. She turned and walked back to her desk, smiling at Michelle's fierce chewing and bulging cheeks.

Hours later, after Mrs. Johnson had left for the day. The general walked out of his office.

"Yes, sir?" Lieutenant Ryuk said, coming to her feet.

The general said nothing. He smiled and gestured down the hall with his head. Ryuk fell in behind him and they walked to the StarScope Chamber guard desk.

"Good afternoon, Vish," the general said as he and the lieutenant walked into the dark chamber. Nothing was projected at the moment. Michelle always felt like she was walking around the bottom of a deep missile silo when the room was in this dimly lit state.

"Good afternoon, sir. Good afternoon, Lieutenant Ryuk."

"Did you learn anything new while we were on the road?" The Geek asked, taking a seat at the conference table. Ryuk sat across from him.

"I'm afraid so, sir."

Michelle glanced at the general.

"What is it, Vish?" The Geek asked.

The inner solar system blinked into existence above them. The sun floating in its normal spot, dead center of the conference table, several feet above. Asteroids hung in the air around the edge of the room, many of them seemingly embedded in the wall. The inner rocky planets hung in their normal locations, as did the familiar yellow and read course lines, surging out from Earth's orbit.

But something different shone deep in the faint cloud of uncertainty. It looked like a small, bright white star.

It caught Hartwell and Ryuk's attention immediately.

Hartwell's eyes narrowed.

"I found two indications of a nuclear explosion in our most recent data upload," Vish said.

Michelle watched the general as he pushed back from the conference table and stood up.

"I have indicated my best estimation of where the explosion occurred," Vish continued. The small white light in the cloud of uncertainty blinked several times as Vish called attention to it.

"What were the data sources?" The Geek asked, walking slowly toward the small nuclear explosion.

"One civilian moon-based radio telescope that happened to be pointed in the right direction. It did not capture a direct image, but did capture significant information consistent with the electromagnetic pulse of a nuclear explosion. The other was from an unmanned cargo freighter on its outbound leg to the belt. The freighter's radiation detection equipment recorded a spike in gamma radiation consistent with a nuclear explosion."

The general came to a stop below the bright white light, suspended in the air between the Earth and Mars. The faint red cloud of uncertainty expanded for hundreds of millions of kilometers around it.

"I am sorry, sir. The data I was able to obtain from these two sources is sufficient for me to hypothesis, with a high degree of confidence, that the origin of the nuclear explosion was the *Odysseus'* power and propulsion system."

"How confident are you?"

"Ninety-seven point oh three two percent, sir."

Michelle waited for the general to react. But he stood. Motionless and silent, staring at the hologram of the nuclear explosion.

After a long moment, Michelle got up from her chair quietly and walked over to the Geek.

The holograms put a soft glow on his upturned face. A single tear ran down his left cheek.

Michelle didn't know what to say. So she just stood next to her general in silence.

* * *

Later that night, after eating dinner with Brianna, Susan took a big towel and walked off post, across highway A1A, and out to the beach.

"Hey, guys," she said to her husband's two bodyguards. They were trying to maintain a respectful distance while still keeping him in sight.

"Good evening, ma'am," the lead sergeant said. He smiled and pointed her in the general's direction.

The Geek was sitting just past the scrubby palms in the sand with his shoes off. Susan approached quietly and then spread the big towel on the ground next to him. She sat on it without speaking. The Geek joined her on the towel and they fell asleep looking at the stars.

Chapter Sixty-Six

The car carrying Thane turned off the main road onto the Babcock estate. After passing through half a mile of dense woods, the driveway emerged between two expansive pastures. A split-rail fence lined the driveway on both sides.

A faint mist, already dissipating, hung over the property as Thane rode toward the main stable, which sat in the distance next to a large pond.

Thane looked at his watch and gritted his teeth.

It was almost 6 AM. He had left the city at 4:30 AM to get here before Fiona departed for her ride. What would have been less than half an hour in the air after a civilized wake-up time had been over ninety minutes in the car after a way-too-early alarm clock buzzer.

But Fiona had forbade him flying. She came to this place to get away and did not want to hear the sound of an aircraft landing. The horses didn't like it either.

The Babcock's were long time family friends of the Malloys. They had fallen into her grandfather's profitable slipstream long ago and had drafted behind him ever since. About ninety miles northwest of the city, their four-hundred-acre horse ranch had become a haven for Fiona. She kept her horse, Sirocco, there and the Babcocks let her use a particular guest house whenever she wanted. The horse ranch was one of Fiona's favorite places, second only to Eugene's villa, which she had not been to in a long time.

Fiona came to the horse ranch often, staying there whenever she had a stretch of time she could manage via conference calls. Taking a flight from her building's platform directly to the ranch's landing pad, she could be on Sirocco in less than an hour.

Sirocco was a black Carthusian. His thick mane, long neck, and broad chest gave the seven-year-old a fierce appearance. He was gentle and responsive to Fiona, though. As if he sensed why she came. To be around him. To be in silence.

And to run.

The pair went on long, solitary rides when Fiona visited. At times walking across pastures together, at times tearing through the woods, they would be gone for hours. Fiona and Sirocco ranged all over the estate and surrounding area, cutting across property lines with indifference. The sight of the trim lady on the beast of a horse was recognized by all of the Babcock's neighbors. The pair made an impression. No one objected.

After they returned, Fiona would walk next to Sirocco in the stable's paddock, making sure he had cooled down. Then she would brush him, head to tail, checking for any scrapes or cuts or injuries from their adventures. After making sure he had fresh water and hay, Fiona would retreat to her small guest house, spent.

She was looking forward to riding her today. Fiona had just checked Sirocco's hooves and was about to tack him up as Thane walked into the stable. The horses looked at him warily, heads poking out from their stalls, as he walked down the central aisle.

Sirocco pinned his ears back as Thane approached. Fiona placed her hand on his soft, black cheek.

"Good morning, ma'am," Thane said.

Sirocco pawed at the ground behind his stall door.

"Good morning, Cyrus," Fiona said, hand still on Sirocco's cheek. "What was so important you had to come out here this morning? I assume its bad news."

"That depends," Thane said with a smile. "Is me taking your account back bad news?"

Sirocco jerked his head up and kicked his stall door. The sudden movement startled Thane. He took a step back.

Fiona looked at Sirocco.

"Easy, Rock," she said softly, rubbing his cheek and then running her hand gently over his nose. "I'll be right back."

She shot an irritated glance at Thane and gestured at him to follow. They walked down the aisle out of the stable toward the pond.

"I thought Max was your boy?" Fiona said. "Remember? He was going to make me forget all about you."

A split-rail fence separated the stable paddock from the pond. Thane leaned his back against it. Fiona stood, hands on her hips, facing Thane.

"Max is no longer with the outfit," he said.

Fiona studied Thane's face.

"This is sudden."

Thane shrugged.

"It had been building for a while," he said.

"Well, he knows a lot about me and about Determined End States. How we operate. What we are working on. Everything. Should I be worried about that? About what he knows?"

"You don't need to worry about that at all," Thane answered.

Fiona studied Thane and then nodded once. She looked at the pond for a long moment and then stepped next to him at the fence. He turned around, and they both leaned on the top rail, looking at the pond. A pair of ducks swam along the edge, looking for breakfast.

"He kept asking about Pruden," Thane said in a low voice. "He was digging around. Figuring out things. And not in a good way."

"I see."

She glanced at Thane. His eyes were fixed on the horizon.

"Well, I'm sorry, Cyrus," she said, looking back at the pond. "I know you two went back a long way."

"Thanks. We did. He was like a little brother to me."

One of the ducks dove under the water in a smooth vanishing act that hardly disturbed the surface of the pond. The other paddled slowly, waiting for it to surface. The mist around the property was nearly gone now, and the blue cloudless sky reflected off of the smooth pond surface. Fiona and Thane watched the spot where the duck had submerged.

The duck resurfaced gracefully and shook its head. Drops of water dappled the smooth surface of the pond around it. Its companion swam closer.

"I appreciate you coming out here to tell me this, Cyrus."

"Of course, ma'am," he said.

"And I appreciate…" her voice trailed off. It seemed better not to say it. *You killed your friend to protect me.*

She looked at Thane.

Thane turned his head and met her eyes.

Fiona reached over and placed her hand on Thane's.

"Thank you," she said softly.

Thane looked at her small hand resting on top of his. Hers was fairer skinned, without the signs of age and war. He wanted to grasp it and pull her in. After a few heartbeats, he looked back into her eyes and said, "When it comes to you, Fiona. To your safety, I will never hesitate. I will always do what must be done. Always."

Fiona blinked. Her cheeks flushed, and she took her hand back with a nod.

The pair stood in silence, leaning against the fence. Fiona thought about her grandfather and what she wanted to do. She was ready to confide in Thane and ask for his help. He would do it, she knew. And she had already trusted him with her worst. The two of them were going to hell, no doubt. This one last thing would be the least of their sins. It might even fall on the good side of their ledger, she thought ruefully.

Thane cleared his throat and shifted on his feet before she could get herself to say it. He took his hand off the fence and turned to face her.

Fiona turned her head and looked at him.

"But there's more, isn't there?" she asked.

"Yes, ma'am. There is."

Fiona turned her head back to the pond, her eyes following the two ducks as they swam away.

"You remember Musashi's odd reference to *Odysseus*?" Thane said.

Fiona nodded.

"Turns out the *Odysseus* is a Company freighter making runs to the belt and back. It's gone missing. The Company lost all communication with it a little more than a month ago. It's actually the second Company freighter to go missing. They are going batshit trying to find them. But guess who is on the *Odysseus.*"

"I'm not in the mood to play guessing games, Cyrus," still watching the ducks paddle away.

"Paul Owens."

The ducks, spooked by something that Fiona did not see, took to flight, surging into the air with just a few flaps of their wings. Their webbed feet touched the water a few times, leaving splashes the birds quickly outran. They flew low, wingtips breaking the pond's surface before climbing up above the trees at the last second.

When the pair of ducks disappeared in the distance above the treetops, Fiona pushed back from the fence and turned to look at Thane.

He stood facing her, one hand on the top rail of the fence.

"I served twenty years in the military," Thane said. "Most of that time in front line combat leadership roles. I fought at Santiago and in a bunch of other patches of hell that you have never heard of. Statistically, I should not be standing here. I should be pushing up daisies in Arlington. There are much better men and women that are. A hell of a lot better.

"I'm not standing here because I am smarter than they were," Thane shook his head. "Far from it. But there is one thing about me I have learned to trust. My gut."

Thane put his fist against his stomach.

"When it tells me something is fucked, I listen to it. And I take fucking action."

Fiona crossed her arms. Hearing Paul Owens' name had caught her off guard. Now Thane's intensity concerned her.

"I took Musashi's ranting when Max found him to be a bunch of bullshit," Thane said, leaning closer to Fiona. "All that crap about the sphere being 'Far from here,' 'Run, *Odysseus*, run,' and 'Adauchi.' Now, though, after years of unsuccessfully scouring the earth looking for that memory sphere, Paul Owens being out there somehow, two Company freighters lost, and Musashi's ties to the space industry…"

Thane's voice trailed off, and he shook his head.

"My gut is screaming at me, ma'am."

"And what is it screaming, Cyrus?"

"Kill Paul Owens."

Fiona turned and leaned against the fence, her face tight.

"Do you think Owens has the missing sphere?"

"No. Well, honestly, I don't know. But it does not seem possible to me. In any case, he is a loose end we should have taken care of years ago."

"He was supposed to be locked away at Leavenworth for the rest of his days," Fiona said, not looking at Thane. "How the hell did he get out?"

"Doesn't matter now."

Fiona looked at the pond. The water was smooth and reflective. No trace of the departed pair of ducks remained.

"The firm has resources in the belt," Thane said. "I have alerted them to be on the lookout for the *Odysseus*. Lost commo is not all that uncommon, so the ship could be fine and underway. Judging by the timeline, she would be only a little more than halfway to the belt by now. Maybe nine months left to cross. If she does make it and docks at the belt, they will take care of Owens."

Fiona nodded, not taking her eyes off the pond.

"I have also initiated an intelligence operation targeting the Company as well as their insurer, Infinity Cargo. They are both going to be extremely motivated to find the *Odysseus*. The Firm's hacking team is burrowing into both of them as we speak, and we have also started human intelligence efforts. We will know the instant the Company or

Infinity Cargo finds the ship, or learns what happened to her.

"Finally, DredSkill also has ways of taking direct action between Earth and the belt," Thane said. "I am energizing those resources now, putting them on standby for when we locate the target."

Thane studied Fiona's profile as he waited for her to respond. She looked tense, her jaw clenched, despite the tranquil setting.

Fiona stepped back from the fence.

"That all sounds very thorough, Cyrus."

"Yes, ma'am," Thane said with a nod.

"It all sounds very expensive also."

"Yes, ma'am. We can talk about throttling back some—"

"No! Of course not, goddamnit."

Thane felt his body assuming the position of parade rest.

"Do everything you believe we need to do, Cyrus," she said. "But I would ask you to discuss the matter with Miss Stone."

"I keep the boss lady apprised of everything regarding your account, ma'am. She is supportive of everything I have laid out for you."

"I'm sure. But I was referring to the cost implications of these actions."

Thane did not respond.

Fiona smiled.

"Do you know what 'Adauchi' means, Cyrus?"

"Yeah. I do. And I don't want you to worry ab—"

"You think it's just me that has to worry?"

Thane's head cocked, he shifted on his feet and released his hands from behind his back.

"I read up on adauchi after Max's debrief." Fiona stepped forward, slowly closing the distance between them as she spoke. "It's pretty stark shit. All about avenging a wrong, particularly the death or dishonor of a family member or master. I tell ya, once you start reading about it, there are just so many stories about loyalty, honor, and the willingness to sacrifice oneself for justice, to exact adauchi."

Fiona stood in front of Thane now, looking up at him, so close they could kiss. She placed one hand on his muscled belly, then the other. "I would have thought this super sensitive gut of yours would be screaming at you now. Like, red fucking alert. You really think Owens would stop with me?"

Thane, surprised and aroused, put his hands on Fiona's shoulders. His head bent towards her to kiss.

"Because it seems to me, Cyrus," Fiona said quickly, taking a step back, out of his hands. "That, given the firm's historical involvement in these matters, our aligned desire to keep them buried in the past, and the possibility, however minute, that an experienced war veteran may be angry and inclined to seek revenge on us all, Miss Stone might consider a modest fucking discount."

Fiona turned and walked back to the stable.

Thane, left standing in his arousal, chuckled ruefully and shook his head. He watched Fiona walk away, appreciating the form fitting riding pants she was wearing. His eyes lingered until she disappeared into the barn.

He turned back toward the pond and leaned against the fence. Thane rubbed his eyes. He was not looking forward to that discussion with Eris Stone. He was also not in a hurry to get back in the car for the long ride back to the city.

Moments later, Thane heard a galloping sound behind him. He turned in time to see Fiona and Sirocco streaking across the pasture in a breakneck gallop. He watched the black horse with its rider until they disappeared into the woods.

ODYSSEUS

Chapter Sixty-Seven

Adauchi Book One
Circa 1510
Translated from the Japanese

The river carried me far.

I washed up on its rocky bank a mile away sometime after the moon had risen. The next morning, I was found by a kind farmer who hid me in his barn and nursed me back to health, though I cursed him for doing so.

When I was strong enough, I thanked the farmer and walked to the closest village.

I needed a katana to commit seppuku, but I had no money. So, I determined that I would steal one. My failure and dishonor were so black, common thievery would leave no mark.

Before setting to my task, though, I asked passersby what they knew of the recent battle between Clans Hayato and Shingen.

They regaled me with tales they had heard. Hayato withstood the Shingen siege for months. Hayato himself suffered a great loss when his only son and the leader of the Elite Guard was slain by Hiroaki and his one hundred bandits. It was only through the great wisdom of Lords Shingen and Hayato that disaster and more bloodshed were averted. Why, they asked, should two great houses bleed themselves to death? Samurai must be mastered, and war is too important to be left to the generals.

The bloodthirsty Hiroaki and his one hundred bandits were thankfully destroyed, and wiser heads prevailed.

Peace was made.

There was much talk of the marriage between Hayato's only daughter and Shingen's son, uniting the two clans that had been at war for over a century. Tales of conquests by the Shingen-Hayato alliance were spoken of everywhere and written about in every paper. It seemed that none of the other clans could resist their advance. There was talk of the dawn of a new shogunate.

Despondent and awash in lies, I went to the village crossroads and sat by the well to wait for a victim. I hoped to find an elderly man carrying the katana from his youth who I could ambush. Once I had his blade, I would leave the village, walk into woods where no one would find me, and disembowel myself.

With no second in attendance, it would be almost all that I deserved.

There were also many posters proclaiming all graduates and associates of School Hiroaki outlaws and wanted men. Rewards had been placed on our heads.

It was dizzying. I alternated between rage, confusion, and sadness.

No matter. I planned to be dead that evening.

I did pull the hood of my kimono over my head, though. I wanted to remain free to kill myself, after all.

I waited all day, but a suitable victim did not pass by.

As the sun set, three young rōnin walked into the village square. They stopped to drink at the well. They each wore both a katana and a shorter wakizashi. But, weak as I was, I would be no match for one of them. Much less three.

Stealing their blades was not possible.

Nonetheless, I sized them up from the shadows. Perhaps if they dozed off or otherwise lowered their guard. As I did, the tallest of them left the well and walked across the street to the inn.

I listened to the other two as they drank from the well.

"This is the tenth village we have stopped in with no luck," I overheard one say. "Perhaps we have gone too far?"

"Or perhaps we have not gone far enough," said the other.

"You're right. Who knows how far the river swept him along?"

"Or maybe he drowned?"

"No. I do not think so. No body was ever found."

"Perhaps it was," the fellow said. "But they did not recognize that it was the body of Manji Saito."

I froze at the mention of my name.

When it became clear that they were paying me no notice, I stood up slowly. When I was sure that they had not noticed, I turned to go.

As I turned, I came face-to-face with the tall rōnin as he came back from the inn.

"It's you!" he said to me. "It's him!" he shouted to his comrades. "Right here! It's him!"

They approached me slowly, from three different directions.

I was done.

I had no weapon.

I was in no shape to fight.

But I was determined to exact a price for my capture. I threw off my kimono and assumed a ready stance.

"Very well, traitors," I said. "Draw your katanas and come at me. I will show you what Hiroaki Ashikaga taught me!"

"Shhh!" the tall one said, raising his finger to his mouth. "Don't say that name!"

None of them drew his sword.

"It is against the law to speak of him," another said. "And we graduates of the school have been deemed outlaws."

"We must stick together," said the third. "In secrecy."

I was confused. My wounds, fatigue, and sadness were a heavy fog encircling my mind.

They could see my confusion. The tall one stepped closer. I flinched at his movement.

He gestured with his palms down. "It's OK. We mean you no harm. We were sent to find you."

"Find me?" I stammered.

"You are Manji Saito, are you not?" he asked, taking another step closer.

My own name made me tremble. I was heartbroken and bewildered at its mention and all that had happened.

"Only survivor of the Battle of the Covered Bridge?" he said to me, almost in a whisper, as he put his hand on my shoulder. "Student of School Hiroaki? And friend of Hiroaki Ashikaga himself?"

"How do you know this?" I asked.

"Many know, Manji," he said in a low and respectful tone of voice.

The three of them smiled and then quickly blanked their expressions.

"We were sent to find you," the tall one said.

"By whom?" I asked.

"There are many of us," one of them said.

"We are resolved to exact adauchi for Hiroaki and our comrades," said the third.

"The time of being pawns to lords, shoguns, money, and politics is over," the tall one said.

"And you must lead us."

Chapter Sixty-Eight

Paul walked under the flagpole at their compound on Fort Bragg. The sun was setting behind him, and his shadow stretched to his front, far beyond his footsteps. It was early summer, and the Carolina evening was comfortable and breezy. The smell of roasting venison grew stronger as Paul walked forward. Chief had been at it for a few hours, and it smelled close to ready.

Paul heard the voices of his soldiers ribbing each other and talking about the toils of the day. He heard Kata also, laughing loudest of all.

The fire came into view as Paul rounded the corner of Filson's command building. A large deer rotated slowly on a spit.

Chief, adorned in a grease-stained white apron over his olive-drab T-shirt and cutoff camouflage shorts, tended to the cooking animal. Stainless-steel tongs hung out of one cargo pocket, a large, dirty rag out of the other. Chief's biceps bulged under the T-shirt, as did his gut. Spotting Paul, he gestured at his sizzling handiwork and smiled with just-like-you-taught-me pride.

Paul held both thumbs up in approval as he walked toward the group.

Stuntman stood in front of the crowded wooden table, foot on an ammo crate, gesturing dramatically. His wavy golden-blond hair and thick mustache were not in regs and made Paul chuckle. Stuntman whipped one hand through the air to get his point across as he held a beer in the other without spilling a drop.

Mia rolled her eyes at him, her lithe body leaning back against the table, short brown hair pulled back. She never believed the braggart.

Dragon One and Magellan sat next to each other, arms crossed, regarding Stuntman with bored skepticism. Their katanas leaned against the table next to them. D1 wore his trademark Ray-Bans and, despite the warmth of the summer evening, his leather flight jacket. His short black hair was gelled into a perfect spiky flattop, and his silver dog tags hung in front of his chest. Paul shook his head at the sweat drenching D1's white T-shirt. No one loved flying or being a pilot more than D1, but Paul thought D1 loved *looking* like a pilot even more. He'd seen D1 wearing that damn leather jacket in August in 100 degree heat.

Magellan jotted notes in his small black notebook. Paul didn't have to read them to know they were full of random observations and tactical thoughts. He was always surprised by that kid's brain. But Paul learned not to let the glasses and relatively slight build fool him; Magellan was deadly on the battlefield.

D1 spotted Paul first.

"Evening, sir," D1 said to Paul, giving him a jaunty salute with one finger. "Beer?"

"Yes, please."

D1 reached over and yanked a beer from the large bucket of ice at his feet.

"Long day, wasn't it, sir?" Magellan said.

"It surely was," Paul said, taking the beer from D1.

"What took you so long?" Kata said, standing up from her seat at the end of the table.

"Got hung up, is all," Paul said, opening the beer.

"Well," Kata said, walking over to Paul and holding her beer out to him. They knocked the cans together. "Better late than never, partner."

They each took a large swallow of beer.

"The colonel is here," Kata added. "Said he had to go grab something. Not sure what. But he should be back soon."

"Filson is here?" Paul asked, startled. "Really?"

"Yeah," Kata said, puzzled by his surprise. "Why wouldn't he be?"

Paul nodded. He knew it was a good question. But he was overcome by the ache of familiarity and couldn't think straight.

"Sir, you made it!" Top called out as she rounded the corner.

Paul turned to see his first sergeant walking toward him in a black utility tank top and olive-green cargo pants. Her pants and boots were covered in mud, and she carried a large cooler.

Over six feet tall with broad shoulders, Top had the build of a professional basketball player. Her sandy-blond hair was pulled back into a thick braided ponytail that betrayed her Norse bloodline, as did the runic shield knot tattoos that covered the length of her arms.

She handed the cooler to D1.

"This thing is heavy," D1 said. "What's in it?"

"Vegetables."

"Thank God," Magellan said.

"Last time we did Chief's meat-only dinner, you guys nearly destroyed the latrines," Top said.

"That is the truth," Kata said, giving Paul a knowing glance.

"Well, I'm not having that again," Top said.

Top looked around the table, pointing at each soldier in turn as she said, "Everyone will eat their veggies this time!"

Grumbles ran through the table, but no one dared argue.

Top looked at D1. "Would you mind taking a break from your posing and taking them over to Chief?"

"Roger that," D1 said, popping up from his seat and walking toward the fire with the cooler.

"Sir, your seat is over there at the head of the table," Top said to Paul, pointing.

Kata walked around to the other end, where she had been sitting.

Paul stepped behind his chair and looked around the table. All twelve of Alpha and Bravo Companies' leadership were there. Kata talked intently to her first sergeant at the other end of the table. Reynolds and Chamberlain argued with D3 and Mia about something stupid.

Emotion welled within Paul.

"Take one and pass them around," Chief said, stepping up to the table with an armful of plates.

He returned a minute later with a large coffee can full of forks, spoons, and knives and placed it in the middle of the table, along with a pile of napkins.

"We're ready, sir," Chief said to Paul. "I'm going to serve it all up at the fire when you give the word."

Chief gestured over his shoulder. The deer now hung on the edge of the fire, while the vegetables grilled on a large metal grate positioned over the flames. The aromas smelled wonderful.

"At ease!" Top said.

Conversation at the table ceased.

"The floor is yours, sir," Top said with a smile, standing next to Paul.

All heads swung to look at him.

Paul fidgeted. He wanted to say how sorry he was. How heartbroken. But it didn't seem like the right time. He was frozen by emotion.

"Sir?" Top said. "Don't you want to say something to us?"

Paul opened his mouth, but he could not speak.

"Sir?" Top said, putting her strong hand on his shoulder.

Paul looked at Kata. Her smile had faded.

D1 crossed his arms in disappointment.

Chamberlain shook his head.

"Sir?" Top said again, this time shaking Paul's shoulder. "I need you to say something."

Paul struggled to focus on Top, but her face was fuzzy now.

She shook him again. "Sir!" she said in a loud voice. "Sir, I need you to say something."

The fire vanished, and night fell in an instant. Paul was freezing. It was dark and he couldn't see the table or anyone at it.

Top shook him again.

"Focus on my voice, sir. Can you hear me? I need you to say something."

Paul opened his eyes.

He was floating in the *Odysseus'* amputated bridge. It was cold. He could see his breath.

A large robot held him by the shoulders.

He blinked in disbelief.

It was a shorter version of Top. There was no advanced ceramic-composite armor and accompanying iridescence. She was all metal, but she was identical in features and slender with powerful proportions.

He knew it was her.

"There you are," she said in a familiar voice. "Can you hear me, sir?"

Paul's eyes widened as he tried to comprehend.

The void loomed outside the bridge's wide window behind his first sergeant.

Paul looked around to confirm for himself again that he was on the bridge. He spotted Althea floating a few arm lengths away, wrapped in blankets. She was motionless and her eyes were closed. Two soldierbots like the one in front of him held on to her.

The last thing Paul remembered was the tug engines giving out and weightlessness returning to the bridge. They'd wrapped themselves in blankets to share body warmth.

After a few cycles, it had been clear that Althea was not coming out of rest mode. Paul had kissed her on the forehead and bound himself to her with a few power cords before taking another hit of hibernation drugs and falling asleep for the last time.

But that was a long time ago, it seemed.

He looked at Top and then back to Althea with concern.

He tried to speak, but his voice croaked.

"She is fine," Top said. "She is in a deep rest-mode setting. We will be able to revive her aboard the ship."

Paul blinked. His eyes darted around.

"Here," Top said, holding a squeeze bottle in front of Paul's face. "Take a sip of water."

He opened his mouth, and she gave him a squirt of water.

It helped.

"I don't understand," he said.

"I know," she said. "But you will."

"How long?" Paul asked, his voice cracking again.

Top gave him another squirt of water. "I don't know. But the mission clock over there says it's the six hundred and eleventh cycle. When did you cut loose from the *Odysseus*?"

"I'm not sure," Paul said. "Maybe four twenty? It's fuzzy."

"That sounds about right," Top said. "We detected a large explosion around then. Had us worried. Especially when the *Odysseus* didn't show at the rendezvous. We started a search pattern but had to be careful. We're supposed to be a lost ship, after all, and we're trying to stay that way."

Top started to unfold the blankets around Paul.

"It's a miracle we found you," she continued. "But whoever put you on this course knew what they were doing. You're right between where we were supposed to link up with the *Odysseus* and where we are going. Nonetheless, we were shocked to find this…"—Top looked around the bridge and then back to Paul—"whatever you call this thing you are traveling in."

"But how are you here?" Paul asked, confusion and anxiety gripping him.

"The *Perseus*," she said, while waving an arm to beckon one of the other soldierbots.

"No," Paul said. "I mean, how are you alive?"

The other soldierbot handed Top a pressure suit. She opened it as Paul's anxiety increased.

"The maintenance boss," Paul said as the thought raced into his head. "The navigator. They were working for you? How did you…"

Top gently took the last blanket away from Paul's naked body. "Get into this pressure suit, please, sir," she said, pulling one of his legs into the suit, then the other.

"The maintenance boss and the navigator!" Paul yelled. Confusion started to suffocate him. Panic surged. "How did they know?"

He kicked his legs free of the pressure suit and pushed away from the first sergeant.

Paul floated away from her, his back toward the large window.

"Tell me what the hell is going on!" he yelled.

The other two soldierbots looked at Top, who was gesturing at Paul with her palms down, trying to exude calm.

"I will explain it all, sir," Top said in a reassuring voice. "But first I want to get both of you transferred to the *Perseus*. You've been drifting on this freezing wreck for too long. We'll get you warmed up and fed and flush the hibernation drugs out of your system. They are contributing to your agitation."

"You'll tell me now!" Paul shouted. He had drifted across the bridge, his back now against the large window. His naked body glowed pale against the black void.

Top regarded Paul for a moment and then said, "OK, but I don't have all the details."

Paul waited for her to speak, oblivious to the cold.

"Colonel Filson saved my memory sphere when he dove into the broken and dying pile of us after we were ambushed on Outpost Devil," she began. "Somehow, he got the sphere to Dr. Musashi, who got it smuggled on board the *Perseus*. The doctor used every trick, connection and bribe he could to get specifications, code, and other supporting Ōkami systems hacked into the *Perseus*'s factory so it could rebuild us on the way to the belt.

"We had just taken over the *Perseus* and were executing our plan when Dr. Musashi learned you were joining the crew of the *Odysseus*. He set in motion a scheme for us to rendezvous with the *Odysseus* so that we could get you back. I can only guess that it was the maintenance boss and the navigator you are talking about. The doctor must have bent them to our purpose somehow."

"Why?" Paul asked in a whisper.

"The doctor realized that he... That we had been betrayed by Fiona Malloy. And that, at his age, he did not have long enough to protect and avenge his own. He entrusted that to you."

"But... but why?"

"Because you are our leader. He trusted you. He believed in you. I do, too."

"But I failed," he whispered. "Do you remember what happened?"

Top nodded but said nothing.

"I'm so sorry…"

"The time for sorrow is over, sir. Now you must lead us."

The End

Spirit Of The Bayonet

Book 1: Betrayal

Book 2: Odysseus

Book 3: Sacrifice

All books available now, in paperback and for Kindle®, from Amazon.

For updates on future books in the series, sign up for Ted's newsletter via his website:

tedruss.com

Acknowledgements

Like Book One, the acknowledgment for this one feels a little unusual, since some of the people who helped shape the book haven't thought about it in over six years—back when I was grinding away on the first version. But their contributions were foundational. The spirit of *The Spirit of the Bayonet* started with their help. (Sorry… couldn't resist.)

Whether it was version one or this latest run, my trusted band of beta readers and thought partners were invaluable. No indie writer has it better. Period. James Aiken, Kirby Andrews, Amber Lilyquist, Ted Miller, Adam Parrish, Jennifer and Dan Ruiz, Kevin Virgil, Russ Watson, Morgan Watson, and David Weinstein.

The finishing crew on this one: Chris Evans and Mark Thomas. True professionals.

Thanks to my wife, Anna; to my parents; and to George and Susu Johnson—writing gets weird and lonely sometimes. Knowing you're in my corner means everything.

Finally—and again, and always—Anna. Partner. Best friend. Farm Boss. I'm so lucky.

Ted Russ
April 2025

OTHER BOOKS

BY

TED RUSS

DUTY'S COST

Val Rafter's luck may have finally run out. Kidnapped by Russians and held at gunpoint on a ship crossing the Black Sea at night toward Crimea, Val is forced to confront the events and decisions that brought him to this desperate moment. Part of a top-secret US Army human intelligence program, Val is an expert at recruiting and running spies. Years ago, while training at the CIA's legendary Farm, he met Sydney, whose beauty, intelligence, and ambition made her a formidable agency covert intelligence officer. The attraction was immediate, but their timing was terrible. Soon after, while serving in the cauldron of Kosovo, Val forged an unlikely friendship with Alexei Volkov, a Russian army officer. When the three are sent to the prestigious Marshall Center for Security Studies in Germany, they become entangled in secrets that will haunt them for the rest of their careers. As global tensions rise, duty and loyalty conflict and propel the three old friends toward a disastrous reckoning in Ukraine in 2014...

In a globe spanning story that takes the reader from top secret CIA training, to Kosovo, Eastern Europe, Iraq, and Syria, Russ weaves a tale that is as thrilling as it is thought-provoking. Exploring the demands of duty, honor, and friendship in a world that often puts them at odds, this is an unforgettable novel that will leave readers questioning the nature of loyalty and the cost of Duty.

Available now, in paperback and for Kindle®, from Amazon.

SPIRIT MISSION

To honor bonds forged twenty-five years ago at West Point, Lieutenant Colonel Sam Avery leads an illegal mission deep into ISIS-held territory.

An MH-47G Chinook helicopter departs formation in the Iraqi night. The mission is unauthorized. Success is unlikely. But to save a friend, Sam Avery and his crew of Night Stalkers have prepared for one last flight.

ISIS operatives in Tal Afar, Iraq, have captured American aid worker Henry Stillmont. Avery knows Stillmont as "the Guru," the West Point squad leader who taught him about brotherhood, loyalty, and when to break the rules as a young cadet twenty-five years ago. Sam will risk his career and his life to save him.

As they near their target, Sam reflects on his time in the crucible of the United States Military Academy. West Point made Sam the leader he is. But his fellow cadets made him the man that he is. The ideals of duty, honor, and country have echoed throughout his life and drive him and his comrades as they undertake their final and most audacious spirit mission.

Available now, in paperback and for Kindle®, from Amazon.

ABOUT THE AUTHOR

Ted Russ is a writer living in the Carolina mountains with his wife, Anna, their dogs, Charlie and Ripple, and a bunch of chickens and bees.

In a distant prior life, he served as an army officer after graduating from West Point. Ted left the military in 2000 with experience as a special operations helicopter pilot and a philosophy degree.

Possessing no marketable skills, he went back to school and got an MBA. His 25 year journey through the business world was winding - from startups to fortune 500s, domestic to expat assignments, general management and sales to M&A.

He discovered writing late in life, publishing his first novel in 2016 and now tries to make a living writing full time.

Exploring themes of identity, loyalty, and the complexities of the human experience, Ted's works span contemporary fiction and thought provoking sci-fi. Readers praise his novels for their gripping narratives, authenticity, and moral depth.

For new stories, updates, and dispatches from the Ridge — sign up for Ted's newsletter at his website:

tedruss.com